THE FIRE OF MILAN

In this powerful story the author has concentrated upon the tragic web which enveloped four characters all comprised in a single household. The chief characters are Melania Mèrici, a wealthy and still beautiful widow, daughter of a naturalised German banker with a town house in Milan, famous for its musical parties, and a remote villa in the foothills of the Lombardy Alps; her only son Donato, known as Donatello, the artist *manqué* who, after military service at the front, returns home a neurasthenic invalid, contemptuous of, yet absorbed in his malady of inaction; Armida Lenai, her confidential friend; with her lover, Gaspare Della Morte, a determined anti-Fascist conspirator. To these must be added the sinister figure of Falaride Narenza, a friend of Donato, a political informer by profession, a 'product of the times', whose fixed purpose in life is to save his own skin and make his fortune.

THE FIRE OF MILAN

by

RICCARDO BACCHELLI

*Translated from the Italian by
Kathleen Nott*

London : SECKER & WARBURG : *1958*

Printed in Great Britain by
The Camelot Press Ltd., London and Southampton

Contents

Prologue

BEFORE I set myself to the task of relating this tragic human story which was grafted on to the historical tragedy of the great fire of Milan—and so broach a very potent and bitter wine, the record of the tremendous years in which it took place —there is need for a brief explanation.

The actuality developed its own peculiar elements and characteristics among remote events and circumstances, but it unfolded and came to its final precipitation as if following the laws of a dramatic action: and so one ought to preserve upon the printed page the compressed power, the sense of doom, the urgent rhythm and the tumultuous force of the words in which the human passions burst forth when they were let loose to conflict, in face of death.

What I should call this poetic structure of the actual event has impressed itself upon the story, unfolding it in chapters of narrative and acts of dialogue, the first illuminating the second, which in turn reinforce the first: but the five 'acts' could be performed on the stage just as the force of events has produced them.

It might be that a new form could arise from this, but the novelty—if it is one—is entirely due to the facts as they occurred and not to any arbitrary and ambitious invention of my own, for the actuality imposed two movements or *tempi*: that of the narrative, broad and flowing, and that of the drama, intense and urgent, reaching maturity in the city which fate had singled out and reaching its climax in the place which, as one thinks back, seems by its very name predestinate:

romance and tragedy, both of the great fire and of the 'wounded souls', in Milan and at Alma Dannata.

Granted that a life of perfect happiness would be an absurdity, must it not come to one end only, in a drama which waits to fulfil all human existence?

BOOK I

ONCE UPON A TIME

CHAPTER ONE

A Widow and Her Only Son

ON the foothills of the Alps in Lombardy, there stood a house which was known by the unusual name of Alma Dannata, *the Damned Soul*, all that remained from ancient legend. Its owner, Melania Mèrici, was an exceptionally beautiful and well-preserved woman who had been a widow for many years—in fact, almost the whole lifetime of her son Donato, generally known as Donatello.

It was for love of this son that Melania had at one time been unwilling to remarry: her love for him was exceedingly tender and passionate and made many of her friends, among whom there were several who would have liked to marry her, accuse her of remaining a widow through jealousy: which at once made her demand in protest, Whatever sort of jealousy did they mean? Actually, she had wanted Donato not to have to put up with jealousy himself, as he might have had to do if his mother married again and so provided him with a stepfather. But it was no use protesting, they all used to say that she was warmhearted and sensitive, but that her sentiments were at once too lofty and too possessive.

For instead of jealousy, as she did not like the word, they suggested possessiveness: at which she protested even more warmly that that was synonymous with sordid egoism of the most unbridled and domineering kind. They had better not insult her!

As a matter of fact, as the years passed, Donato grew to an

appearance and manner which early began to attract attention among the ladies and steal their affections, and Melania did feel herself seized by an overwhelming passion which was certainly possessive and might well be called rash and un-bridled, because it seemed to have every possibility of causing her disillusion and pain and nothing else. She was not accus-tomed or disposed to deceive herself and, recognising in this passion both jealousy and egoism, she fought it and tried to overcome her weakness, and succeeded at least in hiding it from others and preventing it from being a burden to her adored son.

On the other hand, when one of her friends had fallen in love with Donatello, she did not care to have her about the place, either in Milan or in the country at Alma Dannata (which both for the sake of brevity and euphemism was known as Vill' Alma). And when this happened, she had a way of reconciling jealousy with decorum and with her sense, not only of decency but of the ridiculous: the crazy old harridans, she would say, let alone being his mother's friends, any one of them herself could have been Donatello's mother! And you could leave morals out of it, for she was too much a woman of the world to care about that: and in barring these lovelorn matrons from her salon she had always used the most impeccable tact and a suavely elegant moderation touched with irony.

The tact was so impeccable that when there had been a suitable lapse of time, enough for them to have let off steam and gone off the boil—Donato being fickle and flighty in his loves, anyway till now and as far as they were concerned—a few of them returned to their best friend and took to frequent-ing her salon again, and her social and musical receptions, as if nothing had happened, either with son or mother.

The old friends used to smile affectionately and say with good-natured malice that it was a very sensible and practical idea to make him find his lovers under his own roof without the dangers of external adventure: and they used to say that even this was a kind of jealousy and a way of keeping him under her eye.

When her lady friends had cooled off, Melania always made it appear that she had seen nothing, and showed herself more than ever the tender and affectionate friend and comforter. And so, what with those who had come back to the fold and one or two others who had snatched themselves from the burning in time and a few more who, because they were not much to look at, or had other amorous preoccupations, had kept out of harm's way and had a purely friendly liking for Donatello or were fond of his mother, he would have been extraordinarily spoilt, both as boy and young man, if Melania had not been a wise and severe preceptor, a rare exception among mothers of an only son, and widowed into the bargain.

And so it is needless to say that she hadn't wanted him to grow up like the rest of the youth of that time which, with a wisdom after the event which is as laughable as it is conceited, likes to label itself—'between the wars'. In her opinion these young people were debilitated and incapable of strong passions or serious thought and feeling, and for this she blamed their mania for sport and their excessive devotion to Fascist ideology and discipline which, so she thought, was bringing up a generation of cowardly hypocrites and infatuated fools. Behind this was the slack upbringing of a so-called ruling class which had relinquished its status and, worse still, indeed most pernicious and blameworthy of all, had begun by abandoning the duty of educating its sons, with the hard work and struggle and the arduous and austere satisfactions which that implied: and so these sons were left too soon to be a law to themselves and, in the moral and intellectual sense, they lacked fibre and substance, even if sport had overdeveloped their muscles and their capacities for boasting. And since they were left to the indulgence of every whim, boys and girls alike ended deprived of will-power, before they had even formed any conception of the will to do either right or wrong.

She may have been more or less right, but although they had enabled her to bring up Donato with distinguished manners, dignity and strength of feeling and a lofty intellectual culture, combining sensitivity and toughness, these convictions of hers had resulted in one drawback: that no young people of his own age, either boys or girls, made a habit of coming to the house. The truth was that Melania, who was penetrating and even biting in her judgments, had kept a sharp eye on her son's friendships and ever since he was a boy had been inclined to criticise them and nip them in the bud. By the time he was a young man and could make and keep friendships out of the house and his mother's surveillance, he had become, like her, too difficult to please.

Since she was very sensitive to every aspect of human relationship, Melania was uneasy about this: and she blamed herself all the more because most of her women friends were far from putting up such a wonderful resistance to the years as she had done, either physically or morally. Visitors and friends were well-seasoned, not to use a harsher expression: and in short, to put it mildly, Donato passed his youth among people we can only call elderly.

Melania was then seized with the most illusory of all the aspirations which beset fathers and mothers: that of finding her son's friends for him (the 'boy', as she continued to call him). As she soon discovered, it is more difficult to find friends for your son and daughter than to find them a wife or husband.

But when one of her most intimate and faithful old friends to whom she confided her anxieties suggested that perhaps what he needed was to be freed from his mother's petticoats and given a taste for company of his own age, and hence that it would be a good idea if he took a wife, the very notion gave Melania the old jealous sting, all the more fierce, the more bitter and burning because the poison contained something absurd and extravagant, the fact that she was now middle-aged. And because of her age she had a fixed idea for which she bitterly reproached herself: her son could well wait a year or two until she was dead before taking a wife. She was ashamed of it and reproached herself: to think that jealousy, confused and ill-regulated passion, could disturb her balance of heart and mind when she had always exercised such perfect equanimity and self-control!

It occurred to her that it might be an effect of the so-called 'critical age' and at the mere thought she blushed with rage and a kind of terrified disgust at herself. She had never admitted, and she did so now less than ever, that the disturbances of the age which with delicate euphemism they called 'difficult', the physiological and functional derangements in the glands or whatever organs it might be, could upset the mind and the emotions, the clarity and rightness of moral sentiments and logical judgments. She had always thought, and she still thought, that they might trouble the bodily health but not the spiritual. And now this confused and unbalanced emotion of extravagant jealousy caused an upheaval even in her maternal feeling, that rock on which she had so far built and fortified the security and the intact integrity of her personality, not only morally and intellectually, but, till now, physically, for maturity had only very slightly rounded her out, with a harmless and even attractive and healthy plumpness.

Thus despising herself in what she believed was an act of modesty and conscience, she did not perceive that she was at the same time indulging a paltry pride, a general attitude of contempt and scorn. To think that just because of the 'critical time of life', or, in the squalid language of physiology, the menopause, a woman of her education should be brought down to the level of those innumerable 'spiteful old cats' (she had a pithy dialect expression for this), the women who grow jealous and envenomed with their daughters-in-law, stupid mothers, backbiting sisters-in-law, all the petty and hateful personages of a stupid, petty and hateful farce.

She never entertained any of those doubts and second

thoughts which are so salutary: for instance, that if those petty creatures are so common, she must feel, in claiming that she was exceptional and couldn't be touched by such a widely distributed fate, that she was a very rare being, elect among the elect.

Even her anti-Fascism had an excess of pride and exclusiveness and a fanatical and indeed highfalutin quality which hardened and intensified as events converged and gathered to rush down the slope of destiny between the ephemeral Italian conquest of Ethiopia and the irreversible European disaster of the second world war: and in her salon this encouraged a triviality and inadequacy which she did not rightly estimate: for instance, a flood of words and witticism and argument which were the more empty the more elaborate they were. There was one result from this which had a particular effect upon her son—that her determination to find friends for him of his own age induced her to seek out and invite young people who must of course be anti-Fascist: so that this qualification, being an essential requirement, tended to become a sufficient condition for being made welcome at a good table, to her afternoon teas with plenty of rich pastries, and the warmth and comfort of her drawing-room, in complete disregard of food-cards, fuel restrictions and the rationing and austerity of wartime, of Mussolini's Fascist war as she put it.

Among those who were admitted there were, as there were bound to be, shirkers, fools and fanatics, and even some ardent supporters of the cause of gluttony and a sweet tooth, with one or two informers from *Ovra*. But these were mostly harmless. As a matter of fact, the chief of police at this time was a shrewd man who said that you couldn't start arresting political conspirators because that would mean that Italians would all have to devote their time to arresting each other.

The majority of these young men, and they were far from few, managed to reconcile laziness and cowardice with anti-Fascism by devoting great energy to getting a low medical grade or even exemption from military service by more or less fraudulent and illicit means.

This was a by-product of that continual misfortune which her difficult history has imposed on Italy: that the nation always has to face its critical and decisive moments in a state of political division and party schism, exactly at the point where both the crisis and the right course of action demand unity.

By a harsh and dangerous fatality, the product at once of the most trivial and of the very gravest causes, it is precisely the worst dangers which divide the hearts and the opinions of the Italian people. This made itself painfully manifest in the first world war and was repeated to even graver effect in the second.

In spite of a marked bent towards music, or more precisely because of a propensity for being in conflict with himself and other people, Donato had finished his studies by taking a science degree. When he was called up at the beginning of the war, he openly stated as a rigid principle that he was going to accept all the chances and duties which a soldier of a nation at war ought to expect, whether the war itself turned out well or ill, whether it was reasonable or rash. He said that military duty is only the more binding if, as far as can be foreseen, it is certain that the outcome will be unfortunate. On the subject of the distinction between a good and a bad war or a just and an unjust one, he expressed himself with harsh and savage impatience: there were no good or bad wars; war in so far as it was war was neither just nor unjust; they were either lost or won and that was the only real difference. But however desperate a war might be or even if it was lost, nothing, as long as it lasted, exempted the soldier from the struggle or from sacrificing himself, if that was the will of God, for when all is said and done, war is a judgment of God.

His relations with these young people who frequented his mother's drawing-room had become strained, since they were mostly armchair anti-Fascists or the unfit—who fed like fighting cocks—with some girls and young women among them, not a few of whom were a prey to that hysteria which political passion often assumes in women.

In order to evade Mussolini's and Hitler's war, the young men cultivated every sign of cardiac trouble or palpitation, every shadow of gastric ulcer or pulmonary lesion, however long healed, which might show in an X-ray photograph: if it hadn't been a Nazi-Fascist war, you would have seen them all behind the trumpets, banners flying, sword in hand. The young women spent hours explaining the whys and wherefores of defeats and successes on the war-fronts, demonstrating exhaustively and especially after the event, the inevitability of the rout in Albania, the impracticability of defending Ethiopia and how the German campaign was forced to a halt by the Channel, the African campaign at El Alamein and the Russian in front of Moscow and Stalingrad: and how useless it was conquering Norway: and that the Atlantic submarine war wouldn't undo the effects of 'lend-lease' and the contribution which the United States, that 'arsenal of democracy', was making. And when the U.S. later entered the war, it had turned out just as they'd always said, for Franco would never have conceded transit-rights for an assault on Gibraltar. It may seem strange, but when women are seized with the mania for politics, they are always better informed than we men are, which is saying a good deal. Anyway, if it had been any other than an 'Axis' war they would all have been nursing in hospital, either on board ship or under canvas, and braving the torpedoes and bombs. Some of them actually got to the point of saying that they wouldn't join the Red Cross by way of moral protest against the Axis bombardments and attacks on open cities, perpetrated in defiance of that international law which has only one stable and certain characteristic: that while the war is on, it's violated only by the enemy, after the war it's only the vanquished who've violated it.

Whenever he happened to be there, Donato soon lost

patience. He told them to their faces that their theories and their political and moral judgments were of the same kind and level of satisfaction as the relish they obtained, in defiance of ration-cards, from cream-pastries and ham and steaks and roasts while, coal and oil having vanished from the market, they huddled in the warmth of electric fires, flouting cuts and prohibitions: for from such gestures of rebellion against the oppression of Nazi-Fascist tyranny, they obtained their political and ethical satisfaction: and vindicated the dignity of the human person with pâté sandwiches!

During this period, Benedetto Croce, who was the world's leading philosophical opponent of liberticide and racial doctrines, came to Milan once or twice a year for a short stay. As a general rule, this great polemicist and profound moralist found no great entertainment in hearing his own opinions reproduced in drawing-room language and the accents of high society. And when somebody of either sex who had a smack of theoretical philosophy happened to give him a dose of the ideas which he had treated in his *Logic* and his *Practice*, this acted on him like a sleeping draught and he exercised his philosophic tolerance towards these tormentors in a vague interjection or a nod which looked like assent but was really just due to dozing and good-natured boredom.

Melania too got 'Don Benedetto' to call and take tea in her drawing-room: though she took the utmost care with the list of guests for the occasion, she made two bad mistakes. The first was to arrange for him a performance of modern chamber music as chromatic and contrapuntal as possible, and twelve-tone into the bargain, which, as he was going down the stairs at the end of the performance, elicited the comment that if this was the contemporary fate of music, he wasn't sorry that he hadn't been gifted either with the taste for it or with any sort of ear. The second mistake was to imagine that a very beautiful and striking young woman, who was particularly given to philosophising and playing politics, had given up her habit of

B

spouting her axioms and demonstrations—very aggressively and with far more passion than logic and moreover in a forced and unmusical voice.

Deafened and distracted and indeed somewhat overwhelmed, the philosopher had taken refuge in dozing, yet it wasn't this that checked the female orator but a momentary drying-up of the verbal flux. There was general embarrassment when Donato truculently intervened by saying that this sort of political talk was all twaddle and abstractions, and that the philosopher, if he hadn't been fast asleep, would have said that their kind of idealism was only a way of putting a fig-leaf on the world: which, he went on to suggest, could put it on and wear it of its own accord when it wanted to play hypocritical modesty but which, behind the fig-leaf, always remains a shameless impudent satyr, with nothing much to it but its 'virile attributes', as Mussolini put it.

And annoyed by the very fact that he had scandalised them, he went on and on and said that one kind of politics was as good as another and that there were only two possibilities for successful political ideas: the good ones get worse and the bad ones get better or at least lose their force. They turned on him: so he was prophesying the victory of Nazi-Fascism, was he? His reply was that he didn't make any prophecies about what he considered to be superior ideas, simply because it mattered to him that they shouldn't deteriorate in practice.

The contemptuous silence which greeted the last words of this paradox had the effect of waking the philosopher who seemed to have heard something even though he was asleep, for with one of his faintly snorting laughs, he said to Donato that although you could defend his aphorisms about fig-leaves, their drawback was that they were out of harmony with the necessities of the present moment which didn't even suit with truths of a contemplative kind, let alone more or less vague and elegant paradoxes. He wound up by saying that at the present time history demanded that everyone should make up his own mind and behave as if the good and the true were all on one side and the bad and the false all on the other, even if it wasn't true, even if the very opposite were true. There were times in which you had to leave it to history, if you wanted to serve historical justice, by taking your stand and defending it to your utmost in action and suffering and struggle.

This austere truth was received by Donato with the remark that this was exactly why he intended to carry out his duties, since fate had put him into uniform, even if that involved him in something worse and even more bitter than sacrifice in a lost cause.

These last words were quite enough to make his mother shudder, while someone else asked him what, to his knowledge, could be worse. To which his answer was, making any kind of contribution or sacrifice which aided the victory of a hateful cause.

At this further statement there were signs of ironical and contemptuous smiles all round which were only checked by the philosopher's sigh of approval. This reduced them all to silence, while he added that it is on our own account that we ought to sigh, not history's, for history verifies in the fullest and most absolute sense what was said at the time of the Albigensian massacres—'God will know his own'. History, too, would know its own, but seeking to make a corner in it showed that you weren't among them. One must serve history, not try to be its master.

And so the year which Donato passed in Milan in training and garrison duties thinned and scattered his group of contemporaries. And moreover every day times became harder and gloomier: and, inwardly racked with maternal anxiety, Melania suffered severely.

During the second year and the first half of the third, Donatello went wherever his fate happened to take him and it was nearly always far away.

It was a fate which in retrospect might have seemed playful

or ironic, but which bore cruelly on his mother in her apprehension and distress for her only son who was all that she had in the world and, apart from music, her only solace.

Time and again her Donatello was directed to the most dangerous assignments or destinations and the ones which were therefore likely to cause her the most anxiety: the Russian steppes and the African deserts fraught with catastrophe and disaster: the amphibious and, so to say, triphibious assaults and operations against the fortresses of Malta. And always at the last moment, but only at the last, something happened, either it was something quite unexpected or the order was countermanded and the fate which seemed settled was avoided. Sometimes he had no sooner arrived in whatever area it was, than the front became quiet: once a train was machine-gunned by an aeroplane and the delay made him lose the transport aircraft, which was attacked and burnt with all on board in the skies over Taranto. On two other occasions an unexpected order forced him to leave a ship just as it was about to sail. One of the ships was lost without trace in the Gran Sirte and the other went down in sight of the Sicilian coast, with the two battalions on board drowned to the last man.

The way his own improbable luck persisted, while the nation and its policy and indeed world-civilisation moved ineluctably towards the brink of disaster, bewildered Donato.

He felt as if chance had involved him in an insidious maze and that he was being preserved only by a kind of mockery and as it were at the cost of some incomprehensible cowardice and weakness, while it happened more and more frequently that his nerves played him tormenting tricks: it was sometimes as if he saw the existing moment double, as if every event, word, sensation or thought had been previously experienced; and acute anxiety, as if he apprehended disaster, oppressed and disturbed his mental processes, until this disorder of perception, which was a kind of hallucination, passed.

Actually, after a special medical examination in connection with a proposed expedition against Malta which would have been very difficult, Donato Mèrici was sent home on leave to recover from neurasthenia. This time the operation proved abortive during the preliminary trials and rehearsals, which was fortunate for all concerned.

Then a very disagreeable and unexpected personal experience befell him.

In wartime, the soldier forms a technical idea of danger which subordinates and disciplines his whole nature, not only his fear. Risk is an element of fact which has been reduced to calculations and forecasts and is to be met by defensive ideas and means which have been worked out and studied in advance. Yet despite all calculation of the risk involved it is met with—whether as a threat or a fact, whether passively endured or actively challenged—in conditions which allow for it and make it necessary, just as in any other dangerous profession: and moreover there are no professions which are entirely free from risk, no condition of human life, not even idleness and inertia.

Although fate seemed to have given him a kind of exemption, had even as it were exonerated him, Donato had been at the front and above all he had prepared himself morally and technically for danger. He had become accustomed to being shot at in war, and found this none too difficult since he was naturally courageous and imperturbable, in fact indifferent to danger and the idea of violent death. And being thus courageous with the contemptuous kind of courage which laughs at danger, he imagined that he did not know fear: a belief as frail and illusory as it is rash.

On one of the first nights of his sick leave, when he was still only beginning to renew the pleasure and restfulness of home and of his own room, of his own bed with its fine and freshly-laundered sheets, there was an air-raid on Milan.

It certainly wasn't the first he had known. He had already

experienced dozens and those who panicked at the mere sound of the siren always made him laugh. In other cities, he had laughed often enough at the shelters, generally nothing more than rickety cellars shoddily reinforced, into which people packed themselves so tightly that an incident would produce the maximum number of victims in the smallest space. Not so bad when it was only a question of small bombs, but what about the block-busters? Meanwhile, this sort of shelter at least showed the want of preparation with which Italy had embarked on a serious war: a war proclaimed by Hitler as determining the fate of Germany and the disposition of the globe for the next thousand years. And Germany moreover had prepared herself to meet the demands of this situation, except for being able to invade England, forestalling the Russian winter and preventing the intervention of the United States: which were precisely the three things destined to make her lose the war! But the human mind can hardly conceive a stranger delusion than this thousand-years-programme, when what a man does at this very moment isn't what he thinks it is or what he intended, let alone what may go on in a thousand or a hundred years, or for that matter in a day or an hour. Although admittedly he came to them later, Donato did not in these days draw philosophical or historical conclusions either from words or events. He was distressed by his own forecast already referred to: that either these days would lay the foundations of a new Europe, conquered and unified by Hitler, in which he did not see how he could survive: or indeed the last of the old foundations of Europe were being destroyed and without them he also did not see how he could survive.

And here he himself was being unduly fantastic, for while it is true that history has no concern for the survival either of peoples or individuals, those that do survive manage to live in general conditions which imagination would have judged impossible or unendurable. To bring it down to two hackneyed and comforting saws: 'Time is the great healer', and 'You never know what you can do till you try'.

Anyway he did not mean to go down to the shelters and certainly not the one in his mother's house, an old building in an old part of Milan which was the perfect specification for a death-trap, where you could be blown to pieces and buried all at one go.

Awakened by the dismal wailing of the sirens that night, he turned over and laughed. He could already hear the hubbub of the inhabitants on the staircases crowding down to the shelter from every room in the house. He felt that being the only one, apart from a very few others in the city, to stay in his cool pleasant bed added zest to his satisfaction in it.

Melania however thought differently: in her view, as everyone went down to the shelters, it was odd if you didn't, an eccentricity to be frowned upon. Whether there was any danger or not, she thought that, if anything happened, it would look almost ridiculous, as if you'd tried to be a law unto yourself just through pigheadedness or conceit.

When they discussed it, she had asked Donatello if he really advised her not to go down to the shelter and he had replied that it wasn't a case for advice. In the meantime, Melania passed that night inwardly reproaching her son for his eccentricity, wilfulness and bravado. He had said to her that he would be prepared to go down with her only if it gave her pleasure or made her feel safer. If she asked him to go down with her to keep her company, he would do it, but only for her sake, not for his own. To which Melania answered that there were some things you ought not to have to ask: and privately she would have preferred it if his own feelings had prompted him to come down with her, so that she could be less anxious with him beside her.

This time there was the wonted silence of night after the warning, a silence of human minds in troubled suspense in which you could imagine the anxiety of a whole city holding its breath.

Milan had already suffered a few moderately heavy air-raids, quite enough to give a foretaste of what could happen but, as Donatello said, not to be compared with other cities where he had been.

He could make out the sound of anti-aircraft batteries in the distance but they only made him say to himself with a contemptuous laugh that as usual they were kicking up a great fuss to no purpose: and meanwhile they weren't going to keep him awake especially as the warning had managed to interrupt his first sleep, always the sweetest and deepest, and moreover the firing had stopped and the widespread silence had returned, unbroken and potent. They'd gone, or perhaps they hadn't even been interested in Milan, he thought, with a delicious yawn. The silence weighed sleepily on him again.

And then he heard them: they were right over the roof, right above his head, sudden and violent with a thunderous roar which seemed to suck all the air into itself and took away his breath and made him thrust his head under the sheet with a wild uncontrollable movement. They departed and returned before he had even time to realise that he was afraid, although the time seemed to him unspeakably empty and long drawn-out, since he himself measured its void by fits of straining to hear and by the sudden acceleration of his heart-beats.

But between two bomb-bursts which fell close and shook the house and the bed on which he was lying, he realised his fear. The second burst flung open his bedroom windows on the shining impassive depths of a clear and starlit sky, a sky which was packed thick with stars. It was as if through some un-believable and preternatural effect, the starry night broke into his room and even into his eyes, wide like the windows. And he was almost on the point of asking himself not what had flung them open but who had done so, when he heard the planes hovering in the near-by sky. It sounded as if they were really looking for a particular target, the house, himself. And before he could see how absurd and extravagant this was, there

was a third explosion which lit up that part of the sky which
he could see from his windows with brilliant swords and
arrows of light. The house jumped as if it were cut clean away
from the ground or as if the ground had been snatched from
underneath it. The bed shifted: the beams groaned: he felt as
if something had taken him by the shoulders and tried to throw
him out of bed and then flung him back again and held him
down, weighing upon all his limbs. The house creaked and
groaned again in the silence of the night and this showed that
it was settling down again after the violent shaking, but
Donato strained in the silence in an intense effort of listening.
They did not come back and he realised that he had been
afraid, with bloodless vile humiliating fear.

The idea that the bomb had been meant for him could not
have been more ridiculous and absurd but the laughter which
seized him now wasn't funny in itself. It was sombre hysterical
laughter, which is a kind of natural buffoonery at one's own
fear when the danger is over.

What struck him as at once absurd and unbearable was that
the house with everything in it, that he himself in that particular room in that particular house, were exposed to the bare
incidence of destruction. In any other part of the globe he
would have felt that he had both the freedom and the support
of a powerful discipline: but not here. This room had been his
without a break since infancy and every object in it spoke to
him a silent vivid language and wove a delicate sensuous web
of association of the sort which is sometimes revealed by a
colour, a perfume, a quality of light, a sound, evoking at times
one hardly knows what, whether actual memory or the mere
longing for a vanished memory of something which was never
even real. In this room, thus alive with the sense of past time,
of what had been and not been, of all the dead years and of
those still to come, and now so suddenly full of an inexpressible confusion and suspense, life seemed to be passing, empty
of possibility before it was fulfilled, but always composed

of that infinity which we shall never achieve nor create: life was passing, always finished before it had begun: and he desperately rebelled against an idea so bare and simple as that of dying.

As he lay in this room and on this bed of his, the thing which had nearly happened and which could happen from one moment to the next, war or no war, seemed to him incongruous, not to be admitted, against nature.

It was as if the homely indolent comfort expressed by the phrase 'dying in one's bed' had taken on a harsh ironical meaning: because there he was after all, in his own bed!

Meanwhile what he had felt was and had been fear, the very thing for which, with actual cruelty, he had often made fun of timid people, condemning it for the stupidity, the unfairness and insensibility which made it the worst of all faults, a veritable sin, something unclean: it was like claiming for oneself unfairly and individualistically something to which everyone is subject and which seems quite natural in others: fear would be natural and pardonable if it were not just for this sin of irrational egoism. Was he the only one who had a room and memories? Didn't everyone else have a life to lose, a unique irreplaceable life? It was fear which had revealed to him that all the other lives in the world were of no account, that it was only the thought of his own which gave him that pitiful moral dread and made him lie gasping on his bed drenched with a cold and loathly sweat. He remembered once giving a pep talk to some of his troops and severely reproving one of them who had said 'If I die, the whole world dies.' He'd been a fine one to preach!

Only one thing was needed to complete his cowardice, and now that came to him too: relief that he had been alone and that nobody had seen him and had the chance of laughing at him. And now he also felt afraid that he wouldn't be able to keep it hidden because fear had warped his mind and the warp would remain; from now on there would be a path which the vile thing knew and by which it could return to invest him, when off his guard and without spiritual defence.

It is a bitter discovery, a feeling which for a proud man may be almost beyond bearing. Donato had always lived in the pride of certainty that his spirit could never fail him: the doubt terrified him, the mere doubt now was enough to make him miserably, foully afraid. Moreover this was neurasthenia, that mysterious and insidious disease which Donato for very pride would have liked to be able to attribute to some unusual moral cause, whereas it was merely visceral and could do with a dose of salts.

And since neurasthenia is a disease characterised by its greed of everything which can harm the sufferer, it made him afraid of his own fear and fixed this obsession firmly in his head. And he was always hungry except at meal times, he was always worn out and dropping with sleep except when he was in bed, and so on.

And since he did not remember such simple truths as the fact that if you want your soldiers to have courage you must send them into battle with a full stomach and after a good night's rest—or if he remembered them he rejected them for himself as if he had been of a totally different clay—he forced himself to meet the danger of air-attacks and of death, and to overcome his fear by chaffing and brooding inwardly upon the same thought in a way which weakened and exhausted him.

And so he pined and moped, to his mother's despair, and wouldn't listen to a word on the subject which, to his own harm, was always on his mind, but gave way to violent outbursts of rage of which he was ashamed every time anyone begged him to eat or sleep or cheer up or stop thinking so much: which was just what he couldn't manage to do and what was making him ill. He had no faith in doctors and saw his doctor every day. And after having gone through the usual soundings and thumpings and knee-tappings and examinations and tests, what were they supposed to say to him? Only that he was physically sound enough and that to get well from this sort of illness, you must stop thinking so much, give up worrying, sleep and eat: which is the same as saying that you can get well or go to hell. If he had known how to do what they prescribed he could have done without doctors and medicine, he would have been cured before he was ill!

Well, it wasn't he who had sent for them: at least he liked to try and persuade himself that this was the case so as to have the satisfaction of posing as a stoic and rational individual who has a knowledgeable contempt of the small claims of science in general, and of the infinitesimal ones of medical science in particular: and the more miserable satisfaction of charging his mother with encouraging his illness by her anxious fussing, when he knew quite well that the trouble would go of its own accord or would carry him off, without any help from doctors.

He found his mother's way of looking at him unbearable, the anxiety with which she watched over him and spied upon him and the feigned indifference of her tone when she asked him how he had slept, how he liked a meal which had been chosen specially to tempt his appetite, what he would like to eat: he never wanted to eat anything as soon as she made him think about food. It was just the same as when he was sleepless; striving for sleep only drove it away. And he was irritated by the sighs which his mother couldn't always repress and which seemed to him sometimes bored or impatient.

She said nothing about it but she had a very definite reason for anxiety. Donato's father had been strong and full of energy, a cheerful lively young man right up to the time when she had had Donato, and then almost between one day and the next, without why or wherefore, as we say of those whys and wherefores which we can't make out, he had begun to pine and fade away: and while threatened with consumption he had been attacked by epidemic influenza with a terrifying virulence which was the end of him.

And, with her husband's death in mind, every time that
Melania realised that Donato was at the age his father had been,
she was overcome by anxiety, with a terrible fear moreover of
letting him guess what she was thinking and of putting an idea
in his head which would be worse than superstition, an
association of inevitable doom, of having to die as young as
his father.

She reproached herself severely enough for this superstitious terror, which in any case took no account of Donato's
inner disposition: for he had dwelt on his father's end for a
long time now and not with fear but rather with a kind of
longing. So much so that when he felt angry with his mother,
as he did with anyone who tried to make him pull himself
together, he hugged this longing with a private greed as if it
were a secret treasure or satisfaction or a kind of nostrum: and
when he felt sorry for his mother it was not only to shield her
from distress that he refrained from telling her that he had
penetrated her secret grief, but also so as to cling to the
melancholy sweetness of his own.

He was the only one who did not see how much she actually
suffered, even in health, but perhaps this was also because her
suffering had causes and elements which a son cannot understand or even conceive.

But some further information is required before anything is
said about these.

CHAPTER TWO

A Product of the Times

FOR some time visitors had been coming less and less frequently to Casa Mèrici, even the ones who had been most faithful, and now at the end of the first two years of war, they had practically disappeared: they were either evacuated, or they did not go out much, especially in the evenings.

Among the few who still came was an odd creature brought in by Donato. This man seemed to be the only person whose company gave Donato any pleasure and put him in a good humour: not that Melania felt any more drawn to him on that account, but motherly gratitude made her put up with him.

He was called Falaride: and he used to say he'd like to know what bee had got into his father's bonnet to make him name his first-born after Phalaris, the tyrant of Agrigentum, who put Perillus—who had invented it—into the famous bull and roasted him as its first victim: and the tyrant's modern namesake added that this was extremely ingenious too, on the part of the greatest Dead-pan not only of antiquity but of all time, and that even Tiberius himself had never equalled him, although he was pretty ingenious, too: for example when he let his soothsayers all fall down a ravine because if they'd really known their job they'd never have come walking with him.

The second son had been called Tiberius: the third Attila, but he died in infancy, while Tiberius grew up half booby and all the rest ass. The father of the three tyrants had been professor of Greek and Latin, the last of his kind to maintain, right till his dying day, the dignity of the professorial topper and morning-coat with a white tie. Altogether a model of dignity, not only in his devotion to his duty as a teacher and to his educational mission, but in his refusal to complain of the smallness of his salary, of which he used to say that the bread of learning isn't bought or sold, whether you receive it or break it for others.

Among the pupils to whom he taught Latin had been Guglielmo Marconi, his academic judgment of whom—that he was dull and incompetent—had been fished out of the registers and reports and circulated to the press: and this had caused much amusement behind Professor Evemero Narenza's back. He wrote a reply to the newspapers which didn't do him any good and only made everybody laugh all the more, particularly because Narenza was the most perfect pedant and very strict in his attention to purity of diction and style, so that he always had to try and find a learned circumlocution for every neologism, and when necessity obliged him to use one, he always craved indulgence, not only from the reader but from the chaste muses of the fourteenth-century language.

If his anger and contempt had confined themselves to the statement that he hadn't succeeded in making a shining light of classical scholarship out of Marconi, matters would have remained there without harm to Marconi or to himself, but stung by jibes and goaded by contradiction, let alone wounded by the defamation he had received in the course of this polemic, he armed himself with critical and historical learning on the subject of Hertzian waves and the relative merits of different discoveries and inventions.

He got himself involved in a voluble polemic about Marconi's claim to priority and also about his scientific merits, as to whether or not he really had been the inventor of wireless and the whole credit could be claimed by him alone and not rather by Righi, Branly, Slaby, Calzecchi, Popoff, etc.

Due to his emotional bias, Professor Narenza was unable to examine the question of priority realistically, in terms of the

practical, executive, industrial and political facts which
demonstrated that it belonged to Marconi: and so he went off
the track and discharged his venom in accusations of bad faith
and theft of scientific and laboratory secrets: in particular he
charged Marconi with injuring Calzecchi, who had invented
it, by misappropriating his *coherer*: and also of black ingratitude
if not of actual breach of trust towards the great Bolognese
scientist Augusto Righi.

Whatever the Professor himself thought about it, Righi,
who was a gruff and independent man, wasn't pleased by
Narenza's taking up the cudgels on behalf of scientific history
and very rapidly ceased to put up with it, so that before long
Narenza didn't even receive visiting-cards by way of acknow-
ledgment, either from Righi himself, or from the other
scientific luminaries to whom he sent his pamphlets as a mark
of homage, although he had had them printed at his own expense and at the cost of not inconsiderably upsetting the family
budget: for his studies and researches which were as costly as
they were vain, had also to be made at his own expense. In
fact Righi and Calzecchi were thoroughly annoyed and more
or less finally showed him the door: as for Marconi, he didn't
care, or more probably never knew that he had such a bitter,
relentless and eloquent antagonist, accusing him, in the
footsteps of Valla, the humanist, 'of the fradulent discovery
deceptively accredited to Marconi, self-styled inventor of the
marconigraph, named after him by a barbaric abuse'. One of
Narenza's most constantly repeated tags was *vitam impendere
vero*, with the train of more or less stoic maxims which he
extracted by the sackful from 'the classic page' and culled more
sparingly from the 'modern jargon' in order that the finest
flowers of language and of rhetoric should spring from his own
productions. He saw himself as the 'hammer' (in Latin,
malleus) of Marconi and the Marconian sect, of Marconophily
and Marconism, as if attacking a new heresy. And since no one
took the trouble to answer him, or if anyone did it was some

obscure journalist or someone like himself with a unique fixed
idea, and since there is nothing which makes for verbosity so
much as talking to yourself with no other ears to listen,
Narenza's invective in his diatribes against the man he called
'that dishonest conjurer', *ut ita dicam* "the electrician from Pontecchio", 'insurged' to Demosthenic thunders, to Ciceronian
solemnities, and included delicate Catullan touches of naughti-
ness which if he had imitated them in Italian instead of quoting
them in Latin, might have been something of a stigma in the
eyes of outraged modesty: and he also reproduced the severity
of Tacitus, the indignation of Juvenal, without mentioning the
barbs and sallies which he derived from Dante's invective and
the polemics of Annibal Caro and many others, and scattered
lavishly over the pages with a spate of epithets like 'meet to
be spat at' from Demosthenes and frequent repetitions of the
Ciceronian *quousque tandem*. All this in a lofty and circum-
locutary style with many classic graces which would have
amused if they hadn't first irritated the most patient reader.

He could have wished at the very least that the Marconigraph should be given a different name, because it was even
less justified than calling America after Vespucci. He felt
obliged to remark that even if the great and somewhat fan-
tasticating Columbus was always making wild claims about
having reached the shores of China or Japan, or somewhere
about the mount of purgatory, the actual discovery and
scientific delimitation of the New World belonged of plain
right to the Florentine Amerigo: he did not pursue the comparison but increased the dose of 'objurgations' against the
'usurper' who 'callow and precocious youth' having found *ne
quidem dicam*, or 'should one say appropriated, in the illustrious
laboratory and in the learned, albeit imprudent discourses
of Righi, that eminent master, information germane to his
own purely materialistic and eleemosynary purposes, feigned
a leisurely intention and under the cloak of a faithless abandonment of studies and doctrines in which, sooth to say, he

C

had never shone with a vivid nor peculiar light, sequestered himself in the paternal domain of Pontecchio in the Val di Reno, there to labour in secret towards the merely banausic perfection of that ingenious apparatus for the transmission and reception of magnetic flux on which worldly ignorance and heedlessness has conferred the unmerited name of Marconigraph'.

This style was a contributory cause of the flux of mirth from the very few people who happened to be on Narenza's wavelength, and who even took the trouble to be amused at his expense.

But a day came when he was summoned to the Prefecture, and underneath his air of dignity he went along in a turmoil of bold and confident hopes. It is important to know that he had been, from his earliest youth, a devoted Carduccian patriot and a somewhat nervous Interventionist in 1914 and '15: later, in the critical days of 1919, D'Annunzio at Fiume and Mussolini's Fascism and what it stood for, had appealed to him as redemption for the national ideals and as the preservation of the fatherland for a destiny of greatness and power. And when he heard over the radio that Ethiopia had been conquered and the Empire proclaimed from Rome's 'fateful hills' he burst into tears and abandoned himself to his transports of enthusiasm, as if carried away to the ethereal regions of endless felicity and ineffable patriotic pride. He went so far as to say that Mussolini had been able to confer genius even on Marconi, so that in spite of being a Marconiphobe, he accorded complete faith to the invention which everybody was talking about at the time, a device for putting all internal combustion engines out of action, whether they were to be found in aircraft, landcraft or submarines. And he loudly proclaimed this as one of Mussolini's miracles. He didn't use the word 'clima' (when referring to the political atmosphere) because he had purified his vocabulary of all such neologisms and solecisms and barbarisms, and deplored the havoc they had wrought in the Italian and Fascist tongue, and even in Mussolini's public addresses. But he had nothing else against Fascism or the Duce, and as far as the latter's public speaking was concerned he asserted that it wasn't 'right or reasonable to pick holes' in the parlance of that creative afflatus which both in its denunciatory and its celebratory roles had brought about such great historic events: for example, the challenge to the 'iniquitous sanctions' decreed by the League of Nations, whose envy, rage and impotence, as he averred, had united them against the resurgence of Italy and her ineluctable destiny. And he quoted the well-known phrases to the effect that God alone can deflect our purposes but not men or events: that we had the past behind us and the future before us: and that it is the plough which traces the furrow but the sword which defends it, although there was something in Mussolini's turn of construction here which made him, at least in imagination, reach for the red and blue pencils which he used for correcting exercises, in order to record his opinion that it contained a gallicism, that the syntax was barbaric and the language gravely inelegant. These might nevertheless be excused in the man who could endow even the unutterably stupid Marconi with genius and enable him to invent the machine for stopping engines, thus assuring Italy of illimitable strength and something more than the certainty of victory in any conflict, even though her enemies were to be counted in thousands and tens of thousands.

The result of all this was that having brushed and donned the least shiny of his morning-coats, and surmounted it all with his topper, he presented himself at the Prefecture in a triumphant twitter: actually it was at Government House, as it had been called since the word 'Prefecture' had become too reminiscent of the subjection and division of Italy in the days of Umberto and Giolitti. On the way he formulated two hypotheses, one public and the other private: the first was that the Prefect, perhaps even the Duce himself, wanted his approval of Marconi's invention, and he prepared himself to welcome it with a feeling of resignation, and even contentment at the idea that by air, and sea and in the waters under the sea, it was going to call a halt to all the flights and fleets, to aircraft, ships and armoured vehicles in their squadrons: and in the meantime, so rumour had it, Marconi had carried out an experiment one Sunday and stranded all the cars between Ostia and Rome on their way back from the seaside.

The second theory, which was more unassuming but very exciting, was that after so many years as a simple Chevalier, he was going to be promoted to Commander for his services as a teacher and scholar and even as a bard. As a matter of fact, not long before, one of the wilder of the inventors who had been taken seriously by the Duce and commended to the trusting Italian public by means of press-publicity had been trying to obtain iron—and (unless memory errs) gold as well—by sieving the sands of the Italian sea-shore, and so to benefit a great but poverty-stricken people. Untroubled by doubt, Narenza had produced a celebratory ode in Pindarics, interlarded with epic themes from maritime history, and embodying the Mussolinian conception that 'The sword is bread'. And so he was ready to recognise the merits of Marconi's newly-discovered genius, and in the public interest to keep quiet about these bygone plagiarisms and fraudulent practices.

In this frame of mind he was admitted to the Prefect's office and gave a rigid Fascist salute. His Excellency did not lift his eyes from his papers or return the salute, but left him standing.

In the past, the Prefect had been one of the most violent and impassioned of *squadristi*, and he had remained an explosive person, fond of insult and sarcasm, in which he vented the ancient hankering to beat someone up which had lost its former outlet. With a contemptuous lift of his eyebrows, and of course using the regulation second person plural, he asked whether the visitor was that Professor Narenza whose first name was *Evemèro*, and broke off to inquire sarcastically how one manages to acquire such a name.

The Professor felt obliged to put him right and said it was pronounced Evèmero, but this modest correction only swelled the waters of the prefectorial wrath to over-flowing: he could keep his corrections to himself, they weren't in school now, better not start giving lessons when they hadn't been asked for: and Evèmero or *Evemèro,* it makes no odds, it only went to show that anyone who had such a name and anyone who had given it to him, and the priest who had allowed it at the font into the bargain, were all a lot of silly twerps. I must mention that His Excellency was an anti-clerical and a non-believer and, although he complied with superior directives prescribing conformity to the Catholic religion for political reasons, he strained at the leash. And he also had it in for professors because of unpleasant old associations with school and university, for though he was a 'war-graduate', he had been 'ploughed' by the peace.

After his outburst of fury, he came back to the subject and asked Narenza if he were 'this fellow' who had a grudge against Marconi: and without giving him a chance to reply, enjoined him to get over it, and not to imagine that he had been called there to discuss anything or to go into explanations or even to apologise: it had been simply to tell him that they'd already had enough trouble with the balls he'd talked about other people. Was that clear? Well then, hop it. Right turn, quick march and off you go!

But as usual with violent characters, His Excellency had a simple mind, which at this point was seized with something like pure curiosity. Why on earth should this rabbit, this miserable devil of a professor—with the name *Evemèro* into the bargain—have it in for Marconi? However don't let him start talking about culture: in Germany the short answer to such questions had been put by Goering: if you hear the word *Culture,* reach for your gun! So he could give an account of himself without any cultural claptrap.

Narenza, with his arm aching from the prolonged Fascist

salute, began to stammer that it wasn't that he hated Marconi, he simply cared for historical accuracy. He was promptly interrupted: now if it had just been a wish to show off and advertise himself, it would have been pardonable: but instead it was apparently pure and simple congenital idiocy.

His passion for historical accuracy drove Narenza to rebellion when he heard such a description of his anti-Marconian mission and he raised his voice. 'The electrician from Pontecchio' was at the very most a clever technician and a very shrewd man of affairs who had been able to interest English industrialists and government officials in the great Marconigraph project. And the English had held on to him and his Marconigraph as long as it suited their industrial and military policy: when he'd lost his utility and become a nuisance they'd packed him back to Italy. Marconi 'on the rebound' was a present from the English. And the trick he had played about lighting lamps in Sydney had been a pure swindle, *Sit venia verbo*, for the sake of advertisement, a play on words for the benefit of any of the dolts who could be taken in by it.

He couldn't have touched on a worse subject than the English. Did the oaf know, asked the Prefect, rising in his wrath, that Marconi had been held up as an example to the régime and proclaimed as one of its glories? Did he realise that what he was saying was as good as calling the Duce a fool and suggesting that he could be taken in, by the English into the bargain? Did he even have the faintest idea that at a moment of their political history, which like the present demanded heroism, his was anti-Fascist behaviour of the most perfidious kind, it was defeatism, antipatriotism, fraud and treason? The letter which the Ministry of Popular Culture had sent from Rome—and he waved the document under his nose—emphasised the imbecile folly which couldn't grasp the unseemliness of digging up old disputes about the priority of the invention and credit for developing it. In defiance of Italian claims, the letter read, this credit had been attributed to the English and the priority had been claimed on behalf of the French for Branly, of the Germans for Slaby and of the Russians, communists on top of everything, for Popoff. Narenza could think himself lucky, added the Prefect, that all the reports ruled out evil intentions and stated that he was an exemplary Fascist: so that only one theory remained and now that could be looked on as certain, and nobody was 'playing on words' this time: he was just a perfect moron.

In consideration of which he would be spared the disciplinary measures which would have followed from obstinacy—withdrawal of his ration-card, imprisonment and so on. But he might as well know that not only in the town but in the whole province, the printers had been warned not to print any more antimarconian vapourings from Professor Narenza, Evemèro or Evèmero, however he called himself.

The Professor was startled. That certain forms of bullying and intimidation seemed to him useful, necessary or at least tolerable when it was a question of other people, but smacked differently when applied to himself, was only human. But when it was a question of information received, in other words when he found that he had been spied upon, he was shocked and offended. Moreover, for at least seventy of his seventy-five years, he had been accustomed to respect, even deference, and had acquired the most lofty opinion of his own dignity both from himself and from others. From infancy and primary school days, as child, schoolboy, student and later as a young irreproachable teacher, he had never known what it was to be reproved, either by pastors or masters, or by his own conscience. Such a surfeit of perfection, such a stainless and unruffled conscience had prepared him but poorly to put up with domination, rudeness and scorn for the first time at seventy-five.

He protested on the score of dignity, love of historical accuracy, conscience and truth—*vitam impendere vero* he said: but the spate was dammed in his mouth: he could pack up the

Latin because the 'Boss' didn't understand it and definitely drew the line at it: and at the time when he might have been sitting on a school-bench being taught it by old fogies like Narenza, he had been at the front, and after that he had been out on the streets with his Fascist truncheon in his fist, and if he hadn't been, all Narenza's tiresome nonsense and his silly little pamphlets against Marconi would have been over and done with years ago, along with his idiotic touchy bourgeois self-importance.

But Narenza would not give way. Was he supposed to beg pardon for having acted according to conscience and truth? He was, apart from that, still touched to hear the tram conductor or the milkman address him with the direct Fascist 'Voi' and liked to quote Dante's *Voi, che prima Roma sofferie*: and this also fortified him in resisting outrageous abuse from a man who drew the line at Latin. And he couldn't help saying, with the bitterest sarcasm, that even the Duce didn't know any Latin and the fact added nothing to his stature. Then perhaps in the belief that he was appeasing the Prefect, he added a '*Colendissimo*'—most revered—'*Signor Prefetto*', which opened the floodgates of the Prefect's wrath and started him raving.

Who did he think he was calling '*Colendissimo*'? He'd better take care what he was saying and the first thing to remember was that the Prefect while exercising his functions and within the limits of his own terrain, was entitled to be called 'Your Excellency'. And really he'd almost got to the point when he regretted the days when you could teach proper behaviour by the forcible administration of a dose of castor oil. Every time the poor wretch got to the point of saying that in good Italian '*colendissimo*' is a term of the highest respect, he was silenced in Mussolinian fashion, by a thump on the table and was told to get along with him, and all the other silly twerps. And the summary conclusion was: Marconi could be the biggest fake or the silliest clot in the world: for that matter he might never even have existed, might have been a pure fairy story: but

the Duce had spoken, and had made him President of the
Italian Academy: and so now Marconi was history, Fascist
history, and couldn't be touched: and as for him, Professor-
my-Foot, all he had to do was to shut up, here, now, everywhere and for all times. Goering was quite right. Culture?
Where's a gun? And he could thank his stars that information
received was favourable. And by the way, would he like to
know who had given it? A valued and vigilant political
informer, Falaride Narenza. The Prefect didn't mind rubbing
salt into the wound.

To be spied on by his own son was the final blow and he
felt he was seeing the world for the first time as it really is. He
fled without even saying goodbye, in profound humiliation
and a state of sick apathy: and he took to his bed and never rose
again, carried off very shortly by double pneumonia. Falaride
got himself transferred to Milan and used to say that the
Professor, as he called his father, in choosing three such names
as Tiberius, Attila and his own, had merely intended to induce
salutary reflections in his sons on the subject of the cruelty of
tyrants, but in fact he had thus vented his pedagogue's un-
conscious lust for domination. And that was why the first
snub he had received from a tyrant so much less ferocious
and monstrous than Phalaris, Tiberius and Attila, had proved
not only indigestible but fatal—although pneumococcus had
admittedly helped.

This Falaride was a strange type. He had reddish hair, a
pasty freckled skin and cold and glaucous eyes with a sharp
determined expression. He was skinny but had great powers
of resistance and a good supply of vices which he indulged
with a kind of circumspect sobriety. He used to assert that it
wasn't enough to work for money and power, you had to get
yourself into the intimate confidence of those who are in
control of these forms of influence. For a poor wretch who
was the son of the Marconiphobe, there was no profession
better suited to this end than that of agent and political

informer. But all this on the one condition of not compromising his future chances in the event that the money and power should come to change hands.

And when Donato betrayed his scruples and some moral distaste, he brought up the example of his father who had lived a life of the purest and most unblemished virtue and integrity, only to die in a way which was more ridiculous than affecting, since he had even gone so far as to refuse to see his son Falaride on his death-bed because he had given information about him to the police, information moreover which was accurate and justified.

And now at the point to which the various trends in the story have brought us, things had reached a pretty pass, at the end of which this transfer of influence and money he always kept his eye on was certainly due to take place. So without troubling to make a mystery of anything so well-known as his capacities as a political informer, he was on the look-out for anyone who in his judgment might be a favourite in the next transfer. And whenever there were sour faces and contemptuous repulses he didn't allow such signs of disapproval to intimidate him or discourage him in the slightest, in fact he didn't waste time asking for any mercy or excuse for himself, nor intriguing for help or protection, but put himself forward to help and work for these others and be a kind of protector to them. And if you want to know the way of it, he had a memory like a steel-safe for texts, documents and data, and he conclusively demonstrated to the people concerned how often they had shown themselves, both in words and deeds, to be strict and active anti-Fascists, and he expressed his readiness to act as a witness and make this knowledge public and available in a way which would be both useful and acceptable. And he showed himself just as well informed about any weakness or uncertainty or perfunctoriness that there might have been in their professional and political conduct while Fascism was in the ascendant, but here his recollection though no less detailed was more discreet, while his allusions were vaguer and were not carried beyond the degree of precision which the circumstances of the interested parties required, these including their general unwillingness and short memories. But as he said, it's just the man who has a good eye for a straight line who can afford to let himself go in a few curves, provided that they come back to the straight and don't turn round corners or go off at a tangent or worse still turn round in a circle, which is what you would expect from weathercocks, turncoats and opportunists. And on occasions he was quite capable of citing the example of his father whose rectitude, in spite of being so impeccable that he would have been able to hold his head high to that day if only he hadn't been dead, had cost him the bitterest humiliation.

In the end those who had imagined that he had come to try to exonerate himself and do a deal with them about being let off, found that what they had got from him had been a generous and disinterested offer of support and protection the next time the régime collapsed. No matter how furious they got, it made no impression on him. And it was worth seeing this extraordinary man's sardonic self-satisfaction when, as he was quite capable of doing, he would put his hand on the shoulder of one of these characters, who would have expected anything sooner than this sudden absolution, and conclude by pronouncing that they had always been good, indeed impeccable anti-Fascists and that he could and would say so. And when would that be? Ah well, as soon as the rush for recognition began, when some people would have a genuine claim and some only a half-and-half one, while others would have none at all: and then everybody would be putting his own claim forward and of course other people's too, but only in so far as they didn't clash with one's own. And, he'd repeat, there'll be a rush.

And what about himself? asked Donatello. Well, he had no ambitions, political or otherwise, himself: he had only one loyalty, he said with Guicciardini, and that was to his own interest. And he added that he only made one philosophical generalisation: that man is a product of his times: and to follow the times was his only rule.

But when the changeover actually took place, how was he going to arrange things for himself in such a difficult and dangerous moment? And he answered that it would be all very simple: he was going to run away and if necessary hide in Donatello's house, in Casa Mèrici. Did he really think that was such a very safe place, Donato asked him with a laugh? Well, at least it was handy, he said shrugging his shoulders, if it turned out that the thing happened in a hurry.

Meanwhile, after much hesitation and after a heavier air-raid than any they had so far had, Melania Mèrici had made up her mind to evacuate and to move out to Vill' Alma, in the country, with the best of her furniture and effects.

CHAPTER THREE

In a House of Old Milan

MELANIA was the daughter of a prominent German immigrant who had come to Italy without a halfpenny to his name, in the days of commercial and financial expansion under the Wilhelms, when the Milan galleria was full of German commercial travellers and representatives of Krupp's and you could in fact hear German spoken more often than the Milanese dialect.

Her mother, who had been Italian, had died very young. After he was naturalised, it had been by dint of hard work and the application of a strong and steady intelligence that her father, of whom she was the adored only child, had risen from the bank clerk's hard counter to the general manager's soft armchair. He was a man of great abilities who saw himself as standing for something in capitalist society which included the duty of acquiring and augmenting a really high culture and really civilised manners, both in private and public life. After he had been left a widower—and an inconsolable one—she was educated in a well-known Florentine school for girls, and during her girlhood in Florence she had been gently imbued with that kind of humanism so well adapted to privileged classes and to the best international society, which encouraged the growth of a culture more sensitive in matters of taste than of critical understanding: it was as it were delicately resigned to its own sterility and want of productive power.

With a certain wariness in its receptivity, it was Florence that particularly reflected this culture, under the rainbow colours of impressionism and of *fin de siècle* literature, in the

music of Richard Strauss and Debussy, the one both cerebral
and passionate, the other subtle but ephemeral: and in the
splendours and elegances of a D'Annunzio, although here
again with a certain wariness and distance, which was always
ready to offer discoveries, fashions and works of literature of a
more fastidious and esoteric kind, something more enigmatic
and more exacting, as a contrast.

It was reflected moreover in the association between
D'Annunzio's villa, the pagan and Nietzschean *Capponcina*,
and Duse's franciscan *Porziuncola*, whose franciscanism, however, was too futile even to seem sacriligious: and also in
another association—that which existed between D'Annunzio
and Duse, between a florid type of literary genius—which was
poor in creative power however much it abounded in dilet-
tante virtuosity—and an interpretative and mimetic genius
which in its kind was as vigorous and authentic as anything
to be found upon the stage: and it was only lately that the over-
conscious erotic and artistic way of life, with its heroic extra-
vagances which had been publicised by these two, had brought
its illusions to a head in an all too human misery and woe.

The effect of this association was manifest in D'Annunzio's
ideological celebration of power and joy, while his poetry
expresses the melancholy of inward defeat and a desperate fear
of the void and of death: and in the histrionics of Duse, an
actress who dissipated and distorted her natural abilities,
projecting them from the stage on to real life, which meant
carrying over the illusion with all its falseness and futility
and vicious affectation: and this was in every way unfortunate
and still further reflected the weakness of this society which
laid too much emphasis on show and magnificence and excelled
chiefly in interpretative artists, often greatly gifted, virtuosi
and executants and performers of all kinds, in music and letters
and the theatre.

Although the school was well shielded from the sounds of
worldly gossip and scandal, it did receive some very discreet

echoes of them not unaccompanied by a faint odour—only the more seductive in being prudently filtered and purified—of that aestheticism which went with a civilisation based on inheritance, privilege and propertied comfort, and which flattered its indolence: a civilisation which was destined to destroy itself through its stupid inability to grasp the foundations on which it had been built at such lavish cost of arms, money and culture.

That civilisation lasted till the end of June 1914 and bore its fruit in July, which has been strikingly and fatally revealed in the fact that though in its unconsciousness between the two wars it had been open to every other possibility—even self-knowledge and despair—it could not halt on the precipitous slope whose bottom it has not yet reached.

Melania's feminine intellect combined vitality with ease and nimbleness and had received a vigorous training from her father, based on his solid and penetrating experience of men and events. He had however allowed her to be brought up a Catholic out of respect for her mother's wishes and for the freedom and tolerance in matters of religion and thought into which his original protestantism had become transmuted.

In a fresh and sincere young mind and heart, such as Melania's, the recognition of suffering which she had obtained from her father's profound bereavement developed into a sober and vigorous feeling for the dignity of human personality, into an active and faithful and indeed almost religious cult of the artistically and poetically beautiful which had for her its native earth in Florence and its heaven in her beloved music: and this derived also from the doctrine and practice of a moderate catholicism, more social perhaps than charitable in the strictly theological sense, but certainly highly developed in its discretion, its intelligence, its enlightened indulgence and its sensitive emotional control: and from a near-religion of culture which had arisen on a lofty traditional basis of Spinozan metaphysics, Cartesian logic and Hegelian history, with a strong strain of Goethe and all the thousand and one forms of contributory nourishment from the century of culture, and even from the very aestheticism of the age, although this was in a sober and purified form and freed from its vices.

Both she and her father had that kind of affection for Italy which people feel for an adopted country—it may not be stronger than the one they feel for their original fatherland but it is often more jealous and more enthusiastic. In her father this love had been devoted to an ideal Italy, of ancient fame and history, which the real living contemporary Italy preserved like a museum or a ghost, while its own role as he conceived it, in politics, economics and culture, was submission to German hegemony or, to use a milder expression, to that of the Triple Alliance. When this collapsed, the old stalwart had nothing left, nothing more he could understand or do or take an interest in and he very soon actually expired. His daughter's love for the country, on the other hand, had developed into an exaggerated idealism which saw Italy only in terms of the poets, scholars, philosophers and musicians and their imaginative creations—as the home of all ideal beauty, harmony and sublimity.

And it was Germany which had revealed that Italy to the world both as its heir and its defender and had constructed, even by force the spiritual and historical alliance between the continental Europe of the Teuton and the Mediterranean Europe of the Greeks, the Romans and the Italians. And it was in the bitter loss of so much illusion and hope that Melania's contempt for our own vain and petulant local variety of Fascism had originated and her hatred, for so it was, of Nazi Germany, the Germany which had first *let* itself be nazified, and which had oppressed, betrayed and spurned all the ideals for which she stood. To use her own words, she had been forced to recognise that when with what to her was the culmination of her bitter bewilderment, they signed the 'Steel Pact', it was the levity and giddiness of Italy and the recklessness and menace of Germany which were actually in league.

But always before she reached this point she could turn to music and she had done so from the time when she had been left a widow. It was that one indescribably happy year of marriage which hour by hour her music enabled her to relive, not as a mere memory but a dream.

And her father, that stern man so remote from any mysticism, from any sense of the mysterious or supernatural or, as he put it himself, from any form of superstition, had said something, too, which had conduced to this.

When her husband had died, her father had held her in his arms with a deep inward impulse of despair and told her that he was oppressed by a kind of terror and guilt, as if this blow which had befallen her and was exactly the same as the one he had himself received when his own wife died, were the sign and revelation of a predetermined fate, a horrible and fearful doom which should have prevented him from ever bringing her into the world.

On that day Melania had been young and full of overflowing with pain, anguish and lament which are the outbreak of passion, the venting of wild emotion, and thus perhaps a form of consolation in themselves. It was not then but later that she had understood her father's desperation, realising the un-emotional stress of those words, their horribly cold despair.

As for music, she had filled not only that happy year of her marriage with it, day after day, hour after hour, but her whole subsequent life.

Her husband belonged to an old family of minor aristocracy whose simple 'Don' was worth a good many more resounding titles. When Melania fell in love with him, just after leaving school, the Mèrici family was in a condition not far short of poverty. To bring them wealth had been one of Melania's joys, although by no means the greatest, rather the least significant. At that time the Mèrici were living on the rent of their town

D

house which they had owned for several centuries—they had
had to let the second floor, leaving themselves with the mez-
zanine. The engagement, which was short, had been signalised
by the 'liberation', as they called it, of their home: whether or
not it was due to prudence—more probably it was the impatience of lovers—the young couple hadn't wanted to employ
builders in their apartments: the alterations you make to
houses while you're living in them are always the best, apart
from being the most delightful, especially for lovers.

Of young Mèrici, either then or later, there is nothing
important to be recorded except the ineluctable incurable
passion of love which dazzled and pierced him like a lightning
stroke as soon as he first saw Melania. According to all reports
he had very fine eyes although nobody seems to be able to
describe their shape and colour. People used to shrug their
shoulders and say that nobody had ever seen such a light of
love in any human eyes. And when after only three days he
succumbed to an attack of influenza and bade his last farewell
to Melania with a feeble fluttering of his eyelids—the fever
was so fierce that he was too weak for anything else—his eyes
were brighter than ever with that light, they were overflowing
with love.

It may be that Melania was more in love with his love than
she was with him: and it may be too that this helped her to
overcome the pain of loss and reach the term of her pregnancy,
although for some days the doctors feared for her reason. But
she was very young: and that means that this immensity of love
had irresistibly pervaded her and filled her with bliss but not
that she responded to it because any particular and irreplaceable quality in him, either of virtue or shortcoming, had
aroused it in her.

On the other hand she passed the rest of her life resigned to
the belief that no one would ever love her so well again or
look at her with that light of love.

Perhaps she had been able to foresee this in that moment

when he had given her his last gaze, otherwise reason or life might well have succumbed.

In memory of that year and of her husband it had been her wish to keep the house as unchanged and untouched as possible, even in the things in which it was old, uncomfortable or worn-out, and which moved them to loving mockery as they made plans for what they called both restoration and renewal, for what would have been almost a second founding of Casa Mèrici.

Since the Mèrici had not been the kind of family to build themselves a *palazzo*, their house had a very insignificant exterior. It stood on a narrow dark street which was not much more than an alley, in one of the oldest parts of Milan where it would be useless to look for it today, or even to try and imagine what it was like, because the fires of mid-August 1943 found an excellent fodder in the ancient beams and have destroyed not only that particular house, but the whole quarter, which was beautiful but with an inconspicuous and withdrawn beauty, and which after years and centuries had become worn and faded. It all vanished in plaster and rubble and only the solid structure of nineteenth-century cement and iron was left, and that has given place to the intolerable dreariness of twentieth-century rationalism and functionalism: the first has nothing of art but its artificiality: the second, nothing of realism but its tedium.

Through the main door, which was unassuming, there was a small low entrance hall which was closed with one of those wooden shutters, called *pusterle*, which are very common in Milan: they have a monasterial look and are actually used in cloisters.

Casa Mèrici's, in contrast with the modesty of the main entrance and with the floorings, which were made of worn and uneven flagstones, was of the most handsome and massive walnut, which had lasted for three centuries and kept its carvings and filigree-work bright and shining in their lavish elegance: in fact time seemed only to have refreshed them. And there was also the peep-hole, another piece of fine workmanship in brass and wrought iron.

The coutryard was not large, in fact it was on quite a small scale, with a straight architrave, three of its porticoed sides supported by slender columns of grey granite, which in their extreme, almost rustic simplicity, achieved a certain elegance rather than mere sobriety.

An old family friend of the Mèrici used to say that they were like those of the Lazaretto before they were destroyed and the pillars of that courtyard and colonnade where Renzo roamed in search of Lucia and met Fra Cristoforo went under the hammer.

But similar low colonnades were common in buildings of all sorts and periods throughout Lombardy, and were frequently characterised by a mild pure austerity in the specially sober Lombard style which has an air of shy reserve and is always chaste and unexaggerated even when on a grand scale.

The rear colonnade facing the entrance, which had similar pillars but round arches, was open and gave on to a garden and a kitchen-garden. It was certainly more kitchen-garden than pleasure-garden, but in order not to lose a pleasant effect of unruliness, the hothouses, which had been brought to a high pitch of perfection so that a great variety of rare blooms could be cultivated, were very skilfully arranged to be unobtrusive. All this used to remind old family friends that the young Mèrici had been passionately fond of growing flowers. The house itself had central heating but this had not made them give up the old friendly stoves for which, with their cheerful flickering on the andirons, everyone had an old-fashioned esteem.

When the family's most intimate friend, who was called Gian Battista Sessa, was pursuing a vein of melancholy paradox which always characterised his reminiscences and was typical of his kind of wit and sensibility, he sometimes recalled

with a smile that the older-generation Mèrici had had a
struggle and had even had to deprive themselves of many
things so as not to yield to the temptation of selling this
kitchen-garden as a factory-site. Although Sessa was a man of
taste who had read and travelled widely, and always with
intelligence and discrimination, he had certain tricks of speech
which had a touch of perversity about them, and he did not
say 'sell' but 'sequester' or 'hypothecate'—with a mocking and
sardonic delight in this way of speaking. Asked why, he replied
that there were some expressions which were choicer and more
out of the way than others: and then, in the real Manzoni tradition, he began inquiring how one would put it in Tuscan: more
often than not the question was a trap to lead up to the answer
that the word was the same even if the pronunciation was
different: and whoever he happened to be talking to he would
say to him with the utmost seriousness that one might as well
just put up with it and resign oneself: and when they asked him
what to? he would say, to the fact that Tuscan has so many
words in common with Milanese although this was difficult
to see because of the pronunciation. Anyway he used to say
that Manzoni had a bee in his bonnet about the Florentine
dialect: better resign yourself to talking broad Milanese and
keep your sanity.

But speaking of resignation, one of his sayings had become
famous among his friends: after he had got over influenza and
they were congratulating him on his recovery, he'd said Yes,
admittedly he'd got over it but wasn't that rather a pity? What
did he mean, why was it a pity? they'd asked. Well, it was all
over, everything according to plan, the doctor had given up
pestering him, the priest had come for the last rites, you could
say he had more or less passed over: but not at all, he'd got
better and now everything would have to be done all over
again right from the beginning. Rather a pity! (this was a
phrase he was very fond of). They all laughed.

But his first call, while he was still weak and could barely stagger out of the house, had been upon Melania who had been widowed for only a few days: and he asked her to forgive him. Forgive him for what? For not having the courage to say anything to her. But he broke off brusquely and then said that he was the one who should have been taken off by influenza since he'd got nobody in the world but himself and he was useless and weary. And he sat down by the fire with dry eyes and a constricted throat, grieved to his very heart. There had been no one, either on that day or at any other time, with whom she spoke so little or so rarely of her dead husband because she knew that no one else remembered him with such close affection. And Sessa had been her best friend, watchful and trustworthy, and no one else gave her such good advice with so much probity and penetration and good sense. And after years had gone by and he saw that she was sad he asked her if she minded if he said something silly—she ought to get married again. And she answered him by turning the tables on him saying, Rather a pity, wouldn't it be? And with mock gravity he had pretended he was angry and made the sententious pronouncement that it wasn't the slightest good pretend-that life could be all pleasure and that was why a young and beautiful widow ought to make a fool of herself two or even three times if necessary. And to this she answered That would be rather fun, wouldn't it? and they both laughed. But his memory harked back to the time when the hothouses which always provided Melania's house with such rare and beautiful flowers had been built, and his smile turned to a sigh as he recollected that they had come into being just as salvation had arrived, that is at the last possible moment: the Mèrici were just on the point of having to 'hypothecate' the kitchen-garden when Melania turned up to save them. There were old debts still in existence, there had been unfortunate enterprises which never came to birth, mortgages: negotiations which turned out badly: bad luck in spite of probity, the fact being that they were irreproachable people whose credit on all markets was such that it made Lombard silk something like a gold standard. But to anyone who felt like saying that honesty is always the best policy, the answer must be that even Don Abbondio began to believe that he was henceforth to be immune from earthly woe when he first met Melania and received a hint that a certain marriage was on the way.

For in fact with due regard to the will of Him who alone knows why He wills as He does, and keeps it to Himself, Sessa saw no other use for earthly justice except to provide him with a queer metaphor: that is there was an old Milanese expression for drunk, which he liked to use: 'Fuddled as justice.'

But to return to music, when Melania's drawing-room became an extremely distinguished salon known to amateurs even outside Italy, Sessa politely excused himself. It was possible that he might have come round to taking a pleasure even in pure music, but it was an effort which he preferred henceforth to spare himself.

He contented himself with a moderate enthusiasm for the Scala Opera, and with the ballet where there was always the chance of some pretty ballerinas. That artistic gifts don't always coincide with health and beauty is perhaps unfortunate but we have to accept it: however, as he said, he didn't like his ballet-dancers rickety: when choreography with poetical, aesthetic and philosophical pretensions became the thing, he quietly gave up going to the theatre. He confessed that he couldn't stand the type of ballet which was aimed at old dandies and used to admit that he was an old dandy himself before anyone he happened to be talking to could open his mouth to say it: so as to save him the trouble, he would add politely.

He had only once been passionately in love and it was a long time ago: all that's known is that it was lasting and violent, but not whether it made him happy or miserable. Once when somebody had put the grand question whether there's more sweetness or bitterness in being in love, he had replied that it's a mixture of whipped cream and black coffee. But anyway he was always so impeccably discreet that something of the same kind was quite spontaneously induced in other people.

When he wasn't being tormented by asthma or one of the acute periodic bouts of his chronic bronchitis, there was hardly a day when he did not pass half an hour in Corso Vittorio at the American Bar or at the Tre Marie or strolled along Monte Napoleone to pass away the time before lunch or dinner, looking at the young things. This was the time when the dressmakers and clerks and models all came thronging out of business premises and works round about those parts: they all had a word for him and were jolly and respectful at the same time, although, as he said, he could have done without the respect. When he wanted to express particular admiration for one or other of the 'giddy throng' he employed a prudent circumlocution: he said he would like it if he could 'think about his own future' by which he meant have one of them for a mistress, but it would have to be done in a very circumspect and delicate way. It wasn't a serious proposition, he added cautiously: but he would have liked it if only the few years which he had to live and the many which she would have in front of her hadn't made such responsibilities inadvisable.

When he thought about public affairs he was given to sighing, for he had been born early enough to have known a time without important historical events and too late not to have spent the greater part of his life in regretting that this was over. But there was one of the historical events and incidents which he had witnessed which he liked to cite.

There was a well-known and respected private banker of great solidity, of the name of Cottalorda who used to be seen standing at the "Cova" corner between Via Verdi and Via Manzoni on the Piazza della Scala every day, from the time he got up till noon, always punctual and irreproachably attired in a top hat and a frock coat which was dark or dove-grey depending on the time of year or the circumstances, with an impeccable waistcoat and a fancy tie which was nevertheless always chaste and decorous. And the style reflected the man. Sessa's story was about one of these days on which the times moved into historical significance. Actually it was May 1915. A band of excited 'interventionists' was rushing about the main streets with a certain Ferruccio Vecchi who was notorious at that time, and the most excited of the lot, at their head. They had already broken a few windows of German business premises, clamorously and successfully demanded the destruction of Ricordi's Bechstein grand pianos and knocked one or two obstinate 'neutralists' over the head or trampled on them, between the Piazza di Duomo and Galleria.

In short, as Sessa put it, history was unrolling itself at full speed, when on the Piazza della Scala they were suddenly confronted with provocation in the shape of the imperturbable Cottalorda, the perfect type of dyed-in-the-wool reactionary, die-hard and open antidemocrat, and so naturally a Germanophile and an Austrophile and a supporter of the Triple Alliance, let alone a 'neutralist'.

Vecchi was holding a tricolour without the royal arms and waved it in his face, springing up on to the pavement and almost under his nose to shout the fateful challenge 'War or revolution!'

"Please yourself," replied Cottalorda who was quite unperturbed and merely turned up his nose. He said it in the Milanese dialect which gives it a sly untranslateable flavour. Vecchi and the other demonstrators went on their way without taking it in or as if they found the sarcasm beneath contempt. And anyway, as Sessa used to add when he told the story, weren't the conservatives, the die-hards, seized with war-fever too? Weren't all of them or most of them subscribing to a revolution in the event that either monarchy or parliament opposed the war? Weren't they all ready to make a fine old bonfire à la D'Annunzio ('Flame is beautiful') and throw political tradition, society and every kind of principle and institution on to it? Well, what about it? That you can't make an omelette without breaking eggs was his own philosophy of history: but as for Cottalorda's comment he would have liked to have thought of that one himself: he envied him his presence of mind, being himself a retiring sort of man who withdrew from hubbub and disturbance into himself like a snail into its shell: and he made even this simile his own when he added that it wasn't because of cowardice or laziness but because he was rather slow-witted.

Politically then he would have been a conservative, if history hadn't been like a runaway vehicle which had gathered such speed that there wasn't even time to try and stop it, for the changes had taken place before you could stretch out your hand to the brakes. In an epoch of perpetual and universal revolution all that was wanted was to stop it all for ten minutes and the world would experience such relief that it would opt for a hundred years of peace and quiet. Speaking of individuals parties and institutions which represented order and which had attached themselves to Mussolini and Fascism after the war, he said that they had handed over the whole lot, eggs frying-pan and breadbasket to a cook who might have been expected to have the decency to let them eat the omelette themselves when it was ready: but that instead he'd had the politeness to dish it up on his own plate so that they needn't so much as singe the tips of their fingers or get a spot of the grease: and it would be the first time in history that anyone had seen that. Remains of ancient Lombard antipathies towards the subalpine strangers from over the Ticino stirred in his mind and he said that even at the time of the Five Days siege of Milan 'right-thinking' liberals and dyed-in-the-wool conservatives had chorussed approval of popular clamour, at least in its original slogan which had been 'Out with the Germans!': but the second one—'Down with the Bosses!' found them frightened and pretending not to hear it and calling upon Carlo Alberto who, as Sessa said, cut rather a poor figure

imself. And then even the Piedmont monarchy itself had
layed revolutions without giving a thought to the fact that
y dint of sawing away the props of other people's thrones,
ou were sawing away your own: the army, revenue, education
nd religion being the props: the first had been crippled, the
ext two thrown away in loans and subsidies, and as for the
ourth, in 1870 the monarchy had seized every implement it
ould lay hands on, hatchet and saw, plane and file, to make
bludgeons and cudgels out of them. Having thus encouraged
fine respect for the papal tiara, they couldn't very well claim
everence for the crown, could they, considering that they
were constitutional monarchs into the bargain, in other words
made out of cardboard? And now, with Carlo Alberto's great-
grandson, they had taken a hand in the overthrow of the
Austrian throne, without considering that in the end it would
bring down the whole house of cards. He once saw an acrobat
walking a tight-rope at roof-level and called him a 'Constitutional monarch'.

He was Catholic and observant and never passed a church
without raising his hat and he used to say that the Lord's
justice was not at all 'fuddled' like the justice of the law-courts
and makes use of the calculating head and the hothead in-
differently, a Cavour or a Garibaldi, a King Victor Emmanuel
or a Mazzini, a Giolitti or a Cavallotti, for the symbols and
trappings of every class are alike to him, 'even the weapons
they use in the struggle, not excepting the knife and the
bludgeon and our contemporary rubber truncheon, which also
has its effectual if distasteful role in history'.

On the other hand, sensing that the feeling against Fascism
ran high in Melania's drawing-room, he said that since there
was a dictator (and they hadn't offered him the job), he would
go on cherishing an ideal and that was that there might be a
liberal kind of dictatorship. He admitted when faced with
protests that it would be the first in history: and then when
there was goodhumoured laughter, he added that if anything

new wanted doing, somebody had to be the one to start.
However he shook his head and concluded that he couldn't
see that the Duce had any liberal temperament. As a bizarre
illustration he said that the Aventino policy and the moral
campaign set on foot by Matteotti's assassination were Sciua
Panera's duel in an inverted but perfected form: instead of
asking your adversary to 'stand still while I run you through'
they asked him to come and impale himself 'while I stand my
ground'. And when someone quoted to him the view that in
the meantime it had given Mussolini a fright, he said that if
you frightened him too much it might only stiffen him, which
was inadvisable.

Finally a boast slipped out which was most unusual in a man
of his modesty: he'd warned them! From now on they were all
puppets and would all go into the same bag when the show was
over. And no one would ever know who was the real puppet-
master.

In short, he concluded—and from this conclusion he never
budged—that he would never have wished Mussolini to come
to power but now he was there there was quite a risk he'd turn
out better than anyone who might take his place.

In the last resort he put his trust in the Lord, although he
did not stress this and one day when some intellectual told
him that his principles were all to be found in Machiavelli,
he replied 'Really'—with characteristic impishness.

When the second world war began he said that nobody
would have dreamed that the mouth of the puppet-bag would
have been so capacious and if it hadn't been an irreverence to
the Lord, he would have said that the real puppet-master who
pulled all the strings was now revealed.

During '39 and '40 he held the view that not even a great
statesman could have preserved Italy's neutrality: and the day
that France collapsed, he said that now Italy, too, had touched
bottom: and that in his old age he had fallen on evil days, but
that he wasn't speaking out of self-pity because fortunately he

1adn't very many left. He said this when he met a friend in
Galleria in the dark on the first night of the war and the
black-out.

During the months which followed, Melania acted as a
comforter with just that touch of condescension and superior-
ty which is inevitable in such a relationship. And someone else
would hopefully tell him that the world would emerge renewed
nd regenerated from the victory of the democracies. But
meanwhile, he'd say, we shall have to put up with defeat
ourselves. And similarly when he heard other quarters pro-
laiming the benefits which would accrue from the victory of
he Axis Powers, he'd say that in the meantime 'those splendid
ystems' ought to win.

When the news of the extermination camps and of the other
chivalries of this greatest of all historical epochs' began to get
ound, somebody asked him whether, as he'd always been one
o 'hang the lot', he wasn't well satisfied now, and he replied
nat the gallows is a political instrument but that massacre
nd extermination are not, they are only the instruments of
loodlust. But however it turned out, win or lose, it would be
ne worse for Italy: a worse to end all worsts. As far as he
ersonally was concerned, he could always fall back on his
hronic bronchitis and wouldn't be here long enough to witness
ne world crashing.

Melania remembered these words some time afterwards,
ecause Sessa's mania for contradiction, as she called it, had
ery often put her out and lately she hadn't been able to forgive
im for being the only person to share Donatello's absurd
·mpathy for Falaride Narenza and to back him up in it. They
ctually told him that the man was an informer, an *Ovra* agent.
ut Sessa had only laughed his quiet laugh. If you were going
o bother about provocation, surely the world as it was, was
rovoking enough, and to spare. The poor creature was play-
g spies, was he? Well, you had to live, life was hard and they
ouldn't all cope as old Gian Battista had done with no greater

effort than making do on his income: and in the end ther wasn't much to be said for that either. Anyway, what harr could Narenza do him? Get him shut away for a year or two fo making a political crack? But at the worst they'd all glorify hir as a political victim, while instead of having to keep himse at his own expense, he'd have a few months change of air an would have done that poor wretch a bit of good, for a poc wretch he must be if he couldn't get a better job than spying which was rather looked down on as a profession, although : was no more dishonourable than many others which the worl regarded as distinguished and which were certainly 'gil edged'.

Melania was annoyed: she even made a few open allusior to the facetious cynicism of the Italians who as a result c continually jeering at public spirit, political morality, citizer ship and the civic virtues, have got themselves where they a and can't very well do anything else but laugh. But if laug they must, it had better be at themselves, she'd say. But the had neither the courage, nor the honesty, nor for that matte the cynicism to do so, so that now they were moaning an groaning about being deceived, betrayed and ruined, and a after having cheered the Duce to the echo. Only too tru agreed Sessa.

But after that he hadn't been seen again, and the days ra their course and were at one and the same time too empty an too full of anxieties, and time dragged and went all too quick] and was wasted in idleness: and so Melania hadn't even notice his absence; and had noticed it even less because all the usage of society were running down and fell every day more an more into abeyance as the months moved on towards disaste

CHAPTER FOUR

Clearing a Music Room of Memories and Furniture

s we said, Melania had been thinking of evacuating and
eanwhile began to pack up. Among the most valuable, as
ell as the most cherished things were some antique musical
struments, collectors' pieces: her two best pianos on which
early all the great pianists who had happened to give recitals
Milan over the last thirty years or more had played, includ-
g Ferruccio Busoni, D'Albert, Pugno and Casella. And there
as not only a spinet but a clavichord which she had locked
ter Wanda Landowska had given a series of private recitals on
and, perhaps so that nobody else should touch it, she had
estroyed the key.

Packing up all these things was slow and delicate work: but
ith Melania it was even more long-drawn-out because she
ad never anticipated how much exquisitely painful feeling the
sk would stir in her.

For a long time every piece had had its fixed and unalterable
lace in the various rooms, even if it wasn't always the most
nvenient or suitable one.

For example, however often anyone said that a certain
cture wasn't in a good light, it was always put back precisely
the same place, although they all, beginning with Melania,
ere always saying that you ran the risk of a stiff neck if you
anted to look at it. An armchair had been placed right in the
ne of a vicious draught because it was convenient if you

wanted to go on reading by daylight, especially when the winter days were so short or when bad weather or the Milan mists made it necessary to have the lights on in all the other rooms.

Sitting in that armchair, beside that particular window every vestige of natural light played on your page and you could take advantage of the daylight to the very last gleam being so short, and because of that very sluggishness in lighting the lamps, it was all the sweeter, and your long-drawn-out reading all the more delightful in the softness and gentle melancholy of the twilight fading beyond the misty panes. That was why she had never been able to make up her mind to put a lamp within reach of the armchair. For as soon as you light a lamp, the evening is upon you with all the things that that implies. In the words of Verlaine, who was one of her favourite poets, *'c'est l'heure exquise'*.

They did their best to check or discourage the draught by means of a Spanish screen which was beautiful though worn and seemed, in its faded silver and vermilion hues, only the more precious because of this very fragility. Although the draught was kept off your neck and shoulders, in some secret way which she had never been able to detect, it turned itself into a current of cold air round your ankles and froze your feet. So that in front of the armchair there was something else which belonged to other days, a foot-muff lined with fur.

The logic behind the arrangement or rather the partial disarrangement of the furniture depended on the two grand pianos: for acoustical reasons these had been given the best positions in the big drawing-room, which would have done for a small concert-hall. Especially when she was alone and was doing it only for her own amusement, she herself used to play in the little drawing-room on a very good upright piano which had become a little too loose in its action and too feeble in tone, but which she liked even for its defects.

Like the pictures and the rest of the furniture, this also left a faded mark on the wall when it was moved.

Melania was aware of this and never tired of repeating that she was actually too much attached to the wallpapers and the upholstery to want to renew them, or only as infrequently and reluctantly as possible. But it was no longer possible to find anything of the same quality or which matched. And even if it had been, they would have that 'new' look, 'it wouldn't be the same'.

All the same it was a luxurious house and, apart from things of sentimental value, it was crowded with priceless *objets d'art*; and it hadn't certainly the fault of being overcrowded and cluttered so typical of houses at the turn of the century. On this as on all other points, Melania's taste had been sure and sensitive. With the furniture and works of art which her father, a fine collector, had given his only daughter on her marriage, and with whatever purchases she had made herself, she had made it sumptuous, but always with restraint. And after her widowhood she hadn't wished to alter anything in those rooms which had sheltered her year of happiness in her husband's immense love for her: for she had loved him greatly in return but, as she said in confidential moments, and would often say to herself, going over it all again, no love, however great, including her own, could compete with one like that. And these memories gave her a kind of humble pride, a kind of happiness in mourning the lost and irrecoverable.

When she was quite alone, she no longer dared to preoccupy herself so much with her memories for she noticed that they filled her with longing and inflamed her passionate imagination. It was indeed always her husband, or rather the sensuous recollection of him, which invested her and tormented her deliciously: but in time this gradually evaporated and disappeared and what was left was a sensual and ardent young woman's desire for love. And she dwelt on it again and again. She was a woman who would have readily yielded to passion but she found help and confidence in music. In music she could commune with herself and with her memories, even with her

E

desires, assimilating them, if one can say so, to music. In music
her fantasy, otherwise too detailed and sensual, evaporated
into warm dreams, a gentle languor, a sweet semi-conscious-
ness. Passion had seized her after another fashion, when the
first fierceness and laceration of fearful loss had been eased
and when she had allowed herself to get into the habit of lying
long between the sheets of the marriage-bed where they had
loved each other, so that she could dwell on her lover. These
sheets themselves had been a temptation not only because of
the man they brought to her mind, but because they themselves
were out of the ordinary. After the ancient custom of the great
days of Lombard silk, they were woven to last, and families
handed them down with house and jewels, in line of primo-
geniture, for as much as four generations: they were light but
thick, cool in summer and warm in winter. They were one of
the few survivals of the former wealth of the Mèrici family, of
whom only Donato was now left to carry on the name.

Unhappily for them, his parents were still alive when their
son died and they survived him for a long time. When he
married, the old Mèrici, according to their wish, had remained
in their own unpretentious and secluded quarters of the
house, to which their straitened means had reduced them.
And they were inclined to keep themselves to themselves
even more than before, because they were the sort of
people who by now were fixed in their habits: but they
expressed themselves satisfied with the marriage, in fact blissfully happy, and with everything which it brought into the
establishment, in the way of 'collections and connections' as
old Mèrici said in his quiet way: and they were pleased that
their son was so much in love and moreover with a wife who
was not only so rich, but beautiful, gentle, well-educated and
good.

But in actual fact it was only the sight of their son's happiness which caused them pure and unadulterated joy. Everything else, including their daughter-in-law's wealth, really

frightened and offended them: all that stuff, they said, coming into the house, it wasn't due to anything the Mèrici had done.

In the expansive good faith of love and enthusiasm and German sentimentality, their daughter-in-law had over-whelmed them, ever since the engagement, with the liveliest testimonies of affection, proclaiming everything in the establishment, in her father-in-law and in her mother-in-law, who was a gentle and timid old lady, as utterly beautiful and exquisitely rare and characteristic. The place was a hovel, her father-in-law had said, while her mother-in-law thought it was a rabbit-warren and better say no more about two old bundles like themselves, who'd got to the point when they hardly ever went out of the house, let alone further than the ancient street: for what was there to see but the new Milan with its great changes, its great era of expansion and wealth which rose to its most splendid heights in the Simplon Exhibition of 1906? They didn't like these changes and the Exhibition bewildered them while they were terrified by the famous fire. And wandering about these new streets at the risk of sunstroke in summer and pleurisy in winter didn't suit them, especially with all these dangerous bicycles. They were on top of you without warning, and the mere sound of the bell or the horn was enough to frighten you into fits! They did everything they could to avoid this splendid and marvellous 'Progress': and on top of everything, the cabbies had taken to driving so fast! Sessa, who was a friend of the two old misanthropes, said that perhaps it wasn't so much the cabs, it was just that they weren't so quick on their pins. They all laughed, but from the time that motor-cars first put in an appearance Sessa too began to admit that there was more road-hogging and dangerous driving every year in Milan.

The only time they went further than the end of the street, was when they went to the crypt of the Basilica to worship the relics of Saint Ambrose, on the appointed days of ancient tradition.

As for Melania's enthusiasm for 'every stitch' worn by her mother-in-law, who had beautiful lace, and her wonder at every dusty corner in the house, and her moods of expansion and her demonstrativeness, they looked on these as 'German ways' and agreed with Sessa in saying that it was no good 'even when a German likes you, he fights you'—they said this in dialect where it rhymes.

Nevertheless if you had been able to go back into the past, in Sessa's family as well as Mèrici's, you would have found people who were very accommodating and greatly attached, since Maria Theresa's days, to the 'other Germans': that is to the Austrians, towards whom the Milanese had very many good reasons for gratitude, although, as Sessa put it philosophically, nobody mentioned it any longer, and they said that they were devoted to the Emperors only because they had to be and to save the business.

The Sessa family who were petty aristocracy and the Mèrici who were great merchants would have said, if they had still been able to speak for themselves, that playing at liberalism was all right for gentlemen and lawyers and intellectuals: and with the people, it was all right for anyone who had nothing to lose and everything to gain by upheavals which were ruin for business. As chance had it, 'Fifty-nine' was a logical consequence of 'Forty-eight'—with King Victor Emmanuel, whom people like the Sessa and Mèrici families had forgiven for being *oltreticino* (otherwise, from Piedmont), because they were thankful to see order restored: and this forgiveness didn't in general come easily to a Milanese quartered in the Navigli, and a Lombard of old stock, in those days.

However, their daughter-in-law was a 'golden girl' and they had perforce to make up their minds once and for all to like her, as a matter of justice even if inclination didn't suffice. But when their son, just once, merely to encourage the inclination and to overcome the touch of restiveness which he divined, had said that, Melania being a rich heiress, Casa

Mèrici would bloom again, he provoked a dusty answer: they said Casa Mèrici was a plant which had never needed grafting with dowries, and that the money which had come in through marriages had always been left intact and secured to the wives. Anyway he didn't think himself that outside money could take root and flourish in the coffers of this old-established concern, did he? This bitterness pained Donato severely but he would have understood it better if he had known that, having overcome a profound sense of humiliation and an even profounder timidity, his father had called in the utmost secrecy on his future father-in-law at the Bank, in the early days of the engagement.

That the great man, who represented the events and customs of an age which the Mèrici had lost touch with now for generations, made Mèrici himself feel humble and intimidated, is to be understood, because poverty does make people feel small and gets under their skin: but as he said, in his Milanese dialect, they had come down in the world but without bankruptcies or having to borrow or loss of face, and they had honoured their word and their signature and paid their debts to the last farthing: it had been poverty if you like, but honourable poverty. The timidity was of more ancient origin, inherited from generations to whom 'appealing to the Bank' meant the same as 'going to the Jews' in remoter times, the first step in a rapid decline which would not halt till it had reached the bottom where failure and bankruptcy were in wait; or where at the very least all the profits and perhaps the whole concern were going to change hands between the indebted owner and the creditor who had provided the loan: all this as inevitable and predictable as lightning after thunder, Lent after Carnival—or reckoning day after bills. And so in the family, banks and bankers were ancient symbols of terror, apart from the fact that without being a Jew himself Melania's father was the intimate associate of Jews: naturalised he might be, but he was still of German blood: a German of the Germans there was no getting past that; related in short to those who, however well they deserved of the merchant class, belonged to the Banking Community and were foreigners. And moreover it was also a fact that Melania's banker-father had crossed the Alps in the first place with the idea of financing all the tricky modern notions which had been responsible for bringing Casa Mèrici down in the world.

Mèrici was received that day with every courtesy and with all the friendship which was due to relationship and interest, just so and no more: he was passed from commissionaire to secretary, all bowing and scraping: and with the dim light and the thick-piled carpets in the hushed corridors and waiting rooms, they seemed to him so many phantoms: and he had expounded the ancient idea of the Mèrici establishment to his prospective relation by marriage: this had been a project for certain silks of a very luxurious kind, handwoven by methods and techniques which were family secrets. When, a half-century before, the Mèrici had wanted to branch out and turn themselves from merchants into great industrialists, it was just this very project which had brought them to ruin.

The good man had thought that he could keep this secret to himself and that it wouldn't matter to the other either as prospective relative or as a banker. And so he was astounded when the banker revealed that he knew the story inside out and rather better than he did himself, both the project and the ruin which it had caused.

And a demonstration followed, itself a fine piece of close weaving, that handicraft methods of production have had their day, and that in the case of luxury articles, of all others, how you produce anything is of less than no importance, if you don't know how to market the product and stimulate a demand, if you can't 'create a market'.

In short, it was a question of fashion and there couldn't be a more difficult market: there couldn't be anything more capricious, dominated as it was by Paris. And so if he imagined

hat it was enough to display a few rolls of silk in a shop front
n Monte Napoleone or Via Manzoni or Corso Vittorio, he
vas mistaken, and that was a fact even if it were the finest silk
n the world as well as in Lombardy, which of course went
without saying. What you had to do was to conquer the world
of *Haute Couture* and of the Jewish Fashion-Houses, the
Konfektions-Juden. Did he know anything about that? And
granted all this—and all these outlandish names were quite
enough already to bewilder the good man—and given that
you'd set your fashion and created your market, still, with
your handicraft methods, you wouldn't be able to grapple with
and satisfy the demand, and so reap your opportunity.

The demonstration had been clear, rapid and exhaustive, all
done with a pencil and a few figures on a piece of paper,
leaving him staggered and muttering excuses for the liberty
he had taken and for the time which he had wasted.

The banker, with the idea of comforting him and treating
him with exceptional consideration as a friend and relation,
patted him lightly with a hand which seemed very weighty,
and said to him in an agreeable tone which sounded bitter in
his ears, that it's hardly ever a good idea to try and resuscitate
businesses which have gone to pieces and that, when an undertaking has ruined two generations, the best interests of the
third counsel them to leave it in the grave with mingled
reverence and mourning.

The 'hardly' was put in as a sop to politeness, to friendship
and relationship. So were the advice and the gesture. And
though they said nothing to his face, the three or four high
functionaries, who were waiting in the corridor with thick files
under their arms, let him be under no misapprehension about
the time which he had wasted, although it had been so little:
and it was the same with the commissionaires who were standing at the door, extremely polite but impatient. They all told
him of it just by looking at him, while the Director-General,
brushing away his obsequious excuses, did him the honour of

conducting him in person as far as the lift which was a machine in which Mèrici had little confidence and which even inspired him with a certain terror, but which he had to enter all the same, backing into it and bowing his regrets and apologies and farewells.

When he had extricated himself, he was seized with the suspicion that he had made a big mistake and that the banker, no matter how friendly, no matter how terribly polite, and however much he admitted the claims of relationship, was still a banker and quite capable of an abuse of confidence and of passing on the project to one of his business associates: for however grand these banks, industries and businesses were, all such top-flight organisations were really one cabal composed of people who were half-rogue and whole tycoon, and all leagued together to the spoil and ruination of the old-fashioned simple sane and honest people who belonged to the good old days.

He confided his suspicion to his wife and of course she said that Melania's father had been perfectly right and the great project was a wild-cat scheme. She was a woman of great gentleness and discretion who from time to time could be inflexible and even cutting. He was startled and worried and became quite convinced that the coincidence of opinion between his wife and such a leading luminary of scientific banking showed that the man hadn't been straightforward: he'd tried to appear too simple. Was it possible that anything which he had said honestly could have been understood or taken in by the good old lady? No question, he smelt a rat.

With these antecedents and the mutual embarrassment which not only continued but grew stronger between mother- and daughter-in-law, Mèrici's parents became more and more estranged and withdrawn, after Melania began to use the house to gather together a chosen band of musicians and amateurs and musical fanatics and to make her drawing-room a musical salon of considerable reputation and very high standard.

Apart from what they couldn't help hearing in good weather when the drawing-room windows were open, music was a dead letter for the two old people: music meant a box at the Scala, performers both male and female under your own roof, all the pomp and perils of eccentric and ruinously expensive parties which were hardly in accordance with middle-class decorum, with devotional duties, with decent customs in general, and with the retirement proper to a widow in particular: it goes without saying that they didn't fit in with religion, and thrift had better be left out of it. When stalls at the Scala became too expensive, the two old people had sacrificed opera to decorum for that would hardly permit them to sit in the 'gods'. Anyway why climb all those stairs just to listen to the sort of singers they had today, when they could remember Patti and Tamagno? And as for the sort of music which was to be heard in concert-halls (not that they ever set foot inside one, but it was the sort of thing which went on in their daughter-in-law's salon) it was what they called 'scientific': and they raised their eyebrows and shrugged their shoulders.

As she got ready to move Melania smiled tenderly at these dear old faded recollections which rose like a swarm every time she moved a piece of furniture: and the poor dear old couple had been dead themselves for such a long time.

And then she suddenly saw that music had betrayed her after all. For a short time this unexpected thought quite took her breath away. It had betrayed her in every way and throughout her life, continually. But how could it, what did she mean?

The betrayal had really been in the way, in the past, it had filled in so many blank hours which without this illusion of occupation would have shown her how empty her life was. Sessa had been right when he advised her to marry again instead of just 'winding up the arpeggio-and-scale machine'. She smiled as she remembered her old friend and his crotchety pretences that he wasn't just referring, and had no intention of referring, to pure music, chamber music: by the 'machinery' he meant nothing less than the great piano works. But after that? it was not unusual for Sessa, believing or pretending to believe that he was unobserved, in the twilight shadows, or late in the evening, when everyone had gone home and she was playing with only the one light on the page and all the rest of the drawing-room dark, to sit and listen to her for a long time, so silent and unobtrusive that she would forget she wasn't alone. And his eyes misted as he listened. And on these occasions he went out without saying goodbye and a mouse would have made more disturbance. He took a fancy to this simile; so much so that once or twice, half in jest half in earnest, he had said that he would like to depart this life quieter than a mouse going into its hole.

On one of these days when she was getting ready to move and was standing among the disorder of her half-dismantled rooms with their discoloured and dusty walls, Melania remembered this and realised with a shock of surprise that it was some time since she had heard anything of her old friend. But it wasn't the first time that he had vanished in this way for a while. And then moving so much valuable and delicate stuff, with all the difficulties at that time of finding the men and the transport, preoccupied her and gave her a great deal of trouble. And she found herself harking back to the early days of the war when people were rushing to evacuate with all their goods and chattels: and the roads were choc-a-bloc with a miserable display of rags and props and pots and pans all piled up on anything that came to hand, with a panicky throng carrying their household goods in their arms, all worn-out before they even got as far as the suburbs and the outskirts of the city, and long before they got to the country or their destination, and it seemed to her as if fear had driven the whole dark story of misery and poverty out into the light of day.

The most extraordinary thing had been that later not a few of these people, who had worn themselves out once already, repeated the process and toiled back to the city with all their traps, as if it simply wasn't true that every day made it only more likely that something worse would happen. Bad things got worse with age, Sessa had said, just as good wine gets better. He summed up his opinion of war in one word: *chores*. And when it's all over, he had added, nobody remembers a thing: has anybody ever seen a place left uninhabited, just because it's subject to earthquakes? It is the same with war, which is the kind of earthquake which you can't escape from anywhere on earth. If people didn't forget about it they wouldn't have any more children: rather a pity, perhaps. Did he really mean that people shouldn't have any more children because of wars and earthquakes? His reply had been a vague gesture which might mean anything or nothing. Melania began to feel tired herself, seized with doubt whether everything that had to be done was worth the trouble: and she didn't know whether she meant just to evacuate or to go on living: but it's always easier to do something than nothing. And *Vill' Alma, Alma Dannata* enticed her with the thought of escaping from the anxiety which was daily increasing in the city and weighed on you more and more pressingly, although that might mean anything or nothing, too.

Music had betrayed her—here was that strange thought again—had betrayed her even in her relation with her son whom she had taught herself from early infancy, and when his remarkable promise was confirmed she had seen to it that he had the most thorough musical training. The result had been to breed resistance and distaste for it and a boredom which turned to actual aversion especially at any sign of pressure on her part. When in order not to make matters worse she no longer insisted and had forced herself to conceal the displeasure and her hope of seeing him return to his allegiance, the boy had taken to making an outright profession of this contempt and hatred of music, particularly for what she held dearest, her heart's delight, one might almost say her life, the music of those great witnesses and prophets of the romantic

spirit: with Schumann an evensong which went winging over
anguish and evil with the sweetness and consolation which only
the disconsolate can bestow: with Schubert, the elect of the
Muses, a quality of innocence which gave him in itself the
strength to contemplate the abyss and soar over it singing:
with Brahms, the worship, faith and love of a latter-day contemplative, acts of homage at a divine apotheosis, incense
offered up on the altar of memory, at a tabernacle sealed for
ever: and with the unique Chopin, the wing-stroke of melancholy and passion in a dawnless night, the courage of desperation, the strength of an integrity which in its nobility, its
serenity and innocence conquers all apathy and woe: mourning for first sorrow, the whispered confidences of first love,
the utterance of the last hour, life as the condemned, health
as the sick man loves it: flight with a wounded but unconquered wing, the song of a sunless day which is yet all light.
But with Beethoven there is nothing more to be said: a world
created new beyond the threshold of silence, beyond all
destruction, after the end of time, after the last words of
humanity, after the most desperate rebellions have reached
their consummation, and victory has smiled upon her last defeat:
Beethoven, the chant of the highest felicity in the expression
of the deepest suffering, of a freedom which is most sublime
when most it feels its chains: Beethoven the man of flesh who
can invoke a destiny on your behalf and say to it—You will
find your truth in the heart that accepts you fearlessly: in the
torment which it bears unconquered: in the terror which you
cannot inflict upon it: Beethoven, the Prometheus who not
only forgives Jove but has compassion on him: peace in the
heart and in the raging tempest, in the seething tumults of all
passion: the Word surpassing the inenarrable, song beyond
speech, a rite of sound which at once opens and seals a new
spiritual world: Beethoven, all of music and nothing but music.
Was this only a super-illusion, thought Melania on one of these
sad despondent days when she was getting ready to move, was

it the vanity of vanities—all of music and nothing but music?

It was just these very masters whom her son Donato detested, and the way he spoke about them wrung a protest from her—he was blaspheming. And he began by contrasting with the Romantics and their abounding sentimentality what he called the honest unpretentious 'musical craftsmen, who were none the less sublime—Hayden and Mozart, Handel and Bach, Palestrina and, apart from all the great Italians from Frescobaldi to Corelli and from Monteverdi to Rossini, all the others who hadn't tried to descend into the abyss or scale the heavens but who had expressed the idea and the force of the sublime while keeping strictly within the limits of art. They hadn't tried to create new worlds but had been content with something which is of greater value, the beauty of proportion. And finally he had said that for a modern even these composers and their music couldn't achieve anything better than an ingenious and artificial neo-classicism. It seemed to her, in her wrath, that for some time he had buried himself in the study and the theoretical demonstration of a kind of music more like mathematics than poetry, purely objective, an extrapolation of its own abstract laws, developed into independent entities and utterly purged of any appeal to feeling and passion: a wholly cerebral music, rigidly unpoetical.

After that, instead of taking his diploma in musical composition, he had taken a science degree: Melania was so annoyed that she couldn't remember in what science, and hadn't even wanted to find out. Did he really believe, she had asked him, that music had nothing more to say to mankind? And he had answered that mankind or at any rate a certain type of person had always demanded and went on demanding something from music which was at one and the same time too much and too little: that music, especially the kind which Melania preferred, had habituated these people to a surrender to emotion and an appetite for it which were not only vicious and idle but insatiable and enervating. It was this sort

of people who clamoured for the continual stimulation of
their demanding and unappeasable appetite for sympathy and
for self-pity and self-love, and who wanted to have the feathers
of their spiritual wings continually stroked, although they were
by now so fragile that it would be better not to open them at
all, so as not to spoil them: people who worshipped themselves but who conceded a weary and possessive adoration to
a few other gods, on condition that the god was an eternal
fount of complacency and pandered to their nostalgic sensuality and passion.

After that she had been too proud to ask him if he were
referring to herself: or if it was because he didn't know or was
pretending not to know that it was music which had given her
the strength not to yield to another love, to remain a widow
and devote herself entirely to her motherhood, that he now
answered her with ingratitude, or perhaps even with actual
intent to wound and offend her? And now there it was: even
in this, music had betrayed her, because if Donatello had
really been alluding to herself, he would have been right
because the flood of emotion in which she had found her bliss
had been a substitute for love and life, its joys and sorrows: a
substitute even for sins which would have been her own and
real: which would have been suffered and paid for in her own
flesh and spirit beneath the warm light of sun and earth
instead of that iridescent lunar halo, that pale reflection of the
joys and sorrows of a Chopin or a Beethoven or all the other
who were the sublime playthings of her long self-deception.

She ought to have married again, she ought to have listened
to the healthy promptings of her feelings, of her fertile flesh
she should have born other sons out of her joy and brough
them up to active life, not this one only, born in sorrow and
reared to a dreaming melancholy. Music had betrayed her
encouraging her to lose her years of fertility, her vital years, to
fritter away her portion of time and natural and creative
energy in a sly intellectual fiction, a prolonged evasion, it

which half-deliberately, half-unconsciously, she was always exquisitely poising herself between delicate alternatives: a continual frustration of the sound and progenitive instincts and desires of the body, a fantasy of passion which although it may have been chaste in actuality, was not so in thought and certainly not so in the obscure dreams and half-dreams, the surrenders and equivocations of her musical ecstasies.

And finally the betrayal had revealed itself in all its meanness and ugliness, in something which was a mere word, and a trivial one at that but enough to repel her in her excessive spiritual refinement. Though still beautiful and exceptionally well-preserved, she had arrived at the years which she had always hoped and believed would be free and disburdened of the perils of the flesh with its desires and torments, and in her hopes she would even have wished to hasten them: and now it seemed that because her abstinence had not been really chaste, but had nursed a hidden and cheated flame which had been smothered but not extinguished, it had kept her full of sensual sap. Just now instead of dying down and leaving her pacified, it tormented her relentlessly, with a profound and desperate repining for time past and dead, and with unpredictable temptations which were not merely gross but disgusting and obscene. She could experience one of these wild irresistible temptations for a strange man she met in the street, for some peculiarity or oddity, it might be a physical deformity, a look, a tone or a gesture, an odour of the human animal. It seemed as if the physical promiscuousness of wartime were specially designed to arouse in her such animal torments, such disturbances of physical desire.

They could happen when she was in a crowd, for instance in a tram, now the use of private cars was forbidden, or in a packed air-raid shelter during a warning, or in the street. She had always been repelled by crowds and contacts, had felt a kind of panic which seemed to her like a presentiment and a warning, now that it was these contacts, often in their most

shameful and repugnant form, which roused in her flesh a
shiver of vile but unmistakable delight: for instance when some
filthy but shamelessly enterprising brute took advantage of
circumstances to make up to her, and was impudent enough
to paw her about. And she couldn't mistake the fact that if
circumstances hadn't protected her she wouldn't have had
the strength to do so herself: the long and the short of it was,
she would have let him have his way. Her very fear and disgust
were a source of attraction, a spur as potent as it was despicable. Needless to say she imagined every time that she had
seen the last of these inclinations, that this aberration of the
senses was over and would disappear as it had come, irrational
and without warning.

But the moral humiliation itself, which had something at
once fearful and delightful because it found an outlet in a
certain defiant irony and bitterness, encouraged her to relapse
into a kind of passive and complacent acquiescence and let
herself become the victim of the difficult age and its hysterical
urges: a case of arrested development, a retarded sexual glutton.

Finding she was suffering from breathlessness and palpitation, as well as flushes and attacks of anxiety, she consulted her
doctor and would have taken him into her confidence if he had
not anticipated her by talking about the climacteric, the
critical years, and glands and secretions and hormones and all
sorts of disturbances: in particular he had given her some
information which though it alarmed her, had also stirred an
impure and secret pleasure: he had said that this condition
could last several years after reproductive capacity had ended
and she would remain a full woman and a beautiful and
desirable one too: for her alarm could not prevent her feeling
a horror at the thought of becoming old and ugly which,
though it was quite absurd as well as altogether physiological,
was only the more terrifyingly intense.

It drove her to the mirror where she inspected herself so
severely that in the end it infected her with a kind of crude

defiance and the idea of letting herself go, of experimenting at least once before it was too late. Why should she repress the desire for pleasure? Just because it was merely physical and sensual? But on the contrary, that made it seem benign, soothing, and a solution: and even if it turned out in practice to be repugnant, still it would have been a purge, a blood-letting. As for ordinary medicine, the sedatives prescribed by the doctor calmed her anxiety and quietened her palpitations but couldn't do anything against the sexual disturbance. When you came down to it, who was going to benefit from all her self-control and deprivation? She wasn't doing it for any moral principle for she saw that she had always acted in accordance with an emotional and imaginative need which had uniquely dominated her and absorbed her life: now it was a question of fulfilling actual sensual demands. Whatever moral principle she had, remained unaltered, in other words it wasn't a principle and it wasn't moral: it was and remained a need. Underneath all the semblance of dignity, what we call self-respect is probably mixture of pride, fear and caution. And there was always good taste, not that that is much help in similar circumstances because it can work both ways: it can be used to make fun of real delicacy and restraint and to indulge the most unbridled license, if it only seems amusing.

There was finally her regard for her son, but Donato had disappointed her, he was remote, detached, sardonic, bitter, sterile: and how unresponsive he was with her! And after all as she argued round and round it didn't seem to her that it would show all that regard either for her son or for herself as a mother if she were to try and make what the psycho-analysts call a transference on to him, and sublimate into maternal love that slight residue of sexuality soured and retarded as it was, a phenomenon of the evening and decline of life, which ought to be discharged and then forgotten. In short she belonged, at least in so far as she was still a woman, to herself, and not to her son.

F

CHAPTER FIVE

Confidences between Two Friends

MEANWHILE she had made a new friend and confidant,
woman who, needless to say, wasn't to the taste of either Sess
or Donatello. But for some time now, as he grew older, Sess
had taken no pleasure in novelties. And Donatello had take
it on himself to import that Falaride Narenza into the house
almost forcing him on her: she had never really cared for hir
and now Donato, when he came home on sick-leave, ha
taken him up again and was constantly in his society and mor
intimate with him than ever. If truth were to be told, thi
dubious character had no objection at all to the frequer
invitations to lunch and dinner, for he was a rootless creatur
always short of cash, and when Melania made it clear that sh
didn't like it, Donato went calmly off to a restaurant with hi
bosom friend and guest: so as not to oblige him to make
habit of it, Melania resigned herself to seeing the other at he
table much oftener than she liked.

Melania's new friend was an object of jealousy and backbi
ing to the older friends who had survived from earlier day
being a certain notorious Armida Lenai, a woman who, as the
say, had had a past but no husband in it: she had however
lover to whom she was passionately devoted, Gaspare Del
Morte, a man of bold and resolute character, and a most activ
member of the conspiratorial *Justice and Liberty* movemer
against the Fascist government. This was an open secret, a
the secrets of conspiracies and secret societies generally are
Falaride Narenza, however, commented on his very strict an

upright personality and his great energy, to Melania and Donatello.

Della Morte showed this strictness on the few occasions when, more to please his lover than anything else, he had felt obliged to accept Melania's invitations, and he did not hesitate to reveal with complete and vigorous frankness his contempt for merely verbal opposition as it was practised in such sheltered little corners of ideological anti-Fascism, as for example the Mèrici salon, which were so full of fighting talk, and which were tolerated with contemptuous patience by the dictator.

In Gaspare Della Morte's view it was better to be a passionate and violent Fascist than a respectable anti-Fascist on sufferance.

He was a man who had passed middle life, of strong build and medium height, very tough and agile: he suffered from jaundice and had the kind of complexion and something of the temperament associated with that disease. But the bronzed appearance of his skin was certainly not in contradiction to the virility of a face whose features were remarkably handsome, well-cut and strongly marked but regular. As a young man his face must have had a surprising resemblance to those of the young heroes of Greek art, with the straight nose, the brilliant eyes, the smooth open brow, the domed head and the small and perfect ears set rather far back. Armida Lenai was so fascinated by him that when she was listening, as she generally did, to the mere sound of his voice which was deep and intense rather than to what he was saying, the incantation showed itself in the pulsing warmth of her face and her dreamy passionate expression.

Gaspare himself had a bitter outlook which he neither dissembled nor regretted. And it was with a scornful inflection that he used to say that after so many years of general acquiescence and loyalty to Mussolini's dictatorship, in many cases enthusiastic, his Italian compatriots were preparing on all sides to desert Fascism and leave the dictator to his fate, now that the war was taking a disastrous turn and Fascist fortunes were crumbling, and that these people filled him with bitterness: rats deserting the sinking ship! And after they'd had not only the bad luck but the stupidity and weakness to land themselves in this sort of war, they'd turned round on Mussolini as if it hadn't been due to everybody's weakness and folly, theirs as well as his: it was all on a level with the baby who gets into a rage with the sharp corner which has hurt him: and he added that an elementary schoolmaster was just the right sort of dictator for a people who were mostly babies. Somebody demurred and said that the fact that the popular support of Fascism was melting away was a first and major success. To which he replied that cheating and making do had made the Italians so slippery that everything ran off them. In his view they'd just worn smooth like stepping-stones. And when someone else said that even floodwaters abate in time, he answered that the stepping-stones would then be left high and dry. On the other hand, though he felt obliged to wish for the fall of Fascism, the fact that it was due to the war being already lost, and had been brought about by victorious enemy armies occupying their country's soil, filled him with horror. And he wasn't one of those brainless idiots who couldn't see this or just passed over through sheer political factiousness.

At first, Donato Mèrici had felt a lively sympathy for him: later something had repelled him and they drifted apart, having got into the habit of mocking and making fun of what each privately recognised in the other as his own best characteristics: Donato, for instance, that having chosen to dedicate himself he had remained loyal: on which Gaspare commented that it hadn't so far cost him as much as a scratch: whereupon Donato said that Gaspare's moral rigidity had at least cost him the breath he wasted in his conceited and bitter moralising. And one was 'Cato on the cheap' and the other Attilius Regulus done up in cotton-wool. According to Falaride they could

have run through the whole of Livy and Thucydides into the
bargain, to find heroic nicknames to tease each other with,
without seeming a whit less like Renzo's chickens, which,
when they were tied together by their claws, to their mutual
misfortune and inconvenience, still had to go on pecking each
other and couldn't even boast that they'd got a hope of going
down in history or mythology.

Armida Lenai was a proud and sensitive woman who,
although she did not show it, had suffered and was still suffering from her unpleasant social situation: and she had responded
to Melania Mèrici's friendship with affection and gratitude and
with a passionate warmth of expression which was typical of
all her feelings.

There was a touch of adulation in her gratitude, her genuine
admiration and affection for Melania, but it was these which
made her able to win her friend's confidences and also to
encourage the other woman with a warm and loving sympathy
for her difficulties and for her feeling of humiliation which was
all the deeper and more bitter because of the unrestrained
laughter and contempt it would have aroused if people had
guessed the cause: that she was suffering from 'arrested
development', a nymphomaniac too, what a figure of fun she
would have been!

And though she was proud and reserved and always mistress
of herself, and all her life had had an inflexible intangible
quality, had kept herself immaculate, like a mirror which
nothing could tarnish, and had thus created, needless to say,
the impression of living in an ivory tower, the very intensity
of her pride in this persona and in her intellectual dedication
to her adored music, was enough to make her fling herself
into another kind of frenzy, and her devotion to Armida became a sort of disembodied passion. At first it had been a
reaction of contempt and anger against her circle of men and
women friends when she found them turning up their noses,
a defence against their criticisms, their lack of sympathy, their

hypocrisy and scorn: as if, Melania had declared, the honesty
and courage with which Armida had accepted the consequences
of taking her liberty and of her past behaviour, and had also
faced up to the behaviour itself—and that you couldn't
attribute to self-interest or to anything but generous impru-
dence—hadn't been a thousand times better than the social
conformism of worldly people, intent on saving appearances
and conventions, which is so often hypocritical and always
calculating and over-cautious. Warming in her defence,
Melania had exaggerated this portrait of her friend till she had
turned her into a fallen angel, suffering and sinned against
much more than was true or even likely.

And she had involved herself even more closely with Armida
as a confidential friend and intimate, because her circle of
friends had been thinned by the war and her son was estranged,
which made Melania suffer much more than she herself
realised, and because she had given up her intellectual interests
and artistic pleasures, and now felt a trace of that loneliness
which seemed to her the forerunner of desolate old age, as
well as the bitter sense that life and music had both betrayed
her.

Armida had become so indispensable to her that she didn't
like to pass a day without seeing her or at least talking to her on
the telephone, while because of air-raid warnings and difficulties or lack of transport and black-out, she had to stay at
Melania's much more often that could have been foreseen. If
she happened to be there after dark, she often stayed the night
one of those long harassed wartime nights. She became one of
the family, she had a room to herself, which was different from
the ordinary guest-rooms and was provided with everything
you needed to stay there in an emergency for days on end
Melania had taken a pleasure in furnishing it, and had lavished
her taste and imagination upon it. She called it 'pleasant-
surprise room' with a kind of coyness and affection which
she had put into the friendship and its demonstrations right

rom the beginning and which had become more marked.
The 'pleasant surprises' were of course her friend's visits,
specially when as it happened she prolonged them for several
lays: she was calling in the end almost every day and when she
tayed it was always for longer at a time so that some people,
ncluding Donato himself, who had once said it outright when
ie was in a bad temper, began to wonder why Melania didn't
ake Gaspare in too, as one of the family, and keep his mistress
iappy.

At this she had flared up into a fury, which like everything
she did and said relating to her friendship, was exaggerated
ind high-flown, and replied that whatever it was it certainly
wasn't because of fear of what the world would say with its
tupidly malicious judgments. She didn't venture to put the
natter to her friend and her friend's lover, not because she
ared what anyone thought but because they might be sensi-
ive! But Armida and Gaspare were living together, and if they
were bombed out, she not only intended to give them hospitality but had promised to do so, had actually invited them,
ind had dealt with their objections by saying that she was not
only hurt but offended by them.

In short, as Donatello had put it with an irritated and ill-
mannered shrug, the two sensitive creatures had accepted the
offer. And Melania had fiercely declared that she'd have liked
to see them refuse! Wouldn't they have come one of these days,
iave just moved in, he had asked sarcastically, even without
being bombed, just through having nowhere else to live? At
his point, Melania's tongue became sharp: what business of
iis was it, how dare he interfere with his mother's affairs?
Hadn't he got his own quarters. If it suited him, and if his
mother's friendships annoyed him, couldn't he have a separate
able and eat by himself? Anyway they hadn't been getting on
together now for some time: it was quite a long time since he'd
given her anything but ill-temper, contrariety and opposition:
and now it had got to rudeness and sarcasm and he had been

offensive to her in all sorts of ways which were not only embarrassing and unattractive and ill-mannered, but naughty and unkind. He could keep Falaride Narenza's friendship—a wretched-looking object and a base political instrument, ready to betray even the people for whom he did the job of agent provocateur and spy—and leave her to her own friends who were of a quite different quality and kind, thank God!

At this point, although her astonished son made several attempts to answer her they were all swamped by the tumultuous pæan which she poured out on the theme of Gaspare and Armida, their love and the heroic honesty with which they were defying society and living freely together: and it all overflowed in a terrific outburst of tears and sobs.

Donato could not remember ever having seen his mother weep: and seeing it now for the first time, he was astonished and bewildered much more than softened and moved to pity: indeed the very strength of her emotions roused him to something like fear, induced in him a painful state of frigidity and insecurity, a wretched and desperate sense of uselessness and unresponsiveness. And his protesting assurances of tenderness and comfort sounded miserably cold and inhibited and inadequate, and he could hear this coldness and inadequacy in his own voice which made them worse; so that his mother dried her tears, ashamed, not of having given way to them, but because she had a son who couldn't put out a hand to dry them for her, who didn't dare to hold out his arms and take her into them, but only became all the stiffer in his very remorse and contrition which to the onlooker appeared like embarrassment and disgust. Masculine poverty of expression is more obvious in sorrow than in joy, but in either case it can be extremely embarrassing and painful.

They both fell silent with one of those silences which reveal the gulf between minds and which is really more terrifying than the infinite distances we imagine between the stars. Such miserable foolish words: on his side he would never have imagined that he would come to feel the need of expression, of explaining himself: and on hers, something even sadder: it was the first and last time that she had irriated him by bursting into tears, like a fool. Senseless miserable words, with all that anguish and taint of mortality they share with all the other kinds of violence and rashness which come between people who love one another, so that whether they are actually near or far, they are driven asunder into common solitude.

Gaspare Della Morte had a gift which is particularly indispensable in secret and conspiratorial undertakings: the sure instinct for people who could be trusted. In response to Melania Mèrici's offer, he said that he would accept it if the need or occasion arose, but he had added without hesitation that, as a gentleman and a man of honour, he must warn her that giving him shelter under her roof might at any time mean considerable trouble and inconvenience, and even serious danger. She made a gesture as if to check something which he had actually no intention of adding, and said he need not explain himself further. The word 'troubles' was one she didn't even want to hear: and as for dangers and difficulties she looked upon them as an honour. If necessary she was ready to give her word, to swear. . . . And with a smile Gaspare had told her she needn't swear.

A fine woman, he had said to Armida, and added, a bit high-flown: the romantic type of female conspirator and revolutionary, a bit '48 and *Cristina Belgioioso,* on the melo-dramatic side nowadays when there was no Verdi any longer to liven up the action with a train of heroic musical flights. Nowadays artists were mostly like that arid hyper-intellectual Donato Mèrici, busy expressing the anguish of abstract numbers and of empty mathematical space and time with an art which was self-generated, like Faust's *Homunculus* in the glass retort. And maybe Donatello was right, artistically and poetically the most genuinely creative thing you could do, was to give up the attempt to express the inexpressible and refuse to traffic with the impossible or fill up the void with desperate cerebral inventions or more likely with feeble-minded pretentiousness.

There had never been any doubt in Armida's mind that Gaspare was a man of universal intelligence, and now here was a woman of Melania's intellect and culture to confirm her, if she had had any need of it, with equal enthusiasm, in her enthusiastic conviction.

She loved him with all possible tenderness as well as with intense passion and this was enough to satisfy her completely in mind and body. She would have been very unwilling to accept her friend's hospitality as often as she did—the pretty gay comfortable bedroom, the charming hours in her beautiful house, and Melania's good table which, having highly developed senses, she could fully appreciate—if for several months now Gaspare had not had to be away, so often and for such long periods, from their miserable little lodgings which were so bare and uncomfortable as well as being in a poor and inconvenient part of one of the poorest and most distant districts, right on the outskirts of a modern Milan, which seemed to be made up almost entirely of such remote slums. When all was said—and she didn't fail to say it to her friend— the two lovers were really very badly off even for food, because they were poor to begin with and, since Gaspare's political activity had taken him away from his profession, his earnings had sunk to a very low level. In these times of high prices and food shortages, whatever will or interest she had felt—and that was slight enough—to improve their diet, vanished completely when she had to sit down alone. On those days she didn't trouble to lay the table but was quite content to eat standing up in the kitchen: and all she had was her ration of wartime bread soaked in watered milk—when there was any— and a bit of warmed-up cabbage or some sardines from tins which had been old when she laid them in and which one of these days might mean food poisoning or colic. On those days she even saved the basic rations so that when he came home Gaspare should have something to satisfy his strong and healthy male appetite. Otherwise if it hadn't been for the lack of physical and mental zest which came from these dull days alone, she would have had an excellent appetite herself. And she demonstrated this when staying with her friend from whom she did not hide either the fact that she had not been bothering to eat, through disgust and boredom nor the pleasure she took in Melania's good table and the good it was doing her.

Once Melania's warm and indiscriminate fantasy had got to work on it, this all appeared heroic and pathetic in the highest degree. She was worried by these shortages and privations and saw her friend already menaced with tuberculosis through undernourishment. And this constant and detailed account of everything which Armida did, and what she had to put up with during the times the two were apart, led on to confidences about her passionate love which became more and more intimate and languishing as the times in which she could give herself up to it became fewer and farther between. The nights when Gaspare actually was at home she passed anxiously awaiting a visit from the political police with her ears pricked up in case they should knock so that he would have time to escape over the roofs even at the risk of being shot. For that would anyway be better than being tortured, which is what the police would have done to him to make him talk. Meanwhile it looked as if they weren't after him or didn't suspect him— unless that was a ruse. In any case, he didn't seem to give it a thought, unless he was hiding it from her, so as not to give her any more anxiety.

In these days, the only kind of conversation which served to cheat and allay this anxiety and distract this longing and discontented lover from it enough to animate her, was provided by her eager confidences about her amorous and sexual intimacies, the desperate passion which burned her and which devoured her with impatience.

Though she was the younger of the two, Armida Lenai herself was no longer in her first youth, and as the two friends talked this lament that they were no longer young and had only a few years left now for loving, and were fading both in mind and body, returned like an obsessive refrain. And Melania responded in her turn with a lament of her own, also on the theme of the lost dead loveless years, which was long and repetitive and even more despairing and like an everlasting *da capo* never achieving the close. And the yearnings of the one for the wasted present and the regrets of the other for a vanished past mingled and became almost indistinguishable in these insidiously sensual confidences.

Sensual however not in an overt but in an implicit sense: for certainly neither of them would ever have had the slightest thought of homosexual contact: and perhaps this vice which allows our age to combine insane perversion with a dulling of sensibility is anyway more theoretical than real, the effect of a demented and exhibitionistic vanity.

The two women indulged in these lengthy and detailed confidences in low voices, sitting side by side with their arms round each other, or lying flat on the bed together gazing at the ceiling with vague and wandering eyes and holding each others' hands which were sometimes feverishly dry and sometimes sweating alternately hot and cold: and what they confided were detailed descriptions of sensual caresses and riotous feasts of love, of unwillingness to yield followed by sudden unpredictable outbreaks of passion, and sweetness long-drawn-out: all this expressed with a lush ardour, and looks which were like caresses and an inclination to weep tender and grateful tears: and this was all in its way the scum on top of a disordered imagination, even if it went off in fantasy and betrayed itself merely as excess of emotion and sensibility, with the pair working off their excitement, and coming finally to tears and sighs, and kissing and embracing in mutual commiseration.

They didn't even know when the habit had originated. It was

something like the way in which the kink for pornographic
books and pictures, which can become a tyrannical obsession,
can be started off by indiscriminate reading: and this is only
through rashness and vanity or something which is even more
vain and stupid, an overweening confidence in one's own
virtue and seriousmindedness, through which one assumes
oneself out of the range of all the more slovenly and sordid
vices: for it always arises insidiously from self-indulgence and
curiosity which appeared venial and insignificant in the early
stages; the most evil and inveterate of habits are always con-
tracted as a result of 'trying just once'.

The very innocence of this friendship, the fact that their
behaviour was blameless even if their words were not, and
that they had not only never done anything wrong but that the
thought had never crossed their minds, so that they confined
all the viciousness of their emotional disturbance to imagination and sensibility, completely concealed from the two
friends how far they were actually off their balance.

But one must understand that Armida Lenai had her man
and she could hope for contentment in the future. But these
excesses had a stronger effect on Melania Mèrici and they
struck deeper roots, and came out in changes of disposition
and taste and indeed in a disgust for all her usual thoughts and
feelings, a profound and distressing upheaval and self-aliena-
tion. And so in her boredom and irritation she took a dislike,
which was at times even hatred, to everything which had given
her pleasure and which she had once loved, in hateful conflict
with herself and with what had given her her peculiar dignity
and uprightness: and she turned against these things as if they
had caused the deception and illusion and had been culpable
and malignant like an unhappy fate which had thus resulted
in her self-frustration. And so she spurned even her husband's
memory as if in that long-vanished year of happiness and in
his own untimely death, he had given her nothing but illusion
and pain.

She even felt that she no longer loved her own son. It wa
not merely because she was angry and disappointed with hin
for intellectual reasons, which might be excusable howeve
ridiculous: not because he hadn't wanted to be a musician
not even for the reason that she was emotionally disappointed
which is only human and always to some extent inevitabl
between sons and their parents.

The accusation, the injury at the back of all her bitternes
and injustice, which quite inexcusably she made a source o
conflict between herself and her son, arose from the mad anc
pitiable persuasion, or rather from the perverted belief, tha
she had irremediably lost and renounced her own life, no
merely for his sake but through his fault: and it is this injustic
which is the root and sign of all our evil, all our sinfulness anc
crime, of every fault both great and small. And the more sh
pitied and admired herself for this final consummation o
sacrifice, the less she was able to forgive him for it or to accep
it from him.

Moreover there was another feeling, as petty as it is commoi
and as incurable as it is mistaken and unhappy, which con
tributed its sour lees of sombreness and bile to her alread
poisoned blood, so that she turned against her son witl
impulses which would have been hatred if they had not beei
a form of madness, certainly the unhallowed folly of a sicl
mind: this was that she had somehow missed and betrayed, ha
wasted by renunciation, a miraculous destiny which was t
have been all the more productive of marvels, the less easy i
was to define. And when she became aware that a remors
which could hardly hope for expiation, was at work withi
her, she blamed Donato for this too, although she could no
really find any fault with him (and this was the very extremit
of woe) except that he had been born, except that she hersel
had brought him into the world. To think that otherwise sh
would have been alone and free and would either have dedicate
her life to the grand passion or been a great artist—or both!

Her friend felt both pity and alarm for these ravings—and some irritation—and tried to cure her of them by reasoning her out of them. But Armida's pity, reprimands or consolations all affected Signora Mèrici in the same way as the language of her own avowals—they worked her up into a state of exaltation, so that she saw herself a Phaedra with no Hippolytus, a Medea without Jason, and hardly knew herself, whether she was most inclined to glory in her role of unnatural mother or be horrified by it. Was it nothing but histrionics? Of course, it was partly so, but we don't even know ourselves how much words and gestures reflexively influence the feelings from which they arise. The scientific explanation that it was disturbance due to the critical age might be the one nearest the truth and so the most humiliating. But both humiliation and science would have vanished before the truth, if Melania had been able to face the consequences of this immoderate and insatiable pursuit of emotion and sensation: of velleities and appetites which are both strange and over-refined, being located in that area of passionate sensibility, between the mental and the physical, of what is called the æsthetic, but should be called the fantastic: and which lead in the end to sloth and corruption and bring to every nature whose sole aim in life is pleasure and opportunity of enjoyment, its due reward in sterility and impotence.

For no matter how delicate and refined the pleasures may be, no matter how exquisite and sensitive the sensibility they reveal, when they are an end in themselves and become the idol at once exorbitant and elusive and as joyless as it is insatiable—of an egoism at one and the same time complacent and restless, their cultivation brings the direst results, the aberrations of miserable and withered senility, of the libertine reduced to impotence and the worn-out but persistent playboy.

What good was it to Melania to recognise the physical disturbances of the critical age when she was also forced to recognise that her whole conception of life in its intensity of

pride had collapsed without chance of remedy? It couldn't
even teach her humility and acquiescence enough to accept
that she was ill and ought to resign herself to medical treatment.

However ineffectually, the feeble pride of desperation had,
through her obsessions and impatience, too strong a hold on
her, compared to the humbler strength of resignation. In short
the trouble was due to the fantasies of a mind which was too
passive and had too little to occupy it and which had been
weakened by trying to get from sonatas and symphonies what
moral conscience and religious faith, when you have them
alone can give.

And solitude, as she experienced it both inwardly and from
the external circumstances of war, made her afraid of herself
it left her as her own victim with nothing but herself to prey
on. And since she couldn't bear even the mere idea of solitude
she felt, when she was forced to realise it, as if she had been
consigned to a cell which shut out all the light, with only her
own shadow for company, so that she became obsessed with
the fear and hatred of it: and the futile attempt to escape from
it only meant that it was there wherever you turned to look,
perpetually renewing an undiminishing fear and horror.

This was why she couldn't be without her friend and confidant, couldn't even bear the thought of being without her
and couldn't make up her mind to go to Alma Dannata, even
after having moved her furniture and belongings out there
Even on this score there was friction with Donatello, for
though he had plenty of rationalisations and common-sense
arguments to disguise his anxiety and the obsessive idea that
the night-raiders were actually looking for him personally
which had assailed him in their town-house—in short, though
he managed to hide the fact that he was afraid of air-raids—he
was in a hurry to move to Vill' Alma. But he had enough
natural and human feeling to be ashamed of leaving his
mother alone in the city.

All this caused the usual bickering: he didn't see what they had to stay in the city for: and she didn't understand why he was in such a hurry to go: and so there was a cloud between them and they became suspicious of each other and of their own shadows, and they lost their tempers unreasonably and spoke to each other sharply and rudely, although they loved each other as much as any mother and son in the world. And since Melania wasn't afraid of bombs, she suspected that Donato, who was totally ignorant on the matter, had penetrated the secret of the emotional disturbance in her friendship with Armida, and she inwardly accused him of intolerance and egoistical jealousy: whereas Donato suspected that Melania, who knew nothing about it, had penetrated the secret of his fear and shame and was actually alluding to that when she said—with what he insisted on seeing as contempt—that he needn't wait for her if he wanted to go, she didn't need him.

It was to this suspected insult rather than to what she had actually said, that he responded with angry words and looks which struck her in her turn as contemptuous: all right, then, he could stay since she was so unreasonable, but she needn't take it upon herself to tell him to go away, which was an idea he couldn't put forward except to annoy him, since he couldn't make out why she wanted to stay. In a word, the usual vicious circle of disputes about nothing.

G

CHAPTER SIX

Mournful Farewells and
Black Forebodings

As she couldn't bear to be without her friend and confidant
Melania was in terror of the loneliness of the country and
would never have made up her mind to leave for Vill' Alma i
Armida hadn't arrived one day, white with anxiety, and bring
ing the news that, at least for the time being, Gaspare Dell
Morte had to disappear from activity and keep right out of th
way.

Melania said that he must go to Vill' Alma immediately
where he could be hidden or at least kept completely out o
sight, and where the caretakers were trusted old famil
servants she could vouch for. Splendid, said Armida, sh
wouldn't have so much as thought of suggesting such an ide
to her, but since she was so brave and generous . . . Melani
broke in, saying that she was happy to have the chance o
showing Gaspare that even a drawing-room anti-Fascist ha
her uses; but they mustn't waste time. How was he going t
get to Vill' Alma, fifty kilometres and more by road? Ordinar
public transport, the railway, for instance, wasn't safe, and i
wouldn't even take him all the way, and he didn't want to b
seen asking his way in the neighbourhood. And moreove
added Melania after reflection, the caretakers wouldn't tak
in simply any stranger who came and asked for shelter: givin
him a letter, apart from being rash, wouldn't be enough t
convince them. And then there was the route which wa

roundabout and off the beaten track, and went over hill and dale following all the ups and downs of the locality, which was what gave it its charm and beauty: but it was easy to lose yourself among them and wander about in a way which would rouse suspicion if you came across any police or public patrol. Armida said that he had forged papers but saw at once that even so it was essential that nobody should know where he was going, least of all anyone to do with the authorities. Then Melania suggested that she should go first to Vill' Alma but time was short and the threat of arrest was hanging over him. There was going to be a house-search that very night. The warning had been given by a contact in the police so that they wouldn't find what they were looking for and Gaspare could get clear. As far as the search was concerned, everything was provided for. But even if Melania went first to Vill' Alma and could get there in time, which wasn't certain, it would still be difficult for him to find his way. Armida seemed desperately anxious, and was wringing her hands.

Donato would go with him on his bicycle, said Melania, quite sure that she could be as good as her word. Armida was doubtful: Donato was so hostile to political activity, almost scornful of it, and to these conspiratorial methods. It might not be due to love of politics, said Melania, but she confidently asserted that with Donato it would be a question of honour to get someone, who had trusted him, to safety. But were the two of them to take the responsibility of letting an outsider into the secret without Gaspare's permission? And where was Della Morte, by the way? He should be calling her any minute now from a public kiosk, just to get in touch with her, but wouldn't be able to tell her anything because the telephone was tapped by the police. What was more serious, she wouldn't be able to pass on Melania's offer, which was in every way the best solution: and would mean, added Melania, that they needn't be separated; and without more ado she invited Armida to come out to Vill' Alma with her. Armida breathed again. She said that they had a code in which she could ask him to meet her before he went.

This was arranged, and after a word with Armida in a street near the house, Gaspare agreed to everything, and Donato also made no objection to doing as his mother asked. Two days later, a basket of early cherries of the very finest quality arrived in Milan from Vill' Alma, and so the two women knew that everything had gone well and according to plan and without any difficulties.

And then their departure for Vill' Alma was delayed for another day by a duty which overrode everything: this was the funeral of Giovan Battista Sessa which Melania felt that she must attend.

Her old friend had died, and as he had said he would wish to, without giving any trouble to anyone. When she heard the news, Melania thought that his tact had amounted almost to stoic heroism. But a mournful and reminiscent smile came to her lips as she remembered how exaggerated he would have found these words: heroic, stoic and so forth. And she remembered Sessa once quoting his favourite author Manzoni, and the death-scene of Don Ferrante, when he was railing against the stars like one of Metastasio's heroes, and how Sessa had said that when his own time came he wouldn't want to cause any inconvenience, not even to the stars. When anyone started talking about heroism in his presence, he had a special sort of smile—and Melania could feel it on her own face now, so vivid and poignant was the recollection: stoic virtue was an idea which simply called out that, '*Rather a pity, don't you think?*' of his. One evening while they were all talking, a man who fancied himself as a wit and *esprit fort,* started severely criticising the practical results of the 'Concordato' and the 'Lateran Treaties' from the point of view both of the liberal layman and of the Fascist state, and then, ever more critical, he had started to look at them from the point of view of the Church: all to Sessa's increasing discomfort so that he tried to withdraw from the discussion but could not break the spell because the other man was a very good talker. So he had put forward a modest opinion of his own, or rather a possible fourth point of view: that of the Meek who, though they existed, were not good at talking. One result of the 'Concordato' was that it had removed a difficulty of conscience for them. This suggestion did not meet with any success and apparently the other man couldn't help calling this point of view a peace-at-any-price Catholicism, a convenient theory for keeping in with all sides. This provoked a sharp discussion, for he said that Catholics of that sort refused to put themselves out right up till Judgement Day, when they called on Christ to do it for them.

Sessa was hurt by this much more than he showed and he sadly murmured that we are all sinners and that he preferred it if people didn't insult the sacraments in discussions in which he took part. Meanwhile he would withdraw from this one. Someone other than he might have shown more patience. His argumentative opponent asked sarcastically if it had really cost Sessa so much patience to hear him out so far: to which Sessa replied that he hadn't made himself clear: when he'd said 'Someone' he hadn't alluded to himself but to Christ whose patience is no less than his charity. And if the other insisted on going on with the argument and forcing him to say what he really thought himself, he'd use the very same words, the fact that Christ 'puts himself out' for those who abjure him right till Judgement Day was the reason why such a creature as himself, in all his unworthiness, believed and wanted to believe in Christ and the Sacraments. And anyway as the other man was so jolly clever and could make out such a good case for himself, he ought to make a good clean job of his life, and Sessa hoped with all his heart that he'd try and do so, especially, too, when it came to dying and presenting himself to that Judgement which exempts no one, clean or unclean.

Then he went home and gave orders to his old servant not to disturb anyone with the news that he was dying—'thanks' to a sharp attack of his chronic bronchitis, which had been brought on by a 'beastly' spring cold. 'Thanks' had been what he said himself and that it was beastly she had seen for herself, but the master's orders had been quite definite and he had stuck to them—in spite of the Holy Oil and the Last Rites— right up to the end: and the old servant sighed and wiped her eyes and said he'd died like a true Christian, and added, 'They don't grow on every tree.' The poor master had even ordered that his death and funeral should be kept from all but the very smallest number of his friends, but that Signora Melania Mèrici, of course, was to be informed first of all.

Armida Lenai wanted to come with Melania to the Requiem Mass and the Blessing of the Bier, and this in spite of the fact that she had never been in his good books, indeed he had disliked her: and that was of course the real reason why she wanted to be there. In Melania's surprised and inquiring look she read a certain suspicion, as if she were wondering whether he would have liked it and whether Armida wasn't being somewhat spiteful and revengeful in wanting to be there. Guessing what she was feeling, Armida said with a confident humility that it only went to show how remote Melania was from herself and Sessa in these matters. She mustn't think for Heaven's sake that saying that implied any reproach or judgment, which would be impertinent; it only meant that, because she and Sessa had had their faith in common, whatever he might have felt while he was alive about her attending his funeral, now he saw her there from Purgatory or Paradise, she was quite certain he would say a *Pater* and an *Ave* for her and her sins.

If there had been time to think about it, a kind of indefinable jealousy in Melania's attitude might have been obvious to either of them, for to be faced with Armida Lenai as a devout Catholic, the first she'd heard of it, and in Sessa's own parish church, came to her as an astounding and disturbing revelation, quite enough to distract her from the thoughts which at that time and place she would have wished to dedicate entirely to her dead friend.

It was an ugly church and had never been anything else, and had moreover been modernised in the most perfectly representative and completely stereotyped contemporary ecclesiastical style. The ornaments on the walls, an oleographed Via Crucis, the altar-pictures, the multicoloured plaster statues of the Virgin and Child, of the Sacred Heart, of St. Anthony of Padua with the Child in his arms, and some other saints Melania didn't know—it was all showy, sickly and extremely ugly, down to the last detail of fixtures and furnishings. Melania could have borne with all this, could, as it were, have adjusted herself, because, given the current architectural style, it didn't cause her any surprise. But what really distracted her was Armida, who had got to the church before her and whom she saw, as she herself arrived, in a black veil, coming out of a massive and imposing Confessional-box in a pseudo-baroque style which couldn't have been more baroque if it had been genuine, with all sorts of adjuncts and ornaments in the most pretty-pretty and florid kind of jesuitical rococo, the sort they make in ecclesiastical furnishing factories.

She was really taken aback, and she was even more surprised when in company with the old servant and a few beggars who were receiving communion, she saw Armida take up a position at the altar-rail. So she had not only made her confession and received absolution, she was now going to communicate. Could it be possible?

Melania would have wished to have concentrated her thoughts in a devout recollection and silently offer up her heart in her own kind of prayer for her dead friend, but she could not do so. Armida Lenai had shocked her, not only in her liberal rationalistic outlook but to the very foundations of protestant and Lutheran principle whose scruples she had inherited, which she would never have believed she still retained, but which now came violently to the surface. Was

Armida simply blaspheming in confessing and taking communion or did it really mean that she was giving up her lover? And the mere idea very nearly made her laugh. And because of this inclination to laugh, which was as bitter as it was out of place, a profound anger was stirred in her towards this friend for having made her confession and towards the priest for having absolved her. It compelled her to pursue her thoughts much further than she would have wished, and she felt distressed and angry with everything, even and especially with the Catholic sacraments and the Church which administered them. So much so that when the priest descended from the altar and proffered the wafer to the kneeling penitent, Melania turned away her eyes, feeling so painfully disturbed that she wanted to go out of the Church.

Melania looked at that black veil on the penitent's head: she had her face in her hands and was deep in her devotions, immobile and bowed upon the altar-steps, and her attitude so convincingly suggested faith and surrender that Melania, in spite of all her previous ideas and doubts, had to admit that her friend was sincere although she couldn't understand how it could be so. And that black veil suddenly reminded her of a fact which she had learnt by chance some time ago—that the covered head is an ancient legal symbol of subjection and submission, prescribed as such for women in church. It came into her head that the elegant black head-dress on the pale golden hair had been specially chosen for the ceremony as a kind of sign of rebellion and ironical protest.

She felt listless and exhausted with all these ideas, the last of which seemed to be bordering on the absurd, and not one of which had been devoted to her poor friend Sessa who now that the Mass was finished, was about to journey on to the grave with only the very humblest sort of funeral train and one which, through current circumstances, was even meaner than it otherwise would have been.

His last journey was solitary for he had left the servant

nstructions that the funeral was to be as simple as possible,
without flowers or mourners. There was something character-
istically tart even about this. He had said to Melania, on more
han one occasion, she remembered, that he had noticed at
funerals that people were always too weakminded to put up
with the strain of keeping quiet once they were out of the
church, and that this applied to himself too; and that funerals,
even if not at all protracted, always finished up with all the
friends and mourners chattering as they went. And even the
chief mourners finish up with a good gossip, he had said, and
burst out laughing: so it was better to make your own way
alone. Yet even he, thought Melania with a touch of impatience, how pernickety and fussy he had been! She wasn't
far off calling him a touchy bigot, and a formalist.

They had to go home to make their final preparations for
departure but they took a long way round on foot, perhaps
secretly wishing to have one more look at the city which they
were about to leave with no idea when they would return, and
so it came to the point when Melania had to ask Armida
how it was she could take the risk of coming to Vill' Alma.

Armida, in astonishment, shook herself out of a peaceful
reverie—which, to Melania in her aggressive and ironical
mood, seemed somehow remiss and sluggish and reminded
her of the slothful sensuality of a cat—and asked where else
she was supposed to go and whatever it was that had put the
idea in Melania's head to ask such a question? Then she
became timid and bewildered and added, Perhaps Melania
didn't want her any more?

And what, Melania asked, had got into her head now? Why
ever not? They stopped, for Melania's first question had taken
Armida's breath away. It was just at the place where there was
an enormous open space between the houses, no doubt due
to a bomb which must have fallen a long time ago, or else
was a clearing where a new construction had been abandoned.
Armida leaned on the remains of a broken railing and with an

air of distress, humbly and modestly explained that she had been afraid Melania might have regretted her invitation and didn't want any scandal under her own roof due to the fact that Gaspere and she were living together or, if you liked, that she was his concubine. And reproach herself as she might Melania could not refrain from inquiring ironically, whether it had been the confessor who had used this great big technical and legal word to her a short time ago? Oh, she said, today wasn't the first time she'd heard it. As she spoke, she bowed her head, timorously, and looked abashed and went pale and blushed by turns in her fear and confusion. Every time she entered the confessional, she had to listen to harsh reproaches and they were not only harsh, but perfectly justified and she deserved them but what was there to be done about it? As she spoke she managed to look passionate and sorrowful at once and the expression was certainly charming.

What are you to do? Melania put in—don't ask her, she said especially as she wouldn't dream of being shocked or taking back the invitation to Vill' Alma. But she added that she had just felt curious: now that Armida had confessed on her knees and been absolved and genuflected at the altar and received communion, how could she take the risk of being with her lover again? Wasn't she challenging temptation? Was she deceiving herself or did she really hope she could resist?

No, it wasn't self-deception—or hope. And before she opened her mouth, her sad and despondent expression answered clearly enough that she couldn't even imagine having the strength to resist passion and temptation.

Well, then, what sort of vows had she been making all the time she was kneeling in the confessional and genuflecting and lying prostrate on the altar-steps and receiving the host And a feeling of shame held Melania back from saying something which would have sounded even crueller: receiving the flesh and blood of Jesus Christ?

But what she had said was enough. Armida gave a

uppressed sob and didn't trouble to wipe away the unwonted
nd painful tears which poured from her eyes. Melania thought,
maybe she believes that weeping is the way to soften Christ
nd God and Our Lady. But suddenly she felt that these tears
were genuine, miserable human tears. And that just because
hey were so they might find their way to the mercy of
God and fall on the last and lowest step of his judgement
eat, where an angel in all his splendour would come down to
ather them. On the other hand she herself—with her relentless
ogic and argumentativeness, her pride and scruples, her
uritanical conscience which would all seem like vindictive
nd idle contentiousness and wrath—would be spurned. And
with something like poetic imagery, it came into her mind that
he faces of the angels who fell through pride had shone with
ternal light until the day of their rebellion and had then
larkened with eternal shadow—and she shuddered, in spite of
erself, although she still felt indignant with her friend and
with herself and with this religion of indulgences and pardons
nd good works.

She heard Armida saying that she didn't deceive herself or
ave any hopes: that she had never had any illusions of being
nything but a poor weak woman, or hoped to be more than
sinner who could weep and pray and repent for an hour—
ut not be lastingly changed and reformed.

Ah, it's all very comfortable, said Melania, and immediately
egretted the unnecessary spitefulness of what she had said,
lthough too late. But although she was hurt, her friend
eceived it without protest or any attempt to defend herself.
Yes, it's comfortable, that too: and she felt she deserved even
hat.

Then, foolishly, Melania would have liked to heal the wound
which she had foolishly given. But all she could find to say
was, Armida must really forgive her but she couldn't under-
tand how you could go into the confessional and then come
straight out and communicate.

While she was still obsessed with her anger and was dwellin
again on these ritual performances, she saw that of the two c
them, Armida could understand her even less than she coul
Armida, who however received accusations and reproache:
whether open or implied, in a spirit of submission to matc
the veil on her head.

It was as if the confessional and the altar-steps, where n
kneeling sinner is ever rejected, had come between her frien
and herself like a barrier, and as if, now that they had bee
evoked between the two of them, they defended her.

Melania remembered having heard it said—she didn'
know if there was any truth in it or if it was just imaginatio
or superstition—that certain confessional-boxes in the gothi
gloom of the apse behind the great altar of the Duomo ha
been given the name 'Assassins' Boxes' by the townspeop!
because they believed that murderers and worse people who'
committed incest and offended against every law, natura
human and divine, were the ones who had recourse to then
But then she started wondering what was all this sudde
uprush of fancies and images—only the feverish sensibility c
an artist manqué, an abortive imaginative urge.

And then she asked Armida to forgive her for having upse
her when she had no reason or right to do so. But as it turne
out her friend understood this even less than what had gon
before: and meekly asked whatever was there to forgive
She'd said these very things to herself so often, always knowin
that they were useless, God and Our Lady have mercy on he!

Melania took her hands affectionately between her own an
said that was just why she asked her to forgive her for havin
taken it upon herself to say them again without having an
right to do so.

There was a certain melancholy appropriateness in the plac
where they had stopped to talk. It was a very large open spac
enclosed on three sides: the walls of the demolished house
looked exactly like the dingy wings of an abandoned theatre

with what remained of the paint and the wall-papers discoloured by rain and torn by the wind, while the pipes and
intimate domestic tackle were revealed in all their squalor
and ugliness. All the space in between the walls was filled with
the remains of party-walls, piles of gravel and rubble, broken-
down steps and planks, and the cavities and broken vaulting
of cellars. And a rank dry voracious grass had overgrown
everything: tall and thick with a savage luxuriance, it certainly
harboured at night a prolific population of vicious and famish-
ing rats which came out of the sewers which here and there
were broken wide open.

Apart from their usual attachment to places, an incredible
number of cats had been attracted by this game, and they
crowded out all the best corners in the quiet and shade, some
of them having originally belonged to the houses which had
stood there and others coming from neighbouring houses
which had been left empty. They had all with one accord
taken advantage of this freedom of the wild to bring forth a
vigorous and flourishing bastard progeny of every variety,
which were basking in throngs and displaying every shade and
description of feline fur. Idly drowsing as usual, but half-wild,
they packed the place. What was startling was the way they
spread over these miserable ruins like a kind of glossy well-fed
velvet which made one reflect with horror that quite apart
from the live rats, there had often been dead people found in
the ruins after air-raids. When anyone stopped to look at them
and they noticed they were being observed, they would stare
back fiercely and looked as if they would have been quite
capable of attacking human beings if they had been angry or
short of food. There were several of them strolling about with
a casual air, appearing and vanishing among the coarse wild
steppe-like grass and the craters.

'What a horrid sight,' said Armida wearily, 'and what a bad
omen for the city.'

Melania recollected some remarks which had been made a

long time ago by her father who, apart from being a banke
and man of affairs, had been so cultivated and, historically
even erudite, especially in the history of his own profession s
that, though he was German, he liked to call himself a Merchan
of Milan. Her friend seemed to be sunk in a brown study bu
she quoted to her what the banker had said in his role o
Merchant of Milan, by adoption and choice. Before 1914 an
in the early years of the century, Milan had been the capita
and the agricultural market of the Lombard plain which wa
so wonderfully rich and fertile both by nature and throug
agelong cultivation. It had been a city of bold enterprise, ric
in ancient arts and crafts and in the new power of industry an
commerce: the first station and what might be called th
landing-place of Genoa. What he had been talking about wa
the Milan of the St. Gothard and Simplon tunnels, of th
Ticino and Adda, the Milan which the great waterway
the rivers and canals, and magnificent highroads, had made th
market, the junction and crossroads for all the goods, wealt
and trade of the peoples, not only of the peninsula and th
Mediterranean but of the whole continent behind the Alp
And because of its central situation, he had said, it had bee
the bank and mart for East and West and exercised influenc
not only among all the nations of the Mediterranean bu
throughout the whole of northern Europe from the Vistul
and the Danube to the Seine and the Thames, in Warsaw an
the City of London alike, in Paris and Constantinople, i
Spain as much as in Scandinavia. He also used to say tha
Milan, both intellectually and materially, had been perhap
more representative of European civilisation than any othe
city, more open to influences and enthusiasms; and this righ
from the time there had been a Europe: right till the Europea
disaster of the first war and all the straits and restrictions an
closing-down of businesses which resulted from it, and i
which he gloomily foresaw, as he lay dying, the ruin and failu
of his own life's work as an Italo-German financier and as

man of action using his influence for a 'European peace' based
on the balance of power and above all on the Triple Alliance.

What would he have said now if he could have seen the
rubble and ruins which were among these results? Perhaps
only that it was logical and inevitable. But perhaps when we
call on the dead to speak we only project upon them what we
have lost ourselves, the courage to make logical and inevitable
answers. One can't help asking how the Milan which they left
will compare, in the minds of these two women who are still
among the living, with the Milan which they will find on their
return—whenever that will be, with all the eventualities and
dangers which lie between.

They moved away from the ruins as if they were fleeing
from the sight, afraid that it would answer with a prophecy of
dearth, an omen of impending evil.

Melania was blonde and tall, and lithe in spite of a large
build. She had a broad open face in which wonderfully regular
features produced an air of serenity and harmony. Her eyes
were the purest Nordic blue and she had a pink and white
complexion. Her beauty and fine proportions, her gait, the
long rhythms of her swift firm step, even her hands which were
not only beautiful but strong, with the wide stretch of a
pianist who is in command of the symphonic range of the
modern piano—all these characteristics harmonised into
something at once gentle and striking, with a touch of the
Valkyrie: not that she was a Wagnerian fanatic; indeed she
reacted towards the composer of *Tristan* and the *Ring* and the
reputation which his decadence and Nibelungslied romanti-
cism had brought him, with considerable reserves and objections. Nevertheless, her black broad-brimmed hat upon her
golden hair did something to bring out a mythological air, a
she-warrior. And a touch of masculinity in the shape of the
shoulders and the straight back, the 'dry light' of her whole
personality, accentuated it too. And with all her blonde white-
ness and her mild air there was nothing insubstantial about

her, nothing soft, sensuous or yielding: either because she
despised it or was temperamentally remote from it.

Armida was a brunette and had raven hair with a few
premature streaks of silver which gave it a pathetic and
poignant charm and inspired a certain tenderness while bringing out its shining vividness. Her skin was brown with a
warm opaque pallor which absorbed the sunlight and gave it
back in this colourless warmth of tone. Sometimes in her deep
black eyes there flashed and faded a fugitive and charming
tinge of warm violet and then they had what is sometimes
called 'the Venus look'.

It was not merely that her face was irregular, you could not
even call it beautiful: the features were too marked and bold,
the nose a little heavy, the nostrils too wide and as sensual as
the wide fleshy mouth if not even more so. But laughing or
serious, her face had an animal grace, but in a restrained sense
of the word, meaning that a shade more would have spoiled
it. And you could feel—perhaps this was even a shade too
intense—the slow fire of sensuous abandonment which
brooded behind it. Her neck, though rounded and soft and
very attractive, was a trifle short and this made her face and
head look slightly disproportionate. She was not plump but
she was rounded and sinuous and the full and feminine grace
with which she was built and which was revealed whatever
she was wearing, and by every movement, was completely of
the South. Whatever she wore looked light and diaphanous, in
spite of the fact that her way of standing and moving and every
gesture and attitude gave an impression of indolence and
sultry languor. Her hands and feet were beautifully shaped
and almost excessively small. And now that she had arranged
her veil like a mantilla, which suited her wonderfully, one
could see what it was that made her irresistible, how graceful
and charming she was and, though without any deliberate
intention, how full of delight in her own attraction and in the
pleasure she gave.

In fact, the mere gesture of throwing back her lace veil had been quite enough to dispel not only all thought of penitence and contrition but any serious thought at all. Melania, on the other hand, though she went out of her way to speak to her in a sweet and affectionate tone, retained in her manner something rather stiff and severe. For Armida was by nature impulsive and totally uninhibited, while she herself could never break the restraints of intellect and reflection. They were both kind and warmhearted but Armida's good impulses were anyhow of short duration while Melania's, because of his difficulty in complete expression, sometimes turned sour.

A man who wrote drawing-room ballads had said that the two of them ought to change names, because Tasso's Armida was blonde and Melania means black in Greek: but after thinking it over, he said that Signora Mèrici would have been an Armida with no Rinaldo to love her and Signora Lenai would have been a Melania . . . he couldn't think how to fill in the missing term of his overstrained and pedantic comparison and got out of it with the much-abused *nigra sed formosa* of the *Cantico*. But certainly Armida gave the impression of a strong and voluptuous physical nature and of being as inflammable as she was inflaming.

When they got back home to the old Mèrici house with its stripped and empty rooms, Armida hurried to finish her packing so that they could leave immediately: meanwhile Melania noticed how old the house looked in its emptiness and nakedness, and thinking of the many years she had passed there she fell into a kind of trance, not like a reverie but sharply sensitive to the point of torment, with an oppressive melancholy which was at the same time both sweet and lacerating, the burden of a thousand associations without one clear recollection.

She brooded on Casa Mèrici and how she was leaving it and what its fate would be, and wondered how and when she would come back to it and how it would look when she returned. And would she ever return home, to Milan?

H

There was an air-raid warning but neither woman took any notice. Melania however observed that the silence of the half-deserted city was so deep that the sound could not intensify it: and so with this old street of Milan which had been for so many years her own street and which had been the centre for so many fine audiences, some of the best and most famous executants and composers, the devotees true and feigned, the genuine amateurs and the specious enthusiasts of music of every kind, ancient, modern and ultra-modern: for her musical salon, which had not only been renowned but had had merits as great as its vogue, had included figures of fun among its serious habitués. And thinking that Melania Mèrici's salon was closed and silent and had come to its end, she smiled, though her heart melted with inward weeping.

Was this a final farewell to her adored music which the rage of war had overwhelmed and silenced, along with everything else? Was this another, the final betrayal, which her passion for music had brought to her? And though it had betrayed her, were there others still left on the globe who could remain faithful to it or was the whole world bleeding and exhausted, struck down and violated by the scourge?

The All Clear was already sounding but that silence, both within the deserted oblivious rooms and out in the street, remained unaffected.

Suddenly, without remembering the actual notes but with a powerful and very accurate recollection of the marks of expression and of the feelings which they had so often stirred, she heard the music of Beethoven, soundlessly singing, rising and overflowing from the primal, the deepest springs of her very heart: Beethoven who, on the margin of a sonata had written the words 'samsara' and 'nirvana', eternal recurrence eternity that liberates and beatifies: torment and peace. Beethoven who, between the waves of defeat and of that heroic energy which broke out from a desperation and a passion in themselves heroic, had made this chant of ineffable sweetness

as a thank-offering for some mysterious healing: it was not
that it exceeded limits, but began beyond the limitations of
all human and poetic expression and delivered the most
crushing sorrow and the proudest revolts of the spirit alike,
into a world of sublime sound, of mourning and joy and ecstasy.

And while with the humility of a worshipper on the threshold
she entered into this mourning and joy, renouncing the ecstasy,
and content only to be touched by the rainbow light of longing
and dream, there came to her suddenly instead, the melody of
that wonderfully simple and pathetic love-song which Rossini
composed in his youth—*Non sai che questa calma è figlia di dolore?*

Nevertheless it was Beethoven who persisted, compelling
her, carrying her away with his overwhelmingly powerful
appeal, the irresistible summons of a courage which masters
fear and fate, with that voice and accent which is his and his
alone and which from the uttermost depths continually sings
those themes of passion and desperation—not only *Sorgi e
cammina* or *Levati e va* but *Prendi la mia mano e andiamo insieme*—
for under all their tumult and ecstasy, they are behests of
friendship, charity and brotherhood to the human spirit.

No, she hadn't been betrayed: and if she did not fall on her
knees it was because she felt that there would be something
artificial and exaggerated in the act. But the tears which she
wiped from her eyes were sweeter than any she had ever wept
or would weep again. She knew this, but still they were tears
of pure gratitude even if for a lost and unreturning happiness.
And gently and softly under her breath she began singing *Non sai
che questa calma* . . . and gently and softly she smiled to herself.

The next day the two friends were at Alma Dannata—or as
people euphemistically preferred to call it Vill' Alma—where
Gaspare and Donatello were awaiting them as arranged. This
was an occasion for great celebration and for a time they
allowed themselves to forget and recuperate, intensely enjoying
the sweetness and peace of the country.

The villa was built on a plateau of the first great slope of the lower Alpine hills of Lombardy and enjoyed a wide view of the foothills to the north, and also a sweeping panorama of the plain to the south but, because of the complex of low hills and little valleys through which it had to be approached, it had the peculiarity of being visible only from a great distance or from the plain itself or from considerable heights. And as there were none of these in its neighbourhood, you could see it only from the summit or the upper slopes of high hills and of the Alpine foothills. This kept it wonderfully secluded. Moreover the slopes which descended from the plateau on which it arose were clothed with a thick woodland which had grown up close to the two long wings of the villa and had been thinned and laid out on either side into a very beautiful park of carefully selected trees. The place had every kind of natural advantage, its air was always fresh and healthy and it was particularly well watered, for there was a copious spring of extreme purity rising in the lower subalpine slopes which was enough to feed a fountain, a few ancient basins, one of which had been turned into a fish-pond, a small lake and a cheerful little rivulet. In front of the house spread a broad fresh meadow rich and dense with vegetation: at the back there was an ample central loggia from which by rustic steps one could descend to the wood which had an agreeable wildness and went down on either side over a steep precipice.

The villa was enormous and largely unlived-in and it was the result of heterogeneous and ill-assorted attempts, which had been continually repeated throughout the centuries but never brought to a conclusion, to complete its construction and unify its style. It embodied the massive remains of a feudal castle, romanesque and tuscan renaissance designs, baroque rotundities and luxuriances, seventeenth-century decorations and puristic neoclassical graces. Whether by accident or design or due to the prescience of some past owner, this highly complex structure had any number of passages, exits, trap-doors and secret chambers, which were very handy for passing a long time in hiding or for hurriedly taking cover from a search. At one time there had been a subterranean passage which had led out into the woods at the rear but the opening had fallen in.

Melania had inherited Vill' Alma from her father who had given up going there before he died, since it had been bought for his dead wife. Melania was very much attached to the villa which she had restored, repaired, partially refurnished and explored in all its nooks.

In former times she had toyed with the idea of using it in the summer holidays as a kind of friends' academy of music including both professionals and amateurs: but that was all in the past.

There was a big high corridor which provided plenty of space and comfort and ran across the main body of the building to connect the front door with the loggia at the rear. It was enclosed with glass so that it was habitable even in the autumn and at one end there was the endless open sky of the plain, at the other the view of the pre-alpine summits. It had several doors leading from it to other parts of the villa and it was big enough to accommodate a good deal of furniture of all sorts which formed various circles and nooks for rest and study, with some well-stocked bookshelves; and now in addition Melania's two pianos, which had been 'evacuated' with some more books from town. There were three big decorated earthenware stoves which were stoked with logs and made it possible to keep the place warm at any season: and it was used as the common living-room, since it was not only the pleasantest and coolest room in summer but the warmest and most comfortable in the cold weather.

As it led to the loggia the same name became extended to it. And it was here that the guests of Vill' Alma used to foregather as the most natural place for recreation and intercourse: and so it became the scene of the encounters and conversations which provide the dramatic texture of the story which follows.

CHAPTER SEVEN

Counting One's Chickens . . .

DONATO MÈRICI AND GASPARE DELLA MORTE

DONATO: Would you mind if we had that radio off?

GASPARE: I don't mind at all. The interference is terrible.

DONATO: Listening to shrieks and howls can't be much fun.

GASPARE: You're always so intolerant.

DONATO: More so every day.

GASPARE: London-calling-Europe was just giving the news.

DONATO: How can you go on listening to all this radio-stuff? Even supposing it was Timbuctoo calling, what does it matter?

GASPARE: Now, my good chap, if you have to go for me too, you must be either very touchy or very insensitive.

DONATO: We've become very good friends in the last few weeks.

GASPARE: And I'm very glad about it, but not enough to want to be like you in all respects.

DONATO: Well, admit that I don't take offence! I'm friendly with you for all the things in you which aren't like me. That's what I respect you for.

GASPARE: You know, it would be so much better for you if, instead of just getting a sour satisfaction out of humouring it, you made a little effort to resist your unhealthy propensity for denigrating yourself!

DONATO: In whose eyes do you mean?

GASPARE: In your own, more than anyone's, that's the worst of it.

Donato: At least that would mean I'm not vain.

Gaspare: Nor am I, I should hope.

Danato: Oh you! You've got too much pride to be vain. It's no virtue!

Gaspare: And what about you? You're proud to madness!

Donato: Maybe. Anyway, if I can't cure myself, I can punish myself.

Gaspare: I know; with some people that's just self-indulgence.

Donato: And if that's the case, it's sterile and morbid. But you can't just rule it out, can you, that I'm honestly trying to alter myself and get better?

Gaspare: On the contrary. I'm quite sure you are.

Donato: And I'll fill in the rest of what you thought which you don't tell me because you're too polite and perhaps too sorry for me: you're quite sure I won't succeed.

Gaspare: You must have more self-confidence!

Donato: If I had I wouldn't be ill.

Gaspare: That's true, too.

Donato: Meanwhile, forgive me for talking to you about myself so much: if I were in your shoes I should find that difficult to tolerate: I do myself, but I give way to it again and again.

Gaspare: Ah well, you know, your nerves are a bit on edge, you're exhausted.

Donato: What with?

Gaspare: If either of us knew that you wouldn't be ill.

Donato: I suppose that's true too. But you're still hanging round the radio. You must be dying to listen to it.

Gaspare: They were just saying that the Fascist Grand Council has been convened at Rome.

Donato: My dear Gaspare, let them convene it.

Gaspare: Yes, but you know . . . the Grand Council . . .

Donato: They can only convene what they can. You can hardly expect the Fascist leader to convene the Roman Senate: he has to make do with the Grand Council! If you're going to cast a statue you have to use bronze: if you've only got clay to bake the results will be terracotta.

GASPARE: Being an artist what you should say is that one can produce a masterpiece even in terracotta. It's not so, but for the sake of discussion . . . ?

DONATO: If you drop terracotta it smashes: you're a politician and don't need me to tell you that.

GASPARE: That's got nothing to do with art.

DONATO: They say that politics is an art.

GASPARE: May be, in a certain sense—the sense that it can't be a science.

DONATO: Naturally.

GASPARE: But it's nothing at all to do with art in the sense of making statues or poems or pictures or symphonies. It's the last thing I'd do, to accept such a comparison, if I were and artist.

DONATO: And I should be just the same if I were a politician.

GASPARE: Well then, we're of the same mind. But I'd be glad if you'd tell me—as an artist—what you feel on the subject of the art of politics.

DONATO: Ah that's soon said: of all possible and conceivable arts, there's none which is such a bore.

GASPARE: Not for those who go in for it.

DONATO: Aha, that's what you say. And you're so vehement about it. So it's a sort of passion?

GASPARE: And suppose I said it is, how would you think about it then?

DONATO: As a passion? That's soon said too: the most pernicious, sterile and rabid of all: and sometimes the most cruel and ferocious: and on top of all that, still the biggest bore.

GASPARE: In the sense you're giving it, you may be right: but it's not the exact sense. Politics is before everything a necessity and a duty.

DONATO: From which, you mean, nobody ought to be exempted?

GASPARE: Anyway, at certain times . . .

DONATO: And you mean times like the present, unquestionably.

GASPARE: I'm afraid . . .

DONATO: It's about me you're afraid, ever since you made up your mind to like me.

GASPARE: Yes, it is about you. Nobody should be exempted.

DONATO: Well then, guess what I'm going to say to you.

GASPARE: Say it. . . .

DONATO: A politician should never like anyone.

GASPARE: And what about an artist?

DONATO: Ah, that's hitting below the belt. Anyway, I've decided to like you too.

GASPARE: Will you stick to the point, just to please me?

DONATO: To please you, but not myself: for an artist, a real one, gives himself out in a rich creative labour which yields him a return of . . .

GASPARE: Oh talk about yielding a return! Are you trying to show me you're a banker's grandson, all of a sudden?

DONATO: That's a pretty poor joke.

GASPARE: Well, wasn't your maternal grandfather a well-known and influential banker?

DONATO: Will you shut up—or do you have to try and be funny? A real artist puts all of himself into his work and when he's finished it as well as he can, he can say 'Now we'll leave each other alone and stop tormenting each other.' And that's the way he really lives his life. Can you bear me talking?

GASPARE: Yes, but I don't want you to feel forced to admit anything too painful.

DONATO: Thanks, but it's too late. There are other people we call artists too, because there isn't a better or more accurate word. And they wear themselves out, to no advantage, in the fantasy of creation. And this fantasy of creation gnaws at the poor wretches like an exhausting toil or rather like an insatiable appetite which never leaves off because it knows

no natural conclusion, and is all-demanding because there'
nothing real that it can have.

GASPARE: Is that really all that there is to be said on th
subject?

DONATO: I gave up art and took to science just to look as if]
were doing something.

GASPARE: Look to whom?

DONATO: Myself. You'll give me the credit that I don't car
what other people think? I've taken to science although I'n
not interested in the way it plays about with mirrors whicl
never decoy the lark—or in other words, the truth whicl
only flies higher and higher out of the radius of science.

GASPARE: *Laudat alauda Deum.*

DONATO: That could be an epigram. If one were religious on
would call it an omen or a warning or a sign. If truth is lik
a lark singing God's praises then science has nothing to d
with it, because God is a notion outside the ken of science

GASPARE: But not of art.

DONATO: Not if it's true art. And the same with politics. . .

GASPARE: If it's true politics, in other words if it recognise
and respects its own limits and has moderation . . .

DONATO: And charity?

GASPARE: That's the word I was looking for.

DONATO: And it occurred to me because it doesn't mean any
thing to me! You see how unfair it all is!

GASPARE: Now, Donato, show yourself some charity—an
other people who wish you well too, and stop being s
bitter: it's morbid and it hurts you.

DONATO: Have you noticed that when my mother is playing
I always go out?

GASPARE: Yes, I have, and I've also noticed that it upsets he
She loves music.

DONATO: She thinks she does.

GASPARE: Where do you take yourself to?

DONATO: Where the music can't get at me.

GASPARE: Why?

DONATO: Because it disgusts me. It makes me sick.

GASPARE: You know, you really are a very sick man!

DONATO: Who said I wasn't? I'm not supposed to be well, am I? What do you think my life is?

GASPARE: Haven't you made your illness your life?

DONATO: I don't know what life means to healthy people: maybe you do, as you're not ill; but sick men do live on their illnesses, that I can tell you.

GASPARE: I thought they wanted to get better.

DONATO: Yes, when they've got honest straightforward physical diseases. But when you're ill in this obscure baffling way which is half physical, half moral, you don't want to get better.

GASPARE: Well, isn't there any sort of treatment for it?

DONATO: Yes, sleeping-pills for example, but they don't do anything to cure insomnia, in fact they make it past remedy.

GASPARE: If that's the case I just have to deal with you as a man, whether you like it or not, and whether it's good for you or not, which is nothing to do with me.

DONATO: I realise that you're trying to talk to me as man to man. However . . .

GASPARE: Well, what? Aren't you a man?

DONATO: I'll tell you: this sort of trouble does womanise you to some extent. However, say what you've go to say. If I were altogether effeminate, I'd be hating you already for all the things you haven't yet said to me.

GASPARE: What would really do you good and reinvigorate you, would be a brisk plunge into politics, especially as they are today when your life's at stake and you really have to risk your skin.

DONATO: Do you mean that I ought to go back to the front— or become a militant Fascist?

GASPARE: That's a pretty feeble joke. There's nothing of the Fascist about you.

DONATO: Where's the joke? We've lost Africa: we aren't goin
to get Malta. Both seas and skies belong to the Unite
Nations; the Channel is more impregnable than ever: a
Roosevelt puts it, Germany is a fortress without a roof; an
as for ourselves, we're giving way in Sicily and we mus
expect a landing on the peninsula itself; and all this is th
result of a policy which has—I won't say brought it abou
for that would be to make it out more forceful than it i
—but has certainly favoured it and not been able to prever
it. It seems to me that if one wanted to reinvigorate onese
by living dangerously one couldn't wish for anything mor
dangerous than becoming a Fascist. Mussolini said 'Liv
dangerously' but that was while we were at peace: I don
know what he thinks about it now we're at war—wit
real dangers: it's Mussolini's advice you're giving me.

GASPARE: Ah well, if you were a Fascist and in the struggl
I'd respect you, as one resolute enemy to another.

DONATO: What you really mean is that you'd be able to respec
me as much as you despise me for what I am now. Yo
don't imagine I respect myself?

GASPARE: Donato, Donatello!

DONATO: Donatello, eh? What my mother used to call me. I
was a pleasant reminder of something in her early days i
Florence, but now even she has given it up. And you se
anyway, that Donatello, the old real Donatello, was a
artist of exactly the opposite kind to the one I am now—
or have been.

GASPARE: You're wandering. You're just trying to run away

DONATO: No: I'm going for you. What do you think you'r
doing here in this Alma Dannata of ours? It makes me ma
to use that damned name. What do you think you're doing
What with one woman who loves you and another wh
admires you and music which you like listening to, an
every spiritual and fleshly comfort and everything arrange
to delight and soothe you, you haven't even got time to b

bored! Do you call that politics? active politics into the bargain—while all the time your comrades, the anti-Fascist rebels, are risking their lives?

ASPARE: If you feel you have to talk to me like that, you really must be turning into a woman.

ONATO: If you're offended by plain speaking, I suppose it means you've got much more manly with all your refinements and self-indulgences. Now just answer me this. Do you deny what I'm saying? Isn't it true maybe that you're not doing anything to remind anybody of your existence—friend or foe?

ASPARE: Friends! That's the whole point . . . !

ONATO: They meant nothing to me. But you spend your time well tucked away here in the villa sitting up to all hours listening to the Voice of America and listening to the B.B.C. I shouldn't like to say how many times a day, and Colonel Stevens being funny and Candidus being sarcastic and all the lectures they give us on politics and history and ethics and all the re-education, and the concealed threats, and the bland promises which depend on our being able to unhitch ourselves from Hitler who even as an ally was very heavy-weight indeed! Promises indeed! As if anyone could foster the slightest illusion that one could make a promise today and keep it tomorrow! And threats! As if we weren't all of us—in Europe and in London itself for that mattter—all strung up together on the same gallows, all in the mass political suicide of Europe!

ASPARE: I don't know whether it's courage or desperation makes you look at it like this, but in such a tragedy of history as this, you . . .

ONATO: It's a tragedy of actuality and I don't know that I've got either the will or the courage to listen to the political farce, whether the acting's good or bad. And it's the best performers which disgust me most, when the real play is about fate—gathering up all the strings and throwing all

the puppets into the drawer in one heap. And what
history doing with us today, do you think, with all of u
living on this rash and woeful continent—more so than ar
that has ever been? Makes sure that our sins will find us ou

GASPARE: *Le metafore il mare han consumato, E convertito
baccalà Nettuno.**

DONATO: Of course, I'm an artist: I think like an artist. An
I can't help remembering something which though it's o
history now was the beginning of our history today-
prepared the noose for our necks and the bloody agor
we're going through. It's something I remember readin
about Wilhelm the Second, Big Willy, who was the first
the windbags who were so good at blowing all the bellov
and the trumpets and generally sowing the whirlwind ar
reaping the hurricane—he felt he had to say something tc
which would go down in history during that famous Ju
1914—and so what he said was 'The times are out of joir
Oh cursed spite that ever I was born to set them righ
Talk about setting them right! Look at it. It would ha
been better if he and all the other windbags who co
historical phrases had had a look at the way everything th
did only helped to put the times even more out of joint!

GASPARE: Have you done?

DONATO: It's time they'd done! Look, if you've managed
find a way out of it all for yourself, you have all my prai
and admiration and gratitude, you and your political friend

GASPARE: Ah, not so much about the political friends! Do
you see I don't like it!

DONATO: Ah, there's so many things one doesn't like, th
hardly counts!

GASPARE: That's what you say! But I'm willing to admit tl
what's happening today, the tragedy of July 1943—is ju
as you describe it.

* *Translator's note:* 'Metaphors have chained the sea: and turned Neptune i
a dried fish.' From a sixteenth-century poem.

DONATO: And we needn't think the Atlantic Charter is going to alter the situation. And as for the Four Freedoms—what a farce! Two of them, the political and religious ones are as near to oppression and bullying as anything in this world, but they do hold up a noble ideal: but the third one, Freedom from Want, is a veritable mockery of human distress. War's a fine way of arriving at the good life! And as for the fourth, Freedom from Fear, it certainly frightens me—I'm afraid I won't be able to stop laughing! Anyway, when I was in the army and before I was taken ill, I wasn't afraid, I didn't mind dying in this senseless war, for the only thing Europeans can really feel about this war—and Italians especially —is that they don't want to see the end of it. I've been at the front—I can tell you this without false modesty—and I didn't know what it was to feel fear. But when I came home—and this is nothing to boast about—and heard the bombs falling on the city—I wasn't prepared for it nor adapted to it, and I *was* afraid. And now I'm disgusted with life and haven't even any longer the will to die. Is it because I'm ill I feel like this or is it because I feel like this I'm ill?

GASPARE: Listen, Donato, I can see now you've got courage and straightforwardness and a ruthless honesty—and that I value and admire in you.

DONATO: Well, then, call me Donatello but don't cajole me and butter me up because it only makes me suspect that you think I'm asking for it and have been trying to get it out of you.

GASPARE: Oh to hell with your suspicions, out upon them!

DONATO: I'm glad you feel like joking.

GASPARE: You were saying something about my political friends. Well, I've a suspicion . . .

DONATO: What, you too?

GASPARE: Now please, this is no joking matter. I've a suspicion that my political friends who were the ones who advised me, in fact ordered me to go into hiding and let people forget

about me for a while, aren't altogether displeased if it goe
on long enough for people to forget about me for good an
all.

DONATO: That's politics all over. They hope that victory
just round the corner and they like to keep their numbe:
down as much as possible, so as to be sure of their share
the loot.

GASPARE: Yes, politics can be like that but it's not the be
kind. I don't know whether I've a real vocation or whethe
it's just illusion, if it's only ambition or passion, but the fa
is that I do feel that I've a call to political life and I've
longing for action. And I even deem myself fitted for i
I've proved myself and claim that I can do it again. And I ca
see that the competitive spirit, supplanting one's rival, th
'get-out-of-the-way-so-that-I-can-stand-there' attitude, a:
part of reality, they're conditions of necessity which te
and select those who have the will to power, and give the:
training and preparation. And so I don't go in for self-pi
and if my fellow-conspirators keep me out of the way an
do their best to see I'm forgotten, all I can say is that it
a tribute to my abilities and shows they're afraid of what
may be able to do when it comes to forming a part in tl
new society which is going to arise on the ruins of Fascisn
And they're afraid of me both for what I've already dor
and for what I have it in me to do. It's human and inevitabl
The man who goes in for politics isn't an altruist, on tl
contrary, he must be a strong, intelligent, far-seeing egois
It's men who are not only courageous, but austere, who ha\
the urge to power and authority, who like to rule; and th
have the passion in the strongest, harshest and most ruthle
form, and also at its most egotistical: but it's an egois.
which is capable of ascetic sacrifice, for they're also pu:
tanical characters who are capable of purging and refinir
their other passions. Don't fool yourself, it's because it
based on election, and jobs going by open competition, th

liberty needs strong strict men. It's the dictatorships and régimes of hereditary privilege which breed soft and sensitive types: don't you fool yourself!

DONATO: Are you talking to me? Or do you imagine you're in a committee or a public meeting already? As far as I'm concerned, I think all forms of government and society are necessary evils: they're the particular examples of a general evil whose necessity I can't follow.

GASPARE: And what you mean by this general and all-embracing evil, is life, isn't it?

DONATO: To be more precise, I mean man himself. And so don't anticipate your future parliamentary speeches for my benefit. They're wasted on me.

GASPARE: And for once you're quite right. But you see this tendency to anticipate myself as you call it has come over me only because I'm kept silent and put out of the way by my friends and comrades and political rivals.

DONATO: And so you want to let off steam? I'm very willing to listen to you, if only to be friendly.

GASPARE: Go on, stop clowning!

DONATO: Didn't I tell you? I'm an artist. And you see even the artist is a formidable egoist. In his loftiest and most sublime expressions it doesn't satisfy him to enchant and intoxicate other people, he has to do it to himself too. Go on with what you were saying.

GASPARE: If my rivals are taking so much trouble to keep me removed from the scene of action, that's a sign that they feel the day of change and revolution is at hand, and that Fascism is ripe to fall.

DONATO: That's what I said: but in the meantime this is what they call counting your chickens before they're hatched.

GASPARE: You said yourself, only a moment ago, that it's a desperate cause, more or less done for.

DONATO: Desperate is one thing, done for is another.

GASPARE: And who do you suppose is going to keep it going?

And don't you see that they're all struggling now to find alibis and excuses, and push their claims for the day after Fascism is liquidated: there's a rush from all quarters!

DONATO: I think there are a lot of people, all those in fact who haven't seen him fighting, or nearly all, who forget that our ally is still in the field. I *have* seen the Germans. Here in northern Italy you've seen a few troop-trains going through —and even that on the quiet. You've seen how they behave in some military post or recuperation centre. I can see how it is that your ideas are so far removed from actuality, the more so because the Germans are beginning to give way on five fronts after setting out to win the war on only one and when the war on two fronts meant they'd lost it already.

GASPARE: And so what?

DONATO: I don't mean that they admit it themselves yet. And before they do . . . and even after . . .

GASPARE: Yes, after . . . and in the end . . .

DONATO: They'll collapse: but only at the point when they can still drag everyone else with them into the abyss.

GASPARE: So that in the meantime I'm counting my chickens before they're hatched, too?

DONATO: You didn't ask to be given this break. It was pure chance. So don't regret it, don't be impatient, but enjoy it. And let the chickens run wild in the wood—even if it's the old Teutonic forest.

CHAPTER EIGHT

The Twenty-fifth of July, 1943

DONATO MÈRICI, GASPARE DELLA MORTE AND FALARIDE
NARENZA

FALARIDE: What's cooking? I hear something about chickens!
I hope I'm not disturbing anybody. It's luck finding you
here. Can I come in?

DONATO: It looks to me as if you have. Make yourself at
home. Why all the precautions? And how on earth did you
get here?

FALARIDE: You promised me you'd stick by your old friend
and schoolfellow, Donato, if the time ever came . . . but
please don't bother to go, Signore Gaspare—and without
even looking at me: unless you feel too scornful and disgusted with poor Falaride Narenza, Signor Gaspare Della
Morte!

DONATO: What's going on? You look to me as if you're
quaking in every limb! It can't be!

FALARIDE: I was till a moment ago. Now I'm trying to pull
myself together, if I can.

GASPARE: It doesn't look very successful to me.

FALARIDE: I can get my breath back and it makes me feel a bit
more hopeful just to be able to talk to you, Signore . . .

GASPARE: We all know that you know all about me.

FALARIDE: I did once—and as one of the ablest and most active
of anti-Fascists. But on the other hand, you ought to recognise that no one's interfered with you out here in your
hideout.

GASPARE: Do the police know about that too?

FALARIDE: The police don't, but I do.

DONATO: Meanwhile, I'd be interested to know who's been playing spies under my roof.

FALARIDE: It's nobody here. Didn't you give your address in the strictest confidence to your most devoted comrade Signore? We all know nothing's less secret than the secrets of secret societies.

GASPARE: Has he betrayed me?

FALARIDE. Now you see, Donato. He gives one shout and out it all comes. 'He's betrayed me!'

DONATO: Because he knows you're only joking and that you're here as a friend.

FALARIDE: Anyway, he's committed a technical error.

GASPARE: It'll be a useful lesson to me for the future.

FALARIDE: Well, please remember who it was who had the good luck to give it to you. Oh I know it was quite un deserved. Live and let live, that's my guiding principle. I've never done any harm to anyone.

GASPARE: Am I to understand that includes your masters, the government you're supposed to be serving?

FALARIDE: Not even to them. All I've denounced were imaginary plots and conspirator's who'd already got away into safety and so as far as I possibly could I've spared them the stuff and nonsense as well as the abominable atrocities which the historians call political trials.

GASPARE: Tools should serve, not criticise.

FALARIDE: There you are, Donato, that's your man of politics They're all made out of the same stuff. He's so indignant a the mere idea that I might give the same sort of service if he were in power himself that he's already contemptuous and forgetful of what I've done for him—the fact that I've saved him from what he could get for plotting against the security of the realm when it's at war—thirty years hard labour or even twelve bullets in the back in a split second. I've jus said they're all made out of the same stuff, Donato; would you care to know what it is?—and what political justice is, at one and the same time? I'll tell you a story from the last war. Somebody told Clemenceau who was a liberal states-man, a radical and a Jacobin—I won't call him in any sense a reactionary—that a certain Bolo Pasha, who'd been accused of trafficking with the enemy, was only guilty of a half-betrayal, and he said that in that case he'd have him shot by a half-squad of six instead of by the prescribed twelve. But the case in point, the one that immediately concerns us, is backed up by another historical precedent, what another well-known old political go-getter said—'Just give it me in writing and I'll hang anyone you like!' Anyway the fact that I arouse so much indignation in Signore Gaspare Della Morte shows he's got a big political future in front of him. As far as I can see, he's in the running for any office, except one.

DONATO: What an extraordinary chap you are. Which one do you mean?

FALARIDE: Chief of the Political Police. They can't do better for their own governments than let suspects get away.

DONATO: Gaspare, do you hear this Machiavelli?

FALARIDE: A bit low-powered!

GASPARE: I'll remember that lesson too.

FALARIDE: When he's in power, I'll get the sack. Never mind! This is what you get for loving your neighbour, and especially for obliging your rulers present or to come.

GASPARE: What I should like to know, Signore Narenza, is exactly how I am in your debt?

DONATO: So should I. You said this chap didn't betray him?

FALARIDE: Oh no, he was arrested. . . .

GASPARE: Now I understand why I haven't heard from him.

FALARIDE: Of course, the house was searched. He had only one fault, but it happened to be a serious one for a con-spirator: his memory was poor. And so they found a note

on a sheet of paper—oh the tiniest little note on the meres
scrap of paper and all it said was *Alma Dannata*. For all
know, they thought it was the title of a rather melodramati
novel. It was kept and put in the files. And just throug
being curious, that's where I found it and I read it and pu
it back to bed in the files.

GASPARE: Well, and then?

FALARIDE: Well, then I put two and two together. I knev
about a certain lady being here—Oh I'm a gentleman, a
far as I'm concerned, a lady's name won't pass my lips eve
here amongst ourselves. But just by putting two and tw
together . . .

GASPARE: Yes, we quite see the point.

FALARIDE: Bright boys! So do I. But another thing you mus
understand is that I didn't let anyone else in on this an
that what I've come to give you now is the facts—incontro
vertible, demonstrable, verifiable. All you have to do is t
ask. I'm not selling you hot air.

GASPARE: Ask whom? The police?

FALARIDE. Police my foot. I do beg you to be a bit more spry
Haven't you got it? Time's getting on. This is the moment
foresaw, Donato: you can be my friend and help me. A
present I can't do anything either to help you or harm you
but you'll admit that I haven't done you any harm and tha
I've helped you whenever I could. . . .

DONATO: You've started shaking again!

FALARIDE: I've got reason!

DONATO: But what is it you're afraid of?

FALARIDE: Are you trying to make fun of me? It's cruel an
mean if you are. I give you my word, Donato, there's n
risk for you if you hide me. I got here without being see
by a living soul and I haven't left anything in writin,
behind me, either at home or anywhere in the city or a
police-headquarters, nothing on paper, not so much as
cigarette packet. There are my pay-receipts but they can'

ruin anyone by me. And if you don't believe me, Della Morte, all you have to do is to ask your fellow-conspirator. . . .

GASPARE: That's fine! At the prison, you mean?

FALARIDE: That's cruel and mean.

DONATO: Why, you're wringing your hands, you're shaking, you really *are* afraid of something.

FALARIDE. I've never said I was brave. But, Signore Gaspare, you ask your comrade!

GASPARE: And I repeat, just where am I supposed to do it, at the prison?

FALARIDE: What's all this about prison? So you really don't know what's happened. The radio . . .

DONATO: We haven't got it switched on: there'd be nothing to listen to but the usual stuff. . . .

FALARIDE: The usual stuff! With all the people shouting!

DONATO: Doesn't get as far as this. Would you like to explain yourself? This man in prison. . . .

FALARIDE: In prison! He's out on the squares haranguing the crowds. They've got him on their shoulders, they're carrying him in triumph through the streets.

GASPARE: Do you know what I think? You've come here with all this rigmarole just as a routine-job, you're still an *agent provocateur*. And you're doing it very badly. And if we're driven to it, these woods all round here give us the best possible opportunity of getting rid of anyone without trace.

FALARIDE: What did I tell you, Donato? Recognise the type? And if you were driven to it, I should have to take it. It's just my good luck that we can get hold of your friend on the Milan squares if he hasn't already taken the train for Rome.

DONATO: For Rome?

FALARIDE: Of course! He'll get a prefecture or an undersecretaryship, if not a ministry straight off. He can take his pick, it's his moment.

GASPARE: Now will you come to the point and explain yourself?

FALARIDE: It seems you don't know him. He's both ambitious and able. Not at all retiring. No false modesty. He doesn't hide his light under a bushel. He can go for what he likes—except, being Chief of Police, that's out for him, too. It's that bad memory!

DONATO: Then are we to understand . . .

FALARIDE: Can't you people get it yet? The fact is you can see I'm shaking with fear and you're just making cruel fun of me.

DONATO: Out with it—or I'll throw you out of the house, back where you came from.

FALARIDE: No, I implore you. Donato, give me your hand, you're my old friend, my schoolfellow. They've got my name down on their lists and someone in the crowds might recognise me and shout it out—think of it, those crowds, after a spy, I'm terrified at the mere idea!

GASPARE: You're really trembling all right.

FALARIDE: How can I help it? If only I could believe you weren't making fun of me. . . .

DONATO: You can take my word, Falaride. Your hands are cold with sweat. . . .

FALARIDE: It's not only my hands, it's all over—my forehead, I'm shivering all down my spine. If only I could believe you —you really don't know?—the Fascist Grand Council . . .

GASPARE: We've heard that it's been convened.

FALARIDE: Mussolini has asked for a vote of confidence, for solidarity. . . .

DONATO: The usual political antics.

GASPARE: Let him go on, Donato. Yes, Narenza?

FALARIDE: And it was turned down. But it can't really be that you don't know? But I see that you don't from your faces. It's impossible, but it must be so. Mussolini has resigned, and the King has accepted. He's nominated a minister with plenipotentiary powers.

GASPARE: I'd better go at once; I must go, Donato.

FALARIDE: I'd better stay where I am. You see now, Donato, don't you?

DONATO: Yes, I do, you can hide here.

FALARIDE: It's never too late. And provided I can always put two and two together, I hope in the end I'll manage to save my skin.

GASPARE: I'm off. Goodbye, Donato. You too, jelly, goodbye to you too!

FALARIDE: I don't mind you laughing at me. Actually, I'm glad.

DONATO: Why on earth?

FALARIDE: Laugh at anyone and you're half way to forgiving him.

BOOK II

THE FIRE OF MILAN

CHAPTER ONE

Ferragosto '43

AFTER Falaride Narenza's wonderful news which he had brought so strangely and with such egotism into the solitude of Vill' Alma, Della Morte hurried off at once to Milan. At Vill' Alma, apart from the fact that Narenza had taken refuge there instead of Gaspare, everything went on as usual, with the lovelorn Armida, on the one hand, growing more and more impatient as she found her lover's absence daily more of a trial, and with Melania, on the other, less and less able to stomach the person of Narenza, who disgusted her with his slack and careless manners, his mock and ironic humility, and his general appearance—tall and bony with a face like a pole-cat and a shock of red hair.

Under the pretext of keeping him safely hidden (although it was obvious almost at once that such precautions were not really necessary), but in fact so as to have to see him as little as possible, she had his meals served to him in his room. Every now and then Donato dropped in to see him and brought him reading-matter of all kinds for which Falaride had developed an inordinate appetite. On the other hand, Donato himself, on the plea of scientific work which he wasn't doing, tried to avoid his company as much as possible, since he was becoming a bore: once the most pressing cause for fear had been removed, he had been seized with anxiety about the future, how he was going to earn a living and find himself another trade. For he said that the one he had lost cut him off from any other

career or way of life: apart from the fact that it was the only one
he knew and all the others would be a bore and too much hard
work—and that was antipathetic, for being bored and tired out
were not only second nature to him, he had been born that way.

From time to time he came out with the opinion that by now
he could stick his nose outside his room without risk to anybody including himself. He showed signs of wanting to take
part in the villa's communal life which, he said, would also
make him less of a nuisance, for he was being spoilt with all
this separate service in his room.

But Donato assured him that they had too much domestic
staff anyway, with time on its hands: it was a good thing to
give it something to do. Falaride sighed and gave a faint grin
and a shrug of his rather rickety shoulders and said that
Signora Mèrici didn't like him. He quite understood and he
wasn't offended. He was too ugly and slovenly for such a refined and artistic atmosphere as you found at Casa Mèrici and
Vill' Alma. And anyway he quite saw that taking in a political
victim like Della Morte had been quite a different responsibility, much nicer anyway and with much more credit attached
to it, than harbouring a police-agent in difficulties, however
little, he added, they might be deserved. He took to complaining bitterly and acidly. And when he stressed certain words—
for example the word 'credit', his grin became really disagreeable. Sometimes he complained of the heat and of never being
able to get out for a breath, although his room was very well
ventilated. It had been Gaspare's and its advantage was that
it led by means of an ingenious trapdoor in the attic to a
hiding-place hollowed out in an aperture of the wall of the
ancient castle tower. Some previous owner in the bygone
centuries who wanted to conceal his wealth from robbers or
to get out of the way when the police or his enemies were after
him had constructed this refuge which was extremely difficult
to discover and whose secret was kept from Falaride because
Donato maintained that there was no reason to take their

precautions to that length. But to stop him grumbling about being bored he exaggerated the advantages and the need of prudence and although Falaride was not taken in he thanked Donato in a similarly exaggerated style which stank a mile off of pretence and sarcasm.

He started to complain about Gaspare Della Morte, too, who, now his luck had turned, and he had every prospect of power and fame ahead, didn't remember him and all he had done. That's the way when people get well known and successful, he said, they're nearly always ungrateful: and good fortune is hard of hearing.

And he began to toy with the idea that he would return to the world and give out that he was a victim of Fascism. He spoke quite seriously and was quite moved by his own words: a victim of the régime, he said. Although Donato knew that underneath his idle cynicism and his logic-chopping there was a soft irrational core, half-fantasy, half-sentimentality, he didn't expect this kind of self-pity. But he was quite in earnest: and he said that now was the time to set up in the persecution-business: for even if you hadn't been persecuted yourself, you should be able to claim persecutions both collateral and in the direct line, either through your father or your brothers or your uncles. Uncles too, why not? In the case of cousins perhaps the title was becoming a bit indirect. But he himself really could boast of having had a father who'd had every kind of slur and insult heaped on him to make him give up the line of historical research to which he'd devoted a lifetime of hard work, probity and self-sacrifice.

And, he added with a grin, he'd exhausted every penny he'd been able to put by from his pittance as a State teacher, in publishing polemics and critical essays against Marconi whose prestige value to the régime had been chimerical, anyway grossly exaggerated. Now the outlay in money and research which the father had flung to the winds, was going to be harvested by the son!

And with a vehemence which was meant more to ally his own doubts than Donato's, he said, Wasn't that violence and intimidation, with the added sting of contempt, wasn't it oppression, outrage against human personality?

When Falaride had anything to say which could be given an absurd or ambiguous twist, he savoured it and mouthed it and showed such a taste for taking off the people concerned that when, as now, his own father's memory was in question, the result was disconcerting and got under your skin. And he mimed and clowned and was more and more tickled the more irreverent he became. And so it was now as he described the diet based on flour and macaroni and beans, which the anti-Marconian Professor's family had had to put up with and which was due not merely to the fact that his salary and pension were small, but to his Marconiphobe researches and publications. And so he amused himself by irreverent exaggerations which had a basis of truth in the way that his father, who had been not only a scholar but a convinced and impeccable Fascist, had been humiliated and made to suffer for his delusions.

Whether he meant to or not, or was aware of what he was doing, the picture he drew was of a grotesque idiot who maybe —in fact it was more than likely (and here he rose to a fine crescendo)—had died in grief: it was certain that he had died a victim of despotism, his faith in Mussolini wounded, and embittered by the unjust ban on publishing his anti-Marconian pamphlets, though about them his son concluded that only one thing was quite certain, that nobody read them, least of all Marconi.

In the end, Donato could not help laughing, although not without qualms, as Falaride described the death-bed scene, adding new and ridiculous particulars every day: how this just man and patriot, this learned intellectual, this blameless victim of tyranny had died downtrodden and oppressed without leaving a halfpenny to pay the baker or the printer or the

loctor or the chemist let alone the undertaker and the funeral
expenses including the grave and sextons.

And as his father's son, and because of his father's inordinate
pride and indomitable spirit, *Frangar non flector*—you could
break him but you couldn't bend him—he had found all roads
to an honest livelihood and a decent profession closed against
him: and through poverty and persecution he had come down
to being an *agent-provocateur* and a political informer.

For this last matter—and surely it was a clear case if ever
there was one—Della Morte ought to have intervened, ought
to have borne witness that, at the risk of getting himself into
worse trouble, his conduct had been such that he had brought
no harm to anyone, including Gaspare himself. But they must
get a move on, time pressed, the propitious moment was
receding rapidly. He could actually see before his mind's eye
the mounting throng of Fascist victims, of all those who had
been persecuted and had just claims on the anti-Fascists. And
with a subfusion of blasphemous mockery he added that these
claimants were multiplying faster than the five loaves and
two fishes. The novelty was wearing off, he said: before long
it would be a bore: and according to the laws of human
behaviour it wouldn't be long before people would be getting
to the point of hankering after Fascism, just because it was
over. And long before that they would get bored with the
'five thousand fishes', otherwise the victims continually
arriving in their staggering numbers to put in their claims.

Why didn't Gaspare look lively then and get back to Vill'
Alma? Was it contempt or pride or was it just simply due to
forgetfulness and ingratitude, now that his fortunes had
changed and he had become a great man at the height of power
and reputation? He ought at least to have sent for Falaride to
come to Milan if only to give him a little agency in the National
Lottery or a salt and tobacco licence, or some sort of little job
by which he could keep body and soul together. And he
summed up by saying that people are the same in every age

and no matter what the system, as soon as their luck change
and they get into power, they're ungrateful: beginning with
his ancient namesake of Agrigentum who, when Perillus had
been clever enough to make him a bull which could be used
to roast people and had turned their spontaneous groans and
howls into artificial bellowings for his amusement, had tried
out this all-too-dædal invention by having the all-too-ingeniou
inventor roasted first. By way of comfort, Donato told him he
suffered from 'paranoid querimoniousness', he found thi
very comforting!

After a few days, Gaspare did give some signs of life: but
this had the effect of putting Narenza right off his rocker. What
he said, a whole fortnight and more had gone by since th
twenty-fifth of July when the Badoglio government had com
to power, and this chap Della Morte had got nowhere, he had
no authority, he was a nobody, he hadn't made either a nam
or a place for himself—not even a hope of them—and this in
spite of being an anti-Fascist of the purest water, one of th
Old Guard, one of the old reliables, who had never yielded an
inch to the temptations of opportunism? And so after all h
was one of those people who always get turned down and
pushed aside no matter who's in power, a born grumbler who'
just made a profession of it. At the very idea that he, Falaride
of all men, had relied upon this scum, this refuse, and had
pinned his hopes on one of these 'ideologues', a term which
expressed the depths of his scorn, he assumed an air of ic
disapproval of himself, which was a joy to witness and made
Donato laugh so much that Falaride was twice as angry a
before, choking and stuttering in his rage that this had hap
pened to him, of all people; he'd put a ne'erdowell on his feet
a sort of political Diogenes: talk about being querimonious

As he wanted to let off steam, he refused to keep to his own
room any longer, although he knew quite well that he wa
unwelcome, but imposed his company, just for spite, on every
one else.

And so he was also present on one of these mid-August evenings after supper when they were on the meadow in front of the house enjoying the mountain breezes and all suddenly noticed a bright light which had appeared on the other side of the plain just beneath the horizon.

It looked at first as if the moon was rising, but right from the beginning the light was more intense and grew inwardly more concentrated and remained steady and fixed at one focal point, not rising as the moon or a comet would have done, but simply increasing in vividness from moment to moment. And it turned vermilion, the colour of flames, of an immense brazier, a lake of fire. And as the light increased in intensity it appeared more sharply defined and more precisely located upon the horizon against the dome of the night sky. And all around it the darkness spread over the face of the earth and looked deeper by contrast, more infinite in the depths of the sky among the faint stars. And round the fierce burning of that pyre with its horrible fascination, the darkness and silence of night and heaven seemed to grow more continually aghast.

They had all known the effect of high explosive and incendiaries near at hand as well as in the distance but none of them had ever seen a great fierce light like this before, a devouring blaze continually replenished.

As usual with air-raids, when there are repeated waves of assault, there were the white-hot flashes of great fires and explosions and these were renewed more than once: but there were not very many, perhaps fewer than usual, and they seemed noticeably few compared with that vast intense light. And they had ceased already but everyone was so concentrated on the fire, on the horrible fascination of that blazing sea of flame which could be seen glowing just beneath the horizon in the direction of the great city of Milan, that no one paid any attention to this fact.

No one actually said 'Where Milan used to be' but that was what they were all thinking—for the sight overwhelmed

K

both experience and imagination. Although the lights and
flashes had ceased for some time, the fire continued and in
creased and gathered strength as if its raging heat generated
its own energy. And it soon became something which could
no longer be properly described as a fire, it was beyond all
human proportions: and as it grew continually it became like
the vast still whirlpool, the self-devouring gulf of volcani
fires and lakes of molten lava. But because it had been a
human city, it was as if the human mind could not take in the
immensity of the disaster but fled, in its terror and shuddering
bewilderment at its very failure in comprehension, to thought
of rivers of fire and burning vortices of bitumen and sulphur
and ancient images of the wrath of God falling upon the cities
he has condemned. And the very fascination of this horror
was somehow inhuman and, seized with fits of a violent and
morbid curiosity, the beholder could forget that there were
men burning in that fire. Still no one dared to say 'Milan is on
fire': perhaps in secret terror that saying it might stir their
primitive depths to idiotic hysterical laughter, not merely
perverse but insane and of the sort which drives some para
noics to fire-raising. The thought of that laughter frightened
and sickened them all.

Meanwhile a vast cloud obscured the sky over the lake of
fire, covering it with a hemisphere of smoke, black, like an
immense cloak against the deep nocturnal blue, and blazing
and sparkling with the thousands of flames which were hidden
by the horizon. And the cloud reflecting the flames looked as if
it were loaded with sparks like the ones which shoot out of
fire when you poke it hard, and it became more and more
obvious that the conflagration was of immense proportions. It
looked as if this cloak, this smoke-cloud was not only the
centre of the city's funeral pyre but even kept it active. Ferra
gosto 1943 and Milan had gone up in flames.

By the clock it had all taken very little time before Armida
Lenai—as if she had awakened with a shudder from a trance

of horror was heard calling out Gaspare's name. There was no need for words, the desperation and anxiety in her voice were enough and her emotion was in the nature of a relief since it infused a feeling of humanity into their inhuman curiosity, their dulled fascination.

Her friend Melania immediately began to shower caresses on her and tried to say something which would be not only affectionate but encouraging, but without success: and it was at once obvious that it would be better to say nothing, as this kind of exhortation only did the opposite of what was intended, since it seemed so impossible that anyone could escape alive out of that inferno.

The poor soul began wringing her hands in her love and despair and crying out that she wanted to go to Milan and look for her lover: but suddenly she herself saw how absurd this idea was and she began to talk differently and said she wanted to go to Milan to be burnt to death, too. But however desperate she felt it wasn't possible for her to go, considering the hour and the lack of transport. And it seemed that she grasped this herself for she gave up suggesting it; but this only increased their uneasiness as the night wore on and between her outbursts of hysterical anxiety they had to listen to her repeating again and again, like a complaining child, that this night was never going to come to an end and that it was God punishing her for her sins.

After a while, her friend could think of nothing more to say to her, except to suggest that she took some sort of sedative or sleeping-pill. But this made her feel ashamed and she felt that it was as good as admitting how feeble everything is which we have to offer in the way of consolation and how short our patience is with the sufferings of others: and she could almost hear her own voice giving away her wish to go and lie down and sleep, for like all the others she was suddenly overwhelmed with immense exhaustion. And so in the silence and dark on the airy meadow while the conflagration still blazed in the distance as though it would never die out, and while the refreshing breeze of night made the thought of the fire only more horrifying, she said to her again that the minute it was possible she would send somebody for news. She would have liked somebody else to say something and give her support, but Donato kept silence. He felt an incredible spiritual exhaustion, he was sickened and disgusted at being alive. It was not only that he felt incapable of doing anything, he felt unable to make the slightest demand on himself either of thought or action, he was totally without will-power. Milan might be in flames or so, for that matter, might the whole world, all he wanted was to stay where he was, at Alma Dannata, and not move or stir out, as in a total and desperate spiritual paralysis. Above all he did not want to know anything, he did not want to have to think or understand anything, it repelled him, it was too exhausting and asked too much of him. It was the kind of longing with which a man in danger clings to the smallest and frailest protection even though it may be utterly useless: the way the drowning man snatches at a straw and a soldier under fire tries to conceal himself behind a rush or a mere leaf. It is a sort of passion of revulsion: and that was what he felt: as if he wanted to sleep on to the very end of the world and have as little awareness or memory of it as possible. And in the mean time a profound and animal slumber, the agonising sleep of nervous exhaustion, began to weigh on him, on his smarting eyelids, but he couldn't give way to it without satisfying another demand of the animal, the hunger which this exhaustion had brought with it and which suddenly seized him. And he was just going to tiptoe out to the larder or the kitchen, very quietly, but through disgust rather than shame to find something to eat, whatever there was, and then go and throw himself on his bed and fall fast asleep, when Narenza began to speak, to the interest and puzzlement of them all.

His opening remark was that in her distress the lady might

hink he was being sarcastic and even more offensive than
isual. And it became clear that quite apart from his general
misanthropy, he was a misogynist too: his aversion from the
female sex was pronounced. He seemed to wander off on this
private theme and said that only a woman would have the
overweening egocentrism and sentimentality to imagine that
in a catastrophe of this sort, God was thinking about her and her
sins and would go to such lengths to punish such trifling follies.
And though it made them all very uncomfortable to listen to
him, he became even more aggressive and, with mounting
bitterness and harshness, he said he'd like to know what the
thousands of innocent people—the ones who had either no
sins to expiate or none which were bad enough to call for the
burning of Milan and were just leading their own lives—could
be expected to say in justification of these delicate consciences
and these wallowings of over-sensibility all demanding expiation for sins which they themselves had had no hand in? And
he said spitefully that it was a a way of brooding on one's own
sins and from one's own point of view was a subtle form of
relishing and glorying in them, while showing the blindest
egoism towards other people. He said he wished he could
believe in a hereafter himself because it would amuse him to
see how many refined and over-scrupulous souls would be
sent to hell on the Day of Judgement. However, he said, he
didn't believe in hell or in any other article of faith.

But at the very point when his spitefulness and malice had
become almost unbearable to listen to, a pitiful streak began to
emerge, which was a reaction to the hatred itself, and although
his tone was still bored and irritated, he said that if you have
love and faith you ought to recognize how great these gifts
are: and if you were a believer you should thank the God you
believed in and pray for salvation for those you loved and
mercy for all and for yourself. To be able to pray, he said, was
there any greater gift, or to speak in theological terms, any
greater grace?

This exhortation through this bitter and cynical mouth
piece sounded so strange that it affected them more than if i
had come from a better source. And further more, Narenza
proceeded to ask Signora Melania if she would provide him
with something to eat so that he could cycle to Milan and ge
back as quickly as possible with the news. He didn't say, new
of Gaspare Della Morte, but simply news: and naturally h
couldn't have promised more, but there can be a uniqu
convergence of mental and physical circumstances—just thos
in which there is really nothing to be done—when there i
both an inward and an outward demand for some activity
no matter what, to break the intolerable anguish of suspense

Armida went on silently praying: and Melania got up t
see to the provisions which in the circumstances he would b
sure to need—the request was modest and reasonable enough
She thanked him in a low voice and the thanks were heartfe]
although Narenza merely replied, 'Don't mention it', in hi
most surly manner.

Shortly afterwards, just as he was getting on his bicycle, h
was seized by the urge for precise detail which was typical o
him and had to explain that he was going back to Mila
feeling quite certain that in such a catastrophe there would b
no one with either the inclination or the capacity to remembe
anything about a poor wretched police-tool: and he though
that even the police would have forgotten about him too.

As usual, this annoyed them but also made them want t
laugh in spite of everything and Donato in fact did laugh at hi
curious way of referring to himself while he carelessly wishe
him Bon Voyage. And Narenza went off sarcastically mutterin
a reply, 'Have a nice time at home!'

CHAPTER TWO

Among the Ruins

ONE of the greatest oddities (admittedly a very human one) of Badoglio's Forty-Five Days—the period from the 28th of July to the 8th of September, that is from Mussolini's dismissal and the end of Fascism up to the time when the request for an armistice had to be made public—was the nation's euphoria when it found itself on the point of getting out of the war, something which looked incredible and yet seemed at the same time so incredibly hopeful: this was the period after the alliance had collapsed, without being formally denounced, up to the time of the surrender which, though it was called unconditional, was actually negotiated: the period of every kind of absurdity, political, diplomatic and military.

Yet it was plain for all to see—and everyone really knew it—that in actuality and even in these expectations, into which reason hardly entered, everything had gone wrong and was moving towards something worse, although this was perhaps too repugnant to think about, let alone accept. The Allies, who were still technically the enemy, were disembarking from the Mediterranean: and the Germans who in spite of still being our allies, were now the enemy, were descending from the Brenner: and we were distrusted by one side and the other regarded us as traitors and in our own country we had a war between strangers both of them equally hostile and destructive.

As far as we were concerned a short-sighted and reckless policy played its part in this euphoria: it was short-sighted in a Machiavellian sense because it assumed that coming to arrangements, finding a way out, expediency in general, were much simpler than they actually are or have any likelihood of being: and it showed how reckless and overweening it was by swinging from the sluggish and despairing fatalism of a state of impotence and cowardice to the other extreme, the puppetry of fantastic rationalisation, which saw the future in a mirage the other side of reality and at least very difficult to achieve for instance, 'getting unhitched' from the Germans who were still far from believing that they were defeated, as well as from actually being so: and also hoping for co-operation from an enemy who was the less disposed to grant it the more he felt that he was winning. In the one case we were powerless and in the other we were useless and it was folly to delude ourselves but there was nothing else we could do. Matters had reached the point when any solution was not only difficult but impossible, and fantastic solutions were as much use as believing that what looked like a reasonable solution ought to be welcomed or effected just on that ground: that is of all hopes the least well-founded.

And so folly and play-acting became necessary, for at least they had a deadening effect. The most remarkable piece of folly which came out of this wild euphoria was an academic scheme for political theory and planning to which various individuals and institutions devoted themselves after the dissolution of the Fascist government: but no matter what policy had been followed, even one of the most realistic and harsh austerity, it would have cost the country no less in hardship.

An open denunciation of the alliance would have demanded an infusion of strength which was exactly what was being refused or begrudged by the other side; and moreover if the clandestine and turncoat demands for peace and assistance aided and even provoked the intimidatory air-assaults of the United Nations, a different and more open policy would have provoked land-assaults from the Germans. You can't have your cake and eat it—if the proverbial expression weren't beneath a

istorian's stylistic dignity. And even for an effort of despera-
ion, one prime and indispensable condition was lacking, that
unity around throne, state and government on which the will
o fight depended. Would denouncing the alliance and making
war against our ex-ally have created it? Once you begin to
alk about what didn't happen, then anything could have
happened: but the things that happened round about the 8th
of September, in the first place the disintegration of the army,
make it doubtful that there was anything one could count on
with any sort of probability, even of the remotest kind. For if
the policy of the Forty-five Days didn't achieve a single one of
ts aims, didn't even force an exhausted nation to make a
surrender—which would certainly have been unconditional
because it would have been made to the German army already
this side of the Alps—it must have been totally inept, demand-
ng from us in fact a capacity for resistance which would have
taught us first and foremost, had it actually existed, to spurn
any idea of unconditional surrender from whatever source it
came. And a policy which, when we asked for help so that we
could at least try to resist, responded by withholding not only
the help but even trust, and finally even patience, and which
demanded a supreme effort of will while doing everything in
its power to extinguish not only all volition but even hope, was
certainly also very odd, at least as much so as our strange
euphoria.

The result was to engender in the great majority of the
population the only kind of reasonable attitude which is to
take things as they come without reasoning about them, as if
they were an earthquake or an epidemic or some other catastrophe like dearth and famine: it's no good asking them what
they mean or whether they have some purpose or motive or
trying to argue with them, if you have faith you submit to the
will of God. And this was also the only kind of attitude which
was capable of saving the people from the disaster of revolution or desperate revolt during those days when the Germans

had the only intelligent policy—they pretended to be quite
unaware that anything had changed and were reinforcing their
military position in Italy to the utmost. But apart from all this
in the whole history of this war—which was not only the last
great European and the first world war, but the last national
and the first intercontinental war—there is only one mistake
though that was both political and military, which we can
attribute to the Germans: and that was that they made the war
at all: and that they planned, declared and waged it in the
name of a doctrine which, when we reflect on it, opens stagger
ing depths of bewilderment and mystery: the mystery is that
nonsense and ideological superstition which could hardly be
sillier, a fatal form of theoretical mania afflicting not merely
one individual but a whole nation, could acquire in both the
political and military fields, the enormous and terrifying
power which was wielded by Hitler and Germany during those
years. Apart from that one error, which, however, touches
bottom in mistaken theorisation, there was nothing in German
political planning and in their conduct of the war which was
not logical and efficient, even though it took place under the
ægis of a fate which was to allot them the exact contrary of
what they themselves had proposed. And so the most powerful
and best organised political and military undertaking which
European history has seen, whose aim was to build world
hegemony on the basis of European unity, destroyed not only
these but Europe itself. While one is obliged to recognise this
intellectually, otherwise it would be the derogation of reason
one must also agree with the feeling which looks for an original
criminality and moral perversion: and it cannot arrive at
anything of the kind because even the worst and most syste
matic atrocities and war-crimes did not depart from rule and
from the ordinary consequences of political and military action
for otherwise, the only supposition would be that the Germans
were merely lying and pretending to believe in a theory such as
Hitler's. But he certainly believed in it himself—he had seen

he light—and he went in for lying and self-deception only in
o far as he turned to the nations with appeals to policy, self-
nterest and reason, until finally the ineluctable conviction that
ie believed himself to be charged with a revelation and a
nission, united the whole world against him.

It can even be shown that the rest of the world itself com-
nitted nothing but political and military blunders and induced
he very opposite of what it wished and hoped, while the
heories it put forward were inept and foolish, for example,
hose of the liberalistic Atlantic Charter, and of Soviet Com-
nunism. But its sacrifices in sorrow, bloodshed and earthly
vell-being and all that it had to pay for those mistakes,
trengthened the one sentiment to which God grants, and will
rant victory, until the end of human history—the sense of
uman dignity, the faith that man is an end not a means.

Hitler's real fault was that he did not dare to proclaim
openly to the world that Christianity and the sense of humanity
nust be systematically destroyed, although this was what was
n his mind: for if he had done so nobody would have followed
iim and he would never have emerged from the dregs of
obscurity in which he originated, although this fanatic, this
charlatan philosopher and beerhouse prophet was endowed
vith a practical genius which, to our utter undoing, was also
oolitical and military, and thus could not have been more
unluckily adapted to European ruin.

After Falaride Narenza had taken his leave in his usual
truculent way, Donato managed to satisfy the pangs of hunger
orought on by emotional stress—but on the quiet, because he
vas ashamed of being greedy—and then fell into his bed,
overwhelmingly sleepy and without even the energy to undress
completely. His mother and Armida Lenai stayed out on the
meadow until far into the night, watching the light of the
conflagration which was a deeper red now and less intense:
every now and then one of them dropped a remark about what

Narenza had done—out of a kindness and compassion whic
almost amounted to charity—which intrigued them since i
could never have been expected from such a surly nature.

That out of mere human kindness he should have riske
getting involved in trouble, perhaps even in the kind of dange
which their terrified imaginations suggested to the tw
women, was another proof that one should never be in hast
to judge one's fellows. And Armida somewhat took heart an
went on praying with greater faith and fervour: for Narenza
too.

He was cycling through the night towards the flaming city
He was in poor training and began to feel tired and uncom
fortable and was already more than half inclined to regret hi
good deed. However, there had been something else t
summon him to Milan and urge him on: an imperious instinc
which had something predacious about it: an obscure feelin
that everything had to be done all over again and carried ou
in a completely new way: the conviction that when there ha
been such a clean sweep as this, a determined character such a
himself, if he could be one of the first on the spot, would mak
certain of a great advantage, an invaluable opportunity fo
gain, and for making his fortune, by hook or by crook.

But he was astonished to find so few people in the street
and began to wonder if they were all dead in the city, while a
he drew near and the dawn began to break and in the thic
smoke and under the wan sky, the light of the fire turned to
greyish pallor, there was a terrible and increasing smell c
burning which had begun already several miles away an
which became continually more and more oppressive an
disagreeable.

As he passed the first suburban houses, he remembered tha
it was the week of 'Ferragosto', in which it had long bee
the custom to go on holiday and leave the city almost empty
In fact, the first shops which he passed were shut and he coul
read the traditional notice 'shut for the Ferragosto holidays

He was astonished at what seemed a striking example of lack
of foresight until he remembered that only twelve hours ago
he would have been like everybody else and done the same.
Moreover, the whole neighbourhood would have seemed,
with all its windows closed, like any other Ferragosto if it had
not been for the stench of burning and if the pavements had
not been so full of holes that he had more than once to get off
his bicycle and proceed on foot, plodding along on legs which
were stiff from the fatigue of pedalling, and cursing the saddle
which had bruised and taken the skin off his buttocks. He
recognised the kind of holes, with the rough edge which had
been made in the asphalt by incendiary bombs, and he vowed
that he would buy a car as soon as possible and not use the
bicycle any more.

The neighbourhood consisted of humble dwellings recently
built in ferro-concrete which meant that they had no wooden
frame, and he suddenly saw in a flash why they had not burnt.
As it was a poor district the houses had no porters or lodges,
and that gave an even more deserted appearance to the streets.
Most of them had no street door but gates through which
could be seen the inner courtyards which were also empty and
deserted.

He rode round the outskirts of the city to look for Gaspare's
house. He found it eventually and went up to Gaspare's flat
and pressed the bell but did not hear it ring. He realised that
the electricity must have failed and he knocked several times
without result: and as his knocking became continually louder,
the internal echo frightened him; in the silence it was like an
image of the emptiness of the city. And the summer morning
light which had already mounted high, looked ghostly to him.
He had the terrified fancy that the door might open of its own
accord, and shivered. For one moment he felt as if he were
having a nightmare and vainly struggled to laugh and to
persuade himself that his nervous agitation was due to fatigue
after his sleepless night: he forced himself to take the steps

slowly as he went downstairs and in his fear it was as if he could feel a ghost staring at him behind his back and following him down from floor to floor and staircase to staircase. It was only when he got to the bottom and out into the street and mounted his bicycle that he managed to laugh: but he had to turn the street-corner before he was able to realise that he had had no impulse at all to look up at the windows of the flat: it was as if he had been afraid that they too were going to open and he would see the thing of horror which had made him shudder even if he were laughing now.

And when he came across the ruins of a few houses which had just been demolished it was almost a comfort to him as if he had been brought back to something which the times had made normal and customary and more like life and human actuality than that sepulchral and ghostly silence.

But there was another thought he couldn't rid himself of: that all the time he had been knocking, Gaspare had been there in the house, not alive, but suffocated and dead. Or perhaps it was his spirit: perhaps he had been crushed to death in some shelter and burnt alive and was present now in those rooms as an invisible phantom upon the threshold the other side of the door: perhaps he had been caught by the fire, trapped by the flood of burning phosphorus pouring from the roofs and running through the houses and streets, the cellars and sewers underneath the streets, a liquid inferno: somewhere in the burning city he had been burnt alive and had returned to haunt his own home.

Narenza had no particular use for courage, it struck him as an infatuated and irrational form of vanity in the face of danger. But he thought that fear ought to be rational, it should arise from real material dangers and circumstances; fear of the irrational and mysterious he did not admit and despised it in himself. All the same as he sat on the new-made debris and tried to recover his breath and drive away his fear of ghost and phantoms, his disturbed and heated imagination was

preoccupied more vividly than ever by the picture of the city
inundated by liquid fire, by rivers of flame.

He thought that either Gaspare Della Morte would never
return to Alma Dannata and that not seeing him again Armida
Lenai would come, of her own accord, to the conclusion that
he was dead, or else Gaspare would tell them himself that he
was alive and there would be no need for him to go back to
Vill' Alma himself. And then he went on thinking, disagreeably
tickled at his own mischievous ideas. Suppose Gaspare were
alive and didn't want to take up life again with his girl-friend?
—well that was their business and he didn't propose to enter
into it. They said you shouldn't come between man and wife:
fancy trying it with lovers. The real fact was that he didn't
want to go back to Alma Dannata because in the solitude of
the deserted city he felt a kind of vitality and power rising
within him as if the city and all the wealth it contained had
been left ownerless just for him: as if all he had to do was to
stretch out his hand. It was the wild itch of the looter and the
marauder, which battlefields and the ruins of cataclysms, and
now air-raids, have always called out, tempting them to pick
up what they can in the spoils of disaster and death. The word
'spoils' reminded him how people did not seem to be able to
help quarrelling about any inheritance, even if it was no more
than a bundle of old clothes: and he thought of the covetous-
ness round death-beds which seems more than anything else
the urge to satisfy a powerful primitive instinct, to grab hold
of whatever the dead has left behind as if it belonged to anyone
who could take it, in a kind of mockery and sacrilege against
the one who has died. And he thought it was this urge—and he
felt it surging up within himself—which drove men to take
advantage of the air-raids and loot houses and corpses, careless
of danger and punishment, including the risk of being shot if
they were caught in the act.

However it was not that kind of operation which he proposed to go in for. But he did feel that the city belonged to

him and that the time had come to assert himself and make his
fortune one way or another. He felt like a savage in the
primeval forest when right meant nothing but being stronger
and more cunning than anyone else. Why and how he had
come he no longer remembered: he was just there, and this
gave him a sense of power and arrogant liberty, as if nobody
existed but himself. He felt a wolvish voracity stirring within
him, but this was due less to hunger than to the sleepless
night and the exercise which he had had, and he quietened it
with a few ham rolls, but ate with moderation, thinking that
it would be sensible to keep a supply of provisions.

Among the debris there was a piece of cardboard and
plank with nails sticking in it. On the cardboard he wrote
'Gift of the liberators' and planted it among the rubble. There
was no political implication in this slogan. It was simply the
whimsicality and irony of it which amused him and which was
typical of his usual humour. And then, rather more vaguely,
he felt as if the disaster had really made him a present of the
city, to get what he could out of it. This was probably the
first use of a propaganda-slogan which became more widely
spread and influential than any other during the period of the
Republic of Salò and the resurgence of Fascism—which
Narenza was certainly very far from thinking about. It was the
thought of all the people it would annoy which gave him so
much satisfaction as he erected the slogan.

He moved on and began to find houses with windows and
an occasional shop open and people on the streets, with nothing
to say in the great silence, but not seeming stunned or bewildered or incapacitated but rather very busy and attentive
at their own affairs. But the mere thought, the faintest suspicion, that their intentions might be similar to his own, was
enough to make him hurry. If there was anything to be done
he must get on with it immediately. He cycled towards the
centre of the city through a paved street where the incendiaries
had been extinguished without damage except for slight

scorching. But the stench of burning was growing stronger and more oppressive and this made him curious because the street through which he was threading his way, which was an ancient row of fine town houses, looked as if it were undamaged as far as he could see in passing. Then he saw that the upper windows had all been blown out and the empty pallid sky was showing through. The impression was so stupefying that he had difficulty in making sense out of it. The smoke which had poured out of those windows had left traces on the walls. And some wisps of smoke were issuing still, thin, pale and sluggish. Here the ancient wooden beams which were very dry had given the fire something to bite on and the houses had collapsed from within, piling up the lower windows with rubble. The street-doors, which had been closed, were clear. Every now and then someone went into or out of the emergency-exits of the cellars which were used as shelters.

And once again he grasped the magnitude of the disaster— for the first time in fact: but he asked nobody any questions— for the most part there was nobody who seemed to want to talk. And suddenly, near the Piazza della Scala, he found himself in front of a heap of plaster which blocked the street and reached to the second floor of the ruined houses. And here there was something like a crowd of people climbing up and down, so that a beaten track had already begun to appear in the debris.

He began to find the bicycle and the packet of provisions something of an encumbrance and as he was rather afraid that it might occur to someone to make off with two things which were presumably so scarce as a bicycle and food, he turned back with the idea of looking for the street where his own house had been, so as to hide his possessions. Getting there was a slow business for he found that there was more rubble and that the streets were damaged or had collapsed and were flooded with water from the mains, and that the sewers were exposed. And the sky stared through the window-frames of the houses

L

which had burned and collapsed within, with that merciless limpidity which suggested a final judgement, one might almost say a condemnation without appeal and without hope. The city of death, the death of the city. Though he had small Latin, the ancient words came into his mind: *civitas depopulata* and *Quomodo sedet sola civitas*—as if only in Latin or the Bible the words could still be found to match this awe and horror which had fallen on the heart and on the things of the world.

But on the other hand the street and the house where he had lived in a furnished room were undamaged and there were enough people about to make them almost cheerful by contrast. He found the house-porters, an old man and his wife who were very talkative and kept on telling him how surprised and glad they were to see him again and wanted to tell him all about the hell they had gone through that night; and then suddenly went off on another theme and a long grumble about a police regulation which had come into force, obliging porters to stay at their posts. And this roused them to endless complaints: it wasn't fair: everybody else was bolting, even the few who hadn't gone already; in fact there wasn't a soul in the place; and even after they'd obliged the landlord and the tenants by putting out the fires started by the incendiaries on the roofs and all round the neighbourhood, it hadn't been the slightest use looking for anything more than a tip which made you almost more ashamed to take it than anyone should have been to give it; and the police were in too much of a hurry to give their orders: suppose, just by way of example, obeying them had meant that he lost his life or she lost her sight or a limb, the government hadn't promised either of them twopence in the way of compensation or pension. It's a new government, said Narenza, to cut short the flood of grumbling; to which they said that a new government was the same old government, all governments were the same as far as the poor were concerned. But they seemed a little uncomfortable about the word 'poor' so that Narenza was reminded that they had

nade themselves a nice little competence on the black market:
nd he laughed in their faces which was quite enough to make
hem change the subject: they said they had relatives in the
:ountry, dear, kind, affectionate relatives who were ready to
ake them in: regulations or no regulations the two of them
vere going to evacuate themselves like all the rest of Milan.

To live on the fortune they'd made out of the black market,
aid Narenza, and looked them straight in the eye: they needn't
:rouble to try and take him in, he said. This confused them and
hey were terrified when they remembered, too late, that he had
)een a police-agent or in the confidence of the police. Narenza
ook advantage of this and offered to take on the caretakership
.nd so release them from their duties, but he must have it in
vriting. They began to be profusely grateful, but he checked
hem coldly: it wasn't something for nothing: they would have
:o lend him a sum of money which would be repayable when
he war was over: and they needn't bother to say they hadn't
:ot it, he added, rubbing salt into the wound. Between the
ear of blackmail and the fear of bombs he had them by the
hort hairs and they submitted: and it was a nice tidy little
:um. We don't need to go into what they said about him the
ninute they were on their way to the country. But Narenza
:ould imagine it and had a good laugh as he moved in, settling
limself in the best rooms which had belonged to the landlady,
vho was also a moneylender and equally grasping at both
:rades, and who had now taken flight. The vile poverty and
:qualor of the dwelling had often depressed and irritated him
)ut now it put him in high spirits just to think he had some-
vhere to live after seeing so many fine houses burnt to the
:round. That gave him a further idea: that wealth was chang-
ng hands: Fortune was giving up the bank: the whole social
)rder was changing: all to the good for anyone who knew
10w to make the most of it. He looked round the rooms and
ictually there was nothing left except a few straw mattresses,
:or the grasping old wretch had taken everything else away

with her, but Narenza had had the foresight to make the porters give him linen and some essential furniture before they left.

It was a humble street in an old poor quarter. At first Narenza thought that no one but himself was left: but he soon ran into a young man he knew who lived two doors further up and who confided to him, in a state of great excitement, that he was in possession of a motor-bike and sidecar which could be used for transport-purposes, and of a small motor-van which by innumerable precautions he had managed to keep from being requisitioned. This was clearly the long-awaited moment: this was where you made good, for if you had a vehicle you could make pots of money taking the people who had waited till now to evacuate out to the country and bringing back a load of any sort of foodstuff there might be. The enterprising youth even knew where to get hold of petrol; there was a soldier in the car-park who would let him have some but it was very dear and the man wanted cash. And he worked himself up into a state of excitement because fortune seemed to be eluding him just as he had her by the tail. *Fore-lock*, Falaride corrected him, remaining plunged in profound meditation. How's that? the lad asked. Fortune had a forelock, not a tail and she was bald behind. This didn't matter to the young man: forelock or tail, neck or crupper, there was no way of getting hold of her because he lacked hard cash. But Narenza had concluded his meditations: and the cash which he provided served to set going a very profitable trade which the two later bombardments, followed by attacks on alternate nights so augmented that in those three or four weeks up to the 8th of September, the two partners really did make pots of money, taking hold of fortune by the forelock and the tail and anything else the dirty bitch let you get hold of, to quote the young man whose own tongue was not precisely clean.

He and his assistant, in spite of martial law and the orders calling for arms to be handed over, had duly provided themselves with a machine-gun and were determined to use it if they ran into any tight spots as they careered the streets with the combination and the motor-van. Narenza dealt with the business-side which took him into the town-centre, among the ruins of Galleria which had lost its roof, of the Palazzo Marino and the Scala Theatre which had been burned down.

And so on the morning after the third air-raid he was standing in front of the ruined theatre which had been so dear to the whole of Milan, and he was feeling typically delighted with a notice which some 'Friend of the 25th July' had placed at the entrance of the theatre. It read 'We want Toscanini'. As usual Narenza was laughing to himself about the 'Music Maniacs' who had been so busy having a good time all the while this chaos had been impending, and while he was still laughing he heard a voice close beside him, someone addressing a small group of silent listeners. The voice said that this wasn't the end of the matter: not only what remained of Milan but the rest of Italy would go up in flames or be overrun: that war must be declared on the Germans and that they must accept the punishment which their mistakes and sins and cowardice had brought on them and they must redeem themselves by fighting, if necessary rising against Badoglio and the King.

Narenza was more interested in the speaker than in what he said, having recognised Gaspare's voice. And in spite of his own important and pressing preoccupations, he went up to him.

The speech, or as Narenza described it to himself, the harangue, did not seem to be having much effect on the rather dull audience: and none at all, it goes without saying, on Narenza who, however, didn't mind spending a little of his valuable time waiting for Gaspare to finish. As soon as he saw that Gaspare was by himself and was going away looking very angry and depressed, he went after him and stopped him when he had just crossed the corner by the Filodrammatici where there was no one about. He told him briefly that he had

come to look for him and relieve Armida Lenai's anxiety a
she waited for him at Vill' Alma. He even adopted a discreetl
intimate and authoritative air and reproached him for being
so negligent while the poor woman was being driven to th
verge of endurance and while he himself had been going t
his house to look for him and had even knocked five time
without answer.

For five days and nights, said Gaspare, he hadn't been home
he'd been trying—he stopped short and Narenza finished th
sentence—he'd been trying to help people who were in need
His expression as he said this was so serious and concerned
that if he wasn't sincere it disarmed criticism. And once he had
found out that Gaspare had never been back to his house, he
piled one lie on top of another to give colour to the story so
that in the end it came out that he had been to look for him
at least ten times, even at night time with the bombs falling
And if Gaspare wanted to know why, it had just been from a
sense of his duty as a human being: he didn't say, Out of
friendship. Actually running into this strange creature could not
have happened at a moment which would have suited Gaspare
worse, tired out and dispirited as he was, with everything and
everybody. He was standing with an air of bewilderment
Narenza following his gaze saw a number of slogans written
one beneath another, on a ruined wall: one was 'Viva Mussolini' changed into 'Down with Mussolini' by putting a stroke
across the first letter: there was a 'Down with Badoglio', a
'Long Live the Italian Communist Republic', and finally a 'Long
Live the Liberators': here someone had crossed out the 'Long
live' and in a hasty scrawl, substituted the words 'Thanks to'
which spoke volumes. Gaspare pointed to it, and muttered
'Already?' in a bitter tone, but Narenza showed no signs of
being impressed. He told Gaspare that if he had said 'again'
instead of 'already' it would have done just as well: what it all
amounted to was 'just as usual' because history shows there
is never anything new. And furthermore these scrawls were as

good as whole volumes of contemporary history: and the least Gaspare could do was to let them know at Vill' Alma that he was alive. Gaspare said that he'd go at once if he had any way of getting there, especially as he'd lost all hope and didn't know what he was staying in Milan for. To which Narenza replied that he could offer him a lift there in a side-car. In the circumstances it was a gesture of splendid generosity—with one element of calculation. He told Gaspare that when he got to Vill' Alma he was to load the combination for the return journey with provisions, and pay for them at a fair price. Those peasants had the stuff while the city was starving. He'd got a little business together simply because you had to live, whether there were wars and revolutions going on or not. In short, without pretending to be a philanthropist or a public benefactor, he was fulfilling a useful economic function. Gaspare thanked him but asked him where he got the petrol. This curiosity upset Falaride who asked him dryly whether even supposing he'd said it was stolen, would that be a good reason in these times for leaving your loved ones to worry? And why should you anyway? Just because you wanted to stay and preach politics: Gaspare's kind was no worse and no better than any other but that 'Thanks to the Liberators' had been an answer to it which implied more than you could work out. Finally Gaspare could no longer put up with his fatigue and its resulting nervous excitement which made him unable to eat, and kept him awake if he lay down, although he was so sleepy he was swaying on his feet. In this condition he let them put him on Narenza's combination and went off with the third partner driving, a genial and talkative young man. He described himself as a black marketeer by profession, and took a pride in it and even boasted about it, with the result that Gaspare, although almost in a trance, felt enough curiosity to ask him what there was in such a profession to boast about? The other man replied by demanding to know, with great emphasis, what finer profession could there be than one in which, with a bit of cunning and every now and then a bit of determination, you could get yourself a fine living all by fair trading and all without losing sweat or needing to soil your hands by working? Fair trading? asked Gaspare doubtfully. Certainly it was just the same as any other business: no deception, you robbed no one: just buying and selling, selling and buying: and if people didn't like it they weren't forced to do it. Gaspare thought, He's only got to start talking about the laws of supply and demand, to sound like a classical economist. However he felt obliged to remark that the Government had made that sort of business illegal: and for answer he got a delighted laugh. He was a well-educated man, didn't he know who made the black marketeer's fortune? It was the government did it, and all you wanted was a ban, or a price-control or something else to be rationed, and whatever the product was it promptly went up in price: and everybody could see that it would vanish at any moment and bought up far more than they needed. He is an economist, thought Gaspare, a real economist, and he was amused in spite of the fact that he was so agonisingly sleepy that he was nodding. The trade got people fed, the black marketeer went on, and that was all the politics you wanted in times like these, it covered everything from A to Z. There was too much scandal talked, he said, and personally he didn't listen to it. Suddenly he broke off and begged pardon. But what for? asked Gaspare. Well for the way he'd been talking to an important man and a friend of Signor Narenza's, who certainly knew much more about all these matters than he did himself, being nothing but 'one of the troops'. Gaspare realised that he had picked up this expression from the Fascist sporting-press. However he couldn't help laughing to think that the great respect the black marketeer showed him was due to the fact that he was a friend of Signor Narenza's and evidently passed as a 'big shot' on the black market, one of its V.I.P's, if the precious combination had to make a special trip just for him. It struck him that it was the first time he'd been in a position of prestige and authority and he even had to admit that it's the same with everybody, it invariably tickles people's vanity, even with men like himself. So true is it, as they say at Naples where they still keep the ancient shrewdness and acumen, that bossing is better than f——ing.

By the time he arrived at Vill' Alma he was in such a state that Donato had to prop him up: and he couldn't take anything in, all he wanted was to sleep, apart from first falling into a bath to rid himself of the stench of sweat and dust and soot which was still in his nostrils and which still clung to him from the fire which had also blackened his face and hands: and it mingled in his recollection with the stink of choked and broken drains and with the fug of shelters packed with a foul humanity who had lost all restraint in the physical and moral anguish of those sultry and terrifying nights. Stink and foulness, they hung upon him and he could smell them still in his nose, now that he could breathe the pure sweet air of the country.

While he was in the bath he dozed and nearly slipped under the water, and once he was in bed, the freshness of the sheets on the downy mattress was transmuted into a wonderfully light and relaxed feeling of delight which gave him a blissful sleep until far into the next morning, some eighteen hours on end.

CHAPTER THREE

'You Wanted to die'

GASPARE DELLA MORTE AND ARMIDA LENAI

GASPARE: My dear, however long have I been asleep?

ARMIDA: I can't say exactly: but certainly from yesterday afternoon till late this morning.

GASPARE: I was completely worn out. And was it you who got them to bring me my breakfast in bed this morning?

ARMIDA: That was just Melania being a considerate hostess.

GASPARE: It may seem a trifle but what a lot these things mean when the whole of civilisation seems to be collapsing. I can tell you that I'm quite ashamed of the greed with which I fell on it. But I can't say how long it is since I managed to get anything to eat—certainly since the fire started in Milan —except for a few bites, I've no idea what or where or how. I couldn't get the food down in spite of being so hungry, and before long I didn't even feel hungry, I only felt tired and sore. And if I was standing or sitting, I found myself dropping with sleep and if I threw myself down just where I happened to be I woke up panting and shaking with nightmare.

ARMIDA: It's not surprising: with all that intense fatigue and so much anxiety and suffering. . . .

GASPARE: It was sheer desperation and remorse. . . .

ARMIDA: What about? It wasn't you who set fire to Milan!

GASPARE: No, it wasn't me—or maybe it was all of us, which comes to the same thing.

ARMIDA: But war . . .

GASPARE: Yes, war is desperation; but the remorse was because there was nothing to be done, because one was doing nothing.

ARMIDA: Well, you could hardly put the fire out all by yourself!

GASPARE: It's no joke, Armida. If you saw the devastation!

ARMIDA: I can imagine it.

GASPARE: It's beyond imagination! You have to see it. But even that won't do if you're to grasp how desperate it is: you would have had to see all those three nights of flame devouring the city one after the other: I couldn't believe it myself, I couldn't imagine that anything would ever rise again on those ruins, that anything could ever be done about it.

ARMIDA: Poor Gaspare! Well, what happened?

GASPARE: I found myself shouting out—If this is war, if it's our fault, if we're doomed to it as a curse and punishment, still we shouldn't just submit to it just as it is. I grabbed hold of people, but they didn't know what I meant, I didn't know myself what I was saying, even less than they did. I only wanted to give them some sort of direction, some idea which had substance, something to make them act. . . .

ARMIDA: And get rid of your own despair. . . .

GASPARE: Yes, mine and theirs too. But perhaps it's truer to say I just wanted to die, perhaps that's all that's true.

ARMIDA: And you never gave me a moment's thought!

GASPARE: You? But you were here, you were safe!

ARMIDA: You see, you forgot me completely! And even now you don't begin to think what would have happened to me if I'd lost you, what would have been left of me. Not even at this very moment when you can see me and hold me and remember how much I love you! Let me go, we're not in our own home and somebody might come in. No, it's no good holding me, just try and explain if you can how you could forget you loved me!

GASPARE: But I do love you, oh so much more than myself.

ARMIDA: But you care more about what happened on those nights, and your own desperation.

GASPARE: Yes, I admit that. But try and understand me. It was like madness, frenzy of mind and heart, one's very senses were in anguish. I do love you. . . .

ARMIDA: Yes, now. But then you didn't. And the truth is you had it in you to be so indifferent to me, that you wanted to die.

GASPARE: If you reproach me, Armida . . .

ARMIDA: I'm not reproaching you. I'm just unhappy.

GASPARE: But I feel it as a reproach. And what you say may be true but I must say in all conscience, it isn't just.

ARMIDA: Possibly. And maybe it's neither true nor just but it's inevitable, because I love you. I love you enough to be able to admit to both of us that when the city was burning the whole frightful disaster spelled only one name to me— your name. It was all one with you, with your danger and my own anxiety. Do you imagine in all those days that I could eat, that my nights were quiet? And it was three times. Three times there was a sea of flame where Milan used to be —and the thought that you were there in the midst of it all...

GASPARE: It's true: I ought to have let you know I was safe, but I didn't know how. . . .

ARMIDA: Be honest, Gaspare. I've forgiven you already, but a lie I won't forgive: you didn't even give me a thought.

GASPARE: I didn't even give you a thought: forgive me.

ARMIDA: My dear love, I've forgiven you already.

GASPARE: And to be absolutely honest, I don't know when I would have begun to think about you, if Falaride Narenza hadn't found me yesterday morning. . . .

ARMIDA: I made him so sorry for me that he had to come and look for you.

GASPARE: I know, he told me. And then he's started some sort of business, he's on the black market and has got hold of some vehicles. He piled me into this side-car.

ARMIDA: And it went back yesterday loaded up with vegetables and sides of bacon and all sorts of foodstuffs, Melania used all the influence she had among the local country-people to buy up food, in return for what he had done. And the driver had orders not to quibble about price.

GASPARE: What a strange chap Narenza is!

ARMIDA: But fundamentally good-hearted.

GASPARE: He told me he'd looked for me all over Milan.

ARMIDA: If he didn't find you straight away but found time to get a business going, that can't be quite true: however when he saw how desperate I was, his immediate impulse was a good one and quite genuine. And do you know there's something which was even odder considering that it came from him?

GASPARE: Tell me about it.

ARMIDA: Before he went he actually gave me good advice. It was the only possible good advice. He told me to pray. I did: and now you're here, Gaspare. And God be thanked for his mercy.

GASPARE: Thank God, indeed. But if I'm to be totally honest, I must say that if it had been just for myself I wouldn't have prayed to come out alive, supposing that I'd been able to pray.

ARMIDA: I know: that's what I've told myself already. You'd have preferred to die.

GASPARE: And if I hadn't come across Narenza on the square in front of the Scala, or rather among its ruins, I'm convinced now that I should have collapsed into some hole among the wreckage of Milan completely done for. To be quite honest with you, my mind was totally preoccupied—or that's what it felt like—and I was walking about in a dream.

ARMIDA: But of course: and I don't in the least blame you for your preoccupations then or now. Only you could have had just one thought for this poor soul as well.

GASPARE: You're right: and you see that's just why it seems to me now that what I was preoccupied with was really nothing, or worse than nothing: a kind of lunacy, a lot of words boiling up from the void: my own obsession with politics!

ARMIDA: Don't talk like that! I've never blamed you for your politics, even if it is an obsession, have I, Gaspare? And you can believe me, it's often made me anxious!

GASPARE: Politics! When Narenza found me I was haranguing a small crowd of people: I see them in retrospect now, I can visualise those faces staring at me and listening to me as if I were talking to someone else: I see myself, haranguing them and exhorting them to be done with passive obedience, to force the government to give up tricks and temporising and hole-and-corner methods; and to revolt and take up arms, turn the war against the Germans and if need be bring down not only Badoglio's government but the king and the monarchy too. . . .

CHAPTER FOUR

Truth and Fact

GASPARE DELLA MORTE, ARMIDA LENAI, DONATO MÈRICI
and MELANIA MÈRICI

DONATO: Badoglio's government! Aren't you trying to turn the Marshal into some kind of scapegoat?

GASPARE: Ah, so you're there, are you, Donato?

DONATO: Yes, I am and I heard you. All about Badoglio, King Victor Emmanuel . . .

GASPARE: And according to you, they're all just scapegoats?

DONATO: More or less.

GASPARE: I might have known it. And so, the way you look at it, nobody's to blame either for what has happened or for what's going to happen?

DONATO: Nobody or everybody which is . . .

GASPARE: Precisely the same thing.

DONATO: That's what I mean.

GASPARE: And so you think even Mussolini's being made a scapegoat, too?

DONATO: Mussolini? Well, what else would you do with him? You wouldn't grant that he had it in him to bring about a catastrophe like the one the world's going through now?

GASPARE: No, but I do blame him for having done so much to provoke it.

DONATO: It's saying quite a lot already, if you think he had much influence on it.

GASPARE: It's just because from time to time he's tried to do something to avert the crash—either because he believed he

could or to make it look as if he could—that I do blam
him. I blame him for not succeeding in doing anything eve
then.

DONATO: Just the same as all the others, my dear chap, jus
the same.

GASPARE: What others?

DONATO: First and foremost, the governments and state
which'll continue to call themselves the United Nation
until they fall apart, and then I don't know what they'll ca
themselves, not that I care. Have they been able to do an
more than he has to keep the peace? Haven't they failed too
just as much as he has? And if he's shown himself incapable
what about their politicians? Did any of them have any ide
how to avert the crash?

GASPARE: But he was a warmonger. His intentions were ba
that's why he failed.

DONATO: And they were pacifists, and their intentions wel
good, and that's why they failed? Just look where th
argument gets you to! But I'd rather you told me what yo
made of the other one, Adolf, the mystical incarnation o
Hitler and his *Führer-prinzip*?

GASPARE: He's crazy.

DONATO: Yes, but you can't say he's incapable: he's not
failure—if bringing about the present catastrophe was ju
what he meant and what he was fated to do. It looks to m
as if he'd really succeeded.

GASPARE: Yes, that's hard to deny. What about it?

DONATO: Well, then, however much the historians may tell
that history and God himself have to make use of huma
genius and great men to lead the world, what they lead it
no one knows before it happens: the great men with all the
genius and successes don't know; and the fools and the ma
men with all their disasters and failures don't know eithe
there's only the event and that's all there is to say about i
in other words, as a great philosopher put it, truth is fac

GASPARE: And so you don't see any reason or justice or hope in actual events?

DONATO: But I do.

GASPARE: How so?

DONATO: In the event itself, in whatever befalls, so and not otherwise: if you like, just in so far as the cause or reason is unknown to me until it's revealed in the event: and so if you're a believer, you can see them in God, your reason and justice and hope: but it's such a weighty truth, so harsh and so incomprehensible that I haven't the courage to call it anything.

GASPARE: Listen! I don't understand metaphysics or theology: and now you make me think about it, I don't feel I've any right to go on meting out praise or blame to other people. But that doesn't mean that I deny my own faults and stupidities or fail to recognise my own shortcomings.

DONATO: And with that of course you've shut my mouth and reduced me to silence. And it's just because you don't deny your own faults or try to get out of the responsibility of doing what you regard as your duty, that you've the right to blame where you do blame, and to fight the people you do fight. And since you can fight, you've earned a right to your enemies. But in my case, all I can see is my virtues which are so exquisitely passive and sensitive and delicate that they stink of corruption and death: and I've no right to my friends.

MELANIA: Donato, Donatello, why do you talk like this?

DONATO: Because otherwise I might say something worse: I might say I'm a loathsome egoist, a sluggard and a coward who cares for nothing and nobody and yet, so as not to have to make the slightest effort, is ready to exonerate everybody and everything: even himself!

MELANIA: My own Donatello, you're so terribly bitter.

DONATO: Don't you say it, Mother, I'm pleased and proud enough with my bitterness, all by myself.

M

MELANIA: You're so cruel to yourself!

DONATO: You don't have to tell me! I'm a real Nero to myself but a stage Nero.

MELANIA: Say what you like: but still I'm your mother and it's cruel and bad of you to talk to me like that.

DONATO: What I wish is one thing and what I can do is another. I am what I am and nothing else, and I can't give other people what I haven't got. And this is all I have got. But what about you, what is it you want from me?

MELANIA: My boy, I only want you to be happy.

DONATO: Mother, what an exorbitant demand!

MELANIA: I'm more convinced than ever that you were a great artist: and you suffer because you've tried to reject and betray your vocation, because you're trying to strangle it and destroy it.

DONATO: I certainly seem to be a rarity, a unique and most extraordinary rarity. Out of all the number who've really had a vocation and managed to rear it to maturity, and out of all the hosts who've ever imagined they had one and kept it going on vitamin pills and benzedrine, I'm the one who's committed infanticide. I killed *my* vocation in the womb, in fact I stopped it ever being conceived. Nero again. *'Qualis artifex pereo'*. Now, Mother, you're the one that's living in a world of fantasies and putting them on to me! Still you can't have a great love without this generosity, or without its illusions. Don't make me say any more, Mother, don't force me to repay your love so cruelly! But what do you want me to do, start clamouring for your pity because I can't love anything or anybody?

CHAPTER FIVE

The Choice

GASPARE DELLA MORTE, MELANIA MÈRICI
and ARMIDA LENAI

MELANIA: Wherever are you going? Why do you run away from me like this? It's no good. He's gone. He's never spoken like that to me before. But I guessed it!

ARMIDA: There was so much suffering behind what he said!

MELANIA: And it's partly my fault—very much so!

GASPARE: How, Signora Melania?

MELANIA: Not warning him, not helping him, but actually irritating him! and not being able just to stand beside him without asking him for anything—not even that he should be happy! What was it he said? A great lover, yes, true enough, but so demanding and ambitious: so full of ideas and obsessions, so puffed up both in head and heart! Music, vocation, glory, greatness—I've made graven images out of them and loved them instead of him. It's a greedy love, he's quite right: the graven images are insatiable.

ARMIDA: Melania, you feel you must torture and blame yourself, but just stop for a moment and remember that he's sick and that when he's better he'll be a different man! And anyway how do you know that turning against art may not be one of an artist's essential experiences?

MELANIA: But it didn't have to be me who provided him with the experience!

GASPARE: Signora Melania—and you too, Armida, all these things which you get so enthusiastic or so disturbed about—

they're all no doubt very beautiful and rare and exquisite. . . .

MELANIA: But you despise them, don't you, Gaspare?

GASPARE: Never! I have respect for them, in fact, if you like, you can say I admire them. I only say that as things are nowadays, they can wait.

MELANIA: Wait? Wait what for?

GASPARE: Well, in the first place till the war's over.

MELANIA: It seems to me sometimes as if this war will never be over, this or something like it or even worse.

GASPARE: Even that, a luxury of imagination which can wait. It's like a fine wine, it won't lose anything by ageing—in fact . . .

ARMIDA: Gaspare!

GASPARE: I don't mean to offend anyone, but the fact is that the worst part of this war may still be to come.

MELANIA: Is it possible?

GASPARE: It is possible: and we must take the facts into account and face them and prepare ourselves. And there's no time to lose!

ARMIDA: Oh Gaspare, why must you be in such a hurry? You've barely escaped from one disaster and already . . .

GASPARE: What I've been through was a defeat—or something worse, a meaningless and ineffectual gesture: all impotent alike, words, deeds and wishes! Suppose I said that I'm still smarting from the feeling of impotence, it would only be another kind of vanity, a purely personal sentiment which I ought to keep to myself. But there's something else I must say and I'm bound to say it and it doesn't brook delay. If you're going to keep me in your house as a guest, Melania, there's something you've the right to know and I've the duty to tell you—that I intend to lose no time in gathering an organisation together—partly new, partly old. . . .

ARMIDA: A political one?

GASPARE: The way you said that sounded weary—maybe even ironical. . . .

ARMIDA: That wasn't what I meant.

GASPARE: It's all the same. But anyway it's a fighting organisation I'm thinking of rather than a political one.

ARMIDA: Fighting whom? Why?

GASPARE: Because now the war's shifted to Italy, it could spread all over the country at any moment.

MELANIA: Doesn't that mean that as far as Italy's concerned, the war's lost already?

GASPARE: What it means is that we may be going to have a new war, maybe that it's begun already. What it means is that if people have any kind of conviction against Hitler's Germany their duty is already laid down, it's already actual, they must get ready to rise and fight—I repeat, Fight. Don't say anything to me, Armida: I know, we still go on plotting and machinating, we always will. Don't tell me I'm the eternal conspirator, because that's just what I'm going to be if I must. And please listen to me, Melania: and you too, Armida. . . .

ARMIDA: But who is it you're plotting and rising against?

GASPARE: What you should say is, Who is it in aid of? And I'll answer you by saying that it isn't going to be a light matter for Italy to get out of this war, it's going to be very difficult, it'll mean a new war on top of the old one. And it may even mean a civil war—Italians fighting Italians.

MELANIA: Gaspare, what are these horrors. . . .

ARMIDA: Yes, what *are* you imagining?

GASPARE: They're facts, not fantasies.

MELANIA: But haven't the Germans lost the war, too, by now?

ARMIDA: They only go on with it because they're desperate.

GASPARE: And are we to be behind them when we hope, as I do, to prove our faith in a cause which we believe to be true and just, even if we can't win? For after all hoping or despairing isn't what matters. If you believe in truth and justice you oughtn't to take into account whether you'll win or not, you must do your duty. It's not a question of success, but honour. And my duty is to get myself ready to support anyone who'll carry on the war I believe to be inevitable and just, whether it's a party or a government, whether it's rebel or loyal.

ARMIDA: Oh it's always war, never anything but war!

GASPARE: It's natural you should be distressed and one must have every sympathy with it. But fate doesn't listen to us crying for mercy, however pitifully.

MELANIA: But why should there be civil war, war between Italians?

GASPARE: Melania, the peace you've got by retiring here isn't real, and you, none of you know what's going on. The Germans are still very strong, maybe very strong indeed: and they're reinforcing themselves here in Italy every day to such an extent that there's one thing we can rule out—the idea that they're sending in such great forces just to go back across the Alps without joining battle and with nothing more than a few skirmishes by way of demonstration or diversion. And they may even win one of these battles—or more than one. And in that case we shall have to expect bad times—possibly expect the worst. And even if it doesn't get as far as that, I still have to come back to what it is my duty to tell you. Giving me hospitality, Signora Melania, will be dangerous. And Armida, it's the same about staying with me. If I stay here, Melania, it may mean death, they can kill us or burn us out. If you come away with me, Armida, you know what is in store for you wherever I go. You can choose. You can let me go: and you can send me away, Signora Melania.

ARMIDA: You call that choice, do you? as if I could stay here without you. What are you trying to do—test me, or insult me?

GASPARE: Neither. But now you must answer me, Melania.

MELANIA: I can't answer you.

GASPARE: Then you have answered me. We'll go today. And, Armida, our house at Milan hasn't been damaged.

MELANIA: Now just listen. Of all the precipitate people! You're the man who forsees everything, aren't you, and you don't see that I must ask Donato what he thinks? Didn't you think of that too, when you thought of everything?

GASPARE: If you answer me with a joke, it's the best proof of your courage. Forgive me, Signora.

ARMIDA: You might ask me for a little forgiveness, too.

GASPARE: I'd no doubt of your love, Armida.

MELANIA: And after all my mistakes with my son, I'm quite sure what he'll answer, too. But you're the one to ask him, Gaspare, not I.

GASPARE: As you wish. But why?

MELANIA: Because something like you're asking . . .

GASPARE: I haven't asked anything. I've simply laid out the facts.

MELANIA: I know: and you had to. But that doesn't alter the situation—that the facts you've laid out allow of only one reply.

GASPARE: Well then, I can tell you, in all conscience, that I shouldn't blame Donato for not wanting to be involved when all he would get would be the risk, danger and trouble when he has no enthusiasm or conviction.

MELANIA: But wouldn't you, in all conscience, despise him?

GASPARE: No, in all conscience, I would not.

MELANIA: I can see this as a brave man's generosity, and a man of action's too—and also as a proud man's jealousy.

GASPARE: Do you hear that, Armida? You've got all the passion and we'll say I'm full of courage and action and still we have to finish up looking like a pair of simpletons. Now I really should like to know, Melania, exactly what you mean when you say I'm jealous?

MELANIA: Now *you're* trying to joke. And by way of answering back, let me tell you, it proves nothing more than we all know already.

ARMIDA: Well, I certainly don't know what you could possibly mean by jealousy.

MELANIA: Oh it's just due to pride. It's what a proud and courageous man would feel for his own courage and self-reliance.

GASPARE: Very well, Signora, I must be honest and admit to you that, to put it in your way, I'm neither as brave nor as proud nor as jealous, nor, to put it in my own way, as sure of myself, as you make out. And to prove it, here's this little phial. It's a quick poison and I always keep it on me. And I feel I must let you into that secret, too.

ARMIDA: Gaspare, you never told me!

GASPARE: It may be that I didn't want to add to your anxieties. But I was certainly ashamed of admitting it, too. Have you heard anything said about the tortures they use to make people talk when they're under suspicion or accusation? They use all kinds—and they may be even scientific or psychological ones. Those who are experienced say that without some degree of painful compulsion, nothing would ever be found out except when people were caught in the act or where the circumstantial evidence was nearly as strong. I'm not arguing about that. If it's the truth, it only increases one's disquiet: and mine's so great already that I've got the poison.

ARMIDA: Gaspare, you make me frightened.

GASPARE: What do you think I am? I'm so frightened that I keep it on me wherever I go. Perhaps now, Melania, you'll see I'm not so proud, not so jealous—and certainly not so brave?

MELANIA: But more human.

GASPARE: That's something to the good.

MELANIA: It's a truer courage. Can I pass on this part of the conversation to Donato, too?

GASPARE: Yes, but under the strictest secrecy.

MELANIA: Why?

GASPARE: Because too much of my courage depends on the poison.

CHAPTER SIX

'Black Market'

A LITTLE more than a week after the fire, Vill' Alma had a visit
from Falaride Narenza: and to everybody's surprise he seemed
to be suffering from so much anxiety that he was incapable of
carrying on a connected conversation or even listening to one,
or of sitting quietly on his chair for more than five consecutive
minutes. At the same time he seemed to be full of an odd
confidence in his own foresight and powers of prediction.
From Donato he wanted to know if there might not be something or other in the way of a hiding place for some lorries in
the woods round Alma Dannato: and if it would be possible
to deposit some rather bulky articles there in one of the natural
caves or in the vaults of the old castle. Donato could give
him only vague details and not many of these: there weren't
any caves that he knew; the underground passage which the
superstitious countryfolk around had made into a legend was
a narrow hole which came to an end a few metres below
ground, having been closed by landslides. The wood however
was thick and of considerable extent.

Narenza broke in—according to what people said there was
an underground vault capable of holding more than a hundred
soldiers on horseback with their equipment. And they also
said, answered Donato with a laugh, that there were spooks
and spirits of both sexes and all ages roaming about Alma
Dannato: but they hadn't put in an appearance since the
electric light had been installed. Narenza shrugged his shoulder
and said he would have to be content with the woods which

anyway had the advantage that you could subdivide the stuff and deposit it in separate scattered hiding-places and so avoid getting your friends into trouble in case of discovery.

What friends and what stuff? Donato wanted to know, and Narenza looked him straight in the eye, a thing which he did very rarely; and seeing that it was a genuine question, he showed signs of impatience: by friends he meant Donato and his mother, Signora Lenai, and, he added, Gaspare Della Morte—who had already been compromised enough on his behalf. Gaspare broke the silence by saying that he was tired and had lost confidence and had given up any idea of political activity. Oh yes, of course, that goes without saying, commented Falaride Narenza: he knew nothing about anything and he didn't want to know except how he could work for his strictly private and personal profit: nevertheless when all was said and done you could see that he wasn't a man to betray his friends. And so even if they wouldn't allow him the honour of calling himself their friend, that was what he was and his behaviour would show them.

At this Della Morte changed his tactics and said outright that he trusted and believed him, and held out his hand. And Falaride took it and the tears came into his eyes and it was obvious that he had to restrain an impulse to kiss it and he said that you had to have known what contempt and suspicion could be like to appreciate a mark of esteem from a gentleman.

They still wanted to know, said Donato, what sort of stuff it was which had to be hidden: hadn't he said something about lorries?

The stuff depended on what he could arrange with the peasants, he replied evasively. There wasn't a peasant in Italy who wasn't adept and willing when it came to hiding every kind of useful object from saucepans and frying-pans, once copper had been requisitioned, to pigs and cows and cattle in general. You don't mean live ones asked Donato laughing Live ones too, he replied. And, with his glance straying ove ie ornaments distributed round the furniture of the room, e added that it would be a good thing to bury or brick up all ieir valuables. And as Donato went on laughing, he showed ritation again; would Donato stop that idiotic laugh just as personal favour?

Anybody could see he'd made money, said Donato, some-vhat vexed, by the fact that he was taking such good care of imself and was so rude to everybody else. He said that he adn't really made money but he hoped to before very long, was simply a question of waiting. Della Morte didn't laugh ut asked him his views on what was going to happen.

All going down the slippery slope, he said, from bad to vorse: and he could see there was going to be a catastrophe, ll public authority was going to collapse and the armed forces rst of all. They were going to have times when a thief's word vould be as good as a gentleman's. He went on to let them into secret, he'd come to an arrangement already with some :oops in a car-park, to take away a certain number of vehicles, s many as he could be quite sure of hiding. As things were oing, any kind of transport would be as good as gold, and etter, because the value of gold was conventional and ariable: what was certain was hunger and want and a rise in ie price of foodstuffs and therefore of freight-costs.

Meanwhile he'd provided the soldiers with identity-cards nd forged discharge-papers and also with a 'secret weapon'.)onato seemed to be even more annoyed now, he said, than efore, when he was laughing, which was even sillier: did he now what 'secret weapon' meant in the current military lang? He didn't? Falaride said he'd explain: it meant a ivilian suit so that you could slip the painter and hide or go ome. Now did he understand?

Had it really come to that? asked Della Morte. Narenza nswered by turning round on him, too. Did he find that urprising? And what sort of state did he expect a defeated rmy to be in when it had been thrown away—with the few good arms it possessed and the lives of its best troops—in the African deserts and on the Russian steppes and at the bottom of the sea and fighting up in the air: and when the weapons which it still possessed were enough to make you laugh, if it didn't make you cry, and when anyway it was completely rotted with the conviction that the war was lost and that the cause for which it had been sacrificed was unjust and crazy. He wasn't going into all that and didn't want to, but he wouldn't admit that those who had worked to spread and intensify such a conviction and the resulting despondency had any right to be surprised if the army couldn't and wouldn't make use of these weapons any more, for it knew better than anyone what they were worth. And furthermore it knew how well the Germans were armed as they came down from the Brenner, day and night, train-load after train-load. They really did have secret weapons, or at least they were getting them ready. But for the Italian soldier there was nothing left but a civilian suit so that he could take his hook while there was still time.

Gaspare tried to counter this attack by saying that it was all a question of changing sides and giving up a bad cause for a good one. But Narenza interrupted him with an opinion which took the wind out of his sails: that armies don't keep going on 'causes' but on discipline and 'esprit de corps': it was just the same as in politics where the only difference which was ever admitted was between success and failure. He'd read Machiavelli while he'd been hiding at Vill' Alma after the 25th of July: and also a synopsis of Hegel's philosophy: as Stalin had read them, he added to his listeners' surprise or as Lenin had read them for him or Marx for both of them. What about Churchill? asked Donato who was now amused. Churchill hadn't been able to make any use of Machiavelli and the result was that he and the British Isles were all on the same slippery slope as they were themselves on the Continent and, when they got to the bottom, they might find it was like slithering on soap, the faster the descent, the more seat they'd have left on

heir pants. And what about Roosevelt? This question put him
n a good temper: Roosevelt had no need to know what he was
oing, for there's a moment when whatever a nation does or
oesn't do, it can't help being great and powerful. And the
United States were at that moment and Roosevelt was the man.
and you might ask what Roosevelt was to do if the Germans
ad gained the mastery of Europe and the Japanese had
onquered China and had made a bloc with Russia. But the
act was that the Germans who had worked everything out to
ne last detail had seen fit to attack Russia in summer equipment
nd the others, the Japs, who were such perfect know-alls,
ad just indulged a whim and sent a few American ships to
ne bottom without troubling to declare war: and so they'd
ompletely played into the hands of Roosevelt and the United
tates. Well, said Donato, would the Russians ever have made
bloc with two such partners as that, one from the East and
ne other from the West? No, he said: and actually they hadn't:
nd so they'd worked for America, too: and that's what makes
or true greatness both in politicians and peoples—when they
et other people to work for them. In short, the moment had
ome for the United States to lead the world. If that was going
o turn out to be a situation which would suit anybody's
onvenience and happiness was another question which would
e seen later when the war was over. As for Mussolini, he went
n, for he was now in full swing, Machiavelli had always
nded his compatriots in the same trouble—people thought
ney were artful when they weren't, and thought it all the more
ne less they actually were and the less they wanted to be
nought so or even to be so. And Machiavelli had made even
nore of a fool of Mussolini: he not only thought he was artful
ut thought he was the only one who was: and moreover he
nid, that was typical of the kind of damage a writer of genius
ould do: how could you help being affected by the language
hen you read *Il Principe* and imagined yourself both the fox
nd the lion, both beast and man, brought up by the Centaur

and capable of either the lower or the higher nature or one beyond both of them?

Hitler was the only theme that remained but Narenza modestly refrained from giving judgment on him, because, as he said, he didn't see what sort of beast or man he might be. And Donato said that he thought himself that Hitler was a species of animal which was something new in history: no doubt he was inspired, some sort of prophet or seer, but the source of his inspirations and prophecies and visions was within himself: a new kind of leader, if you believed in him, even more of a novelty, if you didn't: but certainly a monster however you looked at him.

At this point Gaspare wanted to know what sort of judgement they had to make on themselves, when they could be having an academic discussion on matters of such moment. But a shrug of the shoulders was the only response he got from either. And Narenza suddenly made up his mind to tell Melania that he had unpleasant news for her. With a very few other houses in the same part of the town, where the old buildings burned very easily, Casa Mèrici had survived all three raids and had been standing alone amid tremendous devastation. To anyone who like himself remembered what it had been in the civilised refined old days—not to mention the music—that was rather pathetic. Happening to pass by he had stopped to look at it and had even gone back: and in case they had any doubts of him, he admitted frankly that it had also crossed his mind that he might make use of it for the purpose of hiding black market goods and vehicles. Anyway, Casa Mèrici seemed to have been spared. But the incendiary material seemed to have spread through it and a slow hidden fire had worked for days in the very heart of the ancient beams dried out by the centuries and impregnated with age old ways of living—and even in the end with music, as they say of violin-wood and the timber of the priceless old playhouses of former times. And they needn't be surprised that he had been moved: for the day before when he

ad come back to look at it and to tell the porters to keep a
areful eye on it, the roof had caught fire, literally before his
yes. And it had fallen in flames and brought down the whole
ouse with it and only the main walls remained. And that, he
aid, had been the end of Casa Mèrici. They were no crocodile
ears which he brushed away.

Melania and Donato looked at each other dry-eyed. In these
ays this sort of news neither surprised them nor disturbed
em particularly. What they felt might have been described
s resignation, if a kind of spiritual apathy had not played a
reater part in it and also an inability to take in precisely and
alistically what the news implied for the future now that
veryone was living from day to day, and scattered and out of
ouch. It even stirred in both of them a momentary surge of
lief, as if they had been delivered from a fear and an obses-
ion: and this was not unusual in those days: when something
ou have long dreaded actually happens, there is a kind of
leasure in merely being rid of the apprehension and though
is may be an illusion it hides the hurt and the misery of the
al event for the time being.

They seemed so untouched by the news that the realistic
Varenza was immensely surprised, and asked them if they had
ound out how to make some form of insurance which covered
ar-damage? And against their will this made them laugh
hich provoked him to remark, somewhat touchily, that there
ere some sorts of refinement which he hadn't got it in him to
omprehend even if he admired or envied them. Just look at
, he'd been moved; and there they were, dry-eyed as stockfish!

He really had become more than insolent: but he didn't give
em time to say so because the simile put him in mind of his
wn business-affairs: for among the stuff he wanted to hide
ere actually was a quantity of stockfish and dried cod which
: one time would certainly have been regarded as having gone
ff, but in these days was very scarce and therefore of the highest
uality. He must go now, he said, especially as he had left town

with the idea of finding lodgings with one of the neighbouring peasants. He said why quite frankly. Although the secret police were no longer in existence, his name was still on their lists and he didn't feel comfortable. If the Germans put in some sort of a government and the lists came into their hands he ran the risk of being blackmailed and forced into taking up a profession again which he wanted to have nothing to do with any more, even if it meant poverty or having to emigrate heaven knows where for good. Seeing that they felt he was being honest, as in fact he was, he let them into another secret. He had three nieces left orphans by his brother when they were very small: and they'd not only been left without a half-penny but, what was an even greater risk, they'd grown into very pretty girls. He'd made provision for his sister-in-law and the girls whom he was as fond of as if they were his own family but on the quiet, so that they could receive the help without knowing where the money came from. His sister-in-law was Sicilian and she'd been evacuated some time ago to the island with the two younger girls where she was living with her parents, and naturally since the Allied landing he'd had no more news of her, so that now he didn't know how to provide for the eldest who had remained in Milan and had been employed in a factory which had been burned down and had turned off its employees. She was pretty, he repeated, wasn't quite eighteen, chaste, well-educated, a good girl with a very nice disposition: he wouldn't have thought it was for him to sing her praises if all these qualities hadn't conspired to put him into a quandary over the girl and had made him so fond of her that he had to see she didn't come to a bad end. Maybe they knew him by now and could sympathise with him enough to know what he was driving at when he said that he hadn't a friend in the world he could really trust. Apart from the Mèrici themselves—and this was due to their good nature and condescension—he'd never had to do with anything better in his life than low police scum: and look at the situation now riff-raff, people of no substance, social scum, banditry, to whom was he to entrust the girl? They'd understand and sympathise: it was a big problem. And he looked at them anxiously and inquiringly with eyes which were sharp enough however muddy they looked.

Melania Mèrici didn't press him to say more: he could bring the girl to Vill' Alma, and if she were only half as good as he had described, they would all be very much taken with her.

His eyes filled with tears, and by way of thanks he said 'God reward you' and this was clearly heartfelt; and he added that if he felt any desire to become the sort of person one could know and respect, it had been due in the first place to being allowed to call himself her friend and Donato's.

He was being perfectly sincere but after Signora Mèrici had cordially repeated that he must bring his niece as soon as possible, he blurted out with his usual airy tactlessness that he had brought her already and that she was waiting in the house of a neighbouring peasant. But he was like that: he even took the smiles which his offhand behaviour had provoked for mere good nature. And so he went off to fetch his niece whose name was Alinda.

N

CHAPTER SEVEN

Alinda

ALINDA NARENZA was unquestionably beautiful: in the firs
place she had wonderful eyes of a soft and velvety black whose
sweetness, depth of colour and brilliance were quite dazzling
both in themselves and in the astonishing effect they produced
and since the pupil was of the same hue, you couldn't read
their expression, except that colour and gaze seemed to be
intensified and enlivened towards the centre of the eye. In
shape they were a perfect almond, the iris surrounded by a
narrow shining circle of pure white: and though they were
actually of normal size, they shed so much brilliance that when
she looked at you, it seemed to overflow and they looked
enormous. Her face was a perfect oval, with a very pretty and
delicate forehead and chin, while the mouth and the other
features were clean-cut, but also lightly-drawn and delicate
and thus a restrained mobility of expression, which was non
the less very lively and sensitive, gave a subtle intensity to the
whole face and the luminous pallor of its wonderful amber
skin: and this made a foil for the magnificent eyes, which
would otherwise have been almost too beautiful: a kind of
astonishment at the world was concentrated in their shining and
sparkling depths: and this resembled the beauty of passive
nature, of flowers, of precious stones, of the colours occurring
in the sky and in the animal creation. That they were capable
of laughter, that indeed they could be described as laughing
eyes, implied the full depth and significance which lies in the
fact that of all the human creation it is only the human face

which expresses joy and sorrow in the light and shade of laughter and weeping. You might have called her face too beautiful to be intelligent, but this did not prevent it reflecting and expressing a quick and generous sensibility, a mild grace and rich intuitive penetration whose warmth of feminine fascination made reflective intelligence seem unnecessary. And with all this and all its warmth, it was still the face of a sensible, shrewd young girl—and this by nature not training.

To pay due homage to the great poet, they were eyes like those described by Giovanni Verga, the kind which when they look yielding and responsive, seem so gentle and truthful that they suggest resignation to a pure and lofty destiny: they were eyes like those which made the Sicilian author write, in *Cavalleria Rusticana*, '*Do you not see that I accept suffering and death?*'

In such a nature, modesty of feeling and conduct, sobriety and sensitivity combined with the wisdom of ancient experience to moderate and subdue her intense and vivid predisposition to joy and passion: making her as it were the sacrificial victim of inevitable sorrow, so that ever admiration for her physical attraction turned to an impulse of protection, a warm and gentle wish for goodness and compassion on her behalf. Anyone seeing that face and eyes in their innocent courage and their virginal secret ardour which was like a glow without flame, could not help wishing that life would be good to her and in whatever way she could be spared, would spare her to the full.

She was of medium height and rather slightly built but with that perfection of proportions which is the basis of this kind of unobtrusive physical harmony and gives it its indefinable beauty. But though they were graceful her wrists and ankles were so slender that they gave an impression of almost too much fragility: and that was almost painful, because the gentle passive yielding strength which breathed from the girlish face was so obviously maternal that it put you in mind of the

sufferings of motherhood and made you wonder how anythin
so frail could endure them.

The face of a Madonna: and it had been Donato who ha
said it: as much as to say that prayerfulness had been the lin
between nature and development, so that in this face an ide
of innocence and charity, pity and salvation, hope and love ha
taken on flesh.

It was the cross-grained Narenza who suddenly noticed tha
something was going on, and talked to Donato like a schoo
master, with the request that he wouldn't turn his niece's head
and added that he'd like to see what sort of faces will be turne
out when generations have been thoroughly conditioned b
sex-mad films, by promiscuity and necking, not to mention th
effect of heavy drinking especially on an empty stomach, an
the widespread addiction to dangerous drugs. For apart fror
a hysterical passion for sport, that was what, in his view, th
emotional and intellectual capacities of the average man an
woman have reduced themselves to nowadays when the vas
majority are anyway brutalised by the frustration of misery c
debased and servile labour conditions, at least in the cities
while even the country is becoming increasingly industrialised
However he admitted himself that this kind of harangue was
bit out of date: what had moved him lately, as he put it, t
positive disgust was that in the factory where his niece had
clerical job and which produced bandages and orthopædi
dressings, she had been chosen the local Beauty Queen. H
fulminated against the idea that the manufacture of illusion
and something perhaps worse than illusion, should be publicl
organised in this way. Fascism had been quite right to pu
down this sort of thing, but no sooner had Fascism bee
suppressed in its turn than you found that the little goo
which it had done had been abolished and only the evil re
mained. It wasn't at all a bad thing, he added, that the busines
had been burned down: and he said it with a Savonarola
expression on his sharp little face which made them all burs

out laughing, with the result that he was fairly beside himself and blustered—'Beauty Queen indeed, Miss jock-strap, is what they mean'—referring of course to certain products of the industry.

Meanwhile Melania and Armida had taken the girl to look at the room they had chosen for her: and even these first conversations were on the basis of the liveliest kind of sympathy: while the girl's anxiety, due to having heard nothing from her mother and sisters since Sicily had been invaded, as well as her poverty and her grateful affection for her Uncle Falaride, all only served to strengthen it. Alinda didn't pretend not to know that a great many unpleasant things were said about her uncle: and she wasn't trying to defend him: she only said that people didn't know how kind he was and how much he had always done for an unfortunate widow with three small children and that without even being a rich man and even at a time when he had actually been poor: and when helping them had meant taking the bread out of his own mouth. It wasn't for her to judge anybody, but she couldn't help wishing that all those who had all along been contemptuous of her Uncle Falaride had it in them to do as much themselves. Meanwhile she begged Signora Mèrici to make use of her and give her something to do, no matter what, anything which had to be done about the house, not that she could hope to repay the Signora's kindness, it was just to show her gratitude and keep her from being idle.

Donato fell in love with Alinda at first sight, it was a matter of hours rather than days: and love healed him, it was a kind of rebirth. They all saw it; in Melania's case, with the profound satisfaction a mother must feel to see her son restored to health even if not without some trace of jealousy or envy. They all saw, too, that Alinda remained simple and modest with nothing at all to say for herself unless she was spoken to. When she was asked to express her opinions and beliefs, they were always modest and sensible: they were never in the least out of the ordinary, but it was just this which revealed her good sense, straightforwardness, her profound intellectual honesty and a real native goodness which breathed a kind of moral fragrance.

But in spite of this, her Uncle Falaride now worked himself into a new and uncontrollable state of agitation. And from morning to night he continually had his eye on the progress of the love-affair and was always finding bigger and better reasons for alarm always preaching and holding forth in a way which could hardly have been more absurd, on ignorant and imprudent young people and the risks they ran, on what was coming to girls who got themselves into trouble, and the hideous corruption of the times which he utterly deplored. Except for his niece and Donato, they were all either bored, or laughed at him. He couldn't really imagine that she wasn't letting herself be tempted and led astray. But on the other hand all his affection revolted against the idea that she could be hypocritical enough to maintain so convincing an air of unconcern. But to Donato, without hesitation, he attributed the most dishonourable intentions, the blackest and most criminal tendencies. He wasn't for one moment going to be taken in by the good humour and actual approbation with which this 'black sheep' received his moralising and his social diatribes and Jeremiads: or take them at their face value as quite ingenuous, and typical of a shy and apprehensive lover, who was perhaps already beginning to be jealous. All Narenza could see was the blackest machination on the part of a seducer so wily and accomplished that he could feign not only naïvety but actual inexperience. It was a good job that he himself was there to keep an eye on things. For with all his brain-cudgelling and mental contortions there was only one supposition which never presented itself to him—that Donato's intentions were honourable and matrimonial. And if it had occurred to him it would have filled him with endless mistrust, for he could not believe that that 'libertine' could possibly want to do anything with Alinda except make her his mistress and a lost woman, as he put it to himself in melodramatic terms.

However, in spite of his agitation, he did not neglect his blackmarket operations but applied himself to their development and organisation: and Gaspare Della Morte took advantage of this in the knowledge that he could rely on Narenza's assurances that all his people depended for their lives on secrecy, indeed, on complete silence: don't ask and don't answer: and if you made a mistake, you knew what to expect: and so they all had false papers on them: these weren't times in which a body which had been bumped off in a ditch or beside a road would be likely to provoke inquiry or even much curiosity. On his side, Gaspare did not attempt to ignore or deny that he was in no position to make difficulties about anything which fate had bestowed on him in the way of assistance or necessary instruments. So he gathered together the first nucleus of a band of young men who had made up their minds to go into hiding and carry on guerilla warfare in the neighbouring hills and in the mountains which overtopped them, and which also offered them a chance, if things turned out badly, of crossing the nearby Swiss border.

He had a wireless receiver securely hidden in the villa and a mobile transmitter in the woods. Without coming out into the open or expecting him to do so himself, Narenza had let him know where some of his dumps were in the woods and, he said that supplies of mouth-munitions were always to be found there too, unguarded: but not gun-food, he didn't mean to go that far. Gaspare felt that he could rely on him completely within the limits of his promises.

It was now almost September, 1943, and the months began with the most beautiful weather, typical of what is in fact the most agreeable month of the year in our climate: and at Vill' Alma, the weather itself, during that last week of August and first week of September, the bliss of late summer melting into approaching autumn, diffused among them all a strange peace

which, for all its strangeness, seemed unalterably happy:
Armida and Gaspare felt it as old and tender lovers, and he
felt it personally in having come in his own mind to a new
serenity, just because he had to wait now, to do what he could
to the best of his ability, without wasting himself in planning
and scheming. And Alinda and Donato felt it too and so
did Melania: with a mother's heart, soothed and blissfully
happy to see that her son is healing and returning to life
and hope.

And the young Alinda was so wholeheartedly in love, her
love was so deep and entire that she was not yet even aware of
loving him. There was no reason to know or recognise it, no
reason to put it into words or give it a name. It mingled with
her entire being, it was part of her soul now pervaded by a
peaceful and oblivious happiness which nothing external
could even reach or touch, certainly not disturb. She had no
plans, desires or hopes. She could not have had hopes without
disturbing that superhuman supernatural peace. And since she
was free of having to hope—except that she might go on
loving—and thus from fretting her love by thinking and
discussing, by desire and imagination, this love, untroubled
by hope, had lifted her spiritually to the summit of an intense
bliss and kept her in its warmth and light. She did not wonder
whether he loved her in return. If she had known that she was
loved, she would have had to think about it and thus to be
concerned by it, whereas in her inward depths which were too
deep for thought, loving and being loved were a certainty and
an inseparable unity. Continually every day and every hour
she knew those heights and depths of feeling which come to
the created being who grasps in the fleeting circumscribed
moment the bliss of infinite life beyond space and time.
Intention or disquiet, if she had had them, would have seemed
equally ungrateful and a kind of impiousness. And from day to
day and from hour to hour, even if she became more aware of
being in love and admitted it to herself, speech and knowledge

eferred always to a point which had been reached and passed:
nd the present moment was already far beyond them, ineffable,
nconceivable, in its overwhelming felicity.

If she ever thought of reflecting and letting herself become
ware of what had happened to her, it was the night-hours
vhich she gave over to it, when she could be alone in the
ilence: but in its very sweetness, her bliss exhausted her and
onsumed all her strength and by the time she came to the
evening and her bed she was so weary she could hardly say a
Pater and an *Ave* before she fell into a delicious and dreamless
leep, as deep as it was gentle.

It was her first love; and she was so suited to it that there
vas no outward sign except for the light of serenity and joy
which appeared in her eyes, in her speech and gestures and in
her physical grace which seemed every day more rapt and
winged and joyful, without relinquishing any of the modesty
nd purity which formed so great a part of it. And if it was
not Donato's first love, at least he had learnt from the
others that he had never felt in any of them what he felt in
his.

It was the last week of August and the first of September,
1943 and after the Ferragosto air-raids, the war seemed to have
disappeared from the Lombard skies, in these days at their
most beautiful. There was a natural and human sense of respite
and physical relief—it was in fact only too human and natural.
Although the war had moved into the Peninsula, it appeared to
be fixed in the unfortunate Mediterranean regions as if it were
to be limited to them and remain remote and unrelated. Any
future which could be conceived or foreseen was only something vague and impending whose very obscurity prevented
you from keeping your mind upon it. A kind of oblivion
affected them all, Gaspare with his clear-sighted activities no
less than Donato Mèrici in a trance of love. It was only
Falaride Narenza who went on preaching and prophesying
and proclaiming the imminence of catastrophe; although

even he had no idea what was coming or whence or how.

In the centre of cyclones there is a peaceful zone which sailors call its 'eye'. And that was how time ran in those days—with enormous speed which appeared to be infinitely slow.

CHAPTER EIGHT

The Eighth of September

On the evening of the 8th of September they had all gathered round the radio to listen to the late news when Narenza said he must be going without waiting to hear it. You didn't want a radio, he said, for the kind of news he was expecting. But meanwhile one of them, either Donato or Gaspare, had switched on and they heard it being announced that the Italian government was asking for an armistice and was ordering the cessation of hostilities and instructing the armed forces to resist any attempt to disarm them. But before anyone could take in its implications, this last warning was greeted by Palaride with a shrug, to which however no one paid any attention.

Their initial surprise at the news could hardly be distinguished from what they felt at the tone of the announcer's voice which was professionally unemotional: and one of the women, Melania or Armida, commented wonderingly on this way of making such an announcement. But Narenza, who was perfectly calm and seemed suddenly abstracted, started to argue: how did they think he ought to do it? Didn't they know there'd been a press-campaign about it? Criticisms of the over-emphatic and truculent tone used by the announcers under Fascism, during the 'unfortunate twenty years'? All the radio-announcers had been changed, and now if they wanted to keep their jobs, they had to sound dispassionate, following Talleyrand's advice to the perfect diplomat, That his face mustn't show what's happening to him, even if it's a

kick on the backside. Dealing with the announcers had been
real progress, an essential and necessary reform of the national
customs. His own tone was unemotional, indeed off-hand, and
made them all uncomfortable. It was one of the women again
who asked what was going to happen now? Italy was out of
the war, he said, the war was over as far as she was concerned.
Gaspare broke in and said that this wasn't the moment to be
funny.

Narenza pretended to be vastly surprised: he didn't know
anything anyway: what would he be likely to know about it?
But he seemed confused and there was something like a
tremor in his voice as he went on that the next thing after an
armistice was peace, that everything was going strictly according to international law and that they must trust in the generosity of the Allies and in German forbearance.

It was obvious that he would have liked someone to interrupt him, but Gaspare made out that he wasn't even listening
and this exasperated him; and he turned round on Gaspare
with a kind of muffled fury and said, Yes, of course, there were
the Germans but they'd leave Italy without provoking military
action from the Italians so as not to find themselves caught
between two fires. And when Gaspare asked him whether he
really believed what he was saying, considering that he'd been
the one to provide some of our troops with that 'secret weapon'
of his, Narenza replied that these were isolated cases of
demoralisation due to a number of circumstances which . .
Well anyway, the order was definite, they'd heard it . . . Don't
surrender your arms, resist anyone. . . .

What arms had they got? asked Gaspare, hardly above a
whisper, and they went on standing round the radio, with an
appearance of intense depression in which shame and grief
played equal parts. And Narenza seemed aggrieved, as if
Gaspare had been bullying him, and started saying that there
was no doubt that their weapons were inadequate, and that
they were bewildered and their morale was low, and that a

he Germans had occupied every city and important position
1 Italy with heavily armed forces, they were in a situation to
•e able to impose a war of extermination. And the English
nd the Americans . . . Donato was searching round for another
tation; and now Narenza seemed to be exasperated with him,
oo, and turned round and asked him: Well, hadn't the Ameri-
ans and the English got anything to say?

Then there was a voice from the receiver: from somewhere
•r other it was broadcasting to the Italians, calling on them to
ise against the Germans. Rise? almost shrieked Narenza.
Vhat with? Pikes? Knives? With Mussolini's famous eight
nillion bayonets? Had whoever it was putting out this line
ver seen a German face to face? Well let the Americans and
English advance and drive north first, and push their opera-
ions to a conclusion. Talk about popular insurrection, calling
•n people to come out on the squares and streets, doesn't make
ense any longer, it's asking them to come out and get slaugh-
ered. The thing was so obvious that an appeal like this made
ou suspect that there was malice or sheer military incapacity
o finish the job, on the part of the Allies, underneath it all.
Otherwise it was the government and the army that they ought
o have called on to resist, and said, We're with you, and done
omething to demonstrate it. If they didn't want to do it and
o couldn't say anything, because it wasn't part of their
•olicy, they could keep their mouths shut. But just to call on
•eople to revolt was mockery, a snare and a delusion, if it
ouldn't be attributed to lack of brains.

That was the very reason, said Gaspare Della Morte coldly,
hat there was nothing else to be done. Narenza stared at him
vith a stupefied expression, and Gaspare added that he
nimself thought that it wasn't a case for barricades, a street-
evolution was out of the question. As he was speaking, he
tared Narenza in the eye, not only as if to read his thoughts
•ut as if he wanted to make sure that Narenza understood,
.nd implying some pact between them. Narenza turned pale

and a cold sweat broke out on his forehead. However, he di
not flinch from the look but asked quite humbly for in
dulgence because he was frightened: but he'd stick to hi
bargains, only, he added, within their agreed limits.

But the humility and the desperation with which he spok
were so genuine that Gaspare, having given him a nod in sig
of acceptance, seemed quite anxious to relieve his mind an
encourage him, and admitted that there was certainly some
thing to be afraid of. It was clear from Falaride's expressio
that he saw that it took generosity and humanity to say this
Alinda came up to the poor soul with tears in her eyes an
gently stroked his hand as if she were trying to comfort hin
and show that she was with him. The other two women an
even Donato began taking the line that after all they mus
still hope, they mustn't be totally pessimistic. But here Gaspar
and Narenza saw completely eye to eye: they must expect th
worst and prepare for it accordingly. And to begin with the
must hide the radio without further loss of time, for fear it wa
requisitioned and they wouldn't be able to go on listening
and they must bury or brick-up all the valuables, as Narenz
had already advised, and some tinned foods as well, sinc
raids and looting were possible. In his excitement, Narenz
now became full of zeal, and kept on repeating in a way whicl
would have been pathetic if it hadn't been funny—that the
mustn't only expect everything to go badly, they must prepar
for the worst. Meanwhile, in the distance, from village street
and houses scattered around the countryside, they could hea
sounds of celebration, for people had left their doors open o
the mild September night. One of the servants came in an
said that the peasants were all rushing down to the village inn
to celebrate being out of the war. They had even lit a bonfir
and there were fireworks and dancing in the market-place
When they stood out on the meadow they could actually se
bonfires and coloured lights and flames leaping: and th
singing and rejoicing echoed in the distance.

As Donato said, it made you furious that they were rejoicing
nd yet touched you at the same time. And Armida added
ausingly that she didn't know whether this was just a wish or
whether it was a hope, but there was something so human
bout their rejoicing that it must make for respect or at any
ate envy even in the maniacs who always wanted to go on
ghting. But she broke off, abashed by a sardonic laugh from
Narenza and by Gaspare's contemptuous silence. The serene
arkness of the starry night was full of the fragrance of
ummer passing over into autumn, while September was still
varm and dry on the stubble-fields and ripe in orchard and
ineyard. It was the moment of full vigour just before decline
when the innumerable sounds of insect life with which the
atense short nights of summer are aquiver were growing
ainter, with the days sloping towards the equinox, and with
aost of the birds—especially the ones which are most vocal
a the mating-season—silent in their nests or only to be heard
iping and cooing in short scattered bursts. And against all
ais Falaride's screech of laughter sounded exactly like one of
aose shrieks from some nocturnal bird of prey which shatter
ae stillness of the air or the singing and gaiety of nights of
estivity and love, spreading an anxious and ill-omened silence
a the woods.

Falaride repeated that everything would go from bad to
vorse: and when on top of all the long-drawn-out miseries
nd sufferings of the war there were new and worse ones which
aight last even longer, and when want and hunger and hate
nd fear had made the people drunk with revenge and lust,
vhich were natural and fundamental instincts, they'd see how
aose nice healthy peace-loving peasants who were so simple-
earted with their feasting and singing and dancing and fire-
vorks would start to pick up what they could, even at Vill'
Alma. First of all war, he said, and then civil war, and that
ecessarily implies brigandage, rapine and revenge: and of all
ae varieties of war that's the simplest and most natural, the

least lying and hypocritical. That's what the history book
teach, he said, but who pays any attention to them? Mean
while they'd better bury anything they valued and keep
completely dark from all the dear good people and the
domestic staff who were so utterly trustworthy.

What had they got to be revengeful about? Donato wante
to know, more disgusted than angry at this prophecy: he wa
about to add that he knew these people and they were fir
courageous people and he had played with many of them wh
were the villa's tenants, as a boy in his summer holidays, b
he refrained for fear of making Narenza laugh. Anyway, h
was shouting already: What for? Poverty and ignorance an
envy—revenge on the rich and the educated and the peop
with something to envy. And don't let them start quotin
Solomon and making out that wealth and wisdom don't mak
you so happy as you might think: it's quite enough that the
make for envy and hatred in those who haven't got them. An
he came down from Solomon to the poet Stecchetti, with
great rush: Stecchetti, he said, was a brainless idiot but it
just that sort of brainless idiot who would manage to summa:
ise social progress as accurately as he had done, and also s
prophetically—'Onwards with torch and axe,' he'd said.

At this point Melania and Donato broke in on his harangu
and requested him not to talk beside the point because the
could both tell him with a clear conscience that they had alway
treated their tenants with generosity and benevolence and,
need arose, with charity: and that this was common knowledg

Narenza said that generosity, benevolence, charitablene:
and good conscience were just the very luxuries they woul
want to be revenged on: and the word made him start shiverin
again, while he went on with his Jeremiad: it was the horn
dirty hands wanting revenge on the soft clean ones: and ever
body knew this and if you didn't it was because you didn
want to know. After all they'd had twenty years full of prom
ises and tremendous illusions from a government which ha

failed and had collapsed after losing a war—and what a war—and who was going to make it up to the people for those twenty years?

Here both Donato and his mother protested even more fiercely: nobody could accuse them or even suspect them of having benefited by the Fascist government or ever wanting it: and they'd wanted the war even less; if anyone, it was the people who had cried up the imaginary victories and been taken in by them.

But Narenza hedged and said talking politics with women and artists was sheer waste of breath. And what if the people had been enthusiastic about the victories? Of course they had: and if the war had been won they would have been even more enthusiastic, and just for this reason they'd revenge themselves both in the applause given and for the hand clappings that proved unjustified. And would they mind if he said that he was neither a woman nor an artist and so he understood things as they are. Even conscience, which they'd appealed to, was a luxury of the privileged classes, a kind of 'spiritual white bread' which encouraged hatred and vengeance.

Donato turned off the annoyance he felt at this effrontery into sarcasm and tried to tell him that he was studying chemistry now instead of music but the irritating creature said that it must be some fantastic kind of chemistry, more like alchemy or astrology. Nevertheless, he concluded, that was something he liked him for, in a genuinely affectionate tone which made them laugh and forgive him for having first been impudent and now patronising. And he said that he only spoke to them as he was doing to warn them, and for their own good, because as far as he was concerned nobody was going to look for him and he was quite content if he came through the war and the revolutions with four tanks and sixteen drums of petrol as a start for making his fortune. But for them it wouldn't be so easy to hide or keep safe.

But Donato protested that they had neither wish nor need

o

to go into hiding: and both he and Melania repeated that they
had never approved of Fascism nor wanted the war.

One of Falaride's oddities was that, when other means of
venting his fury failed him, he would let out a sharp and very
prolonged whistle. He whistled now: and he said that there
was a fundamental principle which they ought to keep well in
mind: that when it became a matter of bad luck rather than
good to belong to an élite or a ruling class . . .

Donato broke in with a laugh: as far as they were concerned
they'd never ruled anything. At this Falaride whistled again
even more piercingly: and he said that that was just what you
paid through the nose for. If they'd never tried to rule that
meant they belonged to the class where you have to pay for
not having been able to keep the whole dinner-service rather
than for the pieces which had got broken. To change the
metaphor, if you lost the game the people could sometimes be
merciful and make allowances for mistakes and having bad
cards, but if anyone had the cool cheek to say that he knew
the whole pack and the cards that everyone held, and knew
how the game was going to go, the people—or history if you
liked that better—would see that he was sorry for having done
nothing about it and sorry he'd spoken, and that he'd been in
the know and couldn't act—but more than anything for his
cool cheek. Ask Gaspare Della Morte if it wasn't so and if it
wasn't true that Donato Mèrici standing there in front of them
now, would get the same answer from history as Badoglio
and Victor Emmanuel and for that matter the whole Grand
Fascist Council which had exonerated Mussolini and let him
off when he'd let the whole dinner-service get smashed.

Gaspare emerged from his silence and said that it was so, but
that he didn't personally see the necessity of joining in the
discussion when Narenza's tongue was already running away
with him.

With genuine humility and without the slightest shadow of
resentment, Narenza replied that it was only because he really

had Donato's interests at heart and wanted to convince him
that he absolutely must go into hiding until it became clear
in what his military obligations consisted.

Put in these terms, the thing played directly on Melania's
maternal feelings and this could be heard in her tone of voice
when she said to her son that Narenza might be right. She
added anxiously that surely they were at least entitled to hope
that the Germans would yield to the inevitable and the force
of evidence and would ask for peace terms themselves: and that
at least they might limit themselves to defending their own
territory.

Narenza said nothing, with an air of being tactful, and the
others were silent too, but it was the kind of silence which is
a way of answering questions which don't really merit it, and
therefore seemed unpleasant and offensive. And for this
reason it was broken again by Narenza who said that the kind
of wisdom she hoped from the Germans wasn't one that could
be hoped for even from the other side; that even if the Germans were to ask for peace, the others would refuse it; that the
American and English aeroplanes would clear the way for
Soviet armour at least as far as . . .

The Vistula? interrupted Melania.

The Spree, said Narenza, if they stopped even there. And
moreover there was nothing less like wisdom than to rely on
the wisdom of the clever people who had the job of ruling the
world because they weren't guided by wisdom but by instinct
and necessity and both these factors remains obscure and
unsettled, until events themselves emerged to show which
way they were going, and whatever it was it was never one
that had been foreseen or desired.

Melania anxiously insisted: did he mean that the last word
hadn't yet been spoken? And Donato said that both the first
and the last word had already been spoken. Wilhelm II had
said the first one at the beginning of the war: oh yes, everything had already begun in 1914. What he'd said was 'The

world is out of joint: oh cursed spite, that ever I was born to
set it right!' which was the sort of bombast you might expect
from that sort of swelled head. In answer to that, Hitler had
said the last word: 'God forgive me the last quarter of an hour
of this war', which if he didn't believe in God, was sheer
desperation and which, if he was alluding to some secret
weapon, was just fatuous. God forgive him indeed, not only
the last quarter of an hour of the war but the next ten or the
next hundred years of the peace which was going to follow
it: God forgive everybody, but perhaps even His mercy wasn't
enough to go round.

Well anyway, said Gaspare Della Morte, that both he and
Donato would have to hide themselves for the time being was
an obvious fact. Narenza shrugged his shoulders and said that
that was the only thing he'd been trying to impress on them
and he'd got quite dry in the process. And Melania sent for a
bottle of white wine and an ice-bucket whereupon Narenza
advised her in the strongest terms to see that even the bottles
were bricked up or hidden because they were the first things
the troops looked for when there was a war on and so did 'the
dear good people' when there was a revolution—the regulars
and the man on the barricades, they were all the same, they'd
all got light fingers, he said.

Before noon the next day and for several days after, reports
began coming in about the Italian military collapse, the
dispersion of the army, and deportations into Germany, and
later about how Mussolini had been caught on the Gran Sasso
and forced to resume the leadership which he did very un-
willingly, until with the news of Hitler's secret weapons he got
back enough of his old rash precipitancy to proclaim their
existence to the world. This was in the winter of 1945 at the
Lyric Theatre in Milan a few months before the United States
were to show Japan that they really possessed them and that
they were ready for use. We may now add that referring to the
Duce's triumphant reception when he made his announcement

Falaride Narenza summarised his view of humankind by saying that he'd seen quite as many people rush to acclaim Mussolini when they thought he was on top again as rushed to jeer at his outraged corpse six months later on Piazzale Loreto. And later, he said, there'd be a third phase when you wouldn't be able to find a soul who was willing to remember that he'd happened to be present even by chance either at the triumphant reception or on the Piazzale. But that would be to go outside the bounds of the tragic story of Alma' Dannata which never got as far as the events which provoked this misanthropic commentary. This may make some readers ask why ever it is that Narenza's sombre and desultory kind of worldly wisdom has been given so much prominence in this narrative. The reason may be that the events, in so far as he witnessed and took part in them, were recounted by Narenza himself. And it's well known that all witnesses—especially if they were actively concerned—are always most lavishly circumstantial about their own part in an event. Having said that, we need only add that when he told the tragic story, Falaride suggested that when it was put down in writing, an attempt should be made to preserve that accent of human truth which is equally remote from the soaring rhetorical flights used to celebrate victory as from the groveling circumstantiality which harps on defeat. Bombast and deflation are both kinds of exaggeration. According to Narenza, what was valuable in the story of Alma' Dannata was that its inhabitants hadn't been either superhuman heroes nor subhuman vermin.

Meanwhile, in spite of the terrible events which took place, the breakdown of the Fascist state, the escape of the government and the king, the Fascist return to power and the shootings which followed on the Verona trial, with all the consequences of the difficult long-drawn-out war in Italy, those autumn days of 1943 moving from event to event, seemed days of exhaustion and oblivion; the events indeed seemed gradually to become confused with each other, as if they had lost substance. This was partly the result of the stupefying effect of weariness and anxiety, but it can be due to the fact that events are so grave in themselves and in their consequences that men feel that there is something in them altogether beyond human power of comprehension and endurance, of action and thought.

At Vill' Alma, they all had their individual ways of suffering and absorbing the slow poison of this time of indolence which although it was actually so fleeting seemed endless. Neither Melania nor Armida were to see the time when the Allies would overcome German resistance and bring their anxieties, either as mother or lover, to an end: but since one of them couldn't bear to hear anything said about Allied victories and advances even when they were actual, and the other tortured herself about difficulties and defeats even when they weren't, the result was that they had no other subject of conversation and were always waiting for news and war-rumours. And both of them got bitterly angry with the young Alinda who was the only one of them who listened calmly to the news, for Donato found that love wasn't enough to keep him well and he had relapsed into alternating fits of apathy and anxiety and seemed equally insatiable for news and unable to put up with it—when it was encouraging it must be misleading, and when it was bad it reduced him to despair. Moreover, although he listened to the radio for hours and gathered what he could from Narenza in his secret comings-and-goings, or from deserters, great numbers of whom had fled into the country, or from the local peasants with whom he spent a great deal of time in weary and meaningless talk, the greater part of what he heard was so silly that he was surprised at himself for having talked or listened, and came to a point of miserable and idle inanition in which he could have wished to go back to his music, if his inclination, never real, had not revealed itself as more exhausted and dried-up than ever. So he passed the time wretchedly, continually irritated himself and continually irritating other people, always contradicting himself and everyone else except Alinda, whose silent companionship soothed him, because it was full of her love and compassion: but they had to be by themselves: and this became rare when September came to an end and they could no longer take long walks in the country round about: for with the misty October weather the wood-fires had to be lit in the loggia, which was the only place kept heated. When the thrushes began to migrate they had an old spring-net mended and went fowling with a decoy-bird and nets. And then this came to an end too. Narenza in the style of Machiavelli would have called it the 'Strange and savage pastime' if he hadn't had something else to think about with his business affairs which called for increasing attention and activity and were doing better all the time.

And now even Della Morte had practically nothing to say—not only about politics but about what was actually happening. They hardly saw him and when they did it was only for a short time and purely formally. Donato, although he couldn't blame his friend for having so little time to spare and for being so reserved, was seized with an obsessive spite, and felt offended and obliged to torment himself about it as if it meant negligence or contempt or even mistrust. Knowing quite well how absurd it was, he would make out that Della Morte was trying to persuade him to join the underground movement in spite of being quite well aware that they wouldn't admit anyone who had got into his mental and nervous condition: and in spite of knowing, too, that even if he were invited he would refuse—this of course reveals not only his sick man's illogicality but his sense of guilt. And though he was convinced that Gaspare was doing his duty and risking worse things than death for the only useful contribution which he or any other Italian could make to help their discredited nation in its humiliation and ruin, the fact was that secretly (and it was secret because he couldn't explain or admit it to himself) he was repelled both by the activity and its necessity.

A sort of disgust and a contemptuous pride entered into

this resistance—it was not only the effect of being honestly aware that he was unequal to the task and ill-suited to it: but his melancholy and apathy, his very despair and disgust seemed to him to have some exquisitely rare and metaphysical quality, something sublime like Hamlet's. To take part in events or to be troubled by them struck him as not only irrelevant but almost blasphemous compared with his solemn and preferred image of peaceful death which would consummate his helpless self-torturing imagination in its emptiness of purpose. When there was so much travail and suffering already in the world, even to think of adding anything to the burden, either his own or that of others, made him sick and shaken, both physically and mentally, and so with all effort, desire or activity. These periods of abstract contemplation had a dual effect: on the one hand he would find himself descending into vulgar and practical calculation: how unlikely it was that anything useful would come out of these conspiracies and guerrilla-movements —of the partisans, as they were beginning to be called—while what was certain was the multiplicity of errors and what was inevitable was hatefulness: and on the other hand his antipathy to them degenerated into a commonplace intellectual vanity in which he felt himself a chosen spirit who had to preserve the pattern and ideal of a lofty vocation which though it was impotent was, just in this, the victim both of the brutish cruelty of the times and of its own refinement. In short, so as not to have to admit that he was a weak, tired man, which would have been honest, he struck an attitude and began to see himself as an artist, and a most unhappy one, the victim and martyr of an exquisitely ironical fate.

Certainly Gaspare did not trouble to understand him or to ask him for anything. As for asking him to take part in what he was doing, Gaspare was so far from giving any thought to the matter that he never even wondered whether he had it in him. Thus it was that he managed to hurt Donato who was already so apt to find ways of hurting himself. And he discovered more than one indication that even Falaride was much more in Gaspare's confidence than he was himself. Within strict limits, in fact, Della Morte found Falaride useful; for instance, for getting information and for providing illegal transport which Falaride let him have with all the demurrals which were necessary to make it look as if he had had actually to submit to what is known as *force majeure*.

Rather meanly Donato was even more infuriated because a good deal of this secret manœuvring was perfectly well known to everyone else in the neighbourhood, so that he got to know what was going on only from casual contacts: and this was the only way he found out that some of the resistance in the mountains had arms: and that at a prisoner-of-war camp for English and colonials, where the prisoners were working on the construction of a dam up among these same hills, they had been helped to get away and hide and then to make their way to the coast or southwards or into Switzerland: and that there had been signalling and radio-communication with allied aircraft which often reconnoitred the zone by night. But among all these people who were so well-informed, there was not one who knew anything about Gaspare, and the very fact that they took so much trouble to avoid mentioning his name, even to Donato, was proof to him that they all knew perfectly well that he was at Vill' Alma. In his worst moods, Donato forecast that things would come to a bad end for everybody, no matter what precautions Gaspare took—keeping himself out of the way, never going out except disguised and then only at night, while he had even laid in a stock of provisions so as to be able to shut himself away for a while without any communication with the outside world. It has already been mentioned that he had a wireless receiver: there was automatic signalling apparatus for guiding aircraft concealed in the woods: and they constantly shifted the position of the radio transmitter so that it should not be found and seized if the men who transmitted Gaspare's messages should be captured. At other times, when

he was bad tempered or bored, these clandestine arrangement
seemed to Donato to be carried out with excessive precautions
it made him feel spiteful and he grumbled to himself that th
Germans had plenty of other things to think about—they'
either win the war on the Italian front and a great many othe
ones too, or they'd lose it on all the lot: and one way or th
other the resistance movement wouldn't count very much. H
said this once to Gaspare—against his will they had got in
volved in a sharp discussion—and Gaspare replied that h
might have forgotten the rest of his Latin but not the ta;
about the martyrs, *Fidem firmavit sanguine*: and there was tha
other saying they'd been taught too, about not loving life s
much that you lost any reason for living. There was a caln
clarity as well as firmness and modesty about his way of saying
this which Donato found humiliating and he was misguided
enough to think that it was meant to be insulting and con
temptuous.

BOOK III
DAMAGED SOULS

CHAPTER ONE

1) DONATO MÈRICI, MELANIA MÈRICI, ARMIDA LENAI and ALINDA NARENZA

MELANIA: I sometimes feel I can't stand it any longer: I feel the war's never going to end.

ARMIDA: You lose all hope and confidence: you get desperate with the way it drags on. And only a few months ago, in the early days when they were landing at Salerno, how hopeful we all were!

DONATO: Gaspare would say that endless complaining doesn't help to end anything.

ARMIDA: There's nothing else *we* can do.

DONATO: And it's not much.

MELANIA: It's worse than nothing.

ARMIDA: Gaspare manages to do more.

DONATO: Even he can't do very much.

MELANIA: But anyway, while we wait for it all to end, you oughtn't to expose yourself so much. Once again I beg and pray you . . .

DONATO: And, mother, once again I ask you—what am I exposing myself to? What *are* these great dangers?

MELANIA: If I knew I shouldn't be so afraid of them. But they say . . .

DONATO: You know what they say round these parts: 'In war-time, lies are thicker than facts.'

MELANIA: And now there's the new Fascist government at Salò, and it must be in control of three-quarters of the country by now. . . .

DONATO: In control. . . .

MELANIA: It's shown itself powerful enough to put people to death when they were running both the party and the state only a short time ago.

DONATO: But it's the others who allow them their powers—or force them to use them—isn't it the Germans?

MELANIA: What does that matter to me? And now there's this call-up order for everyone who's liable for military service.

DONATO: It's one thing to give the orders and another to get anybody to obey them. It's one thing to wipe out a small number or even, for that matter, a large number of people who've neither following nor even influence or credit left anywhere; it's another to get involved in conflict with a whole country—in every town and village down to every house and hillside and thicket—for there's only one thing which would really make people revolt and that would be if there were any attempt to carry out the order now that passionate resistance to the war has become a personal and family matter among the whole population. Alinda, why do you keep looking out of the window as though you expected someone?

ALINDA: God help us!

MELANIA: Donato, what you're saying is all just words. . . .

DONATO: You needn't be in such a hurry to say that! In good times or bad, the Italians have very strong family feeling and today you may say there isn't anything else they do feel.

MELANIA: Don't be in such a hurry yourself! If people resist the order and some of them are arrested and brought to trial and shot, do you imagine anyone will revolt any more than they did for the people who were shot at Verona?

DONATO: But their condemnation was a political example however unlucky it was for them.

MELANIA: And wouldn't it be the same with you—and a handful like you. . . . I can't bear to say it. . . .

DONATO: You mean, of the ruling-classes? Oh yes, I'm a great one at ruling. I'm more interested in what you're looking for out there, Alinda.

ALINDA: Why don't you listen to your mother?

MELANIA: Because I'm right and he knows it!

DONATO: Can you tell me one thing? Why they should be looking for me in particular when there are so many others and only this very minute my mother's been saying that I don't matter to anyone?

MELANIA: Oh Donato, you're just trying to torment me or else you're just benighted with your mania for contradiction.

DONATO: Well, you illuminate me. Alinda . . .

ARMIDA: Since Melania's so squeamish I'll have to say it for her. They might come—not so much to look for you, Donato, as for someone else: and if they didn't find him they might take you in reprisals or as a hostage, and moreover, I can't think why you want to make out that you haven't understood and still don't. I can tell you—and in fact I have Gaspare Della Morte's authority for doing it—that he thinks himself that you oughtn't to expose yourself so much, and that you even ought to go right away across the Swiss border.

DONATO: Who does he think he is? The schoolmaster? And how many other people are poking their noses into my affairs? I see what it is well enough: it's the conscientious man of action, the responsible leader, telling the waster, with no conscience and no sense of responsibility, what to do. All very magnanimous, very kind. But couldn't I say that I serve a useful purpose just by being so thoughtless and heedless? I may draw off their suspicions from this house— and so from Gaspare while he's hiding here.

ARMIDA: Forgive me: I should say that was sophistry—or trying to be funny when it's out of place.

DONATO: Either would be out of place. I can see that too. Well, I'll keep out of the way more and if things take a turn for the worse I'll ask Gaspare to help me get across the frontier.

You see, Armida, I haven't got patience and endurance
I haven't got the sort of fibre which is needed in these days
but if it came down to shooting I think I could do that: an
it would even be a relief if I got one in the head, provide
it was a good shot and finished me off.

MELANIA and ARMIDA: Don't talk such horrors!

ARMIDA: No one doubts that you've got courage—that kin
of courage.

DONATO: Doesn't Gaspare?

ARMIDA: Less than anyone.

DONATO: You think that out of kindness, Armida. But . . .

ARMIDA: I have his authority for it. He actually charged m
to tell you.

DONATO: Well and good, that means I'm under a mora
obligation to do what you ask, Mother. I'll take care an
not let myself be seen about any more. You can keep you
gratitude to yourself, Mother: even that was beside th
point, for, you see, I shan't be doing it for you, so yo
needn't be grateful.

MELANIA: You've got very little idea what it feels like to be
mother, my boy, if you think one's capable of that sort o
distinction. However all that signifies now is that yo
should keep your word and be careful.

(2) DONATO MÈRICI and ALINDA NARENZA

DONATO: Alinda, I still want to know why every time w
mentioned the word danger you started looking out of th
window. But at least there's one thing to the good—
whether there are any real dangers or not, we shan't have t
talk about them any more: that's certainly something gaine
And now my mother's gone you needn't have any difficult
in answering me.

ALINDA: If you knew the hours I spend—and have spen

waiting and watching for you to come back. But you really
are going to keep away from the village and off the roads
now, not let yourself be seen about?

DONATO: I've promised my mother. Do you want me to
promise you too, Alinda?

ALINDA: Who am I?

DONATO: Who are you? Do you mean for me?

ALINDA: Don't say it.

DONATO: And why not?

ALINDA: It would be so sweet just to dream it, so sweet to
imagine that it's true. If you speak, you'll break the spell:
let it go on just for the time being. And you see I'm guilty
even about that. I'm not quite so thoughtless that I can't
see what a terrible time this is: so full of anxiety and stress
and fear: but for me it's a time of dreams and happiness.
I know it must come to an end: I know that I ought really
to pray God to put an end to it quickly; oh it's all so sad. Do
you know what it is that makes *me* anxious? Only that this
time *will* come to an end like a dream that was too beautiful
to last. And I shall spend all the rest of my days remembering
these and regretting and longing for them. But why do you
let me go on? Why don't you stop me.

DONATO: Stop you? If I were the artist I might have been and
may perhaps be yet, I'd write the music for those words
you've been saying. What you might tell me is why you
didn't go on yourself? I was saying nothing: you'd told me
yourself to be silent: and I was listening: it was so sweet:
and even I was imagining . . .

ALINDA: The music for it. Really?

DONATO: Oh yes, the most beautiful music.

ALINDA: Ah well, music isn't life: it has nothing at all to do
with things as they are.

DONATO: Oh why did you stop? And why do you talk like
this now?

ALINDA: So as not to have to say anything about things as

they really are. Anyway, must we? Is it necessary? Don'
they force themselves on us on their own?

DONATO: Nevertheless, music is beautiful, even sad, despairing
music.

ALINDA: You see how remote we are from each other? You'v
been a bit attentive to me; no, let me say what I've got t
say, even if it seems forward: you were attracted by me
must I say more—you actually fell in love with this poor
simple girl Alinda. Oh, I don't say you meant anything
mean or bad. I think enough of myself, I've got enough self
respect, not even to admit that anyone could possibly thin]
lightly of me or treat me without respect. And yet after all
the way I grew up, it wasn't beautiful sad music or just
flower-garden, I know life as it is for a poor working girl
When you've got nothing else in the world but a pair o
fine eyes . . . anyway that's what they tell me, that they'r
not bad.

DONATO: They're astounding, they're marvellous!

ALINDA: Yes, we know, without compare!

DONATO: Absolutely unique!

ALINDA: If that's how you feel about it! But if you don'
mind me telling you what things are really like, they're not
dowry, all in themselves. Don't say anything. No protesta
tions. please! This is where they all start saying that eye
like mine are more than enough—and to spare.

DONATO: And so I'm the sort that runs after money, am I?
didn't expect that from you!

ALINDA: No, not money.

DONATO: Well, then, girls, I'm a deceiver and out to rui
them, is that it?

ALINDA: Now you're forcing me to explain myself: and if yo
don't like it, it's not my fault.

DONATO: I suppose it's mine?

ALINDA: Alas, it's the fault of circumstances. And what they'r
like, you know as well as I do. But you see, don't you, i

your own way you're cruel and egotistical and cunning. Don't force me to say anything more!

DONATO: Anyway you must say something now to justify all these suspicions and accusations and slanders.

ALINDA: You'd like what I said always to sound like music, maybe sad despairing music, but still beautiful. Oh Donato, isn't it fraud and deception, isn't it cruelty and egoism, even if it's the egoism of an artist and a man in love? You're to have all the sweetness of the dream, all the beautiful sad music: and my part is the despair, despair and silence and desolation, and the hard unadorned reality. And if I were to surrender to the dream, the reality would be not only desolate but shameful. Just ruin and squallor, wouldn't it be, Donato?

DONATO: It's not true. This time . . .

ALINDA: Ah this time! That's another thing they always say, too. Do you want to see me in the headlines like the women who drink lysol or throw themselves out of the window, because they've been disappointed in love?

DONATO: But . . . Alinda?

ALINDA: Donato, don't blame me, blame yourself for making me have to talk like this!

DONATO: Nevertheless, I must say you're insulting me.

ALINDA: I should never have wished to, although I could quite well say that if it had all turned out for me in the usual way, for you, being an artist, it might still mean only a sad despairing music which you could compose in memory of a poor girl who'd been betrayed.

DONATO: But you're so hard, so cruel—and with yourself more than anything!

ALINDA: And are you kind yourself? What you're reproaching me for is that I'm not sleep-walking, that I won't let us just share the same dream. The usual dream: we know how it all ends.

DONATO: Still thinking about dowries?

P

ALINDA: That's even worse: you needn't try to be ironical and contemptuous: you don't know what poverty is.

DONATO: Contemptuous? If only you could see into my heart!

ALINDA: It's because I do see that I talk like this, because I think, because I know, that at present you do feel sincere, passionate, loving; oh yes, what you feel is beautiful—at present.

DONATO: Now and always!

ALINDA: Always! That word's been spoilt. You would say it, and now you force me to tell you that it's easy enough to make a fool of oneself for a pair of eyes like mine, but not so easy to put up with the consequences, when the social distinctions . . .

DONATO: Ah, the social distinctions! I wasn't prepared for that!

ALINDA: That doesn't mean they don't exist, does it? Just because you can set them aside and despise them for the time being, do you think that means they're not important? To begin with, may be, let's even say for some time, just as long as there's only the two of us in the world, and we're living out of the world. But we can't go on being alone, we have to go back to the world: and that's when the distinctions begin to make themselves felt. Look, I may seem egotistical, mean, frightened, I have to risk that: the one who is generous enough not to make them felt, may really not be aware of them, but the other, the one in the inferior position, does feel them, and one day will be conscious of the sacrifice which has been asked for and made, and won't be able to help remembering that generosity which the other has wiped out and forgotten. You can say I'm egotistical and mean, but I'm afraid.

DONATO: In times like these when any kind of social life can completely collapse, how can you give a thought to social distinctions?

ALINDA: Dear Donato, I'm not a bit given to imagination!
And ought you to put your hope and trust in social collapses? What I picture—not having any imagination—is
that social life will settle down again just as it does after all
the collapses. And anyway there's still the difference in
education and habits. You may not make me feel inferior,
but your mother certainly does.

DONATO: Let's put the thing crudely: what makes you feel
inferior is our money: or rather my mother's money,
because, you see, my father didn't have anything of his own
except that old house in Milan and that's been burnt down
now.

ALINDA: Money! You see how loftily you can talk about it—
I never could, because I know what money means, and
you'd never know, even if you were left penniless. And
don't you imagine that it worried your father, being a poor
man married to a rich wife?

DONATO: He didn't have time to realise it. He died young
soon after he was married—and very much in love.

ALINDA: I'm sorry. I didn't know. . . .

DONATO: Oh, it's so long ago. But you see, don't you, the
memory which stayed with my mother from those days was
something which kept her from marrying again, although
she was young and beautiful.

ALINDA: And still is, extremely beautiful.

DONATO: And with your harsh judgment, I suppose, you'd be
capable of saying that she's kept such a beautiful memory of
those days, because they were so short?

ALINDA: I think, and I must say, that your mother is much
more generous and courageous than I am. I'm frightened
myself.

DONATO: Do you know what you are? You're just proud,
unbelievably proud.

ALINDA: And I don't deny it. Rich people show generosity
of spirit in forgetting they're rich and poor people in

remembering that they're poor. Let me have my pride of poverty.

DONATO: It's exaggerated pride.

ALINDA: Does it seem so very strong to you?

DONATO: Exorbitantly. Stronger than love.

ALINDA: No, by my pride you can judge what I pay in pain and suffering and sacrifice—and passion too, Donato. Don't speak to me, Donato, don't make me say any more. Don't force me to run away. . . .

DONATO: Run? Where from? What forces you? Where to?

ALINDA: Away from temptation. And I don't know where. But from here. Run away from what you say to me which I don't know how to resist. Oh Donato, for pity's sake spare me!

DONATO: If you did run away you know I should follow you, I should look for you everywhere. Don't you realise that it's too late? Even if you could run away from me and from yourself, everything we've said, both of us, everything which neither you nor I have said but which our eyes speak and sing with laughter and tears. . . .

ALINDA: Oh Donato, Donato, you're wicked. Have you got so much strength now that there's none left for me?

DONATO: Just listen to what I've got to say, Alinda, you proud creature. . . .

ALINDA: Oh good heavens, proud? Donato, for pity's sake don't look at my mouth like that. I know it's trembling. It's because I'm afraid and ashamed. . . .

DONATO: It isn't shame, it isn't fear. It's . . .

ALINDA: Oh, give me a moment's breathing-space. . . .

DONATO: Stay close to me. Don't look out. Don't run away. Don't push me away, Alinda.

ALINDA: Oh, how unsuited we are! Who are they, who are those men?

DONATO: Who? Where do you mean? What men?

ALINDA: There—on the other side of the meadow . . .

DONATO: Yes I see them. They're soldiers.

ALINDA: Germans? German soldiers! And that's the one in command!

DONATO: Yes, it's an officer. You can see that, even at this distance, by the way he holds himself. But there's nothing to be upset about. Their intentions seem quite peaceful.

ALINDA: Run, Donato, hide.

DONATO: It's not me they're looking for. You go—go at once and warn Armida. She must tell Gaspare to hide and be quick about it. I'll hope to hold them a moment or two.

ALINDA: They're coming. I'm so frightened for you I could die.

DONATO: Don't lose your nerve. Go on. Warn my mother too. And don't let's look upset, they'd suspect something.

ALINDA: My love!

DONATO: My dear heart!

(3) DONATO MÈRICI, HERMANN MUELLER and EGISTO REMORSELLA

MUELLER: Are you the master of the house?

DONATO: No, I'm not.

MUELLER: Then would you mind calling him?

DONATO: I'm not the master, but if you want to speak to me it amounts to the same thing.

REMORSELLA: I know what he's up to with his *is* and his *isn't* and his all-the-sames. He's trying to gain time and waste ours!

MUELLER: I'm in no hurry; and you speak when you're spoken to, Remorsella. Meanwhile sit down.

REMORSELLA: Have I your permission, master or not?

DONATO: Do sit down, as far as I'm concerned.

MUELLER: Let me make myself clear. I gave you permission and that's all that's required, unless my superior officer were here. Anyway it's an order—if that's what you want. Understand? Sit down.

REMORSELLA: You make it all so clear, I can only obey.

MUELLER: Next time be quicker about carrying out orders. And now ask this gentleman to explain his oracle.

REMORSELLA: I'd want an explanation myself first. I don't know where oracles come in.

DONATO: *Ibis redibus non morieris in bello.* Oracles are ambiguous answers.

REMORSELLA: If Latin comes into it too, you'll have to work it out between you.

MUELLER: It's not difficult or unusual Latin.

REMORSELLA: But I don't even remember if I went right through the elementary school!

MUELLER: Never mind. Anyway I see there are a lot of good books about. A cultivated home! Ask the gentleman if what Latin and Roman history they still know in Italy wasn't taught them by German scholars?

REMORSELLA: Is it true? I'm only obeying orders: for all I care . . . is it true?

DONATO: Up to a point. But if it's a question of taking orders from a German soldier I can bow to force and keep my mouth shut. Not if it's a question of stuck-up German pedants and professors.

MUELLER: What do you call this sort of thing in Italian?

REMORSELLA: *Menare il can per l'aia*—Much cry and little wool.

MUELLER: A vivid phrase. Anyway a certain gift for racy expression is the last thing a people loses. In fact, poverty and subjection are always very expressive and vocal, whether it's in the form of wit or pathos. *Galgenhumor* is what we call it, gallowshumour. If the slaves owned by the Roman capitalists had had the courage to write on the walls of the *ergastula* we should have had some curious documentary evidence. It's what they say about the ghetto Jews who were first-class at making up biting epigrams and witticisms. This gentleman has read so many books he must know the famous Spengler and he'll know what I mean when I tell him that now they've been reduced to fellaheen, the descendents of the ancient Egyptian conquerors probably beguile their fatigue and boredom and servitude while they draw the Nile-water and work the irrigation-system, with the same fanciful and satirical sayings as the ones the ancient Hebrews of the time of Joseph and Moses used to exchange while they were making bricks for Pharaoh.

DONATO: However . . .

REMORSELLA: However? No *howevers* about it!

MUELLER: Don't you dare speak for me again: don't let it so much as enter your head! But when you said 'However', you no doubt meant that the Italians aren't yet in the condition of the Egyptian fellaheen, didn't you? That depends on how they behave towards us.

DONATO: I meant that to be conquered and humiliated demands compassion, if not charity, and so does servitude, even if its ignominious.

MUELLER: Compassion is a virtue of slaves and at one time the weak succeeded in imposing it on the strong—but that abuse is ended.

DONATO: In the strong, the happy and the victorious it's a virtue to show consideration for the weak, the unhappy and the defeated.

MUELLER: We're strong, but we're not yet victorious and happy. When your misfortune and unhappiness are quite complete we might even be compassionate. In the meantime, you're just former Allies who've betrayed Germany.

DONATO: And Italy, too.

MUELLER: That depends.

DONATO: I can be forced to hold my tongue—not to speak.

MUELLER: Suppose I asked you to, what would you say?

DONATO: That if I were an Italian soldier I should have betrayed Italy, because I don't know how to fight for her.

MUELLER: Very subtle; another oracle! You mean that your duty would be fighting: with us or against us you don't say. Do you get the oracle, Remorsella?

REMORSELLA: I've explained already—I'm too ignorant.

MUELLER: Anyway it's nothing to do with me. I've no orders or instructions about the Italian military.

DONATO: As if they didn't exist, eh?

MUELLER: Something of the sort. If they do, it's a kind of existence which only affects themselves.

DONATO: *Propter vitam vivendi perdere causam.*

REMORSELLA: What, Latin again? You can see they're educated people in this house. All those books!

DONATO: Oh, that's not difficult or unusual Latin either.

MUELLER: No, but it's true there are a lot of books and what's more important, a very fine selection.

DONATO: Is it a soldier or a man of letters I'm talking to? Are we in the Teutoburger Wald with Arminius or sitting on the benches of a German university?

MUELLER: You say. Which do you think?

DONATO: That would be surrender without fighting. Spiritual on top of physical compulsion—it's too much.

MUELLER: Anyway, I'm speaking as a soldier now. Remorsella, as this isn't the master go and find whoever is.

DONATO: Don't trouble. I'll go myself.

REMORSELLA: The fact is he's trying to gain time and waste ours.

DONATO: The fact is that it is a lady who owns the house and it seems to me that a lady's entitled to consideration. Unless we're under suspicion and you're claiming the right to use force. Even so I must ask to go and warn her; it's my mother.

MUELLER: Granted: we don't suspect you more than any other ex-ally. And provided you obey my orders, we'll co-operate in a friendly way.

DONATO: And what are your friendly orders?

MUELLER: They're simple: my men are quartered in the village: I'm moving in with my batman and two telephonists. Out of consideration for the lady I shan't make any more disturbance than is necessary but of course it's understood that I shall take the rooms I like best. It'll be most agreeable to have a holiday in this delicious spot after two summers in Africa and a winter in Russia—like Tityrus I shall be able to say *Deus nobis haec otia fecit*. Meanwhile . . .

REMORSELLA: I'm going now.

MUELLER: No, we can wait. We don't want to upset or frighten the lady. But here she is, if I'm not mistaken. Isn't it so?

DONATO: Yes, here she is.

MUELLER: Extremely distinguished!

4) DONATO MÈRICI, HERMANN MUELLER, EGISTO REMOR-SELLA, MELANIA MÈRICI, ARMIDA LENAI and ALINDA NARENZA

MUELLER: Good day, Signora . . .

REMORSELLA: Mèrici, Signora Melania Mèrici.

MUELLER: I needn't apologise for disturbing you since I'm here on duty. Your son already knows what's to be done and can tell you. To go on with a pleasant little joke which he started, I may say that I'm Arminius, not Brennus who was a stupid Celt anyway.

MELANIA: If you find it easier to speak your own language, my son and I both speak German.

MUELLER: That much I know from these books: but I like to practise my Italian.

DONATO: Especially as we've had to learn most of our Italian philology and history from the Germans, too.

MUELLER: You don't like that?

DONATO: I've no feelings one way or the other: and it's even partly true—or was.

MELANIA: Well then, Signor . . .

MUELLER: *Hauptmann* Hermann Mueller.

REMORSELLA: The Italian is *Capitano. Hauptmann, Capitano.*

MUELLER: Nobody is in need of your erudition: but my name seems to surprise you, Signora?

MELANIA: But . . . why should it?

MUELLER: You made a startled gesture. And yet Mueller is one of the commonest German names—like Meyer.

MELANIA: Well, that's just why I was surprised.

MUELLER: This isn't the first time this has happened to me.

DONATO: What's there to be surprised at, Mother?

MELANIA: If I said, it might look like flattery or showing-off

MUELLER: You can say it: I shouldn't suspect anything of the sort. It often happens to me: and let me assure you, Signora it doesn't turn my head, I don't get any frivolous or worldly satisfaction out of it. Do you know Germany?

REMORSELLA: Does she know it? Why she's even got relatives there.

MUELLER: *Donnerwetter!* If you interrupt me again, I'll teach you to behave yourself! However, to return to our selves, . . . I'm well aware that my name doesn't go with my appearance.

MELANIA: Actually I did expect an aristocratic name.

MUELLER: Baronen or Freiherren von Rhein or von Branden burg or Pomerania, or the Pripet Marshes, Baltic Baron descended from the Teutonic Knights, isn't that it?

MELANIA: Yes, something of that sort.

MUELLER: I know, something heraldic and historical and noble. And instead it's Mueller, plain Mueller and there are thousands of Meyers, and that's just what I'm proud of.

DONATO: May I ask why?

MUELLER: No difficulty at all. If there's a country—Germany to be precise and more particularly Prussia where I was born—where plebeians who, like myself, are sons of plebeians, are being born with the moral and physical

characteristics which at one time distiguished an unap-
proachable and exclusive aristocracy, it means that these
characteristics are becoming general: they're no longer
aristocratic, in fact, they're popular, no longer a matter of
class but national, no longer merely cultural, they're in the
blood and stock. I'm talking about innate, instinctive,
hereditary characteristics: characteristics of style which
you're born with and can't acquire—except after many
generations.

DONATO: I ought to have known!

MUELLER: What?

DONATO: Blood-and-soil mysticism grafted on to the old
military and scholastic pride would produce a eugenic
theory.

MUELLER: I'm not talking about eugenics but about a spontaneous mutation, which becomes innate. For instance isn't
it a fact that for centuries good manners and excitability have
both been more or less inborn with the French? And there's
the English genius for politics and colonisation and trade and
navigation? And aren't the Italians artistically gifted,
especially in melody and sense of form? And we Germans
have a natural bent for forcefulness if now it's become a
matter of style, it means we're developing into a people
who have a right to aspire to power and domination.

DONATO: And to *Lebensraum!*

MUELLER: *Lebensraum!* That's a pauper's idea! space for conquest, dominion, pride of life! *Imperium!*

DONATO: I see. The *Herrenvolk*.

MUELLER: Precisely: a master-race. And that's exactly what's
implied by the fact that I'm called Mueller, and that I'm the
son of modest middle-class professional workers, and the
grandson of artisans and the great-grandson of peasants
and the descendant of feudal serfs. Nowadays a Mueller
can be born with the same manners and feelings, the same
kind of body and mind, the same instincts and bents as if he

were of the blood of the Counts and Margraves and princes who founded the Mark of Brandenburg, the Kingdom of Prussia, among the rivers and woods and right into the marshes, where I may have had ancestors among those savages whom the Knights of the Sword and the Teutonic Knights used to hunt for sport, as if they were wild water-fowl or forest-game.

DONATO: And idolators and heathen into the bargain.

MUELLER: Oh converting the natives to Christianity was a mere formality. The Knights conquered them after they'd thrown away the dream of the Crusades, just as the Hohen-zollerns built the Prussian State after they'd freed themselves from subjection to papal and catholic Rome. Luther's theology had the same significance as the Cross carried by the Knights of the Sword, and in any case, as I and my like understand things, having freed ourselves from every vestige and symbol of Christianity, the German of today doesn't carry a cross any longer, he only bears a sword.

DONATO: Doesn't he even have a crooked cross, not even a Swastika?

MUELLER: Not even that.

DONATO: So strictly speaking, you're not a Nazi?—you didn't originate in the Hitler Youth?

MUELLER: My origins are much deeper and darker than that. Even Hitler is both mystical doctrinaire and practical politician, both cause and means, which are necessarily transitory: the means can fall short and the cause can be set aside both before or after they fulfil their task or arrive at the goal for which they were intended. If you're still in need of a philosophical formula, I should be a pure existentialist —using the term in its fullest force—if I weren't a pure German—using that term also with all its force.

DONATO: And where does it get its force?

MUELLER: You know that already: in the art and practice of war, in the sword of a warrior people, to whom—maybe you don't know it but it doesn't matter—the life of what, with great vagueness and want of definition, is called Europe—has been entrusted. Anyway, if we have to perish, Europe will perish with us and so will the world dominion of the European white race and it will be split between the Anglo-Saxon Americans and the Asiatic Slavs. Meanwhile Europe submits to us and hates us and we tolerate Europe and despise her. Do you want any more?

DONATO: Nothing—or at least not much: you seem—if I understand you rightly—to admit the possibility of a German defeat?

MUELLER: One? ten. And not merely a defeat but a total rout.

DONATO: We know. One wins and the other loses.

MUELLER: That's mere worldly wisdom, Man-in-the-Street Machiavellism. If you go to war first with the idea of winning you don't even make a good adventurer, you're a mercenary, a mere war-usurer, a common profiteer. The tragic nobility of war is in the conscious acceptance of danger, in meeting it with one's head firm and unbowed.

DONATO: So that total defeat . . .

MUELLER: Yes, as at Jena a century and a half ago or at Verdun thirty years ago. . . .

DONATO: Or like the Teutons two thousand years back when Marcus bled them to death, and the Teutonic Knights six centuries ago at Tannenberg.

MUELLER: I see you know your German history. Yes, the Knights, the heroic rout, the tremendous carnage—that was the perfect example, *l'esempio calzante*, isn't that the expression you use?

DONATO: You speak good Italian. Yes, that's what we say. But it was a defeat, and in defeats . . .

MUELLER: It is a matter of spirit, which either submits to them or rises above them: it is in defeats such as these, more than in victory, that honour and duty are no longer sacrifice and martyrdom alone, but the supreme affirmation of force.

And death, inflicted or suffered, holds a terrible feast upon
the battlefield: and the whole of human sense and conscious
ness is consummated and exalted in a supreme intoxication
in pride and joy, and in passionate surrender to its fate—
Amor Fati.

DONATO: *Thus spake Zarathustra*.

MUELLER: This trick of quoting bookish and literary tags is
the typical vice of a culture in its Byzantine phase. And if
there's one thing that's incompatible with what I've been
describing—the heroic vocation—it's that sort of vicious
liberalistic culture.

DONATO: And I'm typical of it—you don't say so, just out of
politeness.

MUELLER: No, but because it would be merely superfluous to
say it: perhaps you'd rather I told you why the line of
German Kings and Emperors which lost the Prussian throne
and the crown of the Reich in 1919 won't ever regain them.

DONATO: If you've got time and inclination . . .

MUELLER: I can spare them. When it came to the supreme
moment on the battlefield, a band of his loyal followers
made the traditional request to the last crowned Hohen
zollern, that they should all march together to the death as
the Grand Master of the Order had done with his Teutonic
Knights at Tannenberg. Wilhelm's reply was that these
things belonged to the past. What do you make of that—did
it make sense? Was it good politics, realism, Machiavellism.
Was he right, do you think?

DONATO: It's not so easy to answer. Wilhelm certainly claimed
divine right and so . . .

MUELLER: He wasn't entitled to finish up like any ordinary
democratic constitutional monarch: we're agreed about
that; and it's because there were millions of Germans who
wouldn't say that these were things of the past, that Germany
has risen again from the hills of Verdun and the plains of
the Marne and the Ypres marshes. You think that's funny.

DONATO: The fact is that Wilhelm was right after all, and the gesture would have been merely ridiculous.

MUELLER: Laugh if you want to: the King of Italy's recently imitated the King of Prussia—but the Italians didn't know how to imitate the Germans, now or then.

DONATO: That's an insult. But I can't demand satisfaction.

MUELLER: Nevertheless, I'll grant satisfaction to friend or foe —but he must be open and honourable.

MELANIA: Donato!

DONATO: Don't be afraid, mother—I can swallow insults. Anyway the war will be over one day, and maybe it's in our stars that Captain Mueller and I should meet again.

MUELLER: Since the meeting may be of the kind you suggest, I've laid down my conditions and I insist on them.

DONATO: And I on the other hand am going to take advantage of this sneering patience of yours to say that the whole harangue you've thrust down our throats is rubbish. And it would be better if you showed some humility or if that's too Christian a virtue—some judgment. This mystique of force and swords is pure raving, moreover purely verbal raving, pseudo-artistic fantasy. If Germany is defeated, as the gentleman admits she may be, it will be up to her to learn from the despised art of politics how to emerge from defeat—which means as best one can, for better or worse. Whole peoples in collective suicide is a fairy tale, maybe it's a Nibelungslied, but it's certainly monstrous, and utterly senseless in any case.

MUELLER: You couldn't say anything to me which would be more offensive and distasteful.

DONATO: You shouldn't claim the sole privilege of being offensive.

MUELLER: The only privilege I want at the moment is not to have to talk to you any more, Signor . . .

REMORSELLA: Mèrici, Lieutenant Donato Mèrici.

MUELLER: Ah, you're an officer? I suspected as much.

MELANIA: Donato! Captain Mueller!

MUELLER: Calm yourself, Signora. I shall take no advantage of this. In the first place I've no orders about Badoglio's deserters and in the second, I'm not the one who's been insulted; thirdly, because of the way the information was obtained; and fourthly, because I obtained it under your roof, Signora.

MELANIA: I'm a mother, Captain Mueller.

MUELLER: I've one too, still living: in East Prussia. Do you know what that means?

MELANIA: I can imagine: I think I can.

MUELLER: It means that if we have to fall back on our frontier there, my mother who's an ordinary middle-class woman of peasant extraction, will meet the Russian invasion in exactly the same spirit as the aristocratic ladies of the Borderland knowing quite well that a war between Teutons and Slav is a war of extermination and horror. Do you know what I mean?

MELANIA: Yes, I think so, I'm sure I do.

REMORSELLA: We all know why. The Signora's German.

MUELLER: I should have preferred not to know that.

MELANIA: But why? I'm the daughter of a German who became a naturalised Italian and I am Italian; I was born here of an Italian mother.

MUELLER: That'll do. And anyway I'm not interested in turn coats and emigrants, or mixed races.

DONATO: Now just listen a moment: has it ever crossed your mind that among all the other forms of exclusiveness you've given us examples of, the pure Germans have a streak . . .

MELANIA: Donato!

MUELLER: Let him go on. A streak of madness, he was going to say. I expect slavish misery and degradation to be satirical and I let it pass.

REMORSELLA: It's my dinner-time.

MUELLER: Run along, food-pipe. I'll go and choose my apartments.

REMORSELLA: Before taking my departure, let me introduce myself to the company: I know my manners: Remorsella, Egisto Remorsella. What, nobody deigns to pay any attention? Never mind, we'll be seeing a lot of each other— including Signora Armida Lenai, who's kept quiet so far.

MUELLER: Signora Mèrici, will you show me round?

MELANIA: Make yourself at home.

(5) DONATO MÈRICI, ARMIDA LENAI and ALINDA NARENZA

ARMIDA: Donato, I'm frightened.

DONATO: There's no need: he's just a German eccentric. At bottom he's not a bad sort, he's just theorised himself crazy.

ARMIDA: The one that frightens me is the other one!

DONATO: Egisto Remorsella? Don't make me laugh!

ALINDA: I don't like the look of him either. Don't laugh, Donato. He makes me shiver.

ARMIDA: And there really is nothing to laugh at. He knows much more than he says and he's shown already that he knows a good deal.

DONATO: But Gaspare Della Morte is well hidden, they won't find him even if they look for him: and nobody's going to look for him just here now we've got Germans staying in the house. In fact, it's good luck, it diverts any suspicion.

ARMIDA: And I repeat, that man knows much more than he says: and besides, he keeps on looking at me in a certain manner.

DONATO: Really? I didn't notice.

ARMIDA: But I did.

ALINDA: So did I.

DONATO: Well, after all, it does credit to his good taste.

Q

ARMIDA: How can you have the heart to joke?

DONATO: Now just tell me, all of you, what else can I do? Listen to *Hauptmann* Mueller theorising? It's beyond me. Swallow his insults? That's what I've been doing.

ARMIDA: But what will there be left for me to do, if that Remorsella knows that Gaspare is here?

DONATO: Let him look: he won't find him. And at the first suitable moment we'll get him away.

ARMIDA: Unfortunately that isn't going to be easy: and if they make a thorough search and tap the walls and use the special instruments they've got, it frightens me, Donato, I'm afraid that there won't be any hiding-place good enough. And if they do find him or even if that man knows anything like enough about it, I'm sure he'll try to blackmail me: he likes the look of me and it's Gaspare's life that he'll use to blackmail me with. It couldn't be more unfortunate, there's nothing I might have to fear which would be worse, is there?

DONATO: No, nothing at all: I see that.

ARMIDA: Well, at least, don't provoke him, Donato, don't rouse him.

DONATO: That's quite justified. I've been letting my tongue run away with me, myself, quite stupidly and pointlessly. But what are you to do with an argumentative and unreasonable windbag like Mueller?

ALINDA: Just think of the people who care for you; the people you care for, yourself. Be a little prudent.

DONATO: Dear Alinda, of course you're quite right and I'll remember. I'll keep quiet, I'll even try to be more dignified.

(6) DONATO MÈRICI, ARMIDA LENAI, ALINDA NARENZA and FALARIDE NARENZA

FALARIDE: Are we by ourselves? Nobody can hear us, can they?

DONATO: The German is over the other side choosing his rooms: you know, the Knight of the Sword, all puffed up because he looks aristocratic in spite of having a common name: you've no idea the twisted mentality they've got!

NARENZA: He passed me and I had a look at him: he really is a fine looking chap: hasn't he got a 'von'?

DONATO: Not a sign of one. Common or garden Mueller.

NARENZA: Well, anyway, what does it matter to you whether he's Mueller or von Mueller or Old Nick himself—and may he fly away with the pair of you!

DONATO: You ought to have been here and heard him!

NARENZA: In all probability Mrs. Mueller could give us the simplest explanation but we can't go and ask her who she was playing around with nine months before this Mueller was born.

DONATO: Of course! That's exactly what I ought to have told him!

ALINDA: Donato, what about your promise?

NARENZA: Yes, why do you have to go stirring up trouble?

ARMIDA: That's what I said to him too.

DONATO: All German and more than half mad!

NARENZA: Now look here! You're a quarter German yourself. Would that make you a hundred per cent mad?

ALINDA: Uncle, you tell him too he's not to quarrel with the Germans.

NARENZA: Quarrel with the German? Well, really you know, underneath everything the German's being mighty condescending. After all it means they'll make friends.

DONATO: You're just in a muddle.

ALINDA: But, Uncle, you said something quite different, only a moment ago. Are you trying to egg him on now to quarrel?

NARENZA: I've thought it over. And anyway if one of them is pure German and the other half, it means they're neither of them quite responsible. In these days there are some people who are more dangerous than lunatics. But I haven't got any more time to waste on the subject whether it's worth it or not! I've just come to let you know that I'm off. I'm striking camp and taking a change of air. I'm not looking for trouble, I've got my affairs to attend to on the black market: the minute the war's over I'm going to open a transport agency and make millions.

DONATO: Millions, eh?

NARENZA: You'll see what a million lire are going to be worth when the war's over.

DONATO: I know what you've got in mind. But it doesn't look as though the Germans are going in for inflation at present.

NARENZA: One would hardly credit that people would still go on being taken by surprise when the same things have been happening ever since the human race began. If the Germans don't do it, the Allies will. It's inevitable with war. It starts with buying and selling gold and valuables: it goes on with foodstuffs, and when it's over if you want to make money, you have to hire out transport, land or water: the demand is the same. I've heard that the German and this other chap are here looking for an illegal radio somewhere in the woods and mountains: there were some shots fired in the night. What that means to me is, I don't want trouble and I don't want to be taken for a partisan when I happen to be a black marketeer—and we have to remember that my work is out in the woods too, and I often have to do it at night. So I'm changing my beat. Mind you, I know nothing: but they haven't captured the radio. There might be somebody here who'd be interested in knowing that, Signora Armida—and also that the partisans have taken to the mountains and will be down again as soon as the weather clears. But I'm only speaking purely as a friend and because I'm quitting. What worries me is leaving you, Alinda, but all things considered, this is still the safest place for you. I trust her to you Signora Lenai—and to Signora Melania. Tell her—with my best respects. I'm off.

ARMIDA: Don't trouble about your niece. We're all devoted to her—and she deserves it.

NARENZA: When the war's over, I'll give you a fine dowry, my girl, and you can make a nice respectable suitable marriage with a real gentleman who has his head screwed on the right way. There's this much to be said for wars: nobody's going to look too closely at the way you made your money. But just before I leave, and still merely as a friend and in complete confidence, I'd just like to say that if you should happen to have anybody hidden about the place, see that he stays where he is and doesn't try to get away, at least for the time being, because they're watching all the exits. They're on to something round here. I'm beating it.

ARMIDA: I see, Narenza. Thanks.

NARENZA: What you see I don't know, nor what you're thanking me for: nor for that matter who Narenza is. From now on, the name's different.

ARMIDA: Quite right. And you take after our friend here, Donato, and be careful.

NARENZA: Talking of which, as far as I'm concerned, it isn't the German that frightens me. He's a German and a military man and all he cares about are German military matters.

DONATO: He's a philosopher as well and a man of letters.

NARENZA: So much the better: these people are always harmless at bottom: and after all intellectuals are professionally inclined to let out all they know—and more, very often, a great deal more. And if there should be anyone hiding here, he doesn't want to be bothered with looking for him, or finding him, it's not a soldier's job—or a philosopher's either. . . . That's on the assumption that not the slightest sign leaks out, either here or elsewhere. But there's someone else who's very little to say for himself, but he looks to me as if he knows a lot more than he says. With him, you've got to watch every little thing; he's got a very penetrating and suspicious eye: all this has got nothing whatever to do with me. Nevertheless if I had to stay here it's not the German I'd be worried about, but the other party.

ARMIDA: That's what I think. You need say no more. I share all your suspicions of him—and worse.

DONATO: Who do you mean? Egisto Remorsella? And why exactly?

NARENZA: It's the wrong time and place to be mentioning names.

DONATO: And now you've found your vocation, have you— in the underground-movement?

NARENZA: Me in the underground-movement? I spoke merely because I thought I ought to, as a friend—merely academically.

ARMIDA: And I am, and always shall be grateful to him: and I'm not the only one.

DONATO: But do you really mean to tell me you're frightened of this chap? Another poor ordinary wretched Italian?

NARENZA: Italian's neither here nor there. This is an international type, supernational, subhuman: a criminal—one of Lombroso's types, criminal by nature and vocation.

DONATO: Good enough! This is Vocation-Day!

NARENZA: As a matter of fact, I've just spotted a new one in you.

DONATO: What's that? Failed musician?

NARENZA: Successful scoundrel. Highly successful.

DONATO: Thanks for the compliment.

NARENZA: You can tell a true friend by his frankness: do you think this is the right time for compliments?

ALINDA: Now for pity's sake, don't you two start quarrelling.

ARMIDA: Yes, indeed. Do remember you're leaving us, Falaride. And we . . .

NARENZA: I've got my reasons: I've got to make arrangements to hide all the connections of my business—and my vehicles, too. They make for a lot of envy nowadays: and I might be asked where I got hold of them, too. So I have to see they're scattered—if I left them all together I might lose the lot supposing there were a *rastrellamento*.

DONATO: What do you mean by '*rastrellamento*'?

NARENZA: What they're doing up in the mountains—a combing out—hunting for an illegal radio and the men working it. But if they come across my trucks while they're looking for it, they'll take those too just as I took them myself when the army went to bits and all the dumps and stores were there for the taking.

ARMIDA: But don't forget you're getting away and we women have to stay here alone with things in the state they're in.

ALINDA: Yes, for Signor Donato will have to hide too, and may even have to get out himself at a moment's notice.

NARENZA: Your Signor Donato seems to be very much on your mind!

ALINDA: Oh Uncle!

NARENZA: Haven't you got a very soft spot for the gentleman in question?

ALINDA: Oh, Uncle, is this the moment . . .?

NARENZA: No, but after all even though he's a waster, he's a nice sympathetic waster, the best friend I've got and now I come to think seriously about it, the only one. That means you'll want a dowry that doesn't vanish overnight. I'll see what I can do—it's all the more necessary because some people are going to come out of this war with next to nothing: now I, on the other hand . . . But I'll think it over: and what about your sisters?

ALINDA: Uncle, ought you really to be thinking about me and my sisters, just now?

NARENZA. I can't possibly be unfair to them—they're good honest girls, too, and what's more not half as pretty as you are.

ALINDA: Oh, Uncle Falaride!

NARENZA: Go on with you, you're as red as a poppy in maytime; I won't say it doesn't suit you: and after all it's a good sign!

DONATO: Falaride, you may think I'm a waster, you're entitled to and I think you're quite right. But I'm a gentleman, you know.

NARENZA: Of course, of course, in every kind of way. But when it comes to love, honour's a bad risk: it gets frozen like government bonds in hard times. If this were done by ordinary people they'd be called rogues, bankrupts and scoundrels.

DONATO: If I give you my word as a friend, a gentleman and a lover that I'll marry your niece if she'll have me, whether she's got a dowry or not, you can and must believe me.

FALARIDE: Of course, of course . . . anyway I'll come back if I can and advise the ladies and cheer them up and see how things are going, if you get what I mean. I'll come back as soon as I can and as often as possible. Don't keep me now. I must be off.

ARMIDA: We're relying on you, Narenza. Come back and comfort us.

NARENZA: And now, keep your hearts up. And stop blushing, Alinda. If people blush it means they're either doing wrong or thinking about it. Hearts up, keep your heads screwed on, hold your tongue, and goodbye.

DONATO, ARMIDA, ALINDA: Goodbye, and come back soon!

NARENZA: God willing. But try and keep cheerful and do watch out for that chap who's so sly and mum.

(7) DONATO MÈRICI, ARMIDA LENAI, ALINDA NARENZA and later MELANIA MÈRICI

ARMIDA: God willing . . .

ALINDA: He will protect us, Armida. I'll keep praying.

ARMIDA: I'll try to hope and trust. What a strange man he is, that uncle of yours, courageous in his way and cheerful. A strange man and not a bit heartless.

DONATO: What's very much stranger is that we're engaged. I'm overjoyed. But you seem troubled and uncertain, Alinda. Aren't you happy?

ALINDA: It's all so sudden, so unexpected. . . .

DONATO: Yes, it looks like the will of God, and He will protect us.

ALINDA: God grant it, Donato.

DONATO: Mother, you've come at the right time: great news: we're engaged!

MELANIA: Oh, I'm so glad, so very glad. But what about Narenza?

DONATO: Don't be too startled. He arranged it for us himself and he's even going to provide a dowry. Fancy! But I'll tell you about it later. Now, Alinda, have you forgotten— we want something else if we're to be properly engaged.

ALINDA: I don't know . . . do you mean the ring?

MELANIA: Here you are. Take it Donato. The man has to give the ring. Don't cry, my little girl.

ALINDA: Oh Signora, it all seems too happy to last. It's frightening: and I *am* frightened!

DONATO: Give me your hand. What slim fingers you've got. Mother's got a small hand but it's too big for you. There we are: all that's wanted now is a kiss.

ALINDA: Signora——

MELANIA: You can call me mother now, my dear—and give him his kiss.

ARMIDA: Melania, what's that Mueller doing, the German?

MELANIA: He's picked his rooms—for the beautiful view. He say's he's a country-lover and fond of woods and birds. Thank goodness, the nicest ones—the ones he's chosen— are in the wing which is furthest away from—you know what.

ARMIDA: Yes, I see. It's luck.

(8) Donato Mèrici, Melania Mèrici, Armida Lenai
Alinda Narenza and Egisto Remorsella

Remorsella: Am I intruding? Is this a family-romance? Shal
we be having wedding-bells before long? You needn'
jump every time I come in, it's not worth the trouble. We're
going to be seeing a lot of each other.

CHAPTER TWO

(1) EGISTO REMORSELLA and ARMIDA LENAI

REMORSELLA: I'm always trying to get you alone but you always avoid me. Don't tell me again that you're busy and have to go.

ARMIDA: Now what is it you want with me?

REMORSELLA: First of all, to tell you that when you look angry and contemptuous it makes you look even more beautiful than ever.

ARMIDA: If I must endure your presence, may I at least be spared your compliments.

REMORSELLA: That's even better. The more the sparks fly the better I like it.

ARMIDA: Tell me: just for the information—What sort of rights do you imagine you've got here? And with me?

REMORSELLA: Rights? If you put it like that, I couldn't say.

ARMIDA: Pestering me, for instance?

REMORSELLA: Pestering! That's splendid! Contempt certainly improves your looks—but it might be a bore in the end. I shouldn't like to lose my patience.

ARMIDA: I lost mine a long time ago. And I'm bored to death with you already. Anyway I'd rather see you angry and spiteful than sugary and poisonous.

REMORSELLA: For your own good and that of anybody who happens to be dear to you, I advise you to look for your patience again and find it—and be quick about it. Aha,

you're not busy any longer, you don't have to go? You're
not bored with me any more?

ARMIDA: I defy you to do me any harm. . . .

REMORSELLA: Who's talking about harm? I'm talking about
your good.

ARMIDA: I don't care what you can do to me. But I have to
think what you might do to other people.

REMORSELLA: Now you're beginning to see sense. And who
might these other people be you have in mind?

ARMIDA: Why, the people who own the house, of course—
my friends, who've been such generous hosts.

REMORSELLA: If you were the only guest, there wouldn't be
much trouble. But everybody knows you—Signora Armida
Lenai—you're the lover of a well-known anti-Fascist and at
the moment he's one of the best-known Resistance leaders,
and he's very badly wanted. The famous Gaspare Della
Morte—Old Mortality—it's an unlucky-sounding name for
times like these.

ARMIDA: What about it?

REMORSELLA: Sounding unlucky!

ARMIDA: Stop it! I've never concealed the fact that I'm
Gaspare's mistress. And so . . .

REMORSELLA: And so they're hunting for Gaspare in the woods
and up among the mountains, and in my view, they're
making a mistake. They ought to be looking nearer home,
much nearer, maybe right on the spot.

ARMIDA: Well then, look! Haven't you searched the whole
villa in every nook and cranny, from cellars to attic—and
even tapped all over the walls?

REMORSELLA: In massive old buildings like this there are bound
to be hiding-places which are hard to find. And then the high
and mighty German captain doesn't take kindly to the job.

ARMIDA: Well, find them yourself, if you like the job!

REMORSELLA: You know where he is—the chap we're looking
for.

ARMIDA: I've told you already: he's got over into Switzerland.

REMORSELLA: Perhaps you could let us have a card with his signature and a Swiss stamp?

ARMIDA: Now, you know there's no international post nowadays!

REMORSELLA: There is, through the Vatican.

ARMIDA: I haven't Gaspare's address.

REMORSELLA: Am I supposed to believe that?

ARMIDA: Please yourself. He takes good care not to write to me so as not to get me into trouble. That strikes me as elementary.

REMORSELLA: Yes, that's obvious. Nevertheless, you know people you could turn to, you could ask one of the partisans to slip across the border and look for the party concerned. He'll be among the political refugees and quite easy to trace.

ARMIDA: No doubt. And where do I find the partisan? I haven't the slightest personal contact among them.

REMORSELLA: Well, as far as that goes, we've caught one or two of them in the last few days. To find out where Della Morte is, it would be worth letting one of them go and sending him off for a Swiss holiday.

ARMIDA: You haven't caught anybody. And these are just silly and pitiful tricks to try and get something out of me I don't know.

REMORSELLA: You're ill-informed. We took three a few nights ago; some of Gaspare's men. Ah, now you're listening to me, you're all ears!

ARMIDA: I should have thought that was natural.

REMORSELLA: Perfectly natural: feminine curiosity—a lover's anxiety. . . .

ARMIDA: In short now you're trying to incriminate me?

REMORSELLA: That would distress me deeply. You see, I'd like to save Gaspare Della Morte, not only you.

ARMIDA: He's saved himself, thank God. And as far as I'm concerned, there's nothing you can do.

REMORSELLA: We'll see.

ARMIDA: All this is just a clumsy stupid trap.

REMORSELLA: That remains to be seen. Up to the present, th prisoners aren't talking—or what's better, they're contra dicting one another: one of them says that Della Morte ha got across the border and the other that he's gone south and another one says that he doesn't know anything.

ARMIDA: That's the one I'd believe, if I were in your place.

REMORSELLA: You're a very brave woman if you can laugh As I said, they're not talking: and as I said and repeat—u to the present. But we've ways of making them.

ARMIDA: Ah, you mean torture!

REMORSELLA: We needn't argue about names, need we?

ARMIDA: Are you really as vile as that?

REMORSELLA: A mere matter of names. If you don't like th sound of that one, I'll call them investigatory or persuasiv methods. But if you can't stand the word, how do yo imagine you're going to stand the fact?

ARMIDA: Is this a threat? Is it meant for me too?

REMORSELLA: Not at all! You've got the stuff of resistance i you. And to spoil anything so beautiful and so encitin would be inexcusable waste.

ARMIDA: You'll never be able to understand. . . .

REMORSELLA: On the contrary, I understand very well. . . .

ARMIDA: What?

REMORSELLA: How much you loathe me.

ARMIDA: But—in that case . . .

REMORSELLA: Please—allow me to do the talking—that wa we'll get to the point more quickly. What are you thinking That I imagine you could find me attractive or love me Not in my wildest dreams. You see even my father didn love me, even my mother didn't think I was nice. But the don't you imagine either that I'm in love with you. It'll d

for you that you attract me—very much, that's one thing
certain. That's enough for you.

RMIDA: Enough? It's more than enough. It sickens me.

EMORSELLA: Don't be sarcastic. Even if it's courageous, it's
useless. Still you've a strong motive for being courageous.
Passion: you're in love.

RMIDA: Your tongue befouls everything.

EMORSELLA: Even if it's wasted, your contempt shows a
generous spirit. But just think for a moment. They haven't
any passion at all to help them those three poor wretches,
nothing to inflame their ideas or stir their blood or get them
on the boil or warm up the other parts you cultivated people
don't mention in conversation, but which give people a
strength which staggers you—men and women alike. No
need to turn your nose up at that. You've got passion, but
you tell me what those three have got to help them stand up
to our persuasive measures.

RMIDA: Honour.

EMORSELLA: It's chilly stuff—it's like a plaster without the
mustard, a hash with the pepper left out!

RMIDA: You're talking about . . .

EMORSELLA: Something I know nothing about. I admit
that. But you can take it from me that I'm talking as I
feel.

RMIDA: Your feelings do you credit.

EMORSELLA: That's the last thing I think about. No, I'm
wrong. It's one later.

RMIDA: At least you're honest.

EMORSELLA: And why should I lie for no reason? Suppose I
were to make out to you that I'm a fine character? Would
you believe me? And even if you did, what good would that
be to me? Should I learn to respect you? But that's just what
I don't want. You attract me: I'm quite honest about it. If
I made out I was in love with you, it wouldn't do anything
at all to make you love me. And the only person I should

have got into trouble would be myself. It really wouldn'
be worth it.

ARMIDA: Well, what about the three prisoners?

REMORSELLA: You're quite right. We must keep to the poin
Now is there anything which would keep them going, pu
more pep, more ginger into them—than honour?

ARMIDA: Idealism.

REMORSELLA: Thin stuff. It's just a bag of wind. If you pric
it, it collapses. You'd see, if you had nothing but idealisr
yourself. . .

ARMIDA: I don't have anything to do with politics.

REMORSELLA: Or at least you know how to keep it to yoursel
But that's nothing to do with me. I'm putting my cards o
the table and making you a business offer, a deal. You d
your part and I'll do mine. Think it over and let me know

ARMIDA: I won't listen to any offer whatsoever coming fro
you!

REMORSELLA: We'll see. I'm quite curious.

ARMIDA: Yes, you've even made me curious. Haven't you an
shame.

REMORSELLA: Me? What for? Why look so surprised?

ARMIDA: I'm looking at you as one would at—what shall
say—a cancer, leprosy. I can see that if you're fighting fc
your creed or your side, you can go to any lengths—cruelt
atrocities, cheating . . . but you . . .

REMORSELLA: You mean I haven't any honour or ideas c
convictions—not even a side?

ARMIDA: What? Aren't you even a Fascist?

REMORSELLA: Let me explain. If I wanted to whitewas
myself, I'd say I've got my convictions but though I'
the child of my age, I won't even say that I've been mac
what I am by the times, or the war, or the general collap:
of moral standards or anything of the sort: they're all c
them whitewash and humbug. All times are alike, wh;
you get by fraud in peacetime, you take by force in war: it

all a question of going the right way to work with them. And one thing war always teaches you, that it's all a matter of whitewash and having the nerve to scrape it off.

ARMIDA: And the shamelessness.

REMORSELLA: Peace or war there's only one thing I'd be ashamed of.

ARMIDA: It's something to know there's even one.

REMORSELLA: Yes, missing an opportunity if one turns up, not seizing it, not grabbing it by hook or by crook. I said I was self-made. But the truth is I was born as I am, not made, it's my nature, it's what I'm really like. If I were able to work on my own I wouldn't stay with the Fascists or under the Germans. But it can't be done, I have to fit in and do the best I can. I do as well as I can with the Germans who are on the spot and give the orders and have the power. You see, it's to suit them that I'm a Fascist. Politics! That's their game. But while I'm a Fascist I'm fierce and merciless and bursting with zeal. You people know nothing because in the country nobody ever does know anything. So I'll teach you something. When constituted society is falling apart in this way, there's something—I don't know what but maybe it's just nature—which brings all sorts of people together—different types but with one thing in common— they can do and will do anything. They call us 'gangsters', and that's what we call ourselves: there are people of fanatical conviction among us—and also sceptics like me, the deluded and the desperate and anything up to and including sadistic lunatics and criminals. Probably you'd class me with them: I don't know and I don't care: I keep a cool head and get on with my affairs—within the limits of what's possible—and trying to extend them as much as I can. We suit the Germans because we take on the nastiest jobs—being adventurers and irregulars. One day they may quite well wash their hands of us or even hang us. My dear madam, we've all got to die one way or the other and if

R

you never do anything, you've finished before you've begun
If you like, that's my conviction—I say it in all seriousness
My gang, quite honestly, is a bag of all sorts—I don't have
to tell you. I have to have money—it's the fifth element: if
you can eat well and drink well, that's not to be sneezed at
in these times. And I confess I've a weakness for women
Since I've been active in a gang, I get plenty of all these
things. And I'm crazy for women.

ARMIDA: And now you've shed the humbug and scraped off
the whitewash, what do you want from me?

REMORSELLA: I want you. How many more ways do you want
to be told?

ARMIDA: You must be crazy!

REMORSELLA: I told you. Crazy about women! I'll give you
the demonstration: the German, the high-and-mighty
Hauptmann has been looking, and he's found nothing
because he feels he's a Knight, a *Portaspada*: it's a sort of
vocation like any other, but it makes him want to dodge
certain other less glorious occupations: and he leaves them
to me: he trusts me to carry them out, or rather he forces
them on me.

ARMIDA: It comes easier to you: you do it better than he does

REMORSELLA: I told you that in the country you don't know
what goes on—you blissful denizens of little earthly para
dises. You're not worried, because you're sure that the three
partisans we've captured can't tell what they don't know
and they don't know Gaspare Della Morte's hideout. But
I've no intention of finding out. I'd rather he stayed put
And by the way, let's be quite clear that it's no good him
thinking how he's going to escape. Alma Dannata is being
watched all the way round night and day. To sum up, on
the assumption that Gaspare is in these parts, I take it as
conclusively demonstrated that he's somewhere where he
can't be found.

ARMIDA: Well then, why lavish all this logic?

REMORSELLA: You've every ground for curiosity, even more for anxiety.

ARMIDA: What am I supposed to be anxious about?

REMORSELLA: If you follow my argument, you'll know. I'm not going to waste time looking for Signora Lenai's lover—who can't be found—because I don't want to find him. When I'm trying to snare woodcock, I don't look for owls. If I rout out the owl, I shall miss the other bird.

ARMIDA: You've said quite enough and I'm going to give you away.

REMORSELLA: And to whom?

ARMIDA: Well, in the first place, to the German officer.

REMORSELLA: Oh, he doesn't care for Italian women—no matter how beautiful, even if they're as beautiful as you. You see, he says you can actually smell the mixed race on their very skins—they smell of Mediterranean, Phoenician, low Greek, Jew, Turk—what he means I don't know and don't care.

ARMIDA: Stop this fooling.

REMORSELLA: Fooling or not, that's what he says.

ARMIDA: I shall give you away to him for blackmailing me, and for being ready to betray your employers.

REMORSELLA: Now you stop fooling. You may call it blackmail, I call it business. The German will say that my business deals are just my private affairs as an Italian and have nothing to do with him: and what has betrayal got to do with it? Now you listen to me with all your ears. Bring your whole mind to bear on it—you'll find it's worth your while. This Jerry, this Teutonic Knight, could really say that I was betraying him if what I'd proposed to you had been to let the owl get away. But what I'm trying to do, on the contrary, is to keep him in the nest: and if you split on this business deal—or if you prefer—this blackmail, it's you and nobody else who'll be splitting on Gaspare Della Morte. I may lose the woodcock but I shall have kept the game the Germans are after nice and warm for them in the nest. No betrayal about that!

ARMIDA: Ah, you fiend of hell!

REMORSELLA: I see you're beginning to get me right. Speaking with all due humility, I'm the *Hauptmann's* political adviser for everything to do with Italian affairs. It's little or nothing to him or to his superiors if one or a hundred of us get slaughtered by the Resistance. That's something which they leave to us and it actually suits them if it all makes for greater hatred among us all. That's politics: nothing there to argue about: *divide et impera*, I know that much Latin myself. But there's one thing they don't leave to us and about that they've no intention of showing the slightest leniency. But before I go any further—do you know what they mean by reprisals?

ARMIDA: What's that got to do with it?

REMORSELLA: I thought you were more intelligent than that. It means that if anybody kills a German soldier, the killers must be handed over or they'll shoot hostages. And if that doesn't do the trick and it looks as if there's a conspiracy— as there always is—they shoot up all the local houses and then set fire to them, with all the inhabitants inside, if they think it's necessary to make an example. Yes, I know. When the enemy does it, it's known as an atrocity: when it's done by your own side, you call it necessity: if you have to put up with it, it comes to the same thing. Well let's suppose that it's become necessary to carry out a reprisal and that, in my capacity as political adviser, I suggest that it's not a good idea to go for ordinary peasants and the local working-people and the poor and ignorant part of the population, but that they ought to take in representatives of the upper middle class, and that they shouldn't turn their guns and their flame-throwers only on the cottages, but on the stately country mansions as well, with their books and pictures and pianos and their priceless furniture and their dry and well-seasoned old beams, all very inflammable material. What a bonfire! And it would show they haven't got two standards. Does that hang together? If you can convince me it doesn't, I'll stick to it that it's politics and though I say it myself, politics of a very subtle kind. And if the villa, which is a well-known haunt of the enemies of Nazism and Fascism should happen to have got a Resistance leader tucked away somewhere, the bonfire will toast him and roast him all right if he won't jump clear or isn't quick enough about it. And if he does it'll be a much nastier finish.

ARMIDA: There haven't been any German soldiers killed round here.

REMORSELLA: That was very good: you said that very well—coldly and collectedly. That's something I appreciate and admire. Still there are partisans round here who've got away from the *rastrellamento*, and they're always making raids and ambushes. It's highly probable, if not certain, that one of these days somebody will be killed, even perhaps a German. And the wretched peasants won't even know whom they're supposed to give away, let alone being in a position to hand them over. If that arises you know now what sort of deal I'm proposing to you.

ARMIDA: If that arises I know what Gaspare Della Morte would do: if he were here, he'd give himself up.

REMORSELLA: A fine gesture: but unwise, for it would not only deprive the Resistance movement of one of its strongest elements but it would snatch my game out of my hand and though he might escape dying like a rat in a hole, his end would be much worse. But still none of this has anything to do with me. If there should be reprisals, his fate is in your hands, Signora Lenai.

ARMIDA: And assuming that I were to accept the bargain you propose?

REMORSELLA: I don't have to be better informed than the Germans: I don't have to know where the chap is.

ARMIDA: Ah, now at last you've given yourself away. Now you're the one who's in my hands.

REMORSELLA: My poor girl, how you do delude yourself! I've told you already that if you denounce me it's as good as giving Gaspare Della Morte away: can't you see that you've given him away to me already?

ARMIDA: *I* have? To you?

REMORSELLA: Who else? If he weren't here, is it likely that you'd have listened to me? As soon as I opened my mouth, you'd have laughed in my face. And now instead, I'm the one to laugh. What a nuisance these people are, coming in just now but still I can't stop laughing. Behold the noble masters of the establishment!

(2) EGISTO REMORSELLA, DONATO MÈRICI, ARMIDA LENAI and MELANIA MÈRICI

MELANIA: And a very ugly and evil laugh it is.

REMORSELLA: It's the best I've got.

DONATO: *Subsannatio diaboli.*

REMORSELLA: I don't know whether that's an insult or a compliment but don't bother to translate it for me!

DONATO: You'll take it as a compliment: I said you laugh like the devil.

REMORSELLA: And so the devil can laugh, can he? Well, I'd sooner be like him than the angels, for if I believed in them I should imagine that they were always serious and a bit of a bore. Signora Lenai, that's all I have to say to you. We must wait and see. All in good time. But think it over—and take it or leave it.

ARMIDA: I'll think it over.

(3) Donato Mèrici, Melania Mèrici and
Armida Lenai

MELANIA: Armida, you seem upset: what has he been saying to you. What is it you're supposed to think over?

ARMIDA: That man suspects that Gaspare's here: in fact he's quite sure!

MELANIA: What very bad news for all of us! If they go on searching they can't help finding him!

ARMIDA: At the moment he's keeping his suspicions to himself: he's not giving it away at present, he's trying to make on it and use it to blackmail me. You can't imagine what a vile treacherous creature he is.

MELANIA: Can't you tell us?

ARMIDA: How can I?

MELANIA: You've told us already. You've said he's trying to blackmail you: that's enough.

ARMIDA: You really know what I mean, Melania?

MELANIA: I'm afraid I do. But if it's a question of money, you can count on me.

ARMIDA: He's perfectly capable of asking for money, too. Can you understand anyone sinking to such depths?

DONATO: I certainly thought he was pretty despicable but I wouldn't have put him as low as that.

ARMIDA: If you can't do anything better than speculate, Donato, you can spare me that.

DONATO: Gaspare must be got away.

ARMIDA: We're watched all the way round, day and night. I might as well admit the situation I'm in in all its horror. I I shall have to let myself be blackmailed—give him what he wants. There's no way out.

DONATO: There's one: the vile beast could be wiped out.

MELANIA: Donato! What would happen?

ARMIDA: I'm grateful to you for thinking of it, Donato, but could you do it?

(4) DONATO MÈRICI, MELANIA MÈRICI, ARMIDA LENAI and EGISTO REMORSELLA

REMORSELLA: There's something rather important I forgot to mention to you, Signora Lenai.

ARMIDA: Only to me?

REMORSELLA: It's not a bad idea if your friends know about it too. Suppose, just theoretically, you or the others imagined that getting rid of me would be a convenient solution, it would have no useful results because to meet all the eventualities favourable or otherwise, I'm leaving the clearest and fullest instructions in writing. One doesn't need to dot all the 'i's' and cross all the 't's', does one? 'Just rub him out' wouldn't work. In fact it would only precipitate disaster.

(5) MELANIA MÈRICI, DONATO MÈRICI and ARMIDA LENAI

MELANIA: Was he listening behind the door?

ARMIDA: He's so artful he doesn't need to. As a type he has a kind of perfection.

MELANIA: Could you really have killed him in cold blood?

DONATO: Now it can't be done, it's easy enough to admit I couldn't have brought it off. You know, Mother, this son of yours that you've brought into the worst of all possible worlds, couldn't be worse adapted to it. Don't lose patience, Armida, there's nothing to be done except philosophise and warn Gaspare of the danger he's in.

ARMIDA: Yes, but he mustn't know the danger I'm in. He can't do anything to defend me, any more than you can, Donato. Oh, I don't doubt that God is just—for we can't enter into His mysteries—but has He taken His mercy away from us for ever?

MELANIA: My poor, poor friend, what terrible times we live through!

ARMIDA: Even if we come through, even if I get out of it all scot-free and escape from this nameless filth which I feel on me already and which fills me with loathing for myself, the wound will remain in our very souls for ever. But God created our souls and why doesn't He do anything to shield them?

DONATO: Don Ignazio comes about now for the news.

(6) DONATO MÈRICI, MELANIA MÈRICI, ARMIDA LENAI and DON IGNAZIO

DON IGNAZIO: May I come in? I hope I'm not disturbing you?

MELANIA: Come in, by all means, Don Ignazio. But I'm afraid you find us all greatly distressed.

DON IGNAZIO: Every home is the same. It's a sorrowful time for all of us.

DONATO: And it's gone on for such a long time—and we've no idea how much longer.

DON IGNAZIO: What's the news? That's what I came for. Not very cheerful? It's bad, eh? Mercy on us!

ARMIDA: Now you're here you can tell me why God wants us damned.

DON IGNAZIO: Damned? What are you saying? Have you any idea? Has something happened? Our Lady be with us!

ARMIDA: Don Ignazio, I'll tell you what's happened later, when I make my confession.

DON IGNAZIO: Come whenever you wish. I'm a priest even if I'm unworthy—it's my office. In the meantime . . .

ARMIDA: Don Ignazio, you said that all homes were the same: but not where the persecutors live—there's no distress there, they're all laughter and festivity.

DON IGNAZIO: But not of a kind to be envied. Still, things are going badly. They've taken two more partisans and it's being said they'll be tortured—God forbid!

ARMIDA: There isn't much that God forbids nowadays.

DON IGNAZIO: Signora, are you trying to drive me away? If I must listen to such enormities, it can only be to condemn them. Unworthy I may be but still I sit at the tribunal of repentance.

MELANIA: She's desperate, Don Ignazio. You must forgive her.

ARMIDA: Yes, I am desperate. They've brought me to it. Don't condemn me.

DON IGNAZIO: It's for God alone to condemn and pardon. I'm here to administer the sacraments, not justice.

ARMIDA: Well, then pray for me. I'm in great danger, mortal danger.

DON IGNAZIO: Always, with all my heart: and whenever you want me, I'll be there to confess you. Things have taken an ugly turn locally, as I was telling you. The Germans generally come back empty-handed when they've been out in the woods on a *rastrellamento*: and they seem angrier than usual because they haven't been able to lay hands on the illegal transmitter which is in the woods and is being used to signal to Allied aircraft. And then there's that plane that comes over by itself at night—the people call it 'Pippo'—that makes them wild. For the time being, they don't use the slightest force against anything or anybody: they don't lay a finger on them. If they requisition anything, they pay cash. But that's what frightens me—just that they're so correct. If you haven't heard it already, they've put it about through that Egisto Remorsella that if a single German's found dead in the woods, there'll be reprisals, they'll shoot the hostages.

ARMIDA: Incendiaries and flame-throwers, shooting up the houses with the people inside. Fire and steel.

DON IGNAZIO: So you've heard that, too?

ARMIDA: I've had it said to my face.

DON IGNAZIO: It's the correctness which scares me. If they've said it, they'll do it. They're capable of it. Look at their faces! They get more sombre every day.

DONATO: Apparently they can do it under international law.

DON IGNAZIO: And every *rastrellamento* makes them harder. When I came in, I was hoping for good news—but if there were any you'd have told me already. . . .

MELANIA: Donato, you were just listening.

DONATO: Yes, I was. But what I heard here distracted my attention.

ARMIDA: Oh, in the state I'm in *I* forget the Allies are on the offensive. Maybe they're advancing. Maybe that's why the Germans look so sombre. That's it, of course. If they only will, the Allies can sweep the Germans out of Italy in a few days. And I shall be saved!

MELANIA: If the Germans fall back, the nightmare will lift. We'll be free.

ARMIDA: Free! I can hear that word ringing and singing! Soon you'll know why, Don Ignazio. And then you'll pity me— even in my rebelliousness.

DON IGNAZIO: Now more than ever. Suffering without rebellion calls for envy, not pity. But can't you tell us anything hopeful, Signor Donato? Why don't you say anything? Can't you? Isn't there any change? Nothing good? We need it so much.

DONATO: They say there's no hurry . . .

MELANIA: Who says so?

DONATO: It's the Allied radio.

DON IGNAZIO: No hurry . . . they're in a hurry to say it! They ought to be here in the middle of it all.

DONATO: You're right, they're in a hurry. Well, we may be in the middle of it all, but at least we ought to know better than to expect anything good to come over that damned radio.

MELANIA: Is that what you really mean?

DONATO: I mean so as not to be too disappointed. I mean that you can't expect that any war will be carried on in our interests—certainly not somebody else's war—that's absurd.

DON IGNAZIO: Anyway, you mean there isn't any news? Or that it's disturbing, or at least not very good? Do you mean it's actually bad? Don't keep us on tenterhooks.

ARMIDA: Something really terrible?

MELANIA: It does seem that Fate is against us. Donato, why don't you speak? Is it something terrible?

DONATO: There you see, that's what we're like. Immediately start thinking about something terrible! As far as we're concerned the news isn't encouraging. In itself it couldn't be better.

MELANIA: But hadn't they gone over to the offensive? Didn't it look as though they were going to cut off the German retreat?

DONATO: The offensive has come to a halt. The Germans have fallen back on prepared positions.

DON IGNAZIO: Bad luck for us. We know what that means. Months and months. And that needs patience—but so much, even with God's help. And things here are going very badly indeed.

MELANIA: Armida, don't! You frighten me. Your eyes have a mad look!

ARMIDA: And I feel I am going mad. My mind won't stand it. But, Donato, weren't they saying . . .

DONATO: Saying! They'll say anything. We don't have to believe them! I've believed it all—at least as much as all the rest of you and more. Now they're saying that the Germans have more than one fortified line: and when they've lost all the others, there's still the last of the lot, which is the strongest of all. They call it the Gothic line, the other side of the Appenines. And there may even be one beyond the last— on the Po.

ARMIDA: Oh, we'd much better die!

MELANIA: But why at least couldn't they tell us in the first place?

DONATO: Because you didn't have to know. I can't help it,

because I know what war is. You're fooled or you fool others. Nothing more usual in warfare, in fact it's the rule.

DON IGNAZIO: But fooling poor wretches when hope's all they've got to hang on to. Surely it's too cheap?

DONATO: Yes, it is: but in the circumstances they don't make these distinctions. This campaign in Italy is only a diversion and if they're going to fool the Germans, there's no help for it, they've got to fool us poor wretched Italians too.

MELANIA: And the Italians trust them: and all the Germans do is to laugh.

DONATO: That's been known to happen.

MELANIA: But it's inhuman treachery. It's merciless!

DONATO: It's war. War plus politics—one only a bit more merciless than the other. War-strategy—by cruelty out of cunning!

ARMIDA: And you can talk about it like that?

DONATO: How else can I talk about it? Are we to go on trying to deceive ourselves? We can't even if we want to— not with the best will in the world. I'm sorry, but in fact I must tell you something else. The Allies have announced that they're going to hold up not only their own operations but even their supplies to the Resistance. And so they advise them to come down out of the mountains and pretend they've given up. As soon as the weather improves, they say they can go back to the woods again. Yes, just like that— as if they were talking about country excursions and pleasure-trips. To my mind this is beyond even the regulation treachery and stupidity of warfare, but for us to lay down the law in these times is so beside the point that it becomes completely stupid.

ARMIDA: And what this all means to me is something worse than death. It's like looking in the mirror and finding I've got leprosy—and worse, leprosy in the soul.

MELANIA: My poor poor Armida!

ARMIDA: Anyway, at least don't tell me to be brave. What hav you got to say to me, Don Ignazio?

DON IGNAZIO: We're all in the hands of God.

MELANIA: And may He have mercy on our souls!

DON IGNAZIO: His will be done: on earth as it is in Heaven But Thou, Lord, that desireth not the death of the sinne and hast bidden us to pray 'That we be not led into temp tation' forgive both persecuted and persecutor the evil tha they do and suffer: for they are all thy children, both th good and the wicked.

MELANIA: You seem to me now as if you were almost at peace How can it be?

DON IGNAZIO: When I came in I still had hope in men. Now have none. It's time for me to go. I'm only a poor humbl priest but I may be some good to my flock who are poo and humble too.

ARMIDA: You mean that we're proud—and that you condem us?

DON IGNAZIO: Signora, haven't I told you already that I'n not here to pardon or condemn? These poor people need m —oh no, not me personally—but only to have me with them

MELANIA: What about us? Are we to be left?

DON IGNAZIO: No, but you need much more—somethin beyond my poor powers! The church was entrusted to m and my place is there among my parishoners. I have to d the same as any poor little soldier on sentry-duty. I am poor man as much given to fear as anyone else. In need o comforting too, so as not to lose heart—and God be thanke I have a mother, a holy and immortal mother.

DONATO: Don Ignazio, do you think that the fact that I'n desperately envious of you might count for me with God

DON IGNAZIO: God alone searches all hearts to the depths— and far beyond good and evil as we understand it. But nov I must go. Oh!

(7) DON IGNAZIO, DONATO MÈRICI, MELANIA MÈRICI,
ARMIDA LENAI and HERMANN MUELLER,
(*who comes in and goes out without speaking*)

DON IGNAZIO: Did you see who that was? Just before me?
Did you notice the way he carried himself? Just because he
takes orders from some general or other or some Hitler!
From Antichrist himself if he likes! I take my orders from
Christ and His Vicar: I'm not afraid any longer.

DONATO: Did you notice his face?

MELANIA: It struck cold to my marrow!

ARMIDA: There's no escape now, there's no more hope.

MELANIA: But maybe it's not all said and done with: maybe
there is a way out. . . .

(8) DON IGNAZIO, DONATO MÈRICI, MELANIA MÈRICI,
ARMIDA LENAI and FALARIDE NARENZA

NARENZA: I'm only just in the nick of time, if it isn't too late
already. Quick, quick! You can't get out—there isn't time.

DONATO: What is it, Narenza? What's the matter? Have you
gone off your head?

NARENZA: You're sane of course. You're the only one that's
reasonable. Where's my niece? Alinda, hurry up, you're to
come away with me. Alinda! They've shut all the roads! I
bought a safe-conduct from that fellow Remorsella for
Alinda. Alinda, Alinda! I tried my best to buy one for all
of you but he wouldn't let me. Alinda. . . . Well, really,
where's she got to?

(9) Don Ignazio, Falaride Narenza, Donato Mèrici, Melania Mèrici, and Alinda Narenza

ALINDA: Here I am, Uncle.

NARENZA: About time! Come on, we must go. Just as you are. No *ifs* or *buts* or *whys*! I mean now, at once. We've no time to lose—not a moment!

ALINDA: Without Donato? Donato, not without you!

DONATO: Narenza's right. Your uncle's right, Alinda. Go along with him. Don't wait. Goodbye, Alinda—no—till we meet again!

ALINDA: And what about all the rest of you? And you, Donato?

NARENZA: I told him I'd pay anything. Don't you believe me? I swear that's what I said to him, that Remorsella. I begged him.

DONATO: You don't have to swear, Narenza. We believe you.

NARENZA: He wouldn't do it. He said it can't be done. And he laughed in my face. The German won't let anybody leave except Alinda, because she's not one of the family. But we must go at once.

ALINDA: There's only one thing this all means to me. I must stay.

NARENZA: Donato, it's your fault. Do the right thing, if you love her. And be quick about it, Donato.

DONATO: Narenza, it was useless even to ask for a safe-conduct for us.

NARENZA: So it seems. He laughed in my face. But I had to try. Quick, quick. Get her to come with me.

DONATO: It was useless—but not for the reason you think. I can't give up this place—even if my mother shouldn't stay here. It would be cowardice. And I might have been guilty of it if I'd had nothing but my own strength to rely on: if I'd had the chance to get away. But it's been taken out of my hands and that seems to me a mercy: it's easy to do my duty. Alinda, my own Alinda, don't make it more difficult for me. I know that what I'm asking you is harder than staying, but you must save yourself. Go on, it wouldn't be right for me to keep you: it wouldn't be right even for you to refuse to get out, now that you've been offered the chance. Go with your uncle, Alinda: and wait for me. If God wills, we'll be together again.

MELANIA: You must go, my little girl.

ALINDA: You too, Mother?

DONATO: Before it's too late

NARENZA: Come on, Alinda, come with me, or I'll carry you off by force!

ALINDA: That's the only way you will. Donato, my Donato. . . .

(10) DON IGNAZIO, DONATO MÈRICI, MELANIA MÈRICI, and ARMIDA LENAI

DONATO: I've never seen Falaride Narenza weep before. Don Ignazio, supreme unction's never refused to anybody, is it?

DON IGNAZIO: No, to no one. But do you really believe . . .

DONATO: Here's someone who can answer you perhaps.

ARMIDA: Who?

DONATO: The German's outside. I can see him coming back. Perhaps this time he'll speak to us: and he'll remove any doubts you've got on this point, Don Ignazio.

MELANIA: Yes, Mueller's coming in.

ARMIDA: I prefer him to some people.

DONATO: Yes, indeed, so do I.

ARMIDA: He's really by himself, is he?

MELANIA: Yes.

ARMIDA: So much the better.

(11) Don Ignazio, Donato Mèrici, Melania Mèrici, Armida Lenai and Hermann Mueller

Melania: Surely, Captain Mueller, we're entitled to know what's going to happen to us?

Mueller: Not at all. You're not entitled to anything. You're outlaws. That's enough.

Armida: And can't you even say why?

Mueller: I'm not obliged to tell you that either: but you'd better know that five of my men have been killed in an ambush: you're the parish priest—you can report to your flock: they've got three days in which the killers can either give themselves up or be handed over. Three days from twelve noon today. After that there will be reprisals. You can go. The others are to stay here. From now on nobody's to go out.

Melania: What do you mean by reprisals?

Mueller: There's no point in asking. Either you know, or you'll find out.

Melania: Can't we know?

Mueller: No.

Donato: It wouldn't be such torture to wait. It would be too humane!

Mueller: Exactly, and we don't have to treat you like human beings. You're outlaws. And anyway these are orders. So there's no point in asking why: or in asking for mercy.

(12) Don Ignazio, Donato Mèrici, Melania Mèrici, and Armida Lenai

Donato: And there was no point in telling us either. He just wanted to be scrupulously correct. Now, Don Ignazio, you need have no further doubts.

Don Ignazio: Alas!

ARMIDA: Just one word, Don Ignazio, before you grant us absolution. I want to ask a favour.

DON IGNAZIO: What is it? If I can . . .

ARMIDA: Nobody else can now. Otherwise, I certainly wouldn't be asking you. But you're the only one who can go out. You'll be seeing that man Egisto Remorsella. You can't imagine the depths of iniquity there are in that man. I want you to say something to him.

DON IGNAZIO: Satan too possesses depths—and iniquity is exactly what makes them. If it were not so, he'd have no reason for pride and his evil would not be complete.

ARMIDA: No one but you can help me now. And you must realise, I'm a victim—and desperate. You'll be meeting him. . . .

DON IGNAZIO: Of course: you run into him at every corner: he's watching everything.

ARMIDA: But first there's something you must know. It's true I'm a victim, the victim of a hideous sacrifice, of a loathsome violation. But I'm not sacrificing myself for the love of God: it's for the love of a man, for an earthly carnal sinful love.

DON IGNAZIO: And who shall be found closer to God, my daughter, than one who confesses his own wrongdoing while suffering the iniquity of others? In the eyes of God his affliction shines with a light beyond all that we know of good and evil. What God has created God alone can judge. And who knows but in his secret counsels the vilest sinner on earth may be forgiven, while those who deem themselves numbered here below among the just, may for that very reason be lost and reprobate. Fellow-Christians, on your knees, before God who beholds us!

ARMIDA: Don Ignazio, tell that man I'm waiting for him!

CHAPTER THREE

(1) HERMANN MUELLER and MELANIA MÈRICI

MELANIA: Captain Mueller, it's striking twelve. Two days have gone by.

MUELLER: Exactly.

MELANIA: And for two days I've been trying to speak to you, trying to make you look at me: you can't still refuse to see a mother's anguish.

MUELLER: It's not different from the anguish of all the mothers in the world today: my mother's too, Signora Melania Mèrici: I'm told that religious people, devout Catholics, say an Ave Maria, Mater Dolorosa when it strikes twelve. A poetic symbol!

MELANIA: Mockery is cheap. If you're killed, you die like a free man, fighting. But my son . . .

MUELLER: He's only got to fight.

MELANIA: That's even cheaper. And who is he to fight?

MUELLER: Anybody he likes if he's looking for a hero's death. . . .

MELANIA: One against a hundred!

MUELLER: That only makes it all the more heroic.

MELANIA: Captain Mueller, I thought at one time that there was something big and generous which I could discern in you: in your very ruthlessness which seemed something beyond good and evil. Am I to believe that I was mistaken?

MUELLER: Why?

MELANIA: There's nothing big or generous about jeering at misfortune and sorrow.

MUELLER: I never jeer at anything or anybody.

MELANIA: Really? You really believe that?

MUELLER: I never lie, least of all to myself.

MELANIA: Then imagine that your mother was in my place. Wouldn't she want to know: wouldn't she ask?

MUELLER: Yes, I think so. No doubt she would.

MELANIA: For you mother's sake, tell me. What is going to happen to my son?

MUELLER: Yes, my mother would want to know that too. Well, I'll answer you as I would her.

MELANIA: Oh no, don't answer me, don't tell me anything.

MUELLER: I can't imagine that sort of outcry from my mother.

MELANIA: I can't bear it. I can't. But even if I can't tell me.

MUELLER: If the people who are responsible for killing these men haven't been handed over before noon tomorrow, the order for reprisals will be carried out. You know that . . .

MELANIA: I know it: but my son . . .

MUELLER: Your son is one of the hostages, no different from the others.

MELANIA: But you won't shoot them all, not the whole village? You'll draw lots?

MUELLER: What do you want to know for?

MELANIA: To have some hope—even for a day—a vestige of hope, if only in chance.

MUELLER: You asked for the truth—in the name of my mother.

MELANIA: And I dread the truth, but would she be able to endure it?

MUELLER: It might kill her—but she'd want to know it.

MELANIA: How can you say it? How can you be so ruthless?

MUELLER: Because if I myself were your son Donato, I wouldn't ask my mother to do what you're doing now. I wouldn't want her begging for mercy and pity.

MELANIA: My son hasn't asked me for anything—he knows nothing about what I'm asking you.

MUELLER: That restores some of my respect for him.

MELANIA: My boy wouldn't have it. If he knew, he'd kill . . .

MUELLER: Whom would he kill?

MELANIA: You, Hauptmann Mueller, he'd kill you!

MUELLER: He's only got to try. But I don't see why.

MELANIA: Because it's not that I'm asking for mercy: I'm not asking for anything. On the contrary, I'm making you an offer.

MUELLER: Signora Mèrici: am I talking to a madwoman?

MELANIA: Yes, I am mad—and not only through suffering. But what's in your mind? It's not the sort of offer which should offend you.

MUELLER: Your sufferings must have driven you mad. You must be out of your mind to think you can make offers to me!

MELANIA: It's both mind and blood, Mueller. I've told you it isn't an insult. You can form your own judgment of what I'm offering you. But first listen, find out what it is.

MUELLER: Don't say any more: don't speak. Not another word.

MELANIA: It's true, isn't it, that you're mad for me—you're on fire for me. Don't say No! Not to me! Say it to yourself —you never lie to yourself. But don't try and say it to me.

MUELLER: You're so sure? How can you be?

MELANIA: You'd better ask me, how long I've been sure. And look at me!

MUELLER: No! But if I can't even resist your voice! How long, Signora?

MELANIA: From the first moment of recognition, when we looked into each others' eyes.

MUELLER: This is presumptuous madness!

MELANIA: And so you're afraid of it? And now you're ready to lie—now I'm no longer afraid of the truth? Call it presumption and madness if you like, but it's truth—and it's completely overwhelmed me, my whole heart and mind and body—even my memory. Because if you look at me, you'll see that I've forgotten everything except this passion, this desperate passion which consumes us both, a man and woman utterly alone in a fiery circle of horror and fear and desperate desire. Is it presumption and madness? They *fan* the flames and the fear and desire grow sharper, with the strength of desperation. Look in my eyes—they're not asking for pity: and what you'll read in them isn't fear——except the one fear of my own consuming passion which is raging in my blood and destroying me: and destroying you too: me in my presumption and you in your cowardice —who don't dare look into my eyes!

MUELLER: If I were to, you'd be sorry. But then I'm not going to: I don't want to. You're just lying—it's all rhetoric and playacting, all put on for the sake of your son.

MELANIA: Mueller, what rubbish! And what cowardice! Or are you jealous of my son?

MUELLER: Everything you've said is true—even that I'm jealous. I only wish there were stronger words to equal the passion you arouse in me.

MELANIA: Look at me! Why don't you look at me.

MUELLER: Don't ask me. You'll be sorry.

MELANIA: You still say that? What talk of regret can there be now between us two after all that we've said? Now that we've either taken the leap—or been flung—I don't know which—but anyway now that we've gone beyond pity and mother-love and a son's life, beyond everything human, into a fierce inhuman passion. And are you afraid of it even if it is a crime? I'm not.

MUELLER: Neither am I. Neither of the crime—nor of the remorse.

MELANIA: Listen, Mueller. I don't want to find that I've spoken as I have to a fool. I would rather have confessed myself, have revealed myself in all my nakedness to my son himself. For you're a fool if you talk to me about duty and honour: it will drive me mad and that will be liberation! And you'll hear me laughing at the pair of us—and fate. Look at me. . . .

MUELLER: You'll be sorry.

MELANIA: Look into my eyes. Oh . . .

MUELLER: No threats! There's a risk I might laugh, too. And how do you know I wasn't laughing already—yesterday?

MELANIA: Yesterday? The names have been drawn already? Mueller!

MUELLER: Listen to me!

MELANIA: My boy?

MUELLER: You force me to speak. Be quiet. If there is such a thing as liberation, I'm liberated already. Whether you're a mother or whether you're merely a woman—be quiet and listen. Yesterday when it came to drawing the lots, I made one of the hostages give me his hat. I can see it now: a peasant's old hat: an old peasant stupid with fright. And it all depended on me—on me alone and my single will and pleasure. This name or that—I could put a name in that hat or not, I could choose to write it or not. All I had to do was to make up the number—by my own choice or leave it to chance. And I left it to chance: for they were nothing but numbers and names to me. And if anyone had told me that one was missing, Donato Mèrici or anybody, I could easily have put him up against a wall for his insolence and made up the number that way, of my own free choice and will. I hadn't even written down Donato Mèrici's name.

MELANIA: Because he wasn't a mere number, because . . .

MUELLER: Not another word. I'd made up my mind and I wouldn't even have let his mother know.

MELANIA: But why, why all this?

MUELLER: Because she was a woman—and I didn't want to get her by a trick, a mean squalid process of bargaining. For I wanted her, I was mad for her, but I wanted her to come to me for passion not through this sort of gratitude with its mean subjection. You understand? I loved this woman but I'm a free man and I wanted her freely.

MELANIA: And now you no longer love me?

MUELLER: Don't ask me: the moment has passed. Just listen to me.

MELANIA: I listen with fear and horror: powerless and trembling.

MUELLER: When I touched those names in the hat there was nobody to intervene between my hand and fate: no will, no voice, no existence, no time: it was the darkness of lonely eternity. What I hadn't foreseen was that an icy soundless wind would come out of that darkness to stay my hand and freeze my blood. I wasn't capable of drawing the lot. Hadn't they all become men? He and the others? You understand me? Human beings. In that momentary breath, passion was blown to a terrible flame—but like ice: and all in a moment it burned itself out: and died. Haven't you ever heard that cold can burn like fire? At that depth of cold, passion burned too. If you don't believe me, take your hands from your eyes and look into mine.

MELANIA: But my son—my son's name!

MUELLER: I wrote it down: I put it with the others.

MELANIA: Ah, so that was the price of your freedom? But I'm going to free myself too. My passion is a fire too, and it's burning itself out into hatred and freedom. My son? Tell me.

MUELLER: His name stayed at the bottom. It was never drawn.

MELANIA: Is he safe now?

MUELLER: He's to live.

MELANIA: And if it had been drawn?

MUELLER: That's a senseless question. Didn't I tell you I'd put it with the others in the bottom of the hat.

MELANIA: And what did you hope for during the draw?

MUELLER: What did I hope for, Melania? Nothing, nothing at all! And who was it who forced me to tell you?

MELANIA: You monster, you wanted to see how far passion could twist a mother's nature: if I was completely its slave, and yours! Even if you told me!—even if Donato's name had been drawn! Admit it. Don't be ashamed. It's monstrous, but then you aren't a man. You're a monster. I see it in your eyes.

MUELLER: I knew that there was only one sort of passion which could survive between us—your hatred, Melania. Where are you going?

MELANIA: You fill me with horror. My son, I'm going to my son!—Ah!

(2) HERMANN MUELLER, MELANIA MÈRICI, DONATO MÈRICI

DONATO: Mother, behold your son.

MELANIA: Donato! Did you hear? What did you hear?

DONATO: Not so much. But more than enough. More than I should have wished.

MUELLER: You're alive. You're going to live. That should be enough for your mother.

DONATO: Whom do I owe it to—that's what I want to know—this still being alive?

MELANIA: Not to him, Donato. But not to me either. Not to what you think, my boy.

MUELLER: You owe it to chance, and nothing else. You ought to be grateful to me, Donato. You can live—and live without shame. And you owe that to me because I left it to chance.

MELANIA: Do you hear. He would have let you be shot.

DONATO: Is it true? Well, then he's in the right. But is it true?

MUELLER: It's true. And for the rest of it, ask your mother, if you want to know.

(3) DONATO MÈRICI and MELANIA MÈRICI

MELANIA: You must believe me! Whatever it costs me as your mother, I'll confess it to you. I loved him. An overwhelming passion had sprung up between us. But I swear to you . . .

DONATO: Don't swear. Any perjury is allowed in a case like this—between mother and son—and even condoned.

MELANIA: Oh Donato, don't you believe me? That man would have had you shot. . . .

DONATO: What if he had? By this time I shouldn't be thinking about it any more.

MELANIA: I'll tell you everything. I can. Donato, my boy, my dear boy, look at me, look into my very heart. I don't have to hide anything from you.

DONATO: And you love him. That's terribly sad!

MELANIA: Not now, not any longer.

DONATO: Not any longer . . . because he broke his word, he didn't keep to his bargain?

MELANIA: There wasn't any bargain.

DONATO: Who says so? Does he? He despises me so much he doesn't mind lying to me.

MELANIA: I say so and you must believe me, because if there had been no other way and if it had been possible to save you by doing it, I would have agreed to the bargain, I would have accepted it, I would even have proposed it and I would have kept to it. But you must and can believe me: I loved him, I loved him to desperation.

DONATO: Mother, what you say stirs such an indescribable convulsion of love and resentment in me, that I know I shall always be grateful to you for this—and that I shall never forgive you.

(4) MELANIA MÈRICI and ARMIDA LENAI

ARMIDA: More troubles? And now he's gone. Haven't we had enough?

MELANIA: If you had to confess to Gaspare what you've gone through to save his life . . .

ARMIDA: What did you say? What's in your mind? The mere idea makes me shudder. But why ever do you think of such a thing? What's happened now?

MELANIA: I had to tell him, tell my son, that I'd have done it for him, I'd have done the same as you've done for Gaspare.

ARMIDA: Ah, I can breathe again.

MELANIA: What do you mean?

ARMIDA: Well, you've confessed it, you were able to tell your son.

MELANIA: And you think . . . but you can't talk . . . you haven't got any sons.

ARMIDA: What am I supposed to be thinking? What if it was your son? Now he'll see how much you love him and he'll love you in return because of the sacrifice you were ready to make. And if you'd done it, he'd have loved you all the more. He loves you already more than ever before, and if he can't speak it's because his heart is too full. And to me, a stranger, he can't speak. That's why he went out and didn't answer me. As if he were jealous of such a secret between you and himself. And he's right to be jealous.

MELANIA: How easy it is to talk about other people's sorrows!

ARMIDA: You're not trying to compare yours to mine—this horror in my heart?

MELANIA: My poor, my terribly unhappy Armida, what are these extraordinary things you're saying?

ARMIDA: I thought you were making some comparison. . . .

MELANIA: My wretched Armida, if there's anyone who ever tries to make comparisons . . .

ARMIDA: I would have liked to comfort you, that was what I meant: I wanted to tell you that such a sacrifice . . .

MELANIA: But it wouldn't have been a sacrifice.

ARMIDA: What do you mean?

MELANIA: I loved him, I did love this German, this Mueller.

ARMIDA: You? And did he?

MELANIA: He loved me, he did love me! And Donato, when he came in a little time ago, accidentally heard what we were saying.

ARMIDA: But if you love him, if he's in love with you, you can save us all.

MELANIA: But I don't love him any more. I'd hate him, if the word weren't completely colourless compared with what I feel for him.

ARMIDA: But why?

MELANIA: When he had to draw the lots, this man put Donato's name in with the others. He would have had him shot. It was chance which saved Donato, not he. Listen, do you hear, those were rifle-shots.

ARMIDA: Yes, from the village. One burst and then a second one: oh Melania!

MELANIA: They've given us till tomorrow.

ARMIDA: Yes, tomorrow, that's what they said.

MELANIA: But anyway, imagine it might have been Donato who was up against that wall—and that man would have done nothing to prevent it: and he loved me and I loved him: and he'd have put Donato in front of a firing-squad.

ARMIDA: We're lost, Melania, whatever happens, we're lost.

MELANIA: There's no possible escape for us, no way out. It's the same for all of us.

ARMIDA: You can still say that? Nobody's situation here can compare with mine.

MELANIA: Nobody's? It's my son I'm thinking of—that wall, and the blood on it. It might have been his.

ARMIDA: But it isn't: he's alive.

MELANIA: He's alive—and wounded in his inmost being: and what I've told him has turned him against life in disgust and scorn. . . .

ARMIDA: You think too much about these refinements of feeling, they're spiritual luxuries, idle ones, too. My dear Melania, don't exaggerate your sufferings, your exquisite spiritual torments. They're not mortal sorrows, they're not the death of the heart. Maybe you've fallen in love—maybe it's unhappy, oh, I don't deny it. If you like it's your hair-shirt—but the hair is soft and silky. And your son won't only forgive you he'll come to be grateful to you: for what you were ready to do for him and because now you've come to hate this man. Oh, your son will get back his love of life: his Alinda will give him back life and love. And they'll give you a beautiful old age full of affection and sweet solici-tude. Oh, I know this may be painful for you and for your son and Alinda: but it won't last for ever. And meanwhile Donato's alive.

MELANIA: And isn't Gaspare alive?

ARMIDA: But I wish I were dead. If only we died together!

MELANIA: And now you're talking wildly—and more than I've done. You're desperately hugging this sorrow of yours. It's as if you were drunk with it—and even wanted to be. It's all you, nobody but you, you're the only real victim, the only one who's made a hideous unspeakable sacrifice. But as for the man for whom you made it, can you have a shadow of doubt, can you doubt for one instant, that he wouldn't recognise it, that he wouldn't be eternally grateful? —he couldn't be so unworthy of it!

ARMIDA: He must never know about it!

MELANIA: And do you imagine . . .

ARMIDA: You and Donato know about it: I would never

forgive myself—or you two either, if ever . . . I'd kill anyone who ever told him, and then myself.

MELANIA: You may be unhappy, but you needn't threaten. Of
course we shall keep silence. But you shouldn't be silent,
even supposing that you could, you shouldn't hide it from
him, this terrible and magnificent thing you've done in all
its splendour and horror and love.

ARMIDA: Ah, but my whole soul is darkened. What you're
saying only reveals to me the eternity of despair into which
I've been hurled—and shows it deeper and more endless.
No one can understand me unless they've suffered what I
suffer, unless they've actually done what I've done. I have
to understand myself in loneliness—oh, if you only knew
how lonely! Not only alone in what I've done but having to
understand it alone. Much better if I were dead. But why
should I say if *I* were dead? Better if he were dead: better if
I had the courage to let him die!

MELANIA: But it would have been an inhuman unnatural
courage.

ARMIDA: And what I'm suffering now? Is that human? There's
something you must grasp, if you can, and if I can make
you. I've no doubt already that, if I were to confide in him,
Gaspare would forgive me and be grateful to me and admire
me. But I've been violated, and spiritually, not only in my
flesh. Oh, my body, my subjected and suffering flesh, how
disgust and loathing lacerated it, I couldn't tell you, even
though I experienced it. I couldn't say if I tried. And it's not
worth trying to tell.

MELANIA: It was force—of the most shameful kind.

ARMIDA: In my flesh: but *I* myself submitted my soul to rape:
it was I who did outrage and violence to my soul, irre-
mediable and eternal wrong, and I should not have done. If
I were to tell Gaspare, if he could keep silent and overcome
his loathing of a body which had been possessed and
defiled by another—and by that man: even if he could

remain silent and forgive me, his very silence, his very forgiveness would remind me of what I have done and that I should never have done it: that I had been overweening and arrogant when I ought to have told him everything, put myself in his hands, body and soul. You see, Melania, if what I had done had been done in a fit of madness—how shall I put it—a moment of aberration or abandonment, what he would have felt would be jealousy, rage, passion— but still love. He would have killed me, but he would have killed me for love. . . .

MELANIA: But it was a kind of madness—and well it might be: it was the madness of despair.

ARMIDA: I've argued with myself: and I shall never be rid of it, I shall never be able to expiate it. And even if Gaspare should be able to forget it, I never shall, never any more. Can you imagine what I shall be picturing to myself in our moments of love? What I shall see in those moments? What he would see if he knew?

MELANIA: But he doesn't know—and he won't know.

ARMIDA: But what I shall feel? Can you imagine that?

MELANIA: I haven't the courage to talk to you any longer.

ARMIDA: And there's nothing else you could say to me. And yet I'd give anything for a compassionate word.

MELANIA: Compassion? Oh, my poor soul.

ARMIDA: No, Melania—I turn compassion to ice—even my own, even what I might feel for myself. My despair has become twisted to universal contempt: and now if I heard the voice of Almighty God, and he spoke in my heart and told me he had compassion on me, I should answer that he should have had it sooner.

MELANIA: Do you hear that? They're shooting again: will this torture never be over?

ARMIDA: It seems to me as if it were always beginning anew. I feel as if I can't remember a day when I didn't have to bear it.

MELANIA: They're shooting down in the village—no, in the woods, quite near—and in the distance too. Whatever is it?

(5) MELANIA MÈRICI, ARMIDA LENAI and
EGISTO REMORSELLA

MELANIA: You again? How dare you?

REMORSELLA: And who's to stop me. For you instruction, Armida . . .

ARMIDA: How dare you call me Armida! And how dare you come near me?

REMORSELLA: Oh, this is fine! You seem to have gone up in your own estimation. Why shouldn't I dare?

ARMIDA: I repeat—how dare you? It certainly never crossed my mind that you could be capable of remorse or even of shame: but I loathed you so intensely I was deluded into thinking that it might even have penetrated to you: if it had done so in the slightest, it would have been enough to keep you away from me. Now even that illusion has gone.

REMORSELLA: Frankly, speaking for myself, I don't understand what you mean when you talk about loathing, Signora Armida.

ARMIDA: What did I say, Melania. You see this man? Even he's created in the image and likeness—Can you believe it? Does it seem real? No, it's not possible. It's a dream. It can't be true. Some men were created not by God but the devil.

REMORSELLA: This is no time for gallantry. If it were, I'd say that for my part I thought it really was a dream, what I did with the most beautiful woman in the world.

ARMIDA: Do you hear him, Melania? He can boast about it, he's quite satisfied, he's even happy.

REMORSELLA: With good reason, in my opinion.

ARMIDA: It won't be long before you hear him actually laughing.

T

REMORSELLA: Of course you don't like it round here when I laugh: I remember now: the devil's laughter—oh dear, what affected notions you've got. Not the devil! That's going too far!

MELANIA: Stop it! What is this shooting? Listen. They've started again. Are they shooting the hostages? Is this your reprisal?

REMORSELLA: No, not yet. The partisans have made an attempt to liberate the prisoners. They've been pushed back from the village and now there's fighting going on in the woods. However that isn't important news. But there's a special item for Signora Lenai. The partisans are trying to get to Vill' Alma, Alma Dannata. They're making a great effort as if there were something specially interesting here. They've been pushed back and the Jerries haven't noticed anything unusual. But all that's wanted is a word from me. . . .

MELANIA: To whom?

ARMIDA: I know well enough. . . .

REMORSELLA: So much the better. That way I don't have to waste time in pointless talk.

ARMIDA: Egisto . . .

REMORSELLA: You actually deign to use my name?

ARMIDA: Yes, I want to put myself on your level, wallow in contempt, tear myself to pieces with my own despair. At least be frank—you've come to blackmail me again, haven't you?

REMORSELLA: To be quite frank, I should never have thought I'd have found you so attractive. I'm crazy for you.

ARMIDA: It suits me.

MELANIA: Armida, you must be mad!

ARMIDA: No doubt! But if you can't stand it, go away. I must have a few words with my lover, my lord and master.

REMORSELLA: Oh, this is too much. You're too condescending, lover indeed! And Master! You mustn't be too humble.

ARMIDA: I never thought I should see you again.

REMORSELLA: What a mistake. A woman like you isn't so easily forgotten.

ARMIDA: So I see! And so you're proposing . . . !

REMORSELLA: To distract the German's attention—Hauptmann Mueller's—and from the very thing which the partisans were particularly after.

ARMIDA: Don't tell me what you want for it in exchange—because I know. And moreover I know what you're going to do afterwards, but I'd like to hear it from you.

REMORSELLA: What do you mean?

ARMIDA: What I mean is, when the German has gone away you'll go on blackmailing me, won't you? How long for?

REMORSELLA: That depends. I'm very attracted by you and I don't hide the fact, but I'm fickle with women. However I should think at least a year, something of the sort.

ARMIDA: Do you hear that, Melania. He *has* a kind of perfection. And how are you proposing to go on blackmailing me?

REMORSELLA: It's simple. Infallible! There's someone, a particular person, who must never, for anything in the world, be allowed to know the price his mistress has paid to save him being roasted alive in a trap. It wouldn't matter to me, but it does to you.

ARMIDA: And so you mean, I must . . .

REMORSELLA: There's another thing . . .

ARMIDA: But you swine . . .

MELANIA: Let him go on, Armida. You've no need to sully yourself by talking to him.

REMORSELLA: I'm going by a rule of my own and I see things as they may turn out—even a long way ahead. And Egisto Remorsella isn't one to believe that the Germans are going to win. Oh no! They've got too much on their plate! There's a certain turn events might take before the collapse and I can see the time coming already when it will be worth my while to play a double game. And right at the end, but in good time, I shall go over to the partisans. Signora Armida

Lenai will testify in my favour and won't spare any words. I went in with the Germans because I was forced to, and at the grave risk of being hanged (as I said, no words will be spared) I saved the life of a certain partisan-leader whom we needn't name, in a country-house known as Alma Dannata. Won't that have been very valuable and meritorious? Of course I need the testimonial already referred to—but I'm sure already that Signora Lenai won't refuse it to me. Ah, Remorsella's no fool; and he can see a long way past his nose. And in exchange for the testimonial, I'll keep mum about a certain little secret. After all it's next to nothing, a trifle, I was going to say a bit of fun, which as long as that other person knows nothing about it, doesn't do him out of anything or spoil things for him at all. After all, taking into account that Remorsella himself is quite popular with the ladies, this little affair—provided one doesn't exaggerate certain difficulties—must have given quite a lot of fun to someone else, not only to him—although admittedly he did get a great kick out of it.

ARMIDA: What did I tell you, Melania? He's got everything. Very well. I'll play your double game.

MELANIA: Armida, what do you think you're doing?

ARMIDA: Do you think I've got any choice? Isn't Remorsella my boss—now and for ever? Would you like some money too? You can have it!

REMORSELLA: I hadn't thought about that. But I'm a moderate man and I won't be exorbitant.

ARMIDA: Well, as a mark of gratitude for so much restraint, we'll carry on the conversation in there, between our two selves.

REMORSELLA: With the greatest pleasure. The firing's stopped. That means the partisans have been repulsed. The Germans must be chasing them into the woods. We can have a nice peaceful little time all to ourselves.

(6) MELANIA MÈRICI and DONATO MÈRICI

DONATO: I was just coming in when I heard that man's voice.

MELANIA: That poor woman!

DONATO: I stood and listened.

MELANIA: Poor wretched woman.

DONATO: She'll be avenged. Meanwhile, talk quietly: he's trapped.

MELANIA: What are you going to do, Donato?

DONATO: Gaspare has had a radio message from his men that they're going to try and get him out today.

MELANIA: It's no good. That man Remorsella has found out. And then they were repulsed.

DONATO: No, the first attack was a feint to draw off the Germans into the woods. Do you hear how quiet it is? That means that the feint has come off. Before long they'll be here.

MELANIA: What are you doing with that revolver, Donato?

DONATO: He mustn't come out of that room alive: so that we're sure of getting away. Meanwhile get yourself a pair of strong shoes and something to put over you both, you and Armida. That's all you need, to get out of here. Go on and be back quickly.

MELANIA: But meanwhile what are you going to do, Donato . . . Donatello?

DONATO: He mustn't come out alive. Gaspare is waiting. Gaspare may come in any minute. And he mustn't know.

MELANIA: Yes, let's spare the poor woman that at least.

(7) DONATO MÈRICI, MELANIA MÈRICI and ARMIDA LENAI

ARMIDA: There was nothing else to be done: and he can say he asked for it?

MELANIA: *He* can say? Where do you mean?

ARMIDA: In hell.

MELANIA: *You!*

ARMIDA: Yes, I've done it. The beast boasted how far-sighted he was, but he didn't foresee that I should have a knife with me.

DONATO: It had to be: he had to die.

ARMIDA: Maybe I shouldn't have had the courage: it must have been his bad angel that egged him on; but he added spice to the whole thing by laughing at me. Was I to let myself be defiled by him and go in fear of him and see no end to it all?

MELANIA: Shut that door, Armida, shut that door.

DONATO: Yes, shut it.

ARMIDA: What does it matter? They'll find him anyhow: don't be afraid: I shall take all the blame and you and Gaspare will all be safe. When I'm dead then you can tell Gaspare the whole story: at least he'll know how much I loved him and how much I've suffered: oh, when I'm dead he'll forgive me.

DONATO: Gaspare mustn't know. We're getting ready to make a dash for it. The partisans . . .

ARMIDA: They've been repulsed.

DONATO: It was a feint. And it's come off. Gaspare's waiting, they'll be here any moment.

ARMIDA: Oh, shut that door, Donato. Now you give me back hope, my courage is gone, I'm lost.

DONATO: That's done. It's the end he deserved. Mother, you're singing: that's a good sign: but what for? And why under your breath and as if you were in a dream?

MELANIA: I didn't realise. It's '*Non sai che questa calma è figlia del dolore*'.

DONATO: Lovely! but what words for a time like this! And who knows whether they're a good omen or not? I hope they are. Ah, you'd say those words—which are so true—

had made this great silence which has fallen on the world and this peace in our hearts. Mother there's something I want to say to you, it maybe that through these bitter and terrible experiences I've been able to come to a decision which may comfort you. If we come through, if ever I see Alinda again, you'll know what I mean, Mother, when I tell you that I'll go back to music. I hope I'll be able to tell of these sufferings and this subjection, the joys of deliverance and the return to life, I feel confident that I shall: and oh, if I could only find the music for this calm which has come to us out of so much sorrow: music to fit this peace which vanquishes so much strife: this hope so much stronger than despair!

MELANIA: Oh Donato, Donatello! If only those days would really come. But you know, my boy, it's the same with me, too—hope takes away all the strength which desperation gave me.

ARMIDA: It's the same with me, too.

DONATO: It's a mean giver: chase it away: and look forward to the days to come, Mother—as I do to Alinda and love.

MELANIA: Poor girl!

DONATO: Why?

MELANIA: Because if we come to an end, you and I, we shall die together. But she must live on alone, if she does live! God grant it may never be—when she loves you so much.

DONATO: Don't be afraid.

MELANIA: With you, whether we live or die, I'm not afraid.

(8) DONATO MÈRICI, MELANIA MÈRICI, ARMIDA LENAI and GASPARE DELLA MORTE

GASPARE: Whether we live or die—are you afraid, Armida?

ARMIDA: No, not at all—with you.

GASPARE: Well, then the victory's half ours already. And I feel myself as if being out in the light and the open air, after being shut up for so many days, were a kind of benediction. Donato, have you told them what to do. Are they ready?

DONATO: I told them—strong shoes and something thick to put over themselves for the cold at night.

ARMIDA: We've got them here.

GASPARE: Then let's be going. Out into the woods and the mountains: and long live freedom! there's a gun for you, Donato. If it comes to it, you'll look after your mother and I'll look after Armida.

MELANIA: Give us something so that we can defend ourselves.

GASPARE: Give *you* something! Do you mean——

ARMIDA: Yes: if we fell into those hands alive—yes, we do . . .

GASPARE: You're right. Here you are, for both of you. It's no use to me any longer. I shall die fighting, now——

MELANIA: And so will we. You can throw that poison away.

ARMIDA: So we will. Give us something to fight with.

GASPARE: Very well. You're brave women. We'll do our best to be worthy of you. Meanwhile, I wonder what it means—that it's so quiet outside. Donato, can you see anyone?

DONATO: Not yet. '*Non sai che questa calma* . . .!' Gaspare mustn't hear us singing. Mother. Can you imagine what he'd say about us—artists with their heads in the clouds!

GASPARE: All he'd say is that the spirit which can laugh in such an hour reveals the fine winged courage of an artist—of a true artist, Donato.

DONATO: Did you hear that, Mother? And he's a man of action—who knows about courage!

MELANIA: Dear Donatello, we're going to be saved.

DONATO: It'll all be as God wills: but whatever happens, may He save our souls! There's no one there, Gaspare—only peace and solitude. I remember the games we used to play out there on the meadow, when we were children.

GASPARE: Go on, you two, go and get ready, and be quick.

(9) DONATO MÈRICI and GASPARE DELLA MORTE

DONATO: It gives you a tremendous and terrible new strength when you know you're armed. It gives me a kind of life which I never thought I could get from such things.

GASPARE: It's not being armed: it's in your heart when you aren't afraid any longer. Anybody there?

DONATO: No, there's nobody. . . . Something moved in the woods. Yes, I can see something. It's the enemy, Gaspare!

GASPARE: Are you sure?

DONATO: They're surrounding the house. They're turning something on us, some sort of weapon. I don't know what it is.

(10) DONATO MÈRICI, GASPARE DELLA MORTE, ARMIDA LENAI *followed later by* MELANIA MÈRICI

ARMIDA: I know what that is: it's a flame-thrower.

DONATO: Reprisals: revenge for their dead. It's all over.

GASPARE: Not yet.

DONATO: What else is there for us?

GASPARE: We can die like men. And you two get under cover.

ARMIDA: They're going to set fire to the place. They said they would.

MELANIA: We're armed. We won't be burnt alive. Kiss me, Armida.

ARMIDA: Goodbye, darling.

GASPARE: Perhaps the partisans will attack them from behind. We must resist to the last. If they advance, Donato, fire at the first one that comes within range: what are you thinking about?

DONATO: I was listening to silence: it was a silence beyond the world: and it called me. But I'll do it, Gaspare, I'll fire on the first man that moves.

GASPARE: While we have a shot among us! Our own people may be just coming.

DONATO: Goodbye, Mother. That's the way he talks and he has to: it's his role—to fight to the end. But I feel peace—and it's not of this world.

MELANIA: Goodbye, Donato—for a while. We shall come together in peace. We shan't have long to wait. But why are they so slow, these men?

DONATO: Perhaps the beasts are just trying to play cat and mouse.

GASPARE: Don't rail against your enemy. Don't give him that triumph. They have the power and they use it: that's the essence of war. Looking at it any other way is pride and hypocrisy.

DONATO: They're holding out something white: what can they possibly want?

GASPARE: Surrender. They want the two women. For their sake we ought to accept.

ARMIDA: And for you, Gaspare, what would it be? Torture? No! There's a dead man next door. I've killed him—and they won't spare me.

DONATO: She's right. You'll be tortured. And they'll shoot me.

ARMIDA: You can save yourself, Melania. You're the only one.

MELANIA: I was a good shot when I was a girl. We'll see. My wrist didn't move, he's fallen. Goodbye, Donato: till we meet again, goodbye.

GASPARE: It's the end now.

DONATO: If you say so, Gaspare Della Morte, it is.

MELANIA: The whole sky's on fire.

DONATO: They've set fire to the roof.

GASPARE: Let them have it, Donato. Remember—like men: right to the last shot.

ARMIDA: They're turning the flame on the windows.

MELANIA: Donato, where are you?

DONATO: Mother, kiss me. She's choking already! It won't be
long now, Mother.

GASPARE: Armida, where are you. The roof's burning, the
walls are falling in. Let's get out and die in the open. Armida,
Melania, Donato! They're all gone. May God receive their
souls—and mine!

Epilogue

THE military report of Hauptmann Hermann Mueller, on the subject of the action by partisans in the neighbourhood of Alma Dannata and the reprisals which ensued, does not refer to any corpses being found reduced to cinders by fire and buried in the villa's debris. A certain Egisto Remorsella was reported missing: and it was only when the war was over that Falaride Narenza came into possession of a kind of blackmail-diary which had belonged to Remorsella himself, and from which he was able to reconstruct the main events of this tragic story, while all that was discovered from digging among the ruins was the skeleton of this individual; and between his shoulder-blades there was a dagger from which Narenza was able to make further deductions which seemed likely.

Right to the end of the war, Alinda had waited for Donato, refusing to believe that he was dead, but now she was convinced by these facts and said she wanted to go into a convent and take the veil.

Somewhat to the surprise of those of his acquaintance who were familiar with his inveterate spirit of contradiction, Falaride made no opposition, but he said that with his favourite niece a nun and his only friend dead, he had been deprived of three-quarters of the pleasure of getting rich, as he was certainly doing, from his trade.

Vill' Alma was never rebuilt. There were no relatives and therefore no heirs to claim it: and anyway we all know that the country can't afford the great old houses of former times. After they had taken Remorsella's remains out of the ruins,

Falaride had a cross erected over them which was blessed by the parish priest, Don Ignazio.

But that doesn't stop the local peasants saying that you can hear the ghosts of these dead at night and that they even appear. They say that Alma Dannata was an ill-omened name and that the curse has been fulfilled.

Ivy and thick grass grow there: and every year the scrub grows further over the ruins. When the birds begin to migrate, it would be a good place for fowling, but even in the most brilliant sunshine a stillness reigns there, which is so deep and austere and so funereal, that it keeps the curious at bay and strikes terror to the listening heart, and moves even those who do not know of the grave and sorrowful vicissitudes of Vill' Alma, to grave and sorrowful thought.

Every year on All Hallows' E'en, Narenza brings a wreath and has a mass said for the dead: and this in spite of the fact that he cannot be described as a religious man. Then he goes to the convent to call on his niece and tells her that he has been to visit them: and that when the two of them are no longer alive to commemorate them, these dear ones of theirs will have nobody left in the world. And when he sees how serene Alinda is, he is almost indignant: but although he understands very little about it, he is appeased when he perceives, behind what she can say in the vanity of words, that she is assured of being with Donato again, among the blessed in paradise.

THE END